# THE
# NAMING
# SONG

ALSO BY JEDEDIAH BERRY

*The Manual of Detection*
*The Family Arcana*

# THE
# NAMING
# SONG

## JEDEDIAH BERRY

TOR PUBLISHING GROUP

NEW YORK

THE NAMING SONG

Copyright © 2024 by Jedediah Berry

A Tor Book
Published by Tor Publishing Group / Tom Doherty Associates
120 Broadway
New York, NY 10271

www.torpublishinggroup.com

Tor® is a registered trademark of Macmillan Publishing Group, LLC.

The Library of Congress Cataloging-in-Publication Data is available upon request.

ISBN 978-1-250-90798-1 (hardcover)
ISBN 978-1-250-90801-8 (ebook)

Our books may be purchased in bulk for promotional, educational, or business use.
Please contact your local bookseller or the Macmillan Corporate and Premium Sales
Department at 1-800-221-7945, extension 5442, or by email at
MacmillanSpecialMarkets@macmillan.com.

First Edition: 2024

Printed in the United States of America

0  9  8  7  6  5  4  3  2  1

*For my sister Cait*

MAP TK

MAP TK

# PRINCIPAL CHARACTERS

## THE NUMBER TWELVE

**The courier.** A member of the names committee, tasked with delivering new words.
**Book.** Chair of the names committee, he brought the courier aboard.
**Beryl.** The diviner who finds words for machines and their parts.
**Rope.** The diviner who finds words for flying things.
**Ivy.** A courier who witnessed a vicious attack on Buckle Station.
**The patchwork ghost.** The courier's oldest friend.
**The stowaway.** A fierce hunter of vermin.

## STEM

**Lock.** The courier's father, a researcher of ghosts and monsters.
**Ticket.** The courier's sister, who never responds to her letters.

## THE BLACK SQUARE SHOW

**The Gardener of Stones.** The director of the show.
**The Gardener of Leaves.** A monster who guards the Black Square's train.
**The Gardener of Shovels.** A quiet woman who supervises the making of costumes and sets.
**The Gardener of Trees.** Pilots the Black Square's train and oversees the writing of stories.
**The Two of Shovels.** A monster who resembles the courier's sister.
**The Seven of Stones.** A brilliant performer.
**The Six of Trees.** A difficult young man who writes stories.
**The Scout of Stones.** A ghost who operates the light machine.

## THE DELETION COMMITTEE

**Frost.** A sayer, rising in power.
**Smoke.** Frost's speaker.
**The seekers.** A pair of very old ghosts, identical and relentless.

## HOLLOW

**The glassblowers.** A group of talented artisans.
**The junk dealer.** Buys and sells nameless goods.

## OLD WHISPER

**Hand.** The first namer.
**Moon.** The second namer, first courier of the names committee.
**Needle.** A child, precious to Hand and Moon.
**The scavengers.** Among the first named, seekers of useful objects in piles of nameless junk.
**Bone, Blue, and the other one.** Elders who were children when something fell from the something tree, they remember stories from before the Silence.

# THE
# WORD
## FOR
# TROUBLE

She delivered *echo*. She delivered *echo* into a nameless gorge at the edge of everything she knew. Water dripped from rock walls and from the limbs of trees by the river down there. She called out the word, and the word rolled back to her three, four, five times, the thing calling itself by name: *echo*.

Birds flew out of the gorge. One of the men who'd followed from Jawbone spoke *echo* quiet to himself. He said the word sounded strange to him.

"They always sound strange at first," she said.


She delivered *stowaway*. She climbed aboard a freight train, hid herself in one of the boxcars, dozed as the train rolled east along the canal.

The doors slid open to gray light and the rumble of Hollow's factories. Two watchers peered inside, ghost lenses flashing. She let one of the watchers see her, and he reached for his signal box. Before he could break it open, she stood and spoke the word for the thing she was, *stowaway*.

The watchers spoke the new word, to her and to each other, until they were sure they had it right. Then they helped her down out of the car. The watchers were happy to have a word for those people. Easier to catch them that way.


She delivered *brass*. In an empty house at the edge of Tooth, she found a brass doorknob, a dented brass bowl, a brass cup. She tested their weight, felt the metal grow warm in her hands. She filled the cup with water from her canteen and drank. With the taste of brass still on her tongue, she went outside and made the delivery.

From boxes and trunks, out of attics and basements, people brought brass clocks, brass locks, brass toys, brass rings for the fingers, wrists, and neck. Some made noise with brass horns while others covered their ears or smiled and shook their heads. Nobody knew how to play.

From the factories of Hollow came new things of brass. The couriers of the names committee were issued brass buttons for their uniforms. She sat alone at her desk, working with heavy thread.

. . .

She delivered *moth*. She wrote in her report that she had seen many kinds of moth out there. More kinds of moth, maybe, than they had numbers to number them with.

The diviner who found names for flying things sat with her at the morning meal. His name was Rope, and his arms were long with ropy muscles, and he used a length of knotted rope for a belt.

"We're still finding more birds after all these years," Rope said. "*Moth* could be *bird* all over again."

She wasn't sure how long Rope had been with the committee. Sometimes, when she saw Rope, it took her a moment to remember who he was.

"*Starling, kestrel, magpie*," Rope said, rubbing his head as though the birds were within, trying to peck their way free. His pale hair was bristly, like frayed rope. "And those are just this month."

He was often like this, she remembered. Unhappy and a little resentful. Was it because the others forgot about him, too?

"You seem tired," she said.

Rope sighed and said, "Hard to sleep some nights. Especially since Buckle."

"I try not to think about Buckle," she said—trying, as she said it, not to think about Buckle.

"It's best not to think about Buckle," Rope agreed.


She delivered *harrow*. An old farmer had built one out of scrap and railroad spikes. It was a new thing, or a thing from before that was back again, which was probably more dangerous.

On the southern border, at the foot of a nameless mountain west of the Well-Named Mountains, the courier found the farmer in her barn. She was making modifications with a naphtha torch. The thing was all shadows and sharp points in flashes of hot light.

The farmer lifted her mask. Juniper, her name was. She looked at the courier's uniform and said nothing.

The courier helped her hitch the heavy frame to an old horse. Juniper had no ghosts to work her land. Out in the fields, the courier walked behind, feeling the softness of the broken soil under her boots. She took an unbroken clod in her hand and broke it. She spoke the word for the thing the farmer had built, *harrow*.

Juniper did not repeat the word aloud, the way people usually did.

The courier told her that she should have filed a request. The sayers rarely made exceptions these days. "They told my committee to send someone," the courier said. "They could have sent some of their own."

Still Juniper said nothing. But she took the courier inside and set out two bowls, filled them with potato and onion soup. A moth flew in loops around the lantern while they ate.

She delivered *whiskey*. A sayer's son had distilled barrels of the stuff in an old granary, then sent jars to senior members of the committees. *Samples for your inspection*, he wrote.

Book invited the courier to his office to share his portion of the nameless spirit. "Obviously a bribe," he said, turning the jar in his hand. "Wouldn't be right to drink it alone."

Book served as chair of the names committee. He decorated his office with purple fabric and soft pillows. He owned a stack of phonograph records from before the Silence, along with a phonograph to play them on. He wore gray suits and vests, purple ties and handkerchiefs. There had been no word for handkerchiefs until Book himself requested one from the diviners, so he could stop calling it "that rag I keep in my jacket pocket." There had been no word *purple* until Book delivered it, back in his own days as a courier.

"Let's drink until we're both of us shabby," Book said. Another courier had just delivered *shabby*, and Book liked to use the newest words. He liked to stretch them where he could.

They drank from small tin cups. Book smoked tobacco wrapped in dried tobacco leaves. He had told the diviners to take their time with that one, because sometimes Book liked the taste of something nameless.

He winced with each sip and was happy. As they drank, he told the courier about the assignment. Told her where the young man kept his still. Gave her an envelope containing the card on which was inked the word, divined by a diviner but still unspoken, unspeakable until a courier made the delivery.

"You know I'll just have to drink more when I get there," she said.

"Then you'll need the practice," Book said, refilling her cup.

The courier sank back into the cushions and Book put his feet up on his desk. It was late; most of the committee was asleep. Book wore gray slippers, his softest pair.

"You're keeping up on your training?" he said. "Keeping fit?"

She was. The courier trained every day. She stretched and lifted weights and ran end to end in the committee's small gymnasium. She read and read again what the old couriers had written down. Moon's *Words on Paper*, Glove's *Deliveries*—those texts she could recite from memory. She was the best the committee had, and Book knew it.

"I could deliver this right here," she said.

"Better to go out and make a show of it," Book said. "We can't let the sayers think that what we do is easy."

"Let the sayers think what they want," she said.

Book frowned. He did not like this kind of talk. The sayers stood above all the named, and what they said was law. More than that: their words were the shape of the world.

So he switched to his favorite subject, the latest gossip about the other committees. A daughter of the maps committee chair had run off and taken up residence in the nameless quarters of Hollow, among the thieves and poets whose stray dreams slipped from open windows to wander the streets.

"Of those kids I am perhaps a little jealous," Book admitted.

He smiled, but the courier could tell that something was troubling him. Not this assignment, not the other committees, not runaways. Something about Buckle, maybe. Something about her. She started to ask, but he downed the last of the liquor and interrupted her with a loud sigh. "I hope it's still this good after you've stuck a name to it," he said.

They both knew it wouldn't be.


She delivered *float*. She lay face-up in water and let her legs dangle. She listened to her own breathing. She had done this as a child, in the pond behind the cottage where her father had studied ghosts and nameless things. Now, in another pond on the other side of the named territories, yellow leaves fell from maples and landed on the water. The sun warmed her face and belly, but the water was cold. It rippled from her shivering.

A crowd of people watched from the shore. The water made their voices small. Fish tapped her feet with their mouths. She lay there long enough to forget what she was doing. Then she spoke the word, swam ashore, and put her clothes on.

*Float, floating, floated, floats.* Once the word was delivered, anyone could speak it, or change it a little to suit what they needed to say. *She floated. We saw her floating.*

Her committee employed diviners to find the words in their quiet chambers, using tools and methods known only to them. Couriers to deliver the words into the world. Committee pages to add the words to the next broadsheet, to print and carry copies to every place with a name. To Whisper, home of the sayers. To

Hollow, the largest city of the named, with its booming factories. To Tooth in the Well-Named Mountains, and to Tortoise on the shore of the Lake. To the cities built on top of cities from before; to the towns cobbled long ago from the nameless nothing; to the new towns on the borders, where settlers waited anxiously for words, because words were a better defense against those for whom the watchers watched than all their guns and palisades.

*A cloud floats. Leaves float. The body floated.*

She felt that the world might not keep a strong enough hold on her. A new word was a welcome weight, and each kept her stuck more firmly to the ground. But *float*, when she delivered it, was the opposite of weight. When she delivered *float*, the people laughed to hear it. They went into the pond themselves, some clothed and some naked, to say *float* while they floated, in spite of the cold. It worried her, how easy *float* had been.

She delivered a name for the ninth month. She went out on the first day and wandered. She watched what people did this time of year, and some stopped what they were doing. Stopped canning vegetables, stopped carrying wood, stopped sewing and tinkering and shoveling. They left fields and mills, left dream scraps drifting in the corners of their rooms. They followed the courier. They wanted to know how it would go. They wanted to be the first to hear.

From charts discovered on walls of structures built before the Silence, the named knew that the year was divided into twelve parts. It was the courier Glove who had delivered *month* and then, in his later years, names for most of those months. He had needed no diviner because he named the months for named things, as towns and people were named. *Under, Ink, Copse, Cloud . . .* But each time he named a month, he found it harder to deliver a name for the next. Now Glove was over one hundred years a ghost, and still the month between Axe and Stone eluded the committee. The named called it *After Axe,* but that was not its name. These were dangerous weeks, a span of time that made the nameless bold.

The courier wandered in the hills and in the forests, and the others followed her. They walked the rails, and for a while they followed the River. Rain fell, and she listened to the sound their boots made. She felt the bite of the wind on her face and hands.

In a frigid gully, among tall pines, she stopped walking. It was the last day of the month. She told the others what name to call it by. *Light.*

They were surprised. This time of year, light was something they had less of every day. They were cold and tired from their journey, but few of them left when the courier left. Most made fires by the banks of the stream there, and they hung lanterns in the pines. They tinkered and shoveled and chopped wood and built shelters. Later, when the sayers said that what lay in this gully was a village, another courier came and named it after the month of its founding.

The people who lived in the village had a saying: *In Light, even the dark feels at home.*

For the courier, home was with the names committee, aboard the train called the Number Twelve.

In the booths of the eating car, and between the broad windows of the common car, namers and crew gathered late into the night. They drank beer and wine and mugs of hot tea. Some brought fiddles and drums, and they had a piano, the one to which the courier Glove had delivered the word *piano*. The piano was never quite in tune.

In the kitchen car, cooks worked the ovens while ghosts carried water and cleaned, ducking the pots swinging from hooks. Whenever there was music in the common cars, some of the cooks came out to listen. One had a very good voice, and others would call for him to sing. A favorite was the song about the soldier who went over the border to fight the nameless, then went so far he forgot every word but the name of a woman whose smile still shone in his mind—but even that wasn't enough to bring him home.

Most days, though, few spoke above the creak and rumble of their ancient rolling home. Mahogany tables gleamed under the shaded naphtha lamps of the conference car. In the garden car, rain leaked through gaps between the ceiling's glass panels, dripping onto plants and onto the plaques that bore their names. In the ghost car, the committee's off-duty ghosts stared out the windows, or fiddled with the buttons on their dresses and shirts, or dozed in the way only ghosts dozed: perfectly still, emptying of color until you could see right through them.

When the Number Twelve came to a bend, anyone riding toward the back of the train might glimpse the engine out front, black and gold and spewing smoke, the oldest machine on the rails.

From Tortoise near the northern border, the Number Twelve could reach the mining towns of the south in one week. From Jawbone in the rugged hills of the west, four days to Hollow and the east's green lowlands, its streams and mills. Book and the train's chief engineer worked in secret to plan their route, keeping mostly to the main lines, constructed before the Silence, maintained now by crews of silent ghosts. The train's route was always changing, and the committee stayed nowhere for long. That was old law, spoken by the sayers shortly after the founding of the committees—for the safety of the namers, or so they had said.

The other three standing committees—maps, ghosts, dreams—all had offices in Whisper, and in other cities as well. Their members came and went as they pleased, or as their work required. But the namers were the exiles, the strange people, cast out and feared and on the move forever. Moon, the second namer, who divined and delivered *ghost* and who brought upon the committee its great shame, had written: *We do not belong to the world we name. We are only the words we deliver, and then we are not even those.*

The cars closest to the engine were forbidden to the couriers. These were for the diviners and their work, for the chief engineer and the assistant engineers. The courier never went farther up the train than Book's office, which filled one side of the seventh car.

After each of her assignments, Book summoned her there and kept her up too late. He never went farther from the train than a station bar, and he wanted to hear everything.

"Give me the finer details, won't you?" he said. "Your reports are so dry I have to take them with whiskey."

He drank whiskey anyway as she told him about the flying machines of the watchers, gliding silently into dock at the watchtower in Whisper. About dredgers hoisting sunken boats and old ghosts from the poisoned lakes north of Hollow. About the ghost wranglers, rough women and men, leading columns of their quarry from the border to the auction houses of Jawbone.

When she told Book what she saw while out on her last delivery, they could pretend that this was official committee work, part of her report. And when he talked about his own days with a courier's satchel on his shoulder, they could pretend that it was part of her ongoing training.

Book had delivered *official* and *ongoing*. He had delivered *perhaps* and *however*, *gossip* and *cajole* and *grudge*, *seethe* and *indulge* and *dissolute*. But of all the words Book had delivered, he was most proud of *shadow*.

"We didn't think of shadows as separate from the things that made them," he said. "We hardly even noticed they were there. The nameless still hide in shadows, but it was worse when shadows weren't *shadow*, just places where the light didn't reach, and no one knew to look for them."

The old words were gone forever. The diviners of the names committee found new words, arranged glyphs to capture sounds for them. But before a word could be spoken aloud by others, a courier had to speak it first. And to speak a new word, the courier had to know the thing it named. Had to hold it in mind like a perfect glass bead, had to become that bead—and then had to break it. What had Book done to hold, to become, to break *shadow*? He would never say.

He added a scoop of glittering black naphtha to his stove, and the fire blazed while the wind hurled cold rain against the windows. The courier thought of Hand, the first namer, who had divined and delivered the first word by thrusting one hand into a fire, somewhere in the vast wasteland that was then the whole of the world. *Hand,* said Hand, naming the thing that burned, naming himself. Or herself: Hand had been neither man nor woman, because there was no *he* then, no *she*. Most agreed that if you found the ghost that had been Hand, you would know it only by the scars of that first naming.

Outside, the winds picked up. The Number Twelve rolled alongside a river, the widest river they knew, the one called the Other. The courier knew that towns stood on the other side of the Other, but she could see no towns through the heavy gray rain.

"I wonder if this is what it looked like," she said to Book. "Just after, I mean."

"After something fell?" Book said.

"After something fell from the something tree," she said, which was the closest anyone could get to saying what had happened to make the old words go away.

Book tapped ashes into the tray on his desk and said, "I am pleased to say that I have no idea what it looked like then." But Book usually knew more than he said.


Behind Book's car were the two cars where the couriers had their compartments. Hers was near the middle of the ninth car. Her curtains, stitched from an old dress that had belonged to her mother, billowed when it was warm enough to leave the window open. Now, in the cooler months, she kept windows and curtains closed, and the fabric dyed the light in her compartment blue.

She wrote letters and reports on a desk that folded down from the wall. She kept her satchel on a peg by the door, kept her uniform in the drawer below her bunk. She kept sketches tucked into the bottom of that drawer, and sometimes she took them out and looked at them. In one of the sketches, a man she was supposed to have forgotten stood alongside ghosts in the field, pointing with a stick at something in the dirt. In another, two young girls—she and her sister, who seemed to have forgotten about her—sat at a table with chalk and a slate between them.

The courier did not feel at home here in her compartment, nor amid the cluttered finery of Book's office. If she thought about it—and the courier did think about it—she knew she felt most at home on the walkways above the couplings, with the wind rushing and the noise of the train pounding at her skin, for that moment it took to pass from one car to the next.

She delivered names to children. The younger the child, the easier the delivery. At the stations, parents held their children in their arms, rocked them when they cried, waited their turn on the platform. No one called the children *nameless,* they were only *unnamed.* The couriers consulted clipboards, looked into the children's eyes, saw something from which they might hang a word.

At one stop, the courier named the children Ruffle, Scout, Chisel, Loop, and Onion. At another, Spool, Dash, Quick, and Bet. She named a set of twins Eager and Echo. She told one mother that her son's name was Moth.

"You don't have to give them the newest we have," one of the other couriers snapped.

The couriers were permitted to use any word secure in the archives of the sayers. Most gave names delivered generations before, words sturdy in people's minds. Stone, Run, River, Sun, Gather, Bone. The old names stuck better, they said. Kept a person's feet on the ground.

But the courier chose names she thought the children might ask for if they were old enough to ask. New words with rough edges, names that felt good to shout during games of chase. They had long tethers, those names, and their teachers might struggle with them a little.

As for her name? When the others spoke of her, they called her the courier who delivered trouble. *Trouble* had been one of her first assignments, and they must have found that fitting. They couldn't call her by name, because she was the only member of the committee—the only member of any committee—who didn't have one.

Her father had known Book when Book still made deliveries. He had known others in the names committee, and even a few of the sayers in Whisper, because of his work for the war effort. His name was Lock, and he would have been able to get her most any name she wanted, any name that fit. She might have been Cup or Whistle. Or Troop, or Cap, or Blue—all names she had favored at one time or another.

But when the Number Twelve stopped in their town, Lock never took her to the station to see the namers. Once, after hearing the train's strident whistle, she had run to him and begged to go. But he had only crouched beside her, straightened her collar, and said, "The work is more important than any name. Your work, daughter, and mine."

The work was conducted in Lock's cottage overlooking the pond. He studied ghosts there—the ghosts of mice and rabbits when he could catch them, the ghosts of people when they weren't needed in the fields. He also studied the things that escaped from her dreams at night. And sometimes he studied her.

This was the most important part of the work—she could tell by his silence as he affixed the wires to her head and laid her down on the long metal table, which was cold even with the blanket he let her bring from the house. The wires ran across the floor to a row of bulky machines. Lock watched the machines as they blinked and hummed, and their humming followed her into dreams. She came to understand that her dreams were interesting to him only because she did not have a name. That if she were given a name, he might not be interested in her at all.

Years before she was born, Lock had taken her older sister to see the couriers of the Number Twelve. Ticket, her sister's name was. A sly, quick-moving girl with black wavy hair and freckles on her nose and cheeks. At the edge of the wood, in the shadows of the trees, Ticket had recited old naming songs as though she had invented them—which was, she said, the best way to recite them.

> The bear is woolly and full of blood.
> Red is the blossom, red was the bud.

Ticket had gone to creche in Whisper, where she sang those songs alongside the daughters and sons of sayers. When she returned home to begin her schooling, she pretended not to see the unnamed little girl, who had appeared in their house just when their mother had become a ghost. The girl understood that this had not been a fair trade—that Ticket would gladly have given up her sister to get their mother back. And if the girl asked questions about their mother, Ticket would only tilt her head and frown, as though to say, *Did I hear something?* Then she would return to whatever she was doing—sewing or drawing or looking at maps.

At night, the girl the courier had been would speak her sister's name to herself, whispering so that Ticket wouldn't hear from the other side of their shared room. The girl imagined she could keep her sister with her forever, just so long as she remembered the shape of her name. Ticket was proud of that name. She collected train ticket stubs and put them in an album with the word *Ticket* written on the cover. "You need a ticket to get anywhere," Ticket liked to say.

Now, seated at the desk in her compartment to write another letter, the courier asked about that album.

*Do you still add new stubs when you find them, or are the pages full? Does it sit on a shelf beside the letters I write? Or do you toss my letters straight into the fire, so you can read the flames the way I read your silence?*

She delivered *walnut*. She sat at the edge of a field, in the shadow of the tree she'd chosen for the delivery. The cold had turned its leaves bright yellow.

She ran her fingers along the hollows and ridges of the bark. She gathered the fallen fruit, tore the green hulls, broke shells with a rock, smelled and tasted the bitter, soft kernels.

With her back to the tree, she sharpened the axe she had borrowed from a workshop in the nearest village. She thought she could hear the tree hold its breath.

She swung the axe and felt its bite. She put her face to the wound and breathed the smell of the sapwood. She cut deeper and breathed the smell of the heartwood. She cut deeper and opened the tree's dark pith. In spite of the cold, she began to sweat. She took off her coat and kept swinging.

The people of the nearest village gathered to watch. When the tree fell, the noise of its falling seemed to come from everywhere at once. Into the silence that followed, the courier spoke its name.

"Walnut," the villagers said, trying it out for themselves. They wanted to hear it in their own voices. They wanted to say they had been among the first.

The courier returned the borrowed axe and put her coat back on. She left the wood for the villagers to cut and gather, but she kept one of the seeds—wrapped it up tight in a handkerchief and tucked it into her satchel.

She brought the walnut seed home to her ghost.

The ghost was called the patchwork ghost, and he looked like a skinny man Book's age or a little older. He wore a gray suit and hat. Both had been patched so many times that the gray was barely visible. The ghost's patches were brightly colored: red, yellow, purple, green. Even some of the patches had patches.

She found the ghost at work in the printing car, where committee pages set type for the newest words and inked them onto broadsheets—dozens of copies for every town in the named territories, hundreds for each of the larger cities. The ghost's job was to draw the things the new words named. He illustrated the broadsheets as quickly as the pages could print them, and the drawings were nearly identical from one sheet to the next.

Seated beside him, the courier unwrapped the walnut seed. The ghost's eyes brightened. He shoved the broadsheets aside, set the seed on the table, and took a sketchbook from his jacket pocket.

The patchwork ghost had belonged to her father. When Book brought the courier aboard the Number Twelve, she had insisted that the ghost come with her, so Book had made arrangements. Finding a use for the ghost was easy enough. He was the only ghost who knew how to draw.

While the ghost drew the walnut, the courier reviewed the newest words on the broadsheet. For *cirrus,* he had drawn wisps of cloud above a high mountain peak. For *plum,* a dark round fruit hanging from a branch. She had tasted a plum shortly after another courier delivered the word. The named would like plums, she thought.

A shadow fell over the words. Three committee pages were standing over her. They were young, two boys and a girl. Their uniforms fit awkwardly, and they looked tired. They had probably stayed up too late, likely together in one of their compartments, maybe with whiskey—some of Book's stash had recently gone missing. Now they were rushing to finish the broadsides.

The girl's name was Sun. "He has hundreds left to do," Sun said. "You can take one when he's finished."

The courier wanted to tell the pages that she had delivered half of the words on that broadsheet. That she would take a copy when she wanted one. But then she saw how the boys wouldn't look at her, saw how Sun's hands were shaking.

They were frightened of her.

It had been this way since Buckle.

So the courier took a breath and said, "Of course. You all have important work to do."

She took the walnut and slipped it into her jacket pocket. The ghost blinked and turned from side to side, overcome with panic. The courier closed his sketchbook and tucked it back in his jacket pocket, moved the stack of unfinished broadsides in front of him. A moment later, he resumed work on the illustrations. The panic was gone, but so was the brightness in his eyes.

The boys looked relieved and returned to the printing machine. Not Sun, though. Her friend Wheel had been with the courier at Buckle that day. Sun kept her arms folded over her chest, watching the courier until she stood and left.

In the eating car, the courier listened to the others discuss their assignments. The couriers talked about how long they had been *out there,* they talked about *the word,* about the weight of it, about what they had done to make the delivery. They talked about *those others,* the people without names. How they saw or thought they saw a band of them at the edge of the forest, on the side of the road, by the banks of the river, in the shadows, in *the middle of the night.* How they felt them watching, following.

And they talked about Buckle.

She tried not to listen. But Ivy, who had also been there that day, was seated at the table across the aisle, telling her audience how it happened. How she had been about to leave Buckle Station with a new word in her satchel. It should have been an easy one, Ivy said. But to speak the word now made her shudder.

"Imagine, after seeing what I saw, having to deliver *giggle.*"

The other couriers at her table shook their heads.

Ivy kept her straight yellow hair cut to her jawline, kept her uniform pressed and neat. She had a sharp-looking smile and bright green eyes that missed nothing. Ivy had been born on the Number Twelve. She began training for the names committee on her first day back from creche, and she could trace her family line through generations of couriers. Her mother's mother had marched alongside soldiers on the southern border, naming towns and territories, naming prisoners. Now Ivy, too, had seen firsthand what the nameless could do.

A cold morning early in the month of Ink. At Buckle, a quarrying town on the canal called the Ribbon, the namers let off five of their own, an unusually high number. Ivy, the courier, and three committee pages.

The courier had gone to the watchers on the platform to show them her papers. She had lingered long enough to let Ivy get ahead, knowing she wouldn't want company. Once the three pages were cleared, she walked behind them into the station.

The pages' satchels were full of broadsheets, and they laughed at how strange it felt to walk on steady ground after so many weeks aboard the train. They would travel together through Buckle, then split up to cover the smaller towns along the canal.

Wheel was the eldest of the three. She hoped to become a diviner someday.

Paw never wanted to be anything but a page, though he preferred working the press to delivering broadsides. Thumb had just celebrated his fourteenth name day. He was the youngest member of the committee, and Buckle was his first assignment.

They had just gone out among the benches when the nameless appeared. They slipped into the green light of the station, shadows dividing from shadow. They were seven or eight in number, faces hidden behind plain white masks.

Later, some people would say that monsters had come with the nameless, but Ivy and the courier agreed on this much: there was only the one monster. It looked like a round mushroom the size of a child, but shiny, like something made of glass.

Two of the nameless carried the monster between them. At first the courier didn't think it was dangerous. She'd thought it was something the nameless had captured. She'd thought it was afraid—and maybe it was.

They set the monster on the floor in the middle of the station. One of them knelt beside it and did something. Nudged it, maybe, or caressed it. The courier couldn't see clearly, and Ivy was already at the door to the street.

Now Ivy said to the others, "At first I mistook the screams for a train braking. I turned just in time to see what was really happening."

When the monster woke, it expanded. A thing like a living detonation, gathering the glassy stuff of itself into spines and sharp edges, jagged stalks unfurling. Without a sound it sliced and bounded, spreading through the station in shuddering bursts, the way ice spreads over glass.

Ivy had been standing just beyond the monster's reach. The nameless were untouched—as was the courier without a name. Most others in the station fell.

The pages writhed at the courier's feet, their bodies pierced by spines, slashed by the monster's knifelike limbs. The courier knelt beside them, reaching first for one and then for another, wanting to hold them, to piece them back together.

"Paw, Wheel, Thumb," Ivy said. "All ghosts now. And how many others? The two watchers running from their checkpoint, taken apart before they could open their signal box. Four machinists waiting for the train to Hollow, ghosts before they understood what was happening."

The courier had stared at the nameless, their boots on the limestone floor, their rustling gray robes. She saw them see her, saw them blink behind their masks. She felt their minds seeking hers, wondering at what she was. As one they drew their weapons—then turned their backs on her, going for Ivy instead.

The courier remembered thinking how beautiful Ivy looked as the nameless surrounded her. How her eyes flashed in the light that shone through the station windows. The nameless came at her with knives and clubs, but also with stranger weapons. Hooked blades, metal bars linked by chains, long poles fitted with spikes. All Ivy had were words and the threat of a name that might stick. The courier admired the sound of her voice, the roughness of it. *Dirt* was one of the words she spat at them, and *crooked* was another. *Burn. Split. Break.* Ivy's cap fell from her head, freeing her pale hair as she ducked and wheeled. The courier wanted to help her, but the other end of the station seemed miles away.

So she snatched up one of the watchers' signal boxes and smashed it hard against the floor, freeing the pigeon within. The bird flew through an open window high in the station wall, out over the city toward Buckle's watchtower. The moment the signal was spotted, more watchers would come.

The nameless saw, and they hesitated. For a moment, the station was silent except for Ivy's ragged breaths.

Only then could the courier bring herself to run, but by then the nameless had scattered. Some rejoined the shadows while others fled through the doors and into the winding streets of the old town.

Their monster, spread too thin to sustain itself, struck out with a final convulsive lash before falling to shards. Ivy collapsed to the floor as ghosts rose to their feet all around them.

"Twelve ghosts, I heard," one of the couriers at the next table said, and another, almost to himself as he sipped his tea: "I heard eighteen."

But Ivy was shaking her head. "I met someone from calibration on my last run," she said. "He told me they took twenty-six ghosts from Buckle station that day."

The others were silent. Twenty-six was more than anyone had guessed, more than anyone wanted to believe. The courier, seated alone at her table, turned and looked out the window.

Ivy leaned toward her across the aisle, yellow hair hanging to her chin. "I'm still amazed that you and I made it," she said. "But then, the nameless didn't go after you, did they?"

When the courier didn't answer, Ivy turned back to her table. "They always recognize their own," she said.


Beryl's advice was simple. "Ignore them," she said. "They push you around because they know they can't beat you."

Between assignments, when the courier wasn't visiting Book or her ghost, she mostly kept to herself. When she did invite a woman or a man into her compartment, or to share her bunk, she rarely invited a fellow courier. Most of the time, she invited Beryl.

Beryl had big hands and a big laugh, and she liked to take her hair down the moment she came through the compartment door. She was a diviner, one of those who found new words for the couriers to deliver. Now Beryl lay sprawled over the courier's mattress, bare feet up against the wall. For days afterward, the courier knew, she would find strands of red hair on her pillow and between her sheets. She didn't mind.

"They push me around because I never took a name," she said. "And because they think I'm Book's favorite."

"You're *my* favorite," Beryl said. "That's more important."

The couriers and the diviners had long maintained a rivalry that was not always friendly. The question, usually unasked but always in the air, was who did the real work of naming. The diviners, behind the locked doors of the divining car, employing secret arts to hunt new words and snare them with glyphs? Or the couriers, who traversed city, forest, and field, seeking those things—difficult to find because they were unnamed—to which the words might finally be bound?

But Beryl and the courier didn't trouble themselves with any of that. The courier never boasted of her deliveries, and Beryl never complained the way the other diviners did when the headaches came, never sat in the eating car after divining a new word, sipping thin broth, eyes squinted against the faintest light.

Beryl divined names for machines and machine parts. She kept a pencil tucked behind one ear and her tobacco pipe in her shirtfront pocket. She had divined *cylinder, counterweight, hydraulic,* and *weir.* The courier was rarely assigned words that Beryl divined, but she knew that *harrow* had been one of hers, because they had talked about Juniper, the old farmer who built one in the shadow of those unnamed mountains.

The courier sat beside Beryl and took a deep breath. She wasn't sure what it meant to be someone's favorite.

"Tell me what you're feeling," Beryl said.

"There aren't words for half the things I feel," the courier said, and Beryl laughed.

Each new thing was a danger, a tool the nameless might use against the named, but Beryl was thrilled by them. She told the courier that when the names committee put the Number Twelve into service, no one really knew how the engine worked. Even now, parts of the engine were still unnamed. And because the Number Twelve had served as model for many of the machines built or rebuilt since—for other engines on the rails and for the churning giants that powered Hollow's factories—the named were steaming along on the back of principles they barely understood.

"It's part numbers and part guesswork, built with tools dug up from the other side of the Silence," Beryl said. "It's enough to make you think the world could end all over again."

She spoke this way often enough that the courier was not wholly joking when she said, "You'd like that, wouldn't you?"

"What I'd like," Beryl said—and she finished the sentence by pulling the courier down onto the mattress with her.

Beryl's skin was pale against the courier's hands. The courier breathed in the scent of her, sharp and smoky, like naphtha and cedar burning together. Beryl turned the black curls of the courier's hair on her fingers, searching her eyes, and the courier knew she was seeking a name, trying to claim her as the namers claimed each new thing. It pleased her, this attention, though they both understood that if she were named, she would cease to be what she was. This had grown into a game between them. Undressing on the narrow bunk, they played it without words: a search, a retreat, a surrender.

"You are a puzzle," Beryl said into the courier's ear, speaking the word as though it were the finest word they had. And when Beryl said it, the courier thought that maybe it was.


Alone, she puzzled things over. The body, too, was a machine they did not understand, housing parts, capacities, sensations for which they had no names. The named pretended not to know. The courier tried, too.

But sometimes, especially at night, and especially when the chief engineer got the furnace burning hot, she imagined she could hear a question in the engine's roar, and feel an answer in the ache of her own body. Together, she and the engine made a music, soaring and strange, and she was afraid that everyone aboard the train could hear.

On the other side of the glass, cinders flew with the smoke, flashing orange before they vanished into the ditch beside the rails. She dreamed she was one of those cinders, streaking over the fields, never letting herself land, because if she landed she would burn the world.


She delivered *tapestry*. She delivered *stoat* and *custom, outrage* and *shortcut.* In Book's office, she said, "You could just read my reports. It's a lot of work to write them down."

"It's a lot of work to read them," he said. "Indulge me. I'm an old man, and the sound of your voice is a comfort."

So she indulged him with the story of *shortcut*, telling him of the narrow route, favored by the children of Leaf, that wound through alleyways and under balconies, connecting the center of town to the wooded gully where they liked to swim in summer and sled in winter. But she had only just begun speaking when the roar of an engine on the opposite tracks silenced her.

An army train. Behind the hulking locomotive came flatcar after flatcar, green and gray and black. The cars were freighted with war machines, their ghost-burning engines new from the factories, armor plates gleaming like the shells of beetles in the bright winter sun.

"So many," the courier said.

"Are we at war again?" Book said. "I can never remember." He was trying to sound bored but not quite succeeding.

The wars with the nameless had begun shortly after the rise of the sayers and the exile of the names committee. It was the courier Rain who had delivered *war*, then marched with the first *soldiers* into *battle* against the *enemy*, in the wilderness west of Whisper.

For a long time, the nameless had the upper hand. Monsters, bred in nightmares and seething with hatred for named things, poured over the borders to break walls and buildings and people. Only after the named learned to build and pilot war machines were they able to push the monsters back.

The courier counted three types of machine on the train. The biggest were the brutes, slouched like dozing bears, clawed hands resting in their laps. Only slightly smaller were the mantises, which the courier knew from the stories to be very fast, their forearms lined with jagged blades. Smallest were the lizards, sleek and nimble, serving mostly as scouts.

None of these machines were *primed*. That was the word the committee had delivered to describe the process that made a war machine operable. Each would have a monster burned in its furnace, to transfer something of its spirit into the machine. Only then, with a pilot trained to negotiate with the monster in its bones, could a war machine stand against the living monsters of the nameless. The process had been refined by her father when he worked for the army, years before she was born.

He had told her stories of the battles. Of machines roaring and coughing steam while launching explosive shells and belching flaming naphtha, fields and meadows lit by the burning of monsters the size of train cars. Some of the oldest machines still patrolled the borders and railways, but most had been decommissioned. The cost to keep them running was high. Once the machines were primed, only the ghosts of people, pure and unrefined, were potent enough to fire those great engines.

Instead of sending war machines, the maps committee charted the land. The couriers delivered names to hills, rivers, and meadows. The sayers spoke law and established settlements on the borders. The borders shifted outward, and with them the outposts of the wranglers, who trekked deeper into name-less territory to capture ghosts for the auction houses.

And hadn't the borders been quiet for many years? Most of the monsters encountered by the named were sorry, ragged things—a shouted word would send them scampering into the shadows. Yet here were new machines, the train that bore them stretching on and on.

"Because of Buckle?" the courier asked.

"There have been other attacks," Book said quietly. "Some among the say-ers think the only way to stop them is with a show of force."

She knew which sayers he meant. The one named Frost would be first among them. But Book didn't like to talk about Frost, and neither did she.

"But where are they going?" she asked. "Who will they fight?"

Book looked uncomfortable. "There are reports—which I do not neces-sarily believe—that the maps committee is on the verge of a major discovery. Their scouts speak of a city. A city that stands at the edge of the world."

"I don't understand," the courier said.

"I think you do," Book said. "A *city*. And beyond the city, nothing at all. Nothing to be mapped. Nothing to be named."

There had long been rumors—even before Book delivered *rumor*—of the last great city of the nameless. It appeared in a few old songs and stories, mostly those told by the Black Square Show or swapped by ghost wranglers and dreams committee hunters in their remote outposts and lodges.

"If the reports are mistaken, then why so many new machines?" she asked.

Without thinking, she had prompted Book for something he would not say. To admit that the sayers could be wrong. What the sayers said was law, and it was their law that bound the names committee to the train, that granted Book his power as committee chair. Who was he to speak against sayers?

Still the cars of the army train swept past, the metal skin of war machines flashing in the moonlight.

"Maybe that's enough for now," Book said, closing the cover on her report. "Another one for the archives, yes?"

His voice was steady, but as he swiveled in his chair and drew the curtain closed, the courier could see that his hand was shaking.


She delivered *melody*. She delivered *jumble*. She delivered *oxbow*, and *gibbous*, and *mustard*, and *sanguine*.

"Sanguine," Book said, savoring the excess. He took her by the waist and danced her around his office. "Let's you and I be sanguine together."

Before something fell from the something tree, there were words for everything, and if something new came along, anyone could find a word for it. No names committee, no diviners, no couriers. No ghosts either, some said, and others said that all the borders were more certain before, clear as lines on a map.

But those were just stories, and who could be sure? When something fell from the something tree, the old words went away, and most of the stories went with them.

This much the courier knew: some words were *border words*, and they did something more than name a thing. Only a few border words had been found, but each was a line drawn through the heart of the world, changing it forever. The first was *word*, divined and delivered by Hand long ago, so the named would know what to call the sounds that meant *hand* and *fire*, *light* and *moon*.

Years later, *sleep* was delivered by a namer named Drum, now remembered for little else. At first *sleep* hardly seemed to matter: the named saw little difference between what happened while they slept and what happened while they didn't. Then, years later still, the courier Glove—on assignment and asleep—delivered *dream*. Only then did the named understand that *sleep* had been a border word: a border between us and the place the monsters came from. Some believed that if *sleep* and *dream* had been delivered before Moon delivered *monster*, then monsters would have remained always on the other side of sleep.

It was Book's opinion that all the border words had been found, that none were left to divine and deliver. The courier knew he was wrong. In the corridors of the Number Twelve and in the streets of the named world, she listened for gaps and pauses, for a voice hesitating at the edge of something— something so big, no one knew it was there. She felt it in the air as an empty hole, dumb and hungry. She felt it when she heard new words, those bright jags of sound, rough and warm and strange. She felt it when she heard a word she had delivered—*moth, brisk, calf, trouble*—and the hair on her arms stood up. It was the word at the bottom of everything.

She delivered *gossamer*. She delivered *burdock* and *snoop*. She delivered *switchback* and *glee, fluster* and *twine*.

Some of those words might find their way into the naming songs, for children to sing at creche. But the courier wanted more. Someday, she would deliver a border word of her own. And only then—when she was old and tired, tired of everything she was—would she give herself a name and become something else, something for which she didn't yet have a word.

The other couriers rarely visited the ghost car near the back of the train. The windows were cracked, the walls and floors scuffed and gouged. Here, off-duty ghosts tied and untied their shoes, or tapped their feet in time to the clunking of the wheels, or tried to solve the unsolvable puzzles of wood, rope, and iron the mechanics made to keep them busy. Ghosts just back from calibration sat still with their hands folded in their laps, gazing straight ahead. Others faded like fraying cloth as they slept the not-sleep of ghosts.

Some of the ghosts had been with the committee since its founding. References to them—to the ghost with one arm, to the big ghost with gray eyes—could be found in the earliest records of the named. Some knew how to fix parts of the train, and some knew how to repair track. Some worked in the kitchens alongside the cooks. Some worked with the chief engineer and the assistant engineers, minding gauges and shoveling fuel.

When the patchwork ghost wasn't making sketches for the newest broadsheet, he made sketches of whatever he wanted in the sketchbooks the courier brought for him. Whenever he filled a sketchbook, he added it to the bulging sack beneath his seat.

"Show me the new ones?" the courier said, and the ghost flipped pages so she could see.

In some, the courier found things she recognized. A bridge, a town, a bend in a particular stream. Other sketches only felt familiar. A boy's face in a window. A woman leading a horse from a barn. A man in a heavy coat standing at the edge of a pond. She wondered if the ghost might one day see her sister through his window. If she would find Ticket's face in his sketch of a street, a station, a crossing. That face would be older now, the freckles darker, and her black hair might be ribboned with gray. She hoped for that moment of recognition, but she also felt sick for hoping.

The patchwork ghost sketched more than what he saw through the windows. Sometimes he wandered the train in search of new subjects. He had sketched the piano in the common car, every pot and utensil in the kitchen car, every plant in the garden car. He sketched stray tools, and plates of food, and shoes, and ghosts, and namers. Among his books was a sketch of Beryl in the common car, studying a sheaf of schematics by the light of a naphtha lamp. One of Rope, the diviner who found names for flying things, seated with his eyes closed among the garden car's plants. One of Book standing beside the engine at some station, laughing with two of the mechanics.

Sometimes, in his search for new subjects, the ghost made trouble. He once spilled a barrel of pickled vegetables in storage. He'd torn up plants because he wanted to draw their roots. He stole paper from the printing car when the courier forgot to give him a new sketchbook. The courier knew when her ghost had done something wrong from the particular way the porters pounded at her compartment door.

But nothing she said to the ghost could convince him to stop seeking new subjects. And why would she want him to? Sometimes he sketched from memory, and those were trouble of another kind. Most of them she hid in the drawer below her bunk, because among them were sketches of her father. She was supposed to have forgotten him, but she had not forgotten him, and neither had her ghost.

The courier wondered about the man her ghost had been when he was still alive. She thought she could imagine the sound of his voice, kind but a little sharp, taking care with each word.

She took the walnut from her pocket. "I thought you might want this back," she said.

The ghost tilted his head. She wanted his excitement to return, but he only looked sad, as though from the memory of having lost it. He looked away.

She closed her hand around the walnut and wished she could fall right through the floor of the train. She often wondered if she was being selfish, keeping him with her aboard the Number Twelve. But she needed him here, didn't she? And didn't the committee need him, too? Besides, this was better than being put to work in one of the factories in Hollow, or at some isolated switch on the line.

The courier shoved the walnut back in her pocket. She rose to leave, but the ghost stopped her with a hand on her arm. She watched, surprised, as he turned his sketchbook to another page and pointed to something he had drawn there.

This was strange. Usually, the ghost showed her his work only if she asked. Stranger still was what she saw on the page. Not her sister. Not a member of the names committee, or one of the other ghosts. No one she recognized—at least not at first.

A pair of figures, strangers to her, yet she *did* know them.

But only from one of the oldest stories of the named.

"Look at this," she told Book. "Tell me what you see."

He leaned over the open sketchbook she'd place on his desk. Squinted. Blinked. "The ghost let you take this from him?"

"I have to return it soon or he'll come looking for it," she said. "But you're stalling. I want you to tell me what you see in this drawing."

Book scratched his jaw and looked bored. "I see people with funny marks on their faces. Lines, dots of paint. If pressed, I would say they look a little like—

"They look like Hand and Moon," the courier said. In the stories, it was told how the first namers painted their faces with marks by which they might know one another. Later, Moon used those marks as some of the first glyphs— for it was Moon who devised their system for recording words on paper.

Book seemed doubtful.

"Look where he's drawn them," the courier said.

The pair stood on a city street, the buildings behind them in ill repair. Great heaps of junk lay piled on the sidewalks. "It's Whisper," she said.

"Is it?"

"Not Whisper as it stands now. The Whisper of three or four hundred years ago. Before they fixed the glass, and built the new station, and repaired the roads."

"Perhaps," Book said lightly.

"Perhaps? Book, there's no mistaking it. Hand and Moon in old Whisper, just as they're described in story. The ghost must have been there. He must have seen the first of the named."

Book leaned back in his chair. "Or your ghost has heard the stories, same as you and me. Heard them often enough to illustrate them." He held up one hand before she could protest. "Think this through. If your ghost was around at that time—three or four hundred years ago, as you say—then he'd have been calibrated a dozen times since. He wouldn't remember anything."

But her father had never sent the ghost away for calibration, and when agents of the ghosts committee came aboard to inspect the namers' stock, they left the patchwork ghost uncalibrated. He was the only ghost who could draw, a useful skill. Book knew this, because he had been the one to deliver the word *exception,* shortly after delivering *official,* to explain her own presence aboard the train. The word also applied to her ghost.

Book snapped his fingers. "I have it," he said. "The Black Square Show."

"I don't see what the Black Square has to do with this," the courier said.

"Well, have you seen them *perform*?" He drew out the word as though it could not really describe what the Black Square did.

The show had come to her town when she was a girl, but her father had refused to take her, just as he'd refused to take her to the namers.

"They used to play the Story of Hand and Moon all the time," Book went on. He tore the end off a roll of tobacco and lit it with a match, puffed the ember to life. "The patchwork ghost must have seen one of those performances. Years ago, this would have been, because the Black Square no longer plays that story."

"I didn't think ghosts attended performances," she said.

"Oh, they turn no one away," Book said, ignoring her tone. He flipped back through the ghost's sketchbook. When he found what he was looking for, he patted the pages. "Here we are. Now I'm sure of it."

He turned the sketchbook for her; the courier sat and pulled the chair closer to his desk. It was a drawing of a shabby train, the cars all different sizes. "You must see it now and then, while you're out on assignment?" he asked.

She had caught sight of it several times, most recently on a trestle outside Brick. The cars of the Black Square's train were painted bright colors—red, orange, gold, and blue—but the paint was chipped and fading. It was the Number Twelve's strange sister, though the courier didn't know what the train was called. She didn't think it had a name.

"Listen," Book said, leaning back into his cloud of smoke. "I want you to tell me if you see the train again. I want to know where you see it, where it's headed. I want to know its velocity."

*Velocity* was a new word, and he used it with relish. But he must have realized how strange his request sounded, because after a moment he added, "Maybe I'll arrange for our routes to line up, if the chief engineer and I can manage it. We could all use a little distraction, don't you think?"

She closed the sketchbook and set it in her lap. "The Black Square Show," she said. "Old stories made real again."

"Don't expect too much," Book said. "The Black Square is a ghost of what it used to be."

She had heard the same from Beryl, who had seen it twice, and from a committee page who had caught the show by chance while delivering broadsides. The Black Square once played all the great cities of the named, performing stories of the first namers, of the wars with the nameless, and even wordless stories of the Silence. Now its train traced the ragged edges of the maps, a rambling, worn-out thing, long past its glory, its purpose uncertain.

"What went wrong?" the courier asked. "I've heard rumors, but—"

"Something happened to one of the players," Book said. "This was in Whisper, right where everyone could see. Right where the sayers could see."

"Someone became a ghost," the courier said, remembering.

"A *genuine* ghost, and the show is supposed to be pretend," Book said. "So the sayers spoke new law, banning the Black Square from the cities of the interior." He puffed thoughtfully at his tobacco. "The players never really belonged to the named. But I wonder who they belong to now. If they even belong to themselves anymore."

He sent a cloud of smoke toward the ceiling and watched it rise, blinking as though he could already see those threadbare figures emerge onto the stage, under the naphtha lights.


In the common car that night, she told Beryl about Book's request.

"He relies on you too much," Beryl said. "Let him find the Black Square himself."

"You don't want to see the show?"

"I'd rather we just run away together. We can build a cottage out in the forest where no one will find us. Grow our own vegetables, chop firewood instead of burning naphtha. . . . What? Oh, your ghost can come with us."

The car was loud with music and talk, but still the courier shushed her. Beryl knew as well as anyone what happened to namers who fled the Number Twelve in defiance of the old laws. The stories were few, mostly about pages and couriers who went out on assignment and chose not to return. The frightening part was not that the watchers always tracked them down, but that no one seemed to know what happened next. The stories always ended there, and no one remembered the names of those who were gone—and that meant deletion committees were involved, like those favored by Sayer Frost and his allies in Whisper.

The courier said, "Sometimes I don't know if you mean anything you say." She left to refill their glasses, beer for Beryl, cider for herself. When she returned to their low couch near the back of the car, Beryl was watching in silence as a storm grayed the lightless hills north of Brick.

"Hand needed to find Moon before Hand could find *you* and *I*," Beryl said, taking her glass. It was an old saying, and part of a story that was true.

The courier settled back into the couch, but kept a little distance between herself and Beryl.

"You're angry," Beryl observed.

"I don't think you understand how careful I have to be," the courier said. And she told Beryl how, on certain city streets and country roads, she sometimes heard the nameless speaking. Except *speaking* wasn't the word.

"It's more like a tugging at the back of my skull," she said. "I can hear their thoughts. Especially when it's me they're thinking about."

It was the naming of the ninth month that really got their attention. She had felt the pull of their questions all through those weeks, and the pull had grown stronger since. A woman without a name, but not like them at all—they must have been curious. She was curious, too. She had to be careful not to let them know.

"You're one of ours," Beryl said, trying to reassure her.

"Ours," the courier agreed. But to prove that she belonged among the named, she had to keep the boundaries tight against her skin. Beryl ran her hand along the courier's arm, an apology, and the courier squeezed her hand. They leaned closer, alone again in their territory of two.

Later, in the dark of the courier's compartment, with the rain tapping against the roof of the car, Beryl asked, "How long until you leave again?"

She had never asked before.

"I have another day," the courier said carefully. "Maybe two."

"Maybe two," Beryl said, almost singing the words. She pulled the courier tight against her, and the courier pushed her fear aside, and they both stopped using words until morning came.


Two more days, and then another assignment, and then back to the train. Pages returned from assignments of their own, some with news, with rumors.

In Hollow, four workers had taken a shortcut home from the factory and arrived at the gates of their compound as ghosts. In the forests east of Bridge, a freight train was derailed and looted; by the time the watchers showed up, every member of its crew was gone. Two wranglers with a delivery of ghosts went missing on the muddy road from the eastern border, and the ghosts they had wrangled went missing, too.

Then a fire in Claw, whole blocks of the harborburned—and hadn't a child told her parents, earlier that night, that she'd seen the flash of white masks in the dark behind their house?

With each new story, the talk on the train was of what would happen next, and whether something like Buckle could happen again. When the others spoke of it, the courier listened but looked away, because she knew they were looking at her.

*Trouble*, they said in the common car, when they heard the news at the stations. *Trouble*, when the Number Twelve stopped for supplies or to name local children, and the watchers moved up and down the platform, watching the rails, watching the train, watching for what they feared was coming.

And then, while she was out on her next assignment, the courier found it for herself.

At Hollow Station, she left the train with her satchel slung over one shoulder. She found a glassblowers' workshop, a large open shed leaning against one of the great factory walls. Two people tended the furnace while others worked the glass. They were making bowls, drinking vessels, baubles.

One man's specialty was figurines. The courier watched him turn and stretch the heavy liquid into the shapes of horses and trees, serpents and flowers. He talked while he worked. He seemed to like having an audience. "And now we have wings," he said, "and legs, and claws."

He tugged tail feathers, then a beak, a bird from the red glowing—

"*Gob*," she said, delivering the name for a lump of the stuff, molten.

All seven of the crew were silent, even the one who liked to talk. Then some tried the word aloud. The maker of figurines laughed and shook his head. "*Gob*, what a word," he said. "I'm surprised you'd bother."

He was the oldest member of the crew, his hands crossed with white scars, burns from the glass. From an old boot he drew a bottle, three quarters full. He shook it and said, "Now *this* stuff. This I like very much." From the way he smiled at her, she understood that he knew her as the courier who'd delivered *whiskey*.

The Number Twelve would be at the station a few hours yet, taking on fuel and water, so the courier accepted a glass and sat at a table cluttered with mistakes: birds with one wing or one leg, a lopsided cow, bent carafes, something that looked like a fox with three tails.

"Need a word for what these are," the glassblower said. "Kids come around sometimes, up to no good. Want to buy them or steal them if they can."

"And what do you do with them?"

He opened his mouth to answer, but one of the others called from the furnace, "We smash them. All of them, every night."

The word *shard* was old, almost as old as *glass*. But there were no words for these glittering shapes, which were too much like monsters. Their curves and facets shone strangely in the light.

The old man's smile was kind. But after the courier had finished her whiskey, she turned down the offer of a second pour.

The sun was going down by the time she left for the station. Springtime now, and the nights were still cool. She walked quickly, the whiskey sloshing hot in her belly.

The machines of the city boomed and blared, heaving smoke into the sky. Whistles sounded the changing shifts; ghosts marched in columns from great bay doors, bearing crates to waiting freight cars while ghosts committee drovers looked on. Some of the ghosts, bound for labors elsewhere, stowed themselves among the cargo.

The courier could feel the pavement humming. Workers saw her uniform and stared. She had come this way earlier, but now the way seemed unfamiliar. A knife grinder looked up as she moved to avoid the sparks from his stone. A boy led three ghosts tied with a single rope into a wide brick structure, and a woman inside glared at her as she pulled the door shut. The courier was not where she was supposed to be.

She turned back toward the main avenue, but found herself instead among dilapidated houses and lawns of weed and ash. That whiskey was strong stuff. A few flickering lights shone through the threadbare curtains of the nearest house. Music from nameless instruments swelled from within, and the courier heard laughter, shouting, singing. A woman sat on the stoop, smoking fermented draff from a long pipe.

The courier remembered Book's stories of runaways and dissolute artists. Some found their way to the Black Square Show, some to certain nameless districts of the larger cities, including Hollow. The woman looked up and smiled. The flame of a match illuminated her face. It was painted green and gold.

The courier hurried past. All she could see of the factories were the smokestacks. All she could hear of them was a distant grinding, like ragged breath. She was alone—and then she was not alone.

She felt their thoughts before she saw them, the tingling at the back of her skull. She had felt it a dozen times before. She had felt it that day at Buckle, but even then it wasn't this strong, this insistent. Whispers and questions, threats and warnings, all wordless.

They came from the dark between the buildings, up stairwells, past sagging iron gates. Rustling into the light, they were shadows one moment, something else the next. Their masks were plain and white, each molded to the shape of an identical face with wide expressionless eyes and mouths. She told herself not to run. Then she saw, in the folds of their gray robes, the glinting of long blades.

A cold deeper than the shadows fell through her body. She ran. The masked figures followed, unhurried, seeming to anticipate her route. They hedged her in, forcing her down winding lanes and alleyways as their minds sought hers with rough fingers. She pushed those fingers away, forced herself not to scream. Each time she thought she had found a way free, another mask

appeared on a corner, beneath an archway, on the steps of a fire escape. A
figure dropped from an overhead walkway and landed in front of her, so close
she could smell hot breath from the mask's mouth.

They herded her deeper into the nameless districts of the city, those shifting
neighborhoods that eluded the scouts and cartographers of the maps committee.
Finally, in a narrow alleyway, the figures closed in from both sides. The courier
wanted to shout as Ivy had done at Buckle, spit words to hold them off, but no
words came to her. She was drowning in the shush of their robes, the gloating
whispers of their thoughts.

Were these the same who had been at Buckle? In the station that day, their
monster had either missed or spared her. Sensing her namelessness, the nameless themselves had hesitated. Not this time, though. They drew their shining
blades, their hooks and spiked cudgels, and swiftly closed in.

She wondered how the ghost they made of her would be designated. The
ghost with tired eyes and worn boots? With brass buttons? Whatever the
ghosts committee chose for their register, it would be the closest thing to a
name she'd ever get. But the ghosts committee probably wouldn't find the
ghost she became. Not if the nameless smuggled it away into the wilds beyond
the border, as they were known to do with the ghosts they stole and with the
ghosts they made.

She pivoted, trying to guess which of them would spring first. When one
lunged, she surprised herself by catching the wrist behind the knife. She pulled
her attacker over her outstretched leg and sent them hurtling into one of the
others. Both fell, their weapons clattering against the bricks.

She felt a shift in their thoughts. While the two picked themselves up, the
others moved more cautiously. She felt the hum of a single mind, gathering
itself, focusing. Then the mind's seven bodies moved toward her as one.

A door opened behind her, and from it came light and a draft of cool,
musty air. A short man with a round, stubbled face stood in the doorway.
He wore a gray cap on his head and a gray silk robe over a rumpled blue shirt
and trousers. He looked at the masks, at the knives and stranger weapons. He
looked at the courier and squinted. He didn't seem afraid, only annoyed.

He grabbed the courier and pulled her with him through the door, then
slammed it shut. Hands scrabbled over the other side as though searching for
a latch. The man slid a bolt into place. One of the nameless pounded on the
door, once, twice, three times. Then nothing.

The man gestured for the courier to follow. Taking the stale air in gulps,
she went with him toward what looked like an office. A lamp burned low on a
cluttered desk. In its glow she saw strange shapes, objects stuffed onto shelves
and heaped over the floor.

The courier's vision blurred as she tried to make sense of what she saw. Nameless things, all of them. At first their shapes and colors eluded her, forms falling to shadow when she tried to focus. Then she made out books and bottles, equipment for sports or for war, rolled schematics, lamps topped by bulbs of lightless glass, jars of spices and spirits. She saw bowls brimming with small metal discs, with brightly colored gadgets that might have been toys. A machine with pedals, and two spoked wheels, and a single seat between them. Chunks of wood shaped like monsters. Miniature vehicles, buildings, people in uniform. All of it unmentioned in the naming songs. Before something fell from the something tree, there would have been words for everything here. Now the effort just to look at it started a pounding in the courier's head.

She kept her attention on the few named things in the room. The shabby desk and chair, the naphtha-burning lamp, the papers stacked in a tray. But the nameless things surrounded her and loomed overhead, and their weight was terrible.

Her companion pulled his gray cap low over his eyes. "We should hurry," he said. His voice was soft and light, its gentleness startling. He took her by the arm and guided her past the desk and into the dark on the other side.

Who was he? Not a friend to those who had wanted to make a ghost of her, but neither was he an ally of her committee. A dealer of contraband, an associate of smugglers and their ilk, an operator of the in-between. She wondered at the desires that compelled named people to seek his services, the weird thrill afforded by nameless junk from a broken world. If his goods were confiscated, the names committee would divine and deliver words for everything it could identify, then see the rest burned. He must have known what she was from her satchel and her uniform, but he didn't try to talk away what she saw.

At the far side of the warehouse, a huge door stood open to a sodden yard, choked by ferns and burdock. Three barges were moored in the canal beyond. Ghosts worked the barges, carrying unmarked crates from their decks into the warehouse. More nameless goods, probably.

"Go right, and keep close to the canal," the junk dealer said, pointing. "When the water goes underground, go with it. That will take you back to where you belong."

The courier took a deep breath. She was alive. She would live. But what did the junk dealer expect in return? As though guessing her question, he shoved his hands into the pockets of his robe and said, "You can thank me by never coming back here. By forgetting that we met."

She could hear the low roar of the factories again. Night had fallen, and the nameless were still close. She left the junk dealer in the doorway of his warehouse, ran to the canal. Followed it, as he'd instructed her, to a place where dismal waters dribbled soundlessly into a tunnel. She stooped to enter and followed the waters down.

For hours she trudged along the grimy shore, below the streets of the city. Through drain grates above she glimpsed flickering lamps and the wheels of passing carts. Animals scurried in the shadows. A dozen times she feared herself lost or followed or watched. Finally she emerged with the water into the open air. She climbed a steep bank and found herself in the rail yard behind Hollow Station.

Inside, the ticket windows were closed. A few travelers sat on long benches, pressed close to their suitcases, sacks, satchels, and ghosts. She saw traders, soldiers, artisans, agents of other committees, watchers assigned to the station. The courier avoided their gazes as she tracked muddy bootprints over the gray stone. She sensed the watchers following her.

A few steps from the information booth, she stumbled. She heard shouting, then footsteps and hushed voices. Someone helped her to her feet.

The station master was a lean man with sad, dark eyes. He brought her to his office, gave her biscuits, tea, an apple. She drank the tea and took a few bites of the apple but couldn't bring herself to touch the biscuits. She lay on the cot he gave her. Slept, and heard in her sleep the soft clacking of the schedule boards.

She woke alone, drank what remained of the tepid tea. Outside, the station master was speaking quietly with the watchers. The courier heard him say that the Number Twelve had departed on the Tortoise line. Someone spoke the word *papers*.

She slipped out a back door and followed a winding passage to the platform. None of the watchers saw her board the first train north, though the other passengers stole nervous glances in her direction. She changed trains twice, keeping to the express routes. The conductors let her be; couriers of the names committee were not expected to produce tickets. She caught up with the Number Twelve late that night, in the town of Nod, not far from the northern border.

Beryl was on the platform, pacing. When she saw the courier she ran to her, hugged her hard, and pulled her aboard, pushing others out of the way. A porter said something about Book. "Book can wait," Beryl said.

The courier lay on the bunk in her compartment while Beryl fetched a copper tub from the bath car. Porters brought urns of hot water. Beryl took the urns and sent the porters away, poured the water herself. She pointed and said, "In."

The courier's uniform smelled of ash and stale sweat. She left her clothes in a heap and lowered herself into the tub. While Beryl sponged her back, she told her some of what had happened, about the masks in the dark, about the nameless quarters of the city opening like boxes within boxes. She did not tell her about the junk dealer, about how she escaped.

"I forgot how to speak," the courier said, thinking again of what Ivy had done when the nameless found her at Buckle. "I couldn't remember a word."

"It doesn't matter," Beryl said. "You're safe."

The train began to move. Beryl scrubbed harder, told her she had watched from a window as the train left Hollow Station. She knew something was wrong when she saw Book watching, too.

"He should have made the chief engineer wait," Beryl said.

The courier wondered whether Beryl knew who the chief engineer was. Few members of the committee were permitted to meet with the person responsible for maintaining the engine. Book, the assistant engineers, maybe one or two of the porters.

"Wouldn't want to harm their precious schedule," the courier said.

"I'll burn the schedule if I ever see it," Beryl said, and the courier thought that maybe she meant it.

The water, still hot enough to hurt, rippled as the train clattered around a bend. The courier watched soap and oil chase each other over the water's skin.


Beryl brought trays of food from the eating car, brought mugs of hot tea so the courier wouldn't have to speak to anyone, wouldn't have to answer their questions. Book would be getting impatient, but Beryl insisted she rest. And that night, when the courier couldn't sleep, Beryl told stories of her childhood aboard the train. Of how she and the other children sneaked onto the roofs, smuggled ghosts into the common car, climbed bridges and water towers in rail yards.

Beryl had been born on the Number Twelve, a child of the committee. Her mother, five years a ghost now, had also been a diviner—color, light, and measurement were her specialties—and her father was one of a pair of mechanics who still worked the Number Twelve. Beryl didn't know which, and neither did the mechanics.

After Beryl returned from creche, pages and couriers had taught her glyphs, numbers, and story. The two mechanics who might have been her father competed for her attention. One taught her how to win at games of Hand and Moon and how to smoke a pipe. The other taught her how to work with machines.

As a child, Beryl had seen little of Fern, her mother, because not even the children of diviners were permitted forward of the crew cars. But Fern had eaten with her sometimes, and once she had taken Beryl into Whisper to see the saying stone and the archives. The stone didn't make much of an impression on Beryl—"big rock in a big hole," she called it—but all these years later, she still talked about the archives. Rows of boxes stacked in long, chilly corridors beneath the city, and in each box a card bearing a single word.

"It's so quiet in there, you can almost hear the words whispering themselves," she said.

Diviners had inked those words, and the cards had gone with couriers out into the world, to an unnamed thing and back again. Some were covered with grime, some wrinkled and torn. But the words held.

"The whole thing falls apart without us," Beryl said.

"And with us?" the courier asked.

"Falls apart anyway," Beryl said, and laughed.

The courier wanted to laugh with her, but the laughter wouldn't come. Instead she let herself be comforted by the pressure of Beryl's chest against her back, of Beryl's knees against the backs of her knees, of Beryl's arm over her middle.


When the courier slept, she saw those pale masks again, and in her dreams they hid faces she knew. Her father's, her sister's, Book's. She reached up to touch her own face and found a mask there, too.

She woke before dawn to find dream scraps drifting through her compartment. Parcels of light in the air, whispers bunched under her bunk, shadows in places where they shouldn't be. A dream, when it escaped, could borrow any material at hand to lend itself substance. One might look like a crumpled piece of paper, swelling with breath. Another like a writhing ball of dust. Some were clumps of clotted air, jellylike, hard to see—it felt bad to step on them. *Draff* was the word the namers had divined and delivered for all such stuff, some two hundred years ago.

As a child, she had learned the hard way that she had to be more careful than people with names. Because her father had never sent her to creche, she'd babbled in the secret air of their house, making the place strange with her noise. At night, her dreams had often escaped, and not only as draff. Those angry things had hissed and buzzed in the corners of the room, and some mornings she'd run from bed with the worst of them snapping at her heels.

Monsters. They were small, but they breathed and reasoned and acted according to their own fierce wills, even if only to bite and tear with teeth and claws made of splinters, pins, nails. Nothing so dangerous as those bred by the nameless in drug-deepened nightmares, but the girl's creations could still draw blood. Her father had always taken them into his cottage, to study them.

Now, the courier slipped from bed and went for her dustpan and broom. Sifting through her draff—quietly, so as not to wake Beryl—the courier was relieved to find nothing with teeth or claws. But she usually woke with no draff at all, the line between sleep and waking crisp as folded paper. Because she didn't have a name, she had to maintain vigilance on every border, especially those inside her head.

She emptied her dustpan into the bin outside her door, closed the lid tight on the juddering mass. In the cities, dreams committee haulers would wheel carts of draff to the refineries, where workers processed it into the shining black naphtha that powered the factories, along with every engine on the rails. Here aboard the Number Twelve, porters deposited the stuff into larger bins at the stations, or into a scuttle for one of the train's stoves. She didn't want the porters to see it, though, and she didn't want Beryl to worry more than she already was. So she put on her boots, her cap, and her jacket, and carried the bin down through the sleeping train, all the way to the last car.

She knew where to step to avoid the gaps in the floor. Springs creaked, the axles whined, and the wind stirred heaps of junk in the corners. From the cupola above came the rustling of birds. Rope, the diviner who found names for flying things, had built a dovecote up there. In addition to his regular duties, he oversaw the committee's messenger birds, which flew to Whisper with reports for the sayers.

One of those birds, she thought, would carry the story of what had happened in Hollow. Book still needed that story from her, and she couldn't put him off much longer. She had to decide what to tell him about the man who had saved her life.

Shivering, she knelt beside the stove near the middle of the car. This place had been more important to earlier generations of namers, who had gathered here to conduct their funerals. In those days, the ghosts of committee members were permitted to remain aboard while the living toasted them and traded stories. Now few people visited this place, and when someone stopped being alive, agents of the ghosts committee boarded at the next stop to retrieve them.

Only the courier made sure the scuttle remained stocked. She liked to come here sometimes, to be alone. The only other person she ever saw here was

Rope. Someday, she thought, this car would come loose from the back of the train, and only the two of them would notice.

She emptied her bin of draff into the stove, lit it with a match from a box she kept hidden in the wall. In its unrefined state, the dream stuff produced a lot of smoke when it burned. The orange flames hissed and sputtered, struggling. She added naphtha from the scuttle and the fire brightened.

She had suspected from the moment she arrived in the car that she was not alone. Now, as the air grew warmer, she saw gold eyes staring from the dark at the back. A moment later, the animal padded into the light of the fire.

"There you are," she said.

For generations, the word for this kind of animal had eluded the diviners. Sleek and fast, the beasts traversed parks, alleyways, and rooftops, seeming to prefer the dark corners of the named world to the nameless wilds. They were visible only when darting from one shadow to another, or when they lay dozing in the sun.

After the courier delivered *stowaway*, she began to glimpse this animal more often—slipping through a door just before it closed, blinking at her from under a table. Now she thought of him as *her* stowaway. Her stowaway took care of himself, but sometimes he accepted the courier's affection, or the scraps of food she saved for him. If others knew about the nameless animal, they must have chosen to overlook his presence because he hunted mice in the storage car.

The stowaway pushed his head against the courier's side, brushing her arm with his whiskers and his gray fur. She stroked his arching back and he made a low rumbling sound, as though from a tiny engine deep in his throat.

"You know about secrets, don't you?" she said. "You must teach me how to bear them."

But something had caught the stowaway's eye, something in the dark she couldn't see. And just as suddenly as he'd appeared, the animal was gone again, his leap from light into shadow like a wind blowing out of the world. Not for the first time, the courier wondered what it would be like to go with him.

She watched the trees sweep past the window in Book's office, birch, elm, and maple blurring in the early gray light. This morning the train seemed different to her, as though each car had been replaced with a nearly identical copy of the original. Had Book's purple curtains always been so worn and tattered? Had his desk always been scarred with so many nicks and gouges? She didn't look at him as he read from the report she had written upon returning to her compartment. Some words he spoke as though he barely understood them.

*"A successful delivery . . . satisfactory conditions . . . Return delayed . . . an unexpected encounter."* He tossed the pages aside and said, *"Gob* is a fine word. I know I won't be alone in thanking you for its addition to the archives. But *an unexpected encounter? Unidentified persons?"*

"They didn't tell me their names," she said.

Book let that pass. "How many were they?" he said. "And what triggered this *unexpected encounter?* What were you even doing out there in that"—he struggled to find a suitable word—*"neighborhood?"*

She sat up straight. "I didn't want this to happen, Book, if that's what you're suggesting."

He'd been after a reaction, and she'd given him one. Sometimes she hated how well he knew her.

"They came after me, and I ran," she said, forcing the words even. "I got away."

Book threw up his hands, then started moving things around on his desk. He looked suddenly old to her. She knew that Book had risked a great deal by bringing her aboard, all those years ago. She knew that the risks were greater since Buckle. Many of the named resented her presence among them, while others pretended she didn't exist. Now, what had happened in Hollow would make it harder for them to go on pretending.

"Book," she said, "they were so close I could . . ." But remembering that smell—of sweat mingled with something dry and burning—caused her voice to break.

Book watched her, blinking. He took a breath and his expression softened. After a while, he said, "I've seen other masks, you know."

She said nothing. She had never heard him talk about masks before.

"Those plain white faces?" he went on. "Everyone knows about them. That's what the nameless wear when they go to war. Most of the time, it's the only face they show us."

He settled more deeply into his chair. "The Black Square has their own versions, for when they need to play the nameless, and their masks are fine imitations. But I was out beyond the border once or twice, long enough to see the genuine articles. A few very beautiful. Big feathered faces, bright colors, huge grins. Horns on some of them! It's how they know who they are. Not names, exactly, and definitely not ranks. Who they are can change, you know. Parent can become soldier, farmer become thief, woodworker become judge become maker of monsters. Simple as trading one mask for another. At least that's what your—"

He stopped, catching himself. She knew what he'd been about to say. *That's what your father believed.* She'd assumed Book had forgotten Lock, as they all were supposed to have done. It surprised her to hear him slip.

Book coughed and turned to look out the window. The light dimmed as clouds moved over the sun. She wondered whether he had lost others to deletion committee votes.

"I'm not sure how many there were," she told him. She closed her eyes and saw them again, masks rising up and falling away, crowding close then sinking into shadow. "Six at least. As many as eight or nine."

"They might be the ones from Buckle, then."

"Yes."

"Do you remember anything else that could help us?" Book said. "Anything to distinguish one from another?"

She thought that some of her pursuers had been taller, some shorter. Did one of them limp? In her memory the figures ran together, a jumble of swishing robes and shining blades. She shook her head.

"And in the end," Book said, "you just slipped away."

She had left out her encounter with the junk dealer. She knew that Book sensed the omission, but if she told him now, then he would have to include it in his own report. Watchers would seek out the junk dealer's warehouse, and if they found it, they would dismantle his operation. Then the sayers would almost certainly form a deletion committee to address the problem of the junk dealer himself.

She understood why Book wanted more from her. The watchers would want more from him; so would the sayers. And if he could give them enough, maybe they would leave the courier alone. Maybe they would leave them both alone. But she couldn't repay her rescuer's kindness with deletion.

"I ran until the nameless didn't follow," she said.

.  .  .

After Buckle, Ivy had been summoned to Whisper to meet with the sayers. The courier had seen her the morning before she left, staring out a window of the eating car. She had looked small and scared and very pale, mug clutched tightly in her hands. When the train arrived at Whisper Station, she rose and left without a word. Two watchers escorted her from the platform.

No one knew when she would return. Few spoke of her absence. Couriers and pages, returning from their assignments, shook their heads: no word of Ivy. Days passed. A week, two weeks.

Then, somewhere in the lowlands southeast of Tortoise, on one of the committee's lesser known lines, a ghost raised a red lantern. The Number Twelve braked, eventually halting at the edge of a broad field. Tethered to an old barn was a flying machine of the watchers, floating in the blue sky like a fat gray fish.

Ivy stood alone in the grass. She walked to the train unescorted.

She said little about what she had experienced among the sayers. Eventually, rumor spread of a subcommittee formed to investigate the attack at Buckle. It was said that Sayer Frost himself was to head this subcommittee. Frost, who Book preferred not to talk about.

In his early years among the sayers, Frost had concerned himself mostly with laws governing ghosts and the operation of the factories. He owned several factories, in Hollow and elsewhere, and he also owned many ghosts. Some had complained that the laws he advanced favored his private concerns, but the particulars of those laws were obscure, and they benefited others, too— people whose support kept him safe in his position. Then, in the last ten years, Frost began to advance deletionist policies that most sayers had once regarded with disdain.

But the threat of the nameless was growing again. The attack on Buckle had only confirmed what many feared: that the smaller incursions of the last decade—raids, mostly to steal ghosts and smuggle them over the border— were prelude to something bigger. And so the sayers granted Frost his deletion committees, to track down those who, through malice or carelessness, threatened the security and safety of the named.

The courier had encountered Frost once before, on the day the watchers discovered her, the unnamed girl hidden among the rest of her father's secrets. It was one of Frost's deletion committees who took Lock away in a flying machine. When Book had argued for her place on the names committee, Frost had stood opposed—a debate that ended with one of the sayer's rare defeats.

The few times Book spoke of Frost, he'd spat the name as though it were something he wanted out of his mouth.

After Buckle, when Frost failed to summon the courier to meet with him in Whisper, she was relieved. Later, though, she began to worry. The sayers must have asked Ivy about what the courier had or hadn't done at Buckle that day. Didn't they want to know what she herself had seen and heard?

Ivy returned from those interviews with a new air of importance, her spirit fortified. She was back among her fellow exiles, but for a while she had stood at the center of things.

As for the courier who delivered *trouble*, the one without a name? For now, Frost's investigation remained only that: an investigation. But if he came for her now, she doubted she would ever return.

The courier waited for the train to bend its route toward Whisper, but the chief engineer only took them farther west, out near the border. At each station on the line she expected watchers to board the train and come for her, but the watchers remained at their posts.

No new assignments came from Book, but Beryl had words to divine. With nothing to do, the courier sat with her ghost in the ghost car. She watched him make sketches of fences and fields and old stone walls. The ghost seemed to sense that something had happened. He finished a drawing of three grain silos and put his cool hand on her hand.

She was glad no one else was there to see. That kind of display could get the ghost calibrated, no matter how useful his talents. She squeezed the ghost's hand and set it back on the pencil. The ghost began another sketch.

The courier knew nothing about the calibration process—that was a secret of the ghosts committee—but she knew it served to rid ghosts of the habits they picked up from the living. When wranglers brought new ghosts from the wilds beyond the borders, they were also calibrated before they could be auctioned and put to work.

"A way to remind them they no longer live," her father had explained to her one day.

She would have celebrated eight or nine name days by then, had she been given a name. She was full of questions, questions he usually ignored, but he liked to talk about ghosts. He studied them in the cottage by the pond, where his equipment hummed in cool, dark rooms. A few of his discoveries had been important to the named—he'd improved the design of the ghost-burning engines, and perfected the technique for priming war machines—so the sayers allowed his work to continue. On paper, Lock was an ad hoc committee of one.

The ghosts he studied also worked the land, tending the orchard and the fields. When one began acting strangely—pulling up flowers, digging holes for no reason—Lock sent for the calibrationists. The girl watched from a window on the second floor as two women in brown uniforms bound the ghost's arms with cables and marched it down the dirt road toward town. After they were gone, she asked her father, "Won't the ghost be afraid?"

"Not at all," he assured her. "Calibration rescues them from the confusion of themselves."

They were standing on the front porch that overlooked the apple orchard through which the calibrationists had escorted their charge. Lock must have guessed that she was thinking of the patchwork ghost, because he sat on the top step and gestured for her to join him. She did so, warily, thinking he was about to tell her something she didn't want to hear.

"Ghosts are the dreams we make of ourselves while we live," he said. "When we stop being alive, that's when the dream gets out. The ghosts of animals last only a little while. They turn to dust after a few days—or maybe months, for an animal that has spent its life among people. But our ghosts are stubborn things."

"Like monsters?" she asked.

"Like monsters," he agreed, "but born from memory rather than careless whim or deliberate malice."

Lock had acquired the patchwork ghost the year before, not at auction but directly from a cadre of ghost wranglers, paying them extra to keep the transaction out of their records. He found the ghost's strangeness worthy of study, which the girl was glad for. She knew that if he lost interest and had the ghost calibrated, she would lose her only friend.

"Can monsters be calibrated?" she asked.

"Oh, it's been tried," he said, leaning back on his elbows. "For a while we thought that monsters might be tamed. But nothing worked. Monsters always remain what they are, which is why they must be burned."

The girl thought of the steel barrel outside his cottage, in which he destroyed the monsters she made once he finished studying them.

"Not ghosts, though," she said. "You don't have to burn ghosts."

He sat up and put one hand on her shoulder. Now, she thought, he would tell her the thing she didn't want to hear. "Some ghosts are burned," he said. "They are a potent fuel, even better than naphtha. And every ghost that isn't burned must be calibrated. Can you imagine what would happen if the ghosts remembered what it was like to be alive? It would make them sad, I think, to know how much they've lost."

A change had come over him, then—the cold distance in his eyes that meant he was thinking of her mother. He took his hand from her shoulder, and though they remained seated together, the girl felt small and alone.

Now, seated beside the patchwork ghost, the courier wondered if her father was also a ghost. If so, did he consider his life's work complete? Did becoming a ghost teach you everything you could wish to know about ghosts?

But if he were a ghost then he would have been auctioned off to the factories or the mines. Or assigned to a rail crew and made to lay new track, or to operate a switch on one of these remote lines.

The patchwork ghost was sketching one of those switches now, a bare lonesome tree of iron beside a leaning shed. If the courier saw the ghost of her father in a place like this, would she recognize him? Like every calibrated ghost, he would have forgotten everything he had lost, including her.

Back in her compartment, she sat at her desk and wrote another letter to Ticket.

*Sister, they came for me with knives. In the nameless districts of Hollow they came for me, and I still see their white masks when I close my eyes.*

As children, she and Ticket had walked together to a hill south of their father's farm. From the rocky peak they could see the whole of the town by the river, the town which the nameless girl was forbidden from visiting. Stem, the town was called, and Ticket pointed out her school, the lumber yard, the gray brick train station, the lighthouse in the river to which she sometimes swam with her friends.

*I wonder if you want to know the story,* she wrote to Ticket now. *Do you avoid the stations when you can? Do you look away if you see the Number Twelve drawing near?*

The courier addressed her letters to a certain street in Whisper, posted them from whichever station they stopped at next. Book had given her the address soon after he brought her aboard, but he warned her that the nature of Ticket's work might prevent her from writing back.

Book would not tell the courier what work her sister did, though he hinted that it had something to do with the sayers. Once, while on assignment in Whisper, the courier went to see the address for herself. In a quiet neighborhood at the bottom of a sloping street, she found a narrow building of dark stone with small, barred windows. She peered inside and saw ghosts carting stacks of paper, arranging them into piles, stuffing them into satchels. Not a residence, but a sorting place for messages. Either Ticket came here to retrieve the courier's letters or one of those ghosts delivered them.

Now the courier saw her own handwriting grow ragged. It was late, and she was drinking whiskey.

*I don't know where you are,* she wrote. *I don't know what you've become, or if you are anything at all anymore. I only hope it's worth what you became on the day you left.*

She slept badly, and was woken in the night by a knock at her door. The man waiting in the hall looked very tired.

"What has he done this time?" she asked, thinking the patchwork ghost must have spilled or broken something in his search for new subjects.

"Oh, it isn't the ghost," the man said. "Something else." Only then did she recognize the short bristly hair, the rope tied around his waist. Not one of the porters, but the diviner who found names for flying things.

"Rope?" she said.

"I wish they'd given us more warning, but that's the sayers for you. You'd better come."

She realized the train wasn't moving. She must have looked terrified, because Rope put one hand on her arm. "I think they only want to talk."

"Give me a moment," she said. She closed the door and looked out the window. No town, no station, no platform. Just gray hills under a sky like black glass. And something else: a small flying machine tethered not far from the tracks, its envelope shining like a second silver moon. Not a craft of the watchers, though. It didn't bear their open-eye insignia.

She dressed quickly, then followed Rope toward the front of the car. Rope was a quiet man, and he moved quietly about the train. He had a habit of sneaking up on people without meaning to. No wonder she often forgot he existed until the moment she saw him. "I was up late, tending to the messenger birds," he said. "I saw the signal from the cupola."

She heard others stirring in their compartments as they passed, but no one rose to peer out. Rope opened the door and a cold breeze blew into the corridor.

Outside, a bald man with heavy black eyebrows stood waiting. He wore a dark gray suit with red embroidering on the collar and cuffs. Not a uniform, but a style favored among high-ranking administrators in Whisper.

When he saw the courier, he stood straight and gave a broad smile. "Thank you for coming so quickly," he said. "Will you join me for a walk, please?"

His voice was deep, almost musical. The courier looked around, though she wasn't sure who she was looking for. Beryl? Book?

"I'll wait for you here," Rope said.

The other man offered her a hand, but she ignored it as she descended the rungs of the short ladder.

"I will return her to you soon," the man said to Rope. "Sayer Frost requires only a little of your courier's time."

Frost. Merciless hunter of nameless things and people, convener of dozens of deletion committees. He was known to spend long periods of time away from Whisper, returning only for crucial votes and the yearly recitation of law.

This man had to be Frost's speaker. All sayers employed such agents, people intimate with their designs who could speak more casually than the sayers themselves were able. Whatever a sayer said was law, and a stray remark not in keeping with the will of the assembly might give rise to ambiguities and contradictions. The nameless had exploited such rifts in the past.

"My name is Smoke," the man said, leading her toward the flying machine. "Please understand that this is not an official inquiry. Frost only wishes to clear up a few points of confusion."

A warm light shone from the cab of the flying machine. The courier saw the flash of watchers' ghost lenses. So the flying machine did not belong to the watchers, but they did serve as pilots aboard the sayer's craft.

Smoke gestured to the open hatch. "After you," he said.

The cabin was warm and simply furnished. Cushioned chairs were arranged beneath a glowing naphtha lamp. Near the front, two signal birds were perched in a cage. The door to the cab stood closed. Others at the back probably led to the galley, to private chambers, to the engine room. That would house a ghost-burner, the courier thought, like those that powered the war machines. Somewhere on the craft, ghosts were kept for fuel. How many had Frost burned to make this trip? The humming of the engine was quiet and even.

Frost was seated with both hands resting atop a black cane, a sheaf of white hair brushed thin over his head. His face was clean-shaven. A thick checkered scarf hung past his unbuttoned jacket, fringe reaching nearly to the floor. His eyeglasses flashed as he shifted to look at the courier. He seemed to have barely aged in the fourteen years since he came to her father's farm to investigate rumors of a child without a name.

Smoke closed the hatch behind them and gestured for the courier to take a seat. She sat and removed her scarf while Smoke went to stand beside Frost.

"The sayer has heard much about you over the years," Smoke said. "He admires your spirit, along with the good work you do on behalf of the names committee."

Trying to keep any hint of anger out of her voice, the courier said, "I do not work on behalf of the namers. I am a namer."

Smoke bowed. "And it is to your credit that use these words with such care," he said. "The sayer wishes he better understood your art. How many times each day do we fail to see the unnamed things right in front of us? Or worse"—he tapped the side of his head with one finger—"the unnamed things lurking within. But you see them, somehow. You seek them out, take hold of them, bind them with words."

"You seem to understand my art very well," the courier said.

Smoke was unruffled. "Neither I nor the sayer have any idea how it *feels*. To make the delivery. To reclaim that fragment from the Silence."

"There are no words for it," the courier said.

Now Smoke stopped smiling. Had she gone too far? He turned and looked—not directly at Frost, but at a point on the floor near his feet. He was trying to gauge the sayer's reaction, or waiting for some cue. Frost, big eyes blinking behind rectangular lenses, considered. Then, at the edges of his mouth, the hint of a smile. Smoke looked up and laughed. It was a deep, booming laugh, and it filled the cabin.

"No words for it," Smoke said, shaking his head. "Very good. The sayer is grateful for your humor. His work sometimes leaves too little room for funny thoughts."

The courier kept her eyes on Frost, and she did not smile. She understood now that there would be no mention of their first meeting, all those years ago. How could they speak of that without also speaking of her father, who was deleted, gone from the record and never to be spoken of again? It was only because of the patchwork ghost's sketches and her own abiding rage that she remembered him at all.

"So," Smoke said, "now that we have shared a well-deserved laugh. The sayer does have questions—about your last assignment? And I join him in hoping that you have words enough for the answers."


They had studied her report from Hollow, and studied it carefully. At first Smoke only repeated the details as she had written them: the time of her departure from the Number Twelve, the route she took through the city, the location of the glassblowers' workshop. Smoke was trying to put her at ease, maybe. Or maybe he wanted to catch her in some error. She answered carefully, keeping close to what she had written.

When they came to the subject of the glassblowers, Smoke's manner shifted. He put his questions to her mildly, as though each had only just occurred to him, and he no longer seemed interested in the facts. What he wanted now were impressions.

"And how were you received among those artisans?" he asked. "Were they pleased to be visited by a courier of the names committee?"

She had included a description of the oldest of the glassblowers, his figurines and his white scars, his offer of whiskey, her decision to accept. "Those we encounter while out on delivery are not always kind to us," she said. "But the glassblowers welcomed me in and encouraged me to observe their work. I believe they would have liked me to stay longer."

"You speak as though you expected to be chased away."

"Members of my committee are often treated with suspicion."

Now Smoke looked concerned. "Why do you say this?"

He knew the answer very well, but she would have to supply it anyway. "People want new words," she said. "Many seek to witness a delivery if they can, and to be among the first to speak the new word. But the namers themselves are always outsiders, always strangers. Maybe because people know the story of our founding. Of Hand, of Moon. Of what Moon did to deliver *ghost*."

"Ah," Smoke said. "You speak of old Whisper."

"And of the old laws under which we still live." She glanced at Frost as she said this, but he showed no response. She wished they would get to the questions she knew were coming. About the masked figures, about her escape. Did they already know about the junk dealer?

Strangely, though, Smoke did not ask about the nameless, or about her escape. He wanted to know still more about the glassblowers. "There were seven of them, is that correct? And they had a furnace?"

"You have a flying machine," she said. "Couldn't you go to Hollow and see for yourself?"

Smoke looked again in Frost's direction. When Frost tilted his head, his speaker said for him, "In fact, we have just come from Hollow. We have even been to the place where you reported meeting these glassblowers."

The courier felt uneasy. The conversation was straying quickly from the track of what she knew.

"Now we come to the puzzling bit," Smoke said sadly. "You see, we found no glassblowers in their workshop. No fire, no glass, not even a *gob*. Just an old shed beside a factory, and an abandoned furnace inside. It's almost as though they had never been. Or as though someone pretended to have met them."

The courier sat up straight. She knew the workshop had been real. She had seen the molten glass, felt the smoothness of the stuff when it cooled. She had spoken with the glassblowers, shared their whiskey. She had *delivered a new word* in their company, a fact which Frost knew very well.

"They must have dismantled their operation," she said.

"And why would they do this?" Smoke asked.

But her thoughts strayed to the masked figures, to their robes and knives and stranger weapons. Seven or eight of them, same as at Buckle. And there had been about that many glassblowers in their workshop, too.

Of course. She saw it now. Scars on the hands holding knives in the dark. Burns to match those on the hands of the glassblowers. Whiskey on the breath breathed through a mask. The scent of burning naphtha clinging to shushing robes.

She had thought the nameless spotted her when she accidentally wandered into their strange neighborhood. But that wasn't it at all. They had followed her from the workshop, maybe even nudged her off the familiar route with their needling thoughts.

"Well?" Smoke asked.

"I can think of only one reason," she said to Smoke. "The glassblowers and the nameless are the same people. They must have recognized me from Buckle. Once I left, they put on those masks and pursued me. And when I escaped, they had to abandon their hideout, because they knew watchers would be sent to investigate."

She turned to Frost. "How long have you known?"

Smoke smiled and said for him, "We only guessed. But since you believe it, we believe it, too. We have been seeking this group of nameless for a long time. But you, it seems, are the one to have finally found them."


Silence in their silent places beyond the borders. Most of the nameless avoided words, but these seven were an unusual lot, living among the named, conducting trade, conversing with customers, with suppliers, with fellow artisans.

The courier told them what she could remember about the glassblowers, describing their faces, their scars, the words they used. A tall man, lanky and yellow-haired with eyes set deep in his skull. He was the one who wanted her to know that they smashed the malformed glass every night. A woman with one green eye and one pale as milk; she stayed silent the entire time. The old man with his whiskey bottle, his high-pitched laugh, his gentle good humor. Thinking of his kindness now, the courier shivered.

At some of these descriptions, Smoke looked at Frost, and Frost pursed his lips. Maybe what she told them matched other details they had gathered since Buckle.

Outside, the sky was lightening, and the scrub on the hills threw long purple shadows over the slopes. She heard the watchers in the cab adjusting their instruments.

"The last time your committee encountered these operatives," Smoke said. "What was it, almost a year ago now?"

"You're talking about Buckle," she said, and she felt how changed the word was, how heavy with new meaning. *Buckle* was no longer just a place. It was also something that had happened.

Smoke seemed to choose his next words with care. "It is easy to believe that it happened by chance," he said. "The Number Twelve at the station that day, a stroke of luck for our enemies. But it is rare that the namers leave five of their people at one stop. Rare that you make yourselves so vulnerable."

"So they were lying in wait," the courier said. "Or they picked up on some pattern in the route."

"All possibilities—but not, we think, the most likely one. We believe that the nameless knew your committee would be there that day. That they knew exactly how many would debark. That the attack was planned around this knowledge."

"But they couldn't have known that with any certainty," the courier said. "Not without help."

Smoke said nothing, only nodded for her to go on.

"Help from someone with access to the Number Twelve's schedule," she said. "From someone aboard the train."

As she spoke, the courier felt a gulf open in her mind. Fingers of thought reached for but failed to grasp something for which they had no name. A person among them but not among them, in their midst but in between. Someone whose movements would go overlooked, whose motives might elude them: someone like a shadow before they had the word *shadow*.

Frost removed something from his jacket pocket and handed it to Smoke. An envelope. Smoke gave it to the courier, nodded for her to open it. Inside was a card like those Book gave her with each assignment. She turned it over and found inked upon its surface a new word, unspoken and undelivered.

"The sayer cannot capture our criminal until the crime is named," Smoke said. "Frost asks that you deliver this word to the one who has earned it."

The courier sounded out the glyphs in her mind, feeling their contours. Something menacing drifted below their surface. It was a hidden thing, cool and slippery and hard to see. She wondered who had divined it.

"Why isn't this coming through Book?" she asked.

Smoke frowned, as though the reason should be obvious. And suddenly it was. Book was one of the few people with access to the schedule. He and the chief engineer crafted it in secret, and Book was probably the one who had decided how many namers should depart the train that day. Book was among their suspects.

"No one can know of your assignment," Smoke said. "If the person to whom that word is bound learns of our efforts, we risk another attack. And the next, I fear, will be something rather worse than what we saw at Buckle."

She knew what they expected of her. Tuck the card away, bow, thank the sayer and his representative for trusting her with such an important task. They were giving her a chance to prove her worth. She should have welcomed it without question.

Instead she set the card on the table and said, "If I do this for you, there's something I want in return."

Frost narrowed his eyes. Smoke's expression did not change, but the warmth was gone from his voice when he said, "You desire payment of some kind?" He knew as well as she did that the namers did not own property; it was why her ghost was officially kept with the committee's stock.

"I have a sister," she said. "She's in Whisper, I think, and I think she works with the sayers."

"Go on," Smoke said.

"If I make this delivery, I would like to see her again. It's been a very long time."

"And this sister's name?"

"Ticket," she said.

Smoke looked at Frost. The sayer frowned and looked at the floor, as though he were trying to remember something. Then he gazed directly at the courier. For a moment she was afraid that he would speak. Instead, he gave her a small but unmistakable nod.

"Well, it seems we have a deal," Smoke said, his relief plain. She had her answer and her assignment. She put the card with its envelope into her pocket.


The next minutes passed as though in a dream. Her descent toward the train, a cold wind blowing out of the hills, the realization that she was walking at the edge of an apple orchard. Earlier, in the dark, she hadn't seen the trees or their budding branches. It was as though they had grown there while she sat in the flying machine.

She did not turn to watch the machine take flight, but she heard the soft hum of its ghost-burner, felt its shadow pass over.

Rope helped her back up into the train. Did they speak at all on their way down through the car? She felt weightless and unmoored. Floating. She thought she heard whispers from behind closed doors.

Rope left her at her compartment. She found Beryl inside, standing by the window. The draft stirred a few stray dreams by her feet, pale thready bunches of dust. When Beryl saw the courier, she sighed and pulled her close.

"I thought they'd taken you," she said.

"Only for a little while."

They closed the door and lit the courier's lamp, left it burning on the desk while they lay together. No whistle sounded, but the courier could feel the train moving again.

"Who were they?" Beryl asked. "What did they say?"

The courier wanted to tell her everything. About Frost, about the glassblowers, about her secret assignment, that word like a snake coiled in her pocket. But she remembered Smoke's words after they presented her with the card. *No one can know of your assignment.* Even Beryl was under suspicion.

Yet Smoke had used the sayer's name in front of Rope, so that much would surely be known by the others soon enough.

"Frost had some questions about my report," she said. "It's over now. I'm home."

Beryl squeezed her more tightly, and the courier was grateful that no more questions followed. For a while, she might have slept.

When she opened her eyes, the lantern had gone out, and the morning sun shone blue through the curtain. She was still in her uniform. On her desk were the two pages of the letter she had been writing to her sister the night before. She wondered whether Beryl had seen it. Whether she might even have read it.

She rose from the bunk and took the card with Frost's word from her pocket. She tucked that into the bottom of her satchel, which hung from its peg by the door. The letter she slipped into her desk drawer.

When she turned, she glimpsed Beryl watching her, a puzzled look on her face. But Beryl closed her eyes and pretended not to have seen.

[art tk]

When Ticket ran away from home, she left in the early morning and without a word, taking only food, clothes, and maps, and her album of train ticket stubs.

Lock hardly seemed to notice his eldest daughter's absence. But the girl without a name, alone in the room she had shared with Ticket, found her nightmares growing worse.

With the nightmares came new monsters. Her father, fascinated by what he referred to as *the fresh crop*, collected them carefully, brought them in cages to his cottage, and studied them for days at a time before burning them in the barrel out back.

The monsters were more terrible than anything the girl had dreamed up before. Not because they had bigger teeth, or sharper claws. They were terrible because they looked less like monsters and more like parts of living people. A misshapen hand of wood crawling over the floorboards. A thing like a lumpy head, made all of cloth and buttons, watching and listening from atop her chest of drawers. An almost-baby of jellied air, wallowing in a dusty corner.

The girl woke each morning thirsty and confused, terrified of what awaited her. The days passed in a blur. Sometimes she drifted off to sleep at the kitchen table, in the field, on the porch—and with each sleep came more monsters.

The only thing that helped were the games of pretend she invented for herself and the patchwork ghost. She asked him to play at being a fellow soldier in the war, or a monster to be hunted by the dreams committee, or a watcher patrolling the borders under her supervision. He obliged her, and maybe not just for her sake—his eyes shone with something like glee while she ran and hollered for him.

But at night the girl was alone, and when she was alone the monsters came to join her.

Through her tears one morning, she said to her father, "It's my fault that Ticket's gone. She tried to teach me, but I didn't study hard enough."

Lock had already deposited the new monsters in his cottage. Now he crouched beside her and sighed. "Listen carefully," he said. "I know of some people who might be able to help. People with special techniques for cases like these. If I send for them, they will expect you to work very hard. And if you do, they can make the nightmares stop."

"Who are they?" she asked, wiping the last tears from her face.

Lock looked uncomfortable, as though he wasn't sure how much he should say. "I know them because of my work," he explained. "If they come here, you must do exactly as they say, and you must speak as little as possible. Do you understand?"

She knew what he was really saying. That the particulars of his work must remain secret. That they must not know she didn't have a name.

"I understand," she said.

"Do you want me to send for them?"

She thought he might want her to refuse. To tell him she could bear it, and to keep making monsters for the sake of his work. But he was doing something he so rarely did—offering something just for her, just because she needed it—and for that reason alone she couldn't turn his offer down.

He nodded and patted her head. Later that day, he sent the messenger bird.

They arrived a week later, the people who could help her. They were five in number, all dressed in loose-fitting brown uniforms. The courier, thinking back on them, could only remember the kindness of their eyes, the warmth of their smiles. They moved carefully about the house, inspecting each piece of furniture in her bedroom, looking through each window. She wanted them to see it all, wanted them to understand everything that had happened. But when she opened her mouth to speak—about the monsters, about her sister— her father glared at her, and she was silent.

The days and weeks that followed were a jumble in the courier's memory. She could no longer recall how she learned what she learned. But the visitors, her guides and protectors, kept her company every day, and every night she dreamed they were still by her side in their rumpled brown suits.

Who were they, these quiet, gentle people? Members of the dreams committee, she guessed, to whom her father sometimes sent reports of his discoveries. The dreams committee had hunters to track down monsters, so why not keep people whose job it was to stop monsters from appearing in the first place? *Sleep* was a border word; these were the guardians who patrolled its perimeter. Every night, they gave her a mug of something warm to drink, to help her sleep, and then they tied a short length of rope around her wrist.

The rope was important. Each time she found a dream frightening, each time she felt a monster forming in her mind, she was supposed to think of the rope, to *feel* it there on her wrist. The rope was a reminder to put her fears someplace where they couldn't escape.

At first more monsters came, terrible and frightening as any she had dreamed before. As her father quickly collected and disposed of them, the visitors instructed her to imagine a very boring person, a person like a ghost who has been calibrated. They told her to give to this person each thing that scared her. They told her, again, to feel the rope and remember.

She remembered, and it worked. That other presence in her dreams—a dull, hollow shell in the shape of a man—willingly took each bad thing she gave him. As he grew more solid, she made fewer and fewer monsters. And then, one morning, she made no monsters at all.

The visitors remained another day or two, to make sure the process was complete. The courier could no longer remember where they slept, what they ate. But she remembered knowing they had left, because the pot in which they had mixed the medicine to help her sleep was gone from the kitchen. It made her sad, the sudden departure of those people who had looked after her. They had been quiet and serious, but at least there were other people for a while.

"They'll be back to check in on you in a few weeks," her father assured her.

They never had the chance.


The courier still didn't know who tipped off the watchers about her father's activities. But she had some guesses.

There was the delivery boy who glimpsed her playing in the woods with the patchwork ghost one day.

Or maybe one of those brown-suited visitors, upon returning to the dreams committee, felt it was their duty to report everything they had seen at Lock's farm.

When the flying machine descended into the field, the girl was playing in the garden outside her father's cottage. He'd patted her head and told her, "Wait here." Those would be the last words he spoke to her.

Several watchers debarked from the flying machine, and with them came five others—Frost and his deletion committee, she learned later. Her father did not run.

At the time, Book had just risen to the rank of committee chair. He had known Lock from his work on the ghost-burning engines of the war machines—some of the tools and processes Lock introduced had needed names. When Lock was taken, Book took an interest in the girl, who by that time would have celebrated her eleventh or twelfth name day, had his committee learned of her existence sooner.

But instead of assigning a courier the task of finding a name for her, he went before the sayers and made his plea. It would be foolish, he told them, to name a child of her age. Any name they chose would never sink as deep as bone, never claim her fully. The confusion, he said grimly, would likely lead her to make a terrible decision. Book did not have to explain what kind of decision he meant—many prisoners of war made ghosts of themselves after having names forced upon them.

No, Book said, leave the girl as she is. And let the names committee have her.

The courier imagined him in Whisper, younger and slimmer and tall, standing in his gray suit before the saying stone at the bottom of the ancient quarry in which the sayers held their assemblies. She didn't know the exact words he'd used, but she could guess.

*There is no place more safe for her than the Number Twelve. Let us see if she can defy what she is. Let us see if she can do her part in naming the world.*

It still surprised the courier that Book had been able to sway the sayers— and sway the names committee, too. She'd said so, once, and Book had leaned back as though cushioned by the strange music swelling from the bell of his phonograph.

"I can be very convincing, when anyone bothers to listen," he said.

Still, many had voted against Book's plan, including Frost. And now that same Frost had come for her in the night with his secret plan. Why should she not tell Book, who had saved her and found a place for her among the named?

Because she was being tested, she thought. She was more like this shadow person they imagined than anyone else aboard the train. And if they suspected Book, they must also suspect her. They had chosen her because they wanted her to prove her innocence by delivering the word Frost had given her—or to prove her guilt by failing.


She slept again, and when she woke, Beryl was gone. The courier swept the draff from her floor. She wondered whether it had all come from her dreams, or whether some was Beryl's.

She spent the day moving restlessly about the train. She sat concealed amid the densest foliage in the garden car, breathing the scent of damp soil. When time came for the midday meal, she took her plate alone to the last car of the train. If her stowaway was there, it chose to remain hidden.

In the late afternoon, a porter came for her. "It's time," he said, which was all he needed to say.

Book was waiting for her in his office. He looked tired, as though he were the one who'd been woken in the night to face questioning aboard the sayer's flying machine. "Well?" he asked.

"They wanted to go over my report," she said. "We discussed it in some detail."

"*In some detail*," Book repeated.

"I'm surprised they bothered to come all this way. Frost didn't speak the whole time."

Book leaned back in his chair and squinted at her as though from a distance. "Frost speaks law," Book said, "but he keeps the truth hidden. He'll never tell you everything you need to know."

"Will you?" she asked.

She caught him flinch before he said, "Haven't I always?"

"You want me to report back to you on everything I see, everything I do. But you don't tell me where my sister is. You're too selfish to tell me anything I want to know."

For a moment he looked hurt. Then his face reddened. "Your sister wants nothing to do with you," he said.

She knew that he wanted to hurt her back, but that wasn't what she felt. She didn't feel anything at all.

She turned and walked out of his office. Book shouted after her, but she ignored him. Something had occurred to her, standing there before his desk. If Book really was the one who had worked with the nameless against the committee, he might have sent her into Hollow knowing what would happen. Knowing that *gob* would lead her to the glassblowers—into the hands of the enemy.

Maybe the train left Whisper on time because Book hadn't expected her to return.


She delivered *tarry*. She delivered *tedium*. She delivered *sliver*.

Book was punishing her, giving her words to bore and annoy, even hurt her a little. Others must have seen the flying machine that night, but no one asked her about it. They avoided her, and the courier went through the cars ignored and unseen. She listened to the gossip of pages while they worked in the printing car. Listened to her fellow couriers, boasting of their latest deliveries. To the diviners, when she sat close enough in the eating car.

She delivered *pest*. She delivered *scald*. She delivered *bitter*.

Book was keeping her busy, keeping her away from the train. Keeping her—whether he knew it or not—from the answer to Frost's question. With the taste of bitter leaves still on her tongue, she sat with the patchwork ghost on the deck at the back of the last car. The evening was warm and clear, the fields dark green under a big moon. Her stowaway was behind her, brushing his furry side against her back, curious to see her there. The courier watched the rails while the ghost sketched them.

They were crossing the flatlands east of Jawbone. She saw on the horizon the dark shapes of villages abandoned during the Silence and not yet reclaimed. Their ancient names might still appear on road signs, but the signs would use words from before, like those in the books her father had kept hidden on a high shelf. As a child she'd stood on a chair to take the books down, but when she tried to read them, the glyphs writhed like insects on the page, making her head hurt. If she stared for too long, her eyes would fill with tears as though stung by smoke.

This was after her sister had taught her words, but before she learned that the sayers had outlawed the old books because they were dangerous, like wrinkles in the fabric of the named world. Law dictated that those books be burned, but her father kept them even after he caught her trying to read them. The books burned later, seized by the same deletion committee that took her father.

The train slowed as it neared the village of Spur. A trading post, leaning porches, rusting water tower, gloomy tavern. Years ago, she'd debarked here and gone into a pasture to watch a cow deliver her young, and to that animal she had delivered the word *calf.* She'd seen fewer than ten people in the village then, but now the streets were crowded, and lamps shone from every porch and window. The people must have come from miles around, old and young, farmers, ranchers, their faces bright in the lights of their lanterns.

Leaning over the rails, the courier saw the train of the Black Square Show on a siding near the station, saw its red and green and yellow cars, its engine dark with grime. The show must not have started yet. Surely Book would have seen. At the thought that she might finally see the players perform, the courier's heart beat faster. But the Number Twelve picked up speed again, and the lights of Spur fell quickly into the distance.

Had Book seen the other train? He had asked her to tell him if she encountered the Black Square—because he'd wanted to see the show, or for some other reason? She knew he was hiding something from her—something about Buckle, and maybe something about the Black Square, too. Yet he punished her for keeping a secret she hadn't wanted in the first place.

The stowaway pressed his head against her side. She stroked the animal's head and back as she spoke to the patchwork ghost. "I need you to do something for me," she said.

The ghost looked at her.

"I need you to watch Book while I'm away. If he leaves the train, follow without letting him see. I want you to make sketches of everything he does. Do you understand?"

She saw something shift in the ghost's eyes, like light underwater. It was the same light she had seen there when she was a child and they had played their games of chase—nameless and watcher, monster and dreams committee hunter.

For the first time in years, she saw the ghost smile.


The next morning, she went with Beryl to the gymnasium car. Beryl lifted weights while the courier stretched and tumbled. They both were quiet, savoring the early morning hush. The courier knew that Beryl was angry with Book on her behalf, but for now they spoke only of weights, laps, repetitions. The words they used were old words. The first sayers, recognizing the importance of able soldiers, had urged the namers to divine and deliver words for every part of a training regimen. Those words felt good on the tongue and in the air, strong and supple, nearly as physical as the work itself.

The courier ran from one end of the car to the other, back and forth. "Never enough room in here," the courier said.

"Home is the place where there's never enough room," Beryl said.

The courier stopped near Beryl's bench and leaned forward with her hands on her knees. Between breaths, she said, "I have an idea."

She took Beryl's hand and led her out the door at the back of the car. Here, a column of rungs provided access to the roof. She tested her weight against them, then scrambled up. Beryl hesitated a moment before climbing after her.

The sun shone red and low through a pine wood, and the morning mist clung to the distant hills. The courier usually knew at a glance which town was next on the line and how long till they'd reach it. Even when the train skirted nameless territory and most committee members avoided the view through the windows, the courier knew how far to the next station. This place, though, with its black woods and low hills, she didn't recognize at all. The light was strange here, the shadows long. Even the engine sounded uneasy. Beryl hugged herself, swaying as she breathed.

"Ready?" the courier asked.

At first Beryl didn't seem to understand. Then she shook her head.

"You can run with me, or you can watch from here," the courier said. Before Beryl could respond, the courier jogged away over the roof of the car. A moment later, she heard Beryl's footsteps behind her, slow at first, then faster. The courier grinned to herself.

It felt better than she wanted it to, running in the open air, the smell of pine mixing with burning naphtha. They pounded swiftly over the roof of the gymnasium, but Beryl slowed as they drew close to the gap. Always Beryl poked at the borders, pushing them both to the edge of anything with an edge. Suddenly the courier wanted to test her back. Besides, the train was moving slowly. This would be easy. She ran harder, and Beryl hurried to catch up. "Really?" she asked.

For answer, the courier leapt. The cars swayed and Beryl leapt after her, stumbling when she landed. The courier reached to steady her, but Beryl pushed her hand away. She looked angry, then determined. She stood and ran past the courier. With a wordless whoop, the courier chased after her.

The air felt cool against her face and arms. She wondered if the people in the cars below could hear the thumping of their shoes. She wondered if the sound worried them.

The jump to the next car was easier. Beryl said nothing, and neither did the courier. The rush of the wind, the roar of the train, those were enough. They leapt from the eating car to the common car, and then to the conference car. When they reached the car containing the courier's own compartment, Beryl slowed again.

"We should—" she said, and the courier knew what she wanted to say, but the courier pretended not to hear. She kept running.

They leapt to the seventh car, Book's office. She imagined him looking up from some report and frowning. The train beyond this point was forbidden to the courier. Would she be breaking the old laws if she kept going? She had seen those cars from the outside countless times. What difference would it make to see them from above?

Beryl's face was pale beneath her red, wind-tangled hair. If the courier had a name, she thought, Beryl would have shouted it.

But the courier kept running, and Beryl ran with her. They jumped and landed lightly. The sun had cleared the trees and the dew glowed bright on the pines. The roar of the engine grew louder. When the wind shifted, they had to duck the long rope of smoke.

The courier stopped counting cars. They were above the diviners' quarters, or above the divining compartments themselves. They didn't stop until they reached the front of the train, the car she thought must contain the office of the chief engineer.

Beryl knelt, and the courier put her hand on her shoulder while they breathed. Ahead was the tender, fully stocked with naphtha. The glittery black mass folded and knotted, melting into itself and sending up a stale odor, like something dug from a swamp. Beyond was the engine. Each time the courier saw its great steely bulk, it seemed larger than she thought it could be. From up here, it was the monstrous noise—how it tore and churned the air as it dragged the rails to itself—that left her without words.

The smoke shifted again and covered the sun. When the light returned, a face appeared in the window at the back of the engine's cab. Gray boilersuit, long gray hair, gray hollow cheeks. A ghost, but one the courier had never seen before, not in the ghost car or anywhere else aboard the train. The ghost was looking right at them with clear, bright eyes.

Beryl stood. "We should go."

The ghost disappeared back into the cab and another face replaced it: a living man's, smudged with soot. The courier recognized him as one of the assistant engineers. When he saw her, his expression changed in a moment from surprise to anger.

"Let's *go*," Beryl said, almost shouting now, and this time the courier let herself be pulled away.

They moved down the train in strides and leaps, the cars flying backward beneath them. With the sun at their backs, and the distant trees still sunk in nighttime, the courier felt cold, the joy of the run gone out of her. The engine's whistle sounded a pattern she had never heard before, three short bursts followed by two longer blasts. In her mind she saw herself leap from car to car to car, then fly from the end of the train and disappear into the nothing beyond the hills.

But here was the roof of the garden car, its glass roof glinting. They could go no farther. The courier turned and fell into a crouch, shaking as she breathed.

The whistle sounded again as the train rounded a bend and emerged from the trees onto a riverbank. The water was wide and gray. From an island rose the ruins of an old lighthouse, and just ahead was a village, its station a clump of dark brick near the shore.

Recognizing the place, the courier shook her head. It was Stem. There to the east were the fields that had been her father's farm, and there was the hill that she and her sister had climbed for its view of town. There was no place in the named territories that she knew better, yet she hadn't recognized it at all.

Two figures appeared at the other end of the car, a porter and a mechanic, two of the toughest crew members. Both looked very unhappy.

"There's a word for this, isn't there?" Beryl said.

*Trouble*, the courier thought, but she didn't bother speaking it aloud.


"I'll make a terrible ghost," Book said. "I'm slow, I'm clumsy, my belly gets in the way of everything I do. And look at this."

A shabby heap of papers shifted as the train rocked through a curve. Book steadied them, then selected several sheets and fanned them out over his desk. All bore the circular insignia of the sayers.

Just a decade ago, official requests for words were a rarity, filed with the committee only when the sayers feared an immediate threat from the nameless. Now they were common practice. Book read, *"A piece of glass that divides light into colors. . . . A game that children play by hiding from someone who must find them. . . . A kind of fish that looks like a snake and keeps mostly to river bottoms."*

"Those I've seen," the courier said.

Book ignored her. "Apparently they want a name for an arrangement between two people who agree to spend the rest of their lives in each other's company."

"Book," she said.

"Next they'll want a name for what happens when they change their minds."

"Book."

"They have no idea how this works. There may be dozens of words between what we have and what the sayers want, but they think it's as simple as sending a ghost to fetch your laundry. I may as well make a ghost of myself right now. If I'm lucky, I'll end up in the factories. At least there'll be less paperwork, and fewer people wanting to do my job for me."

She stopped trying to interrupt him.

"And you," he said. "Running across the rooftops, disturbing the diviners, the assistant engineers. What am I supposed to do with you? Send you off to a creche with the other children?"

"Did I break committee law?"

"You *are* broken law. Do you know how difficult it was to find a place for you here? Do you know what I risked to make that happen? The watchers all polishing their goggles since that mess at Buckle, and you, meanwhile, behaving like—"

"Like a child," she said. "You already—"

"Like someone without a name," he snapped.

A cold shock went through her. In her silence, Book went back to his papers, selected one, and found the corresponding envelope sent down by a diviner. "You say you know these fish that look like snakes?" he asked. "They sound horrible. Consider them yours."

She delivered *eel*. She delivered *muck*. She delivered *bleary*. She delivered *toil*. The worst assignments Book could find, he sent to her. In the faces of her fellow couriers, she saw flashes of cruel delight. Book's favorite was being made to suffer; now the one without a name, the one who delivered *trouble*, would finally know her place. She avoided them as much as she could, taking her meals alone in her compartment or in the ghost car.

She delivered *bland* and *bruise*, *whimper* and *bog*. She rarely had to go far to make her deliveries. For some, she never even left the train. Each time Book summoned her to his office, she glared at him with her arms crossed over her chest, challenging him to give her something worse. And he did, every time.

Weeks passed, and she didn't see Beryl. At first she thought the diviner must be avoiding her. Then worse possibilities occurred to her. The committee might have dismissed Beryl for their rooftop run. They might have turned her over to the watchers.

Finally, she found her one day seated in the chair farthest from their favorite spot in the common car. Beryl glanced up from a sheaf of schematics. She looked tired, thin, bleary. When she saw the courier, she smiled and stood. They embraced, but Beryl held her only briefly.

"I shouldn't have pushed you like that," the courier said. "I shouldn't have made you run with me."

"You didn't make me do anything," Beryl said, but her voice was flat, and the words sounded automatic.

They sat together at dinner. The courier told Beryl about her recent assignments. About the stream of horrible words, words that should have been distributed evenly among the couriers or assigned to trainees in need of toughening. "He's going out of his way to hurt me," she said. "My talents are wasted on these mean little words."

While she talked, Beryl looked more and more distracted, until she seemed not to be listening at all.

"Did I say something wrong?" the courier asked.

Beryl set her fork down. "I'm just wondering if you ever paused to think about who might be divining those words."

The courier's meal felt like rocks in her belly. She imagined Beryl in the divining car, those long hours alone, seeking word after terrible word. If they hurt to deliver, then they also hurt to divine.

"Since they caught us on the roof?" the courier asked.

Beryl shook her head. "Since your meeting with Frost."

So Book was punishing Beryl, too. And only because he believed that Beryl knew what the courier wasn't telling him. The courier should have guessed. Should have realized that he would try to drive them apart.

Before she could speak again, Beryl asked, "Have you ever considered taking a name?"

The courier's throat tightened, choking out any words she might have spoken.

"It's still possible, isn't it?" Beryl said. "If you took one willingly? If you worked to make it stick?"

The courier looked at her hands on the table and tried to think of a word to describe this feeling. Not *anger*. Not *grief*. Both those things together, and worse than either alone. Some burying thing, cold and heavy, keeping her silent, keeping her still.

Beryl shrugged and resumed picking at her food.

Later, they walked through the train without speaking. At the door to the courier's compartment, Beryl squeezed her hand. The courier considered pulling her inside, telling her about the word Frost had given her. Her secret assignment, the shadow aboard the Number Twelve. Maybe Beryl could help. Maybe she knew something about Book, or about the glassblowers.

But the moment passed, and she let go of Beryl's hand. The diviner walked the corridor alone, toward those cars where the courier could not follow.

With each new assignment, Book barely acknowledged her presence. She felt like a ghost as she wandered the train. Book receded in her mind as though down a long corridor, into a dim place where the air was thick with tobacco smoke, music crackling like fire in the walls.

Her dreams grew strange. Broken earth and wasteland, nameless machines churning in the hollows, bloodied hands under a hot sun. A vision of the Silence, she thought, when the whole world fell to ruin, and there were no words for *fall* or *world* or *ruin*. A few among the first named had been children when something fell from the something tree, so the Silence could not have lasted more than a lifetime. But that was long enough to undo most of what had been, to break every border, to fill the world with monsters.

Then another dream, stranger and more troubling. Ragged dark cavities, dusty corridors, the rich rusty smell of blood in the shadows. This was the Number Twelve—not the Number Twelve as she knew it, but a labyrinth composed of the places between, where her stowaway traveled, dozed, and hunted.

And wasn't she moving now with the sleek surety of that nameless animal, a shadow with light in its eyes? For hours she wandered the hidden parts of the Number Twelve, feeling the rough wood under her paws, and the signaling, electrical and exquisite, of whiskers brushed by wind. Then a scratch of movement in the darkness, and with her stowaway she stalked her prey: a leap, a rush, a moment of desperate struggle before her claws and jaws closed over a wriggling ounce of fear and heat that flooded all her senses.

She woke with a cry, drenched in sweat. At once she lit her lamp to make sure nothing had woken with her from her dreaming. Only draff, though some with life enough to scratch at the floor with clawlike splinters. She swept it up and brought it to the last car of the train, burned it in the stove while the messenger birds warbled overhead.

Just a dream? Or had she truly slipped behind her stowaway's eyes and under his skin? She'd heard stories of the nameless sharing the contents of their minds, their dreams. Could they do the same with animals? She breathed, tracing the border around her body and mind, willing it to hold.

Dutifully, she made her deliveries. The word Frost had given her was a cold, heavy animal at the bottom of her satchel. Couriers were not supposed to bear more than one word at a time, and now she understood why. With each delivery, she felt that unspoken word steal more of her strength. It was hungry. It wanted out.

Then, in late summer, in the month of Drone, came an unwanted first. The assignment shouldn't have been difficult. She spent a week with her new word, two weeks. She tried to deliver it while gazing at her own reflection in a puddle. She tried with clouds moving over the moon. She tried with a leaky faucet, with a fraying rope, with a cup of water left to dry in the sun. But every time she felt ready to speak, the word retreated, like an animal withdrawing into a hole. She knew the sound the word should make, knew where to put lips and tongue and breath. But when she opened her mouth, no sound came. She returned to the train exhausted, her throat sore from the effort.

"I'll give it to someone else," Book said, swiping the card from her hand.

Later, she heard the other couriers whispering in the common car. She heard them speak the word and knew it had been delivered. Ivy had needed only two days.

*Diminish.* The courier almost laughed to hear it. If the patchwork ghost made an illustration for *diminish*, it could have sketched her, worn and ashen in the margin.

Her next assignment brought her close to the home of the farmer Juniper. Almost a year had passed since the courier delivered *harrow*, there in the old woman's fields near the southern border. Now she had a few hours before she was scheduled to rejoin the Number Twelve in Tooth. She should have gone straight to the station, shown the watchers her papers, and waited. But she decided to visit Juniper instead.

She found the house empty, the windows dark. The barn was empty, too, and vegetables rotted in muddy fields. The harrow was gone, along with the rest of the farmer's tools.

The courier went to the nearest village and asked around. The neighbors wouldn't meet her eyes. They had harrows of their own now: factory-built, with shining steel tines. But no one would speak of the woman who made the first one from railroad spikes and scrap metal, out in the shadow of the nameless mountains.

Back aboard the Number Twelve, the courier went straight to Book's office. He was playing one of his records, his slippered feet up on his footstool. The music was almost inaudible through the scratches. She recognized *brass*. She recognized *drums*. But most of the instruments on the records didn't have names. And whatever kind of music Book played, there was no name for that, either.

She had to shout to be heard. She hardly knew what she was saying, only that she shouted loudly and for a long time. Book said nothing. He kept his feet up. He seemed to be listening more to the music than to her.

Finally he said, "Farmer? We're talking about a farmer?"

"I wrote about her in my report," she said. "*Harrow*. You remember."

"I remember your report," he said. "I remember it covered only a fraction of the time you were away from the train."

The courier swallowed. He was right. The old woman's farm had reminded her of her father's farm, the parts of it she'd liked, and her hands had known the work. So after delivering *harrow*, she had stayed another day to fix fences, dig ditches, pull nameless weeds from the herb garden. She had taken more time than she needed and kept some details to herself. She hadn't thought Book would notice or care.

With the volume of his music still turned high, he leaned forward over his desk, as though to make sure no one in the corridor could hear. "That harrow contraption was only the beginning," he said. "She kept inventing things. Things from before, new things. Sometimes it's hard to tell the difference."

"So the sayers gave her a job, maybe," the courier said, not whispering. "Set her up with a workshop and all the tools she needed."

Book frowned. She was trying to make him talk about something unpleasant. About the lengths to which the sayers would go to keep the nameless from gaining ground. About those ad hoc committees and their orders. About those who carried out such orders. Would Frost form a deletion committee for her if she failed? For Book if she succeeded?

She said, "A boy, a sayer's son, brings back a thing from before and bottles it. He knows who to bribe, so we name it *whiskey*. He must be doing well; I've seen merchants trading jars with his name on the label for good naphtha, for freshly calibrated *ghosts*. Then a lonely old woman builds a new thing to help her work, to keep herself alive. And do you even know her name?"

Book's frown deepened, but she pressed on.

"Juniper," she said. "The farmer's name was Juniper, and she was kind to me."

"*Kind*," Book said, as though it were the most useless word the committee had ever delivered. He sat back in his chair and waved her away. "I'll let you know when we're ready for you again."

Her eyes were stinging as she left. Book's words ground in her mind. *When we're ready for you.* As though he and the committee were the same thing. As though he were only doing his part.

But they knew each other too well for that. It scared him, all that each of them knew. And it scared her, too.

The ghost car was nearly empty. Porters had led most of the namers' stock outside to clear an obstruction from the tracks. But the patchwork ghost was here, working on a sketch. She sat beside the ghost and told him about the farmer, about Juniper.

"We never said much," she said. "Just worked around the house and fields. In the evening we drank tea made from the herbs she grew in her garden."

The ghost kept sketching, but she knew he was listening. If a deletion committee had taken Juniper, then speaking of her now was forbidden. But the words kept coming. "She squeezed my hands when I left. Her hands were rough. She lived out there with so much silence, but she lived."

The courier wished the ghost had been with her, because then he might remember, might now sketch the old woman and her home, her fields.

She put her head on the ghost's shoulder. He was working fast, pencil scratching hard against the paper. He had drawn a room full of tables and chairs, people leaning close over drinks, faces lit by low-burning lamps. A tavern of some kind. Broad windows with a view of tall trees, patrons with their hats pulled low. Not one of the station bars. Not a place the courier recognized. When had the ghost seen such a place?

At the back of the room, in a corner, the ghost drew a table without a lamp. The man seated there was in shadow, but the courier recognized the cut of his suit, the handkerchief in his pocket. It was Book.

She sat up. The ghost's sketching was urgent now, almost feverish. He drew a figure seated across the table from Book. A woman in a short dark coat, dark hair tucked under her cap. The ghost's eyes were shining as he filled in details. The woman's hand, pressing something against the surface of the table. Sliding it toward Book, or accepting it from him. A note, a document, maybe a map.

When the ghost was done, the courier stared for a long time. The woman's features were partly hidden by her cap, but the courier knew her. Knew her freckles and big eyes, knew the worried way she pressed her lips tightly together.

The patchwork ghost had done as she'd asked. While she was away on an assignment, maybe just this last assignment, he had caught Book sneaking from the train. The ghost had followed, and this is what he had seen.

Book in a corner of some strange tavern, meeting with the courier's sister. With Ticket.

The ghost tore the page from the sketchbook and gave it to her. She looked again, just to be sure. Then she folded the paper small and stuffed it into the bottom of her satchel, down with the undelivered word.

The courier lay in her bunk, thinking how dangerous it would be to fall asleep with this much anger throbbing through her body. If any escaped in the night, it would escape as something worse than draff.

How long had Book been meeting Ticket? And why had Book kept those meetings secret from her? She thought of the letters, dozens every year, she'd posted to that address in Whisper. Of her last letter, unsent and stowed in her desk drawer. If Book and Ticket still spoke, he could have given the letters to her in person. The courier could have gone with him, could have sat with them at that table.

Unless Frost and Smoke were right about Book. In the sketch, it looked as though he and Ticket were trading information. That information might include details about the Number Twelve's schedule. Were they both working with the nameless, with the glassblowers in Hollow?

If so, she was ready. She could deliver the word to Book, and Frost would have the criminal along with the word for his crime. But what would happen to Ticket? Would the watchers take her, too? She had spoken Ticket's name to Frost and Smoke, that night aboard the flying machine. Maybe they were already investigating her.

She gasped as something landed beside her on the mattress. Fur, warmth, an insistent rumble: her stowaway. The courier took a few deep breaths as the animal padded back and forth over the mattress. She stroked the thick fur on his back, and finally he curled into a ball beside her.

She thought of that dream or not-dream, when she had gone with him through the train. If it wasn't a dream, had the stowaway known she was with him? Yes, she thought, of course he had known, and she followed him now, down into sleep.

She woke to shouting, to the clomp of boots in the corridor. The stowaway was gone, just a hint of warmth on the blanket beside her.

She rose and opened her door, found other couriers standing in their doorways, blinking. Ivy appeared for a moment at the front of the car. "There's been some kind of attack," she said.

The train wasn't moving. The courier remembered the sight, hazy and dark, of nameless territory outside her window the night before. Still in her night-shirt, she ran with the others down through the train. No one seemed to know what they were running toward, but she imagined cars broken open, masks and blades in the corridors, something with claws, with sharp teeth. She was too late. The nameless had struck again.

In the eating car, someone was screaming. The courier climbed onto a bench to see. A porter was on his knees in the aisle, scraping at his face with both hands. A cook came from the kitchen with a pot of water and doused him. The porter screamed again, and the courier saw red welts rising on his skin. She thought for a moment that the cook had scalded him—but the welts were from stings, not burns.

"He came from the storage car," the cook said. "Those *things* came with him."

Dozens of buzzing black shapes darted and veered through the air, bouncing against the ceiling. Insects, an unnamed kind. Many still crawled over the porter's body. A page tried to brush them off, but she shouted and jumped back as she herself was stung.

The courier opened windows and helped swat the insects out. Others crushed them against the tables with plates and pans. The insects curled into themselves and their ghosts flew up, angry still. Not the nameless, then, but nothing good.

Still on his knees, the porter sobbed and groaned. His eyes were swollen shut, round and dark as bruised plums. He rolled on the floor as his face and hands grew big with poison.


The engineers sent a signal up the line. An hour later, a physician came from Claw in her steam speeder, a compact cab behind its sleek green boiler. Tins and glass bottles rattled under her robe as she climbed aboard.

The porter had been moved onto a bench in the common car. His breath was ragged, his face unrecognizable. The physician knelt and whispered into his ear. The car was quiet enough that the courier could hear some of the words, *still* and *steady,* words to soothe and calm. The porter's trembling less-ened, and his breathing grew easier.

Next the physician mixed liquid from one of her bottles with powder from a tin, forming a green paste. This she spread with her fingertips over the worst of the stings. Book stood close, watching.

The poison was bad, she told him, but not as bad as the shock. "Imagine, to be engulfed by a nameless swarm. Best for now to keep him under. Give him these when he next wakes."

She put two paper packets into Book's hands. "Draff from good dreams," she explained. "Brew them into a tea. The hotter he can drink it, the better."

Rope had been silent this whole time, rubbing his bristly hair with one hand. For once, though, many were watching him, waiting to hear what he'd say, because they knew he was the diviner who found names for flying things. Now he let out a little gasp as he spotted a still-living insect in the curls of the man's hair. He fetched it out with pincers and trapped it in a glass.

"Well?" Book asked him.

"I can try," Rope said. He left in the direction of the divining car.

The physician was intrigued. Book showed her to a seat, and a kitchen ghost brought her food and drink.

When Rope returned almost an hour later, he came cradling his head. "We have *sting*," he said, "and we have *nest*, and *wing*. We have *bee*, which is close, but not close enough. I can get there, but I need another week, maybe two."

The physician looked bored. She put on her robe and said to Book, "I've left enough medicine for a week." She returned to her speeder. The whir of its little engine faded as it steamed north along the rails.

Later, after most of the crew had returned to their duties, the courier found Rope alone in the garden car, staring at a fern.

"Not some new kind of moth?" she asked.

She had meant it as a joke, but the diviner shuddered and stepped back as though stung. His hands were shaking as he brushed past her.


In the eating car, porters still batted the tiny angry ghosts out open windows, though some of the ghosts were already turning to ash.

Book was arguing with one of the mechanics. Book wanted to send a ghost to remove the nest, but the mechanic—his name was Salt, and he was one of the two men who might have been Beryl's father—believed that a ghost, freshly trained for this peculiar task, was unsuitable.

"Might get only part of the nest," he said. "Worse, might bring it back here instead of getting rid of it."

Salt wanted to leave the whole car at the next station, then return for it once the infestation had been dealt with.

"It would be *unseemly*," Book said, using one of his favorite new words, "for the namers to leave an unnamed menace at some stationmaster's door."

The courier stood near the back of the crowd. Around her, the kitchen ghosts washed and dried dishes as though nothing had happened. When she was sure that no one was watching, she slipped past the ghosts and through the rear door.

The train was poised on a steep hillside. At the bottom of the slope, leaf-less trees rose crookedly from a shallow black bog. The shadows of the cars lay huge over the water, and the courier's own shadow was a tall, thin blade passing between.

In the storage car, the air was cool. The courier held still and took shallow breaths until she heard the droning. On a high shelf at the back of the car, she saw the papery nest bulging from a stack of wooden stakes. It was a sad, slumped thing, humming with dull life.

She hoisted open the sliding bay door in the middle of the car. It rumbled loudly on old iron wheels. Alerted by the changing air, the insects began to move. They looked heavy yet hardly there, legs dangling, wings thrumming, a blur of black and yellow.

The courier walked among them, and the insects circled close. She climbed a stool and took hold of the stakes to which the nest was secured, lifted with both hands. The nest tore as she lifted, and more insects spilled out, filling the air.

She felt the first stings at once. She walked slowly to the door and lobbed the nest out of the car by the stakes. It tumbled down the slope and hit the water, floated out among black trunks.

The buzzing grew louder. She stood at the door with her eyes closed, lis-tening, certain the noise had some meaning. More stings now, on her hands and arms, on her neck. But under the rage, the courier heard something else. A warning, or an invitation, or both those things together.

The noise made her dizzy. The living cloud descended.


She woke in her bunk with fire running under her skin. She didn't know how she got here, only that she wanted to scream. She twisted the sheets in her fists. Someone was beside her, whispering, holding her arm. Then she slept again, and the buzzing of the insects followed her into her dreams.

The dreams were formless, a mist through which strange words drifted. For a while she felt her stowaway at the outermost boundary of her senses, a protective presence, warm and fierce. When she woke again, Beryl was touch-ing her face with cool fingertips.

The courier tried to speak, but no words came. Was this how it felt to be a ghost?

"Book said he didn't want to waste the medicine on you," Beryl said. "So I stole a little. Which he knew I would do, of course. Now don't try to speak. Sleep if you can."

Darkness again, and Beryl was gone. The courier smelled burning. It was her own poisoned blood, scorching her veins. No, the lantern on her desk was lit. Had someone been sitting there?

She was going someplace far away, falling backward down a long, dark chute. She wondered how they'd built a chute into a train car. She tumbled, and the masks of the nameless rose up around her, white for war. Through the eye slits she saw black-and-yellow bodies throbbing, saw wings shining like jewels.

The courier fled down nameless streets and into an old warehouse. In the middle of the gray expanse, she found her sister sitting tied to a chair on a dirt floor.

*Ticket.* They had taken her sister, and it was the courier's fault.

She pulled at the rotted ropes until they fell apart in her hands. Ticket's eyes were huge in the dark.

"We have to get out of here," the courier told her.

Her sister nodded, and the courier took her hand; it was dry and thin as paper. They ran together toward a distant square of sunlight, but Ticket fell behind, her body going long and strange in the dark.


The courier woke to the patter of rain against her window. Her head hurt. She was thirsty, her tongue dry and swollen. She ached everywhere. When she moved, she felt sharp, burning points on her hands, arms, and legs. The insects must have jabbed her dozens of times. Her blanket was gone, her sheet torn and thin, worn almost to nothing.

She rolled away from the wall and waited for her eyes to focus. A woman in a ragged blue dress was seated at her desk.

"Beryl?" she said, and the woman turned.

It was not Beryl. It was not a woman at all.

A scream lodged itself in the courier's throat. She wasn't dreaming. She was alone in her compartment with a monster, a monster in the shape of a woman.

The monster stood and strode toward her on spindly legs. When the courier scrambled away, it reached across the bed with its long, long arms, and she was too weak to fight it off. The monster slid one hand under her back and another under her neck, gathering her up. Before the courier could twist free, the monster began to rock her back and forth. From the uneven crease of its mouth came a soft cooing sound.

The courier stopped struggling. The monster wasn't trying to hurt her. It was trying to soothe her. The thing's eyes were too big, the brow too high, the lips too thin, the skin too pale. But the face was familiar, down to the freckles on its nose and cheeks.

Asleep, the courier had told the dream of her sister that they had to escape. And so they had, the both of them together.

She wriggled free of the monster's grasp, got out of bed, and locked her compartment door. How long since Beryl had last been here? If she'd seen the monster, she would have screamed. Anyone would have screamed.

Seated at the edge of the bunk, the thing watched with a frown as the courier went to the window and peered outside. The train was moving through a region of rolling farmland. She reached for the curtains, but the curtains were gone. The monster was wearing them.

Once a dress of her mother's, the curtains were now a dress again. It didn't fit well, the skirt and sleeves too short for the monster's limbs. The courier saw her scissors and thread still out on her desk. The monster must have made the dress itself.

The monster could sew.

The courier went through her desk and found things missing. Most of her paper, the scraps of cloth she used for mending. The desk itself was lopsided, some of its legs shorter and more narrow than they'd been before, and the wood of its surface was warped and worn. Diminished.

The unsent letter to her sister was gone. She drew close to the monster and examined its skin. On its face and hands patterns like wood grain whirled through pale papery textures. On its throat and wrists were darker, fibrous patches. And everywhere were small inky markings, glyphs floating under the skin.

The monster had made itself from the material in her compartment, just as draff might snatch a handful of dust to give itself form. It had taken her blanket and sheet. It had taken the letter to her sister along with the rest of the paper from her desk, and wood from the desk itself. It had taken the books from her shelf and the ink of their words. It had molded all these things into a misshapen imitation of her sister, a thing like the girl Ticket had been when the courier last knew her, stretched strange rather than grown older.

Chasing an itch, the courier reached one hand to the top of her own head. Most of her hair was missing. It was on the monster's head now, dark and curly.

. . .

The trouble with monsters was that they defied naming. They could never be pinned down, never be made to fit. Scraps and oddments, the draff of a common uneasy sleep—these could be put to use. They could be burned, refined into naphtha, even used as medicine. But a dream that walked and clutched and saw and breathed—this was different. Few of the named could make a monster, even if they tried. And when they did, the dreams committee dispatched its hunters to capture the thing, and to investigate the careless person responsible for its birth.

But they wouldn't call the courier careless. They would call her nameless. A threat. A menace. The nameless made monsters for one reason—to break the named world.

The courier felt herself weaken, felt her breath go. The monster, moving with a weird grace, swept across the room to catch her. While the courier struggled to regain her balance, the monster made cooing sounds and stroked what was left of her hair.

Someone knocked at the door. The courier held still, watching as the knob jerked, then rattled. The monster watched, too.

"Are you there?" Beryl called. "Are you awake?"

The courier pushed the monster away. "I'm here," she said. "I'm fine."

The knob rattled again. "Why is your door locked? I have something for the stings."

The courier remembered the cool touch of Beryl's fingertips in the night. She looked at the blotches on her arms. They were covered in a green crust.

"I have enough medicine for now," the courier said. "I'm feeling much better."

The monster approached the door, but the courier pulled it back. When Beryl spoke again, her voice was firm. "You had a fever last night," she said.

The monster pawed at the courier's arm and made soft mewling sounds. The courier pushed it away again.

"Is that animal in there with you?" Beryl asked. She had never acknowledged the stowaway before. The courier remembered how he had flitted through her dreams. Maybe he had visited her compartment while Beryl tended to her.

The knob rattled harder, but the lock held.

"Go away!" the courier shouted. "Go back to your own car!"

Beryl was quiet, but the courier could see the shadow of her feet under the door. The monster kept pawing at her, and its whimpering grew louder. To drown out the noise, the courier said, "Please just leave me alone. I don't want you here, and I don't want your help."

Beryl's footsteps retreated quickly up the corridor. A moment later, the door at the front of the car slammed closed.

The monster leaned its head against the courier's back. "Oh," it whispered sadly, its breath dry and shallow. "Oh, oh, oh."

When she was promoted from page to courier, Book had presented her with a new uniform of gray wool. Her green page's uniform had fit her poorly, the jacket baggy, the legs of the trousers too long. Later pages received new, sturdier uniforms, and no one had asked her to return hers, so for years it had remained at the bottom of her drawer. Now she fetched it out from under her other clothes and held it up to the light.

"Take that off," she told the monster, plucking the hem of the ragged blue dress that had been her mother's. She didn't like seeing it on that thing. "You're going to wear this instead."

The monster looked confused. When it didn't move, she slipped the worn straps off its shoulders. The monster turned its head, suddenly shy. The courier tried not to look directly at its body, but she couldn't help noticing the glyphs from her letter and her books strewn across its shoulders, chest, and belly. She guided the monster's long arms into the sleeves of her old shirt, then buttoned it. She lifted each of its legs and made it step into the trousers. This the monster seemed to find amusing. It grinned and stamped its feet.

"Stop that," the courier snapped.

The monster's smile grew, revealing big teeth of pale wood. Looking away, the courier fastened the buckle at its waist.

Last came the wrinkled jacket, and the monster understood what to do with that, stretching to slip its arms into the sleeves. It tried to work the wooden buttons with its long fingers but couldn't get them through the holes. The courier pushed the monster's hands aside and did them herself while it watched.

The uniform had been big on the courier, but it was too small for the monster. Yet the monster seemed proud of its new clothes. It stood straight, head close to the ceiling, and tugged the jacket snug.

The courier checked the lock on the door again, then quickly changed into her own uniform. The monster murmured, apparently pleased by the similarities in what they wore, its fingers hovering over the brass buttons on the courier's jacket.

She imagined leaving the monster at a crossing or in some wooded place, but she knew she couldn't take that risk. Monsters tended to seek the people who had dreamed them. The dreams committee hunters would use this one to track her down.

She couldn't abandon the monster, and she couldn't keep it aboard the train. She had no choice but to burn it.

The courier cut her own hair, trimming ends left choppy by the monster's theft. When she was done, it still looked terrible. She covered it with her cap.

*Sleep* was a border word, and her vigilance on that border had faltered. Now the monster was her burden, her responsibility. She would handle it on her own, after dark, in the last car of the train. But when she thought of the stove there, thought of how small it was, her stomach turned. She would have to burn the monster a little at a time.

No different from burning draff, she told herself. In all the stories of battles against the nameless, monsters fought even as they burned, and they didn't seem to know they were burning. So this one, too, should feel no pain or fear. There was a danger that some fragment of the monster's spirit would end up in the stove. That usually only happened with furnaces attached to machines—it was how the war machines were primed, granted a monster's spirit for its pilot to master—but when her father was working to refine the priming process for the army, some of his test furnaces had gone strange, doors swinging open on their own, dampers rattling fretfully, legs creaking as though wanting to stretch, to walk. He had dismantled them and buried their parts in separate holes. If something similar happened to the stove in the last car, the courier would have to come up with something.

They waited out the day. The courier picked at the green stuff coating her stings. The monster found the sketches at the bottom of the courier's drawer. It paged through them and then stared for a long time at the one of the courier with her sister. Finally the courier snatched it out of her hands. She took the rest of the sketches, too, and stuffed them into the bottom of her satchel.

"Those aren't for you," she said.

The monster grew restless, wringing its hands and cooing at nothing. She wondered if such a thing could be made to sleep. If a monster slept, would it dream? Could its dreams make more monsters? The courier shivered. She had an idea, though she wasn't sure she liked it.

"Do you want to hear a story?" she asked.

To her surprise, the monster glided across the compartment and sat on the floor, next to the bunk. It gazed eagerly up at her.

The courier's books were gone, but she knew some stories by heart. She began to tell the Story of the Child Who Went Underground. It was one of only a few stories that had survived the Silence, told to Hand by the three oldest of the named—Bone, Blue, and the other one—who had been children when something fell from the something tree. The courier skipped the beginning, about the two children by the riverbank, the older one reading from a book without pictures. She didn't want to use the word *sibling*. She started instead by telling how the younger child followed the fast white animal into its hole.

"The child fell down and down, deep into the ground," she said, "but she landed softly, at the end of a long corridor."

The monster's eyes grew bigger as it listened, and the courier felt steadied by the words. She began to enjoy the telling, gesturing to show how the child grew large then small again as she consumed the strange foods and liquids she found. They had just come to the part about the animal like a worm that sat on its mushroom, breathing smoke, when she heard another knock at the door.

She knew from the sharp rapping that it was one of the porters. "Go away," she said.

"I've brought your dinner," the porter said.

The courier was hungry and thirsty, and she didn't know when she'd next have a chance to eat. The monster stared at her, waiting. She shooed it up into her bunk and covered it with what was left of the blanket. Then she unlocked the door and opened it just wide enough for the porter to squeeze the tray through. Beans, bread, beets, an apple.

Frowning, the porter said, "If you're well, Book needs you. There's trouble."

"There's always trouble," the courier said. She took the tray and slammed the door.

She ate at the diminished table, her door locked. The monster watched, curious, making little tuts of surprise each time a piece of food disappeared into the courier's mouth. The courier offered the monster a slice of apple. The monster put it in its mouth, moved it around, and swallowed without chewing.

The courier couldn't finish her meal. She tried to tell the monster more of the story, but her thoughts were wandering. She was inventing things, changing how the story went, and she could no longer remember what happened next. "The animal like a worm crawled onto her back," she said, "and they went together through the garden . . ."

Her head throbbed. The sun was still over the horizon, but she couldn't put it off any longer. She rose and smoothed her uniform with her hands. She smoothed the monster's, too.

"Try not to make any sounds," she said. "And if anyone looks at you, turn away. Do not let them see your face."

She didn't know how much the monster understood, but it looked very serious as it listened. She pulled the monster to its feet. It stood with its arms hanging limp at its sides. The courier strapped on her satchel and gestured for the monster to follow.

The corridor was empty. The monster stayed quiet, but it moved sluggishly, and the courier had to tug it along by the hand. That reminded her of the dream from which she had dragged the thing, and the pain in her head grew sharper.

In the eating car, a few crew and committee members chatted over mugs of tea. The monster hunched and turned its head as it walked, as though to glance out a window. No one looked up. They didn't see her monster, the courier thought, because they were too busy trying not to see her.

All except Ivy, who was seated with some other couriers at the booth nearest the kitchen. Ivy stood and stepped into the aisle, blocking the courier's way. The monster kept moving. Ivy frowned as it squeezed past her, but as soon as it was through the door, she returned her attention to the courier.

"We never got the chance to talk about what happened in Hollow," she said. "It sounds like you barely made it out of there. The same crew from Buckle, you think?"

The courier, thoughts churning, tried to conceal her panic. What would that monster do if left on its own? "I don't know if they were the same," she said quickly.

She tried to slip past, but Ivy moved to stand in her way again. "You must have been terrified, alone with them like that," she said. "It would have been hard to get a good look at them." She seemed genuinely interested. The others at the booth sipped from their mugs and pretended not to listen.

The courier took a breath to steady herself. "Their masks were the same—"

"Of course, their masks," Ivy said, as though she'd only just remembered that the nameless wore masks. "So did they give you one?"

"Give me one?"

"I thought maybe they would give you a mask this time." Ivy was grinning now, and it was not a friendly grin. "Or did the nameless not want you either?"

The others in the booth chuckled. Ivy grabbed the courier's arm and pulled her close. "I'm sorry you're so alone now," she said.

*Now?* The courier wrested her arm free. Suddenly she wanted to bloody that smile with her fist. Wanted a real monster at her side, a monster from some story of the war. No, she wanted to *be* that monster, with claws and fangs and a hunger to match her rage.

Ivy watched her, eyes gleaming, waiting to see what she would do. But the courier only shoved past, holding back tears until she was through the door and out between the cars, where she could pretend she was shaking only because of the cold.

The monster had gone ahead without her. It wasn't in the kitchen. It wasn't in the storage car either, and it wasn't among the ghosts in the ghost car.

Here, the courier paused beside the bench where the patchwork ghost usually sat. The bench was empty. Nothing unusual about that: it was often required in the printing car, and other times it simply wandered off. But the ghost's sack of sketchbooks, usually tucked below—those were gone, too. That was strange.

*There's trouble*, the porter had told her.

If he had wandered off to draw something, he wouldn't have taken the whole sack of sketchbooks.

*I'm sorry you're so alone now*, Ivy had said.

Had something happened to her ghost?

Some of the ghosts turned to look as she ran past them to the last car. The monster was seated on the floor near the cold stove. It watched the courier search the place. She opened the rear door to peer out onto the deck, then overturned junk in the corners, though she knew it was useless. Up in the dovecote, the messenger birds fussed at the commotion. The patchwork ghost wasn't here.

The courier stood over the monster. "Did you see him?" she asked. "My ghost, the one with his suit all patched?"

She heard the panic in her own voice. She was talking to the monster as though it were someone who could help. The monster only blinked and wrung its hands. The courier knelt beside it and said, "You wait for me here. And if anyone else comes in—"

The monster was listening carefully, eyes wide.

"Hide if you can," she decided. "Under those blankets, or out on the deck. If that doesn't work, you'll have to run. Jump from the train if you have to, and run very fast."

Was she trying to protect the monster or herself? She imagined it trudging long-limbed through the wilderness. Maybe the nameless would find it and take it in. Maybe it would find others like itself, hapless things, the waste of fever and reckless dreaming. But she knew the dreams committee hunters would likely find it first.

The monster's face was blank now, unreadable. The courier told herself that it wasn't a person, its feelings thin as paper, just scraps from her own mind. She was responsible for the monster's destruction, and that was all.

"I'll come back for you soon," she said.

She ran up through the train, ignoring everyone she saw. In the seventh car, she went straight to Book's door and slammed it open.

Book, startled, began to rise from his chair. When he saw who it was, he sat back down. A nearly empty bottle rattled on the shelf beside his phonograph records. A fire blazed in the stove, and the air was hot.

Book was not alone. Rope sat in one of the cushioned chairs. The diviner turned to look up at her.

"Here she is," Book said. He was smiling, but the smile looked wrong. "Our pretty puzzle, our quickening heart. And what does she want from old Book this time?" The record they were listening to was in bad condition, more scratches than music. The noise hurt the courier's ears.

"Where is my ghost?" she said.

"*Your* ghost?" he said. "Which of the committee's ghosts do you mean?"

"Book."

Book and the diviner exchanged a look. "In fact," Book said, "Rope and I were just discussing the matter of the patchwork ghost. Which is, of course, a possession of this committee, and therefore the committee's responsibility. Especially since no one else seems capable of looking after it."

The car jostled, and the needle skipped. The courier wished that Book would turn off the phonograph, but he seemed not to notice the noise.

"Book, what happened?"

Rope looked genuinely concerned. "Beryl didn't tell you?" he asked.

Beryl had wanted to tell her something, the courier remembered, when she'd pounded at her compartment door. But the courier had sent her away.

Rope sighed. "It happened while you were recovering," he said. "I found the ghost in a car near the engine. Car number *three*."

The courier recalled what she knew about the cars closest to the engine. After the tender came the chief engineer's quarters, and the next car was home to the assistant engineers. The third car was windowless and plain, its exterior painted drab gray. It was where the committee kept its most closely guarded secrets.

"The divining car," she said.

"You can probably guess what the ghost was doing," Rope said.

She did not have to guess. The ghost was doing what he always did. Only this time, instead of sketching a view from the train, or a plant growing in the garden car, or a cake of soap in the bathing car, or cutlery or bottles or pickled vegetables, the ghost had sketched something he shouldn't have seen, something that not even the couriers were allowed to see. He had sketched a compartment of the divining car.

"We're only ever just a step or two ahead of the nameless," Book said, "and that's when we're lucky enough to be ahead. Battles are rarely fought between machines and monsters now. Many more are fought in shadow, by those tasked with keeping secrets and those who wish to take them."

"Where is my ghost?" the courier asked.

"Some wanted to feed it directly into the furnace," Book said. "But some, including Rope here, pushed for a rather more *kind* course of action. A vote was called. You may be pleased to hear that Rope's opinion won out. The ghost is to be calibrated."

The courier was sweating under her uniform. She thought of the ghosts that returned to the Number Twelve with blank eyes, knowing nothing of what they had been, needing to relearn the simplest of tasks. Calibrated. *Saved from the confusion of themselves.*

Book's stern look faltered. He cleared his throat and said, "Rope, leave us, please. We'll speak again soon."

Rope nodded and rose from his seat. For an awkward moment, he hesitated before the courier. "I am sorry," he said.

The courier said nothing. When Rope was gone, she said to Book, "This is still about Frost, isn't it?" she said. "You're finding new ways to punish me."

"You brought it upon yourself," Book said. "That ghost has grown worse under your care." More gently, he added, "We both knew this would happen eventually."

She reached into her satchel and took out the sketch of his meeting with Ticket. She unfolded it and laid it flat on his desk.

"Tell me what's happening here," she said.

Book leaned closer. When he saw his own likeness, he went still. "How did you—"

The courier tapped the paper. "Book, where *is* this?"

His watery eyes shone. "You had me followed? By the ghost?" His laughter was almost admiring, but she heard the nervousness in his voice. "No wonder he's grown so bold."

"Where did he follow you?"

Book waved a hand over the sketch, as though to dismiss it. "This could be anywhere, any tavern in any station along the line. Tortoise? No, Leaf. It looks like Leaf."

"I delivered *shortcut* in Leaf," she said. "This is someplace I've never seen. And what about my sister? Book, what are you doing meeting with my sister?"

He swallowed. Turned as though to fetch whiskey, turned back to his desk. The phonograph needle had reached the end of the record and now it looped over the same few scratches again and again, matching then missing the rhythm of the train's passage over the rails.

"Frost put you up to this, didn't he?" he said. "You can't trust him. You can't."

She laughed, louder than she'd meant to, startling them both. "How long have you kept her from me, Book? How much more are you keeping from me? At least Frost—" But she stopped herself.

"What have you done?" he said. "What have you told him?"

She felt dizzy in the heat. She didn't know if she'd said too much or too little—to Book, to Frost, to Beryl. She needed to get out of that office, away from the fire. Away from Book's accusing stare.

She snatched up the sketch and ran.

She had already left the monster alone for too long, but the monster would have to keep waiting. Let them find it, she thought. Let them think what they wanted. It didn't matter anymore.

Instead of returning to the back of the train, she went forward. At the front of the seventh car was the door through which she had seen Book and Beryl pass countless times, the door that was forbidden to her. She opened it and stepped through.

The moment she crossed the gap, a hand closed around her arm. She stifled a scream.

Beryl put a finger to the courier's lips. She led her up the corridor and into a compartment near the front of the sixth car, closing the door behind them.

Beryl's compartment was about the same size as the courier's, but it felt smaller for all the clutter. Tools and machine parts covered the surface of the desk. More lay sorted into piles on the floor. Rolled schematics stood in the corners, and spools of cable, rope, and wire drooped from wooden pegs on the walls. The view through the window was partially obscured by jars of bolts, nuts, and screws, nailed through their lids to the undersides of shelves.

"I knew you'd do something like this," Beryl said.

"Then why didn't you report me?"

Beryl's face was pale in the light from her naphtha lamp, her eyes red from tears or sleeplessness or both. "You're reckless and selfish, and that makes you dangerous," Beryl said. "But I'm not going to report you. I'm just tired of having to look after you."

"And tired of not having a name to use when you're angry."

Beryl swallowed. "Not just when I'm angry," she said.

They were standing very close amid the clutter. Beryl frowned at the courier's cap and started to remove it. The courier yanked it back down, but Beryl had seen.

"Your hair," Beryl said.

"I cut it."

She looked doubtful.

"Help me," the courier whispered. "Please help me this last time. After that, you can forget all about me, pretend I've been deleted. Maybe I will be. Either way, you won't have to look after me anymore."

Beryl took a shaky breath and closed her eyes.

"Please," the courier said.

After a moment, Beryl said, "The reference car."

"The what?"

"Two cars up. That's where they're keeping the ghost." She held up one hand. "Just don't tell me what you're planning to do once you find him."

The courier stepped back. She thought of that cottage on the border that Beryl had talked about, the two of them by a fire as the snow fell, silencing the forest. "You could come with me," she said.

Beryl seemed smaller then, and very tired. And something else, too. Ashamed, maybe.

Suddenly, the courier thought she knew why. "When Book called the vote," she said, "where did you stand?"

Beryl opened her mouth to answer, closed it again. The courier stared at her and waited, leaving a silence for her to fill. The diviner's eyes were bright with tears. "You're so stubborn," Beryl said. "About that ghost. About not taking a name. Don't you understand that I just want you safe?"

"So when he called the vote—"

"Book didn't call the vote," Beryl said. "I did."


The courier thought of the word in her satchel, the one that Frost had given her. She thought she could almost deliver it. To Beryl, if she wanted. To Book, if she believed her worst suspicions. She could almost deliver it to herself, for all she had done, for all she was about to do. But her mind was a puzzle with pieces missing, and she couldn't clear the mess away. Couldn't make space enough for the sound the word should make, for how it should feel to speak it.

So before Beryl could say anything more, she left, and moments later she was out over the tracks again, alone with the roaring wind. She kept moving. The fifth car looked the same as the sixth, rows of doors behind which diviners slept or read or studied. No one came or went, no one tried to stop her. She crossed to the fourth car.

The reference car, as Beryl had called it, was crowded with boxes, chests, barrels, shelves. From racks hung clothing of every cut and fabric and color. In a box left out on a table were clocks, watches, hourglasses, and sundials. She saw shelves containing bones, fur, paper, glass, and stones. Musical instruments swayed on hooks—drums, a fiddle, a bell, a brass horn polished to gleaming. She saw a gun in a locked case, saw bullets on a pillow, saw sketches in boxes labeled *plants and their seeds, animals with fur, animals with feathers, things to eat, things to bury, furniture, weather, weapons*. She saw sacks and crates stuffed with as much of the named world as the committee could fit into one ancient railcar. It was like the junk dealer's warehouse in Hollow, except everything here was named, and to walk among the stacks was like falling through a hundred old naming songs.

> *A ball will roll, a bell will toll.*
> *Dig dirt with a shovel to make a deep hole.*

Did the diviners think of the songs while they browsed these shelves? Did they come here to plan their approach before retreating into the divining chambers? Maybe they needed such objects at hand while performing their work.

At the front of the car, the patchwork ghost sat slumped in an old wooden chair, arms hanging, chin to chest. He seemed broken. The courier had never seen him look so much like a ghost.

Seated beside him was an assistant engineer. It was the same young man who had spotted her with Beryl on the day of their run atop the cars. The courier hid herself behind a rack of shoes and boots, watching as the assistant engineer dealt cards for a game of Hand and Moon. He played his first card and said to the ghost, "I think I may have you this time, friend."

When the ghost failed to take his turn, the engineer chose a card on his behalf. "An interesting play," he said, "but I don't think it'll help you in the end."

The courier tried to work out how quickly and quietly she could close the distance between them. The car was no longer than the gymnasium car. More obstacles, here, but also more places to conceal herself. She thought she could make it halfway through before the engineer would notice her. Maybe she could arm herself along the way. From where she crouched, she could see a hammer, an axe, a pick . . .

The courier breathed to steady herself. Then, as the engineer began to shuffle for the next hand, she made her move, slipping past the shoes, ducking behind a shelf of fabric, spinning around a barrel of tools. She strode quickly up the car, the names of named things heavy in the air around her. *Rope* and *pulley, sieve* and *satchel, clothespin, bucket, lure,* and *twine.* Each seemed about to reach out and trip her, snag her, take her breath.

The engineer dealt the cards and didn't spot her. But before he could finish, before she could reach him, the train's brakes sounded.

The courier lurched forward, nearly falling. She threw herself against the wall between two broad shelves, her heart pounding.

The engineer peered out the window. "This is your stop," he said brightly. He stood and patted the ghost's shoulder. "Thanks for the company, friend."

He collected his cards and tucked them into his coat pocket, then opened the door to the outside. Cool air flooded the car. The engineer waited until the train slowed to a crawl, then hopped down.

The courier ran to her ghost. Outside, the signal lamps of a rail yard glowed red and yellow in the dark. She recognized the station at the edge of Brick.

She took the ghost by the arm. "With me," she said. "Quickly."

The ghost didn't budge. She tugged his arm, but it was like trying to move a statue. Then she saw the shackle. The ghost's right ankle was chained to the nearest shelf, which was bolted to the wall. She knelt and pulled at the chain, but it held firm.

"I need your help," she said to the ghost. "If we pull together . . ."

The ghost didn't look at her. It was as though he had already been calibrated. Thin, diminished, hardly there at all. The courier could almost see through him.

With one foot braced against the wall, she pulled again, first at the chain, then at the shelf. Neither gave. She dropped to the floor and leaned her head against the ghost's knee. She was breathing hard and her limbs felt weak. Force alone wouldn't work. She could search the car for tools, maybe. Find something to dismantle the shelf—no, there wasn't time.

"Please," she said to the ghost. "You have to help me."

She felt the ghost's cool fingers on her cheek. She looked up at him, and the ghost smiled.

"No," she said. "I'm not leaving without you."

The ghost tilted his head as though to say, *What choice do you have?*

She took up the chain, wound it around her fist, and pulled again. The muscles in her arms burned, her head throbbed. She would pull until the train broke or she did.

She heard a creaking noise. For a moment, she thought the bolts were loosening. But it wasn't the bolts. Someone else had climbed into the car.

She turned, expecting another assistant engineer or a brown-suited calibrationist of the ghosts committee. Instead she saw a ghost in a gray boilersuit—the same ghost who had peered from the back of the engine's cab when she and Beryl ran over the cars. Long, tangled hair spilled down past the ghost's hollow cheeks. *Haggard,* she thought. Not an old word, but the right one.

As the ghost stood there with one hand in the pocket of that gray boilersuit, the courier kept very still, unsure if she should run or try to explain. The ghost held something out to her: a key on a ring of keys.

She hesitated only a moment before taking it. She knelt beside the patchwork ghost and slid the key into the lock. It didn't turn easily, but it turned. The shackle popped open and fell rattling to the floor.

The patchwork ghost, suddenly himself again, stood, brushed off his jacket, and straightened his hat. Then he reached under the table to retrieve his sack of sketchbooks.

Outside, a pair of calibrationists were approaching, cables slung over their shoulders. The courier returned the keys to the haggard ghost. The ghost pocketed them and nodded.

"Thank you," she said. "We have to go."

At the door, she turned to see the haggard ghost still watching them. She was certain she hadn't known the living person the ghost had been, yet something seemed so familiar about that sad face, those tired eyes.

The ghost raised one hand: a gesture of farewell from the years of the Silence, maybe, or maybe from before.


She ran, and the patchwork ghost stumbled after her. Her ghost's limbs were stiff, his stride short. When the courier pressed him to hurry, he nearly fell. She tried to take the sketchbooks, but the ghost held tightly to the sack and wouldn't let go.

They passed no one in the fifth and sixth cars. In the seventh car, she saw light shining from under the door to Book's office. The courier walked past it, but the patchwork ghost stopped. He grabbed the doorknob, but the knob only rattled in his hand. Locked.

"What are you *doing*?" she hissed.

The car jolted forward. The calibrationists must have guessed that the ghost was still on board. Harder to escape if the train was moving.

The door at the back of the car slammed open. Ivy, her uniform jacket open over her nightshirt, raised a naphtha lamp and peered into the corridor. She saw the courier and strode forward, dragging some writhing, long-limbed thing behind her over the floor.

It was the monster. It wailed miserably, big eyes rolling in their sockets. Ivy threw the monster at the courier's feet, where it curled its long body around her ankles and whimpered.

"I assume this is yours," Ivy said.

Before the courier could respond, the patchwork ghost hurled itself against Book's door. The door buckled inward, wood cracking. Before the courier could stop him, the ghost hit the door again, and this time it splintered and broke. The ghost went tumbling through.

In Book's office, sheets of paper lay scattered over the floor. Black ink on white pages, some handwritten, some typed on a typing machine. The courier saw maps, diagrams, letters. Most of the sheets were piled near the stove. The door of the stove stood open, and the flames burned brightly.

The rug was damp and glittering with glass shards. Book sat on the floor, back against his desk, face shining with sweat. He held the jagged neck of a broken whiskey bottle in one hand. His other hand clutched his chest, twisting the fabric of his shirt.

The courier stepped free of the monster's grasp and followed the ghost into the hot, smoky air. Book didn't seem to notice either of them. He was staring into the dark at the front of the car, his eyes glassy and strange.

"What did you do?" Ivy said to the courier. She pushed past her to stand over the documents scattered around Book's desk.

"Book?" the courier said. She followed his gaze to the shadows among the furniture. Something stirred there, black and yellow, its movements almost mechanical. Its eyes were gleaming jewels, its legs long stalks, its heavy body covered in thick bristles. Another monster, but nothing like the one she had made. It was like one of those nameless insects from the storage car, swelled with malice to the size of a large dog. The monster spread its wings, and they flashed in the firelight.

Ivy screamed as the monster took flight. She swung her lantern in a wide arc, but missed and fell backward, striking her head against a corner of Book's desk. She hit the floor hard and her lantern went rolling over the rug, naphtha flame spurting.

The monster wheeled in tight circles. For a moment the courier lost sight of it, then it landed on her chest. She stumbled backward, the stings she'd suffered in the storage car flaring anew. She heard the song of the nest, a great chorus calling, drawing her in. The fire in the open stove was multiplied a hundred times in the panels of the monster's eyes. It flexed its stinger.

But before it could strike, something pulled it away, its legs jerking, its wings a blur. Big, papery hands gripped the buzzing thing tight. It jabbed the other monster's arms with its stinger. The monster only grunted, sounding both curious and disgusted. Then it knelt beside the stove and shoved the thing inside.

A high-pitched trill filled the air as monster held monster to the fire. The wings and antennae curled to blackened stumps, and then its body was burning. But those long-fingered hands were burning, too. The courier grabbed her monster by its middle and pulled it away from the stove. She peeled off her jacket and used it to extinguish the flames. The stings had left little gray marks on the monster's arms, and the fire had scorched its hands. The monster's eyes widened as smoke rose from the blackened tips of its fingers.

From the stove burst what remained of the insect thing. It pitched itself over the floor, still burning as it leapt, crawled, and thrashed. Book's papers caught fire, the flames joining those from Ivy's broken lantern.

Through all this, Book still stared into the shadows. The courier went to him and shook his shoulders. "We have to go," she said.

He finally seemed to see her. "It was waiting for me," he said. His eyes were wide, his lips wet and purple. The courier moved his hand from his chest and parted his shirt. Near his heart, a puckered bruise had risen where the monster had plunged its stinger.

The burning thing arced through the air again. It landed behind Book's desk and went still. Flames climbed the curtains.

The courier leaned into Book, shouldering his weight. He rose partway, then fell backward to lay sprawled across the floor. Her monster touched his chest, close to the wound.

"You get her," the courier said, pointing to Ivy.

The monster wrung its hands and muttered. It took Ivy by the ankles and dragged her clear of the flames.

All this time, the patchwork ghost had been searching the drawers of Book's desk. Now he held up what he'd come for. It was a sketchbook, the one in which he must have drawn the divining chamber. The ghost tossed it into the sack with the others.


*Fire.* Hand had seen and touched that hungry light, and the brightness of its hurt had drawn the first words from the first namer's lips, breaking the Silence.

*Hand. Fire.*

Later came *wood*, and *stone*, and *water*, all found and named by the light of *fire* as Hand's scorched hand blistered and cracked.

Now fire reached for every surface of the seventh car. The courier's eyes stung as she looked for something to smash the window. She found Book's footstool and hurled it, shattering the glass. Wind sucked smoke from the car, but the flames grew brighter and hotter.

Ivy's head bounced over the threshold as the monster dragged her into the corridor. The courier grabbed Book under his arms and pulled him after. Her feet slipped on the papers scattered over the rug. She glimpsed clusters of words arranged in bewildering combinations.

*Wolf guards the cave while the serpent seeks the key.*

*Under the half moon, a yellow wind rolls from rock to bramble.*

She coughed and staggered through the door. Her ghost helped drag Book down the corridor to the back of the car, then out onto the walkway.

The train's brakes sounded, and Book's eyes fluttered open and closed. He mumbled words like those on the documents the courier had seen. Real words, most of them old and solid, but spoken in ways that stretched or changed their meanings. Less like committee business, and more like the poems crafted in the unnamed neighborhoods of Hollow, passed from hand to grubby hand on long printed pages, a mockery of the committee's broadsheets.

These were no poems. The meanings that slid below the surface were practical, she thought. A reporting of facts, of movements and plans. These were messages intended for a select few. Hearing the words tumble from his wet lips made the courier shudder. Book was delirious, awake but dreaming, incriminating himself with every breath.

Frost had been right about him. He deserved the word she bore, and maybe her sister did, too.

On the walkway, above the noise of the brakes, she heard the fire roaring as it spread through the car. She saw two streams of smoke: one from the engine, black against the stars, and one from the broken window in Book's office, bright gray and shot through with sparks.

The train came to a halt in a dense wood. With help from her ghost and her monster, she lowered Book and Ivy to the ground. They dragged them away from the burning car, out among the trees. The fire reached through windows and over the roof. Trees glowed in its light, leaves flicking in the hot breeze.

The courier checked Ivy's injuries. Her pulse was strong, but on the back of her head was a large lump. When the courier pulled her hand away, it was coated with blood.

Lanterns moved behind the windows of the cars. A group of mechanics gathered outside, where they began working to uncouple the seventh car from the eighth. Engineers and porters came with buckets of water siphoned from the engine's reservoir. They emptied the buckets onto the flames and steam mingled with the smoke.

The courier called to them, but no one heard. She shouted more loudly, then stopped when Book's hand fluttered against her cheek.

"Let them do their work," he said.

She knelt and touched his forehead. His skin was hot and dry.

"It was you," she said. "You told the nameless we'd be at Buckle. Did you tell them I'd be in Hollow, too?"

She wanted him to confess before she made the delivery. She wanted him to come as close as possible to delivering the word to himself.

Book's eyes widened, but not at the accusation. He had noticed her monster. The flickering half-light softened the strangeness of the monster's face, hid the patchiness of its skin. "Ticket?" he said. "Ticket, what are you doing here?"

"Book, that isn't my sister," the courier said, though she couldn't bear to tell him what it was.

He seemed not to hear. "Ticket, why didn't you report back? No word from you, not even a whisper."

Pain shook him. He ground his teeth, hand going to his throat, but he kept his gaze on the monster. "Did you make it to the Black Square?" he asked.

The courier remembered that other train, each car painted a different color, engine steaming on a trestle near Brick. Remembered it in Spur, the people flocking to the show, their lanterns bright.

Over on the tracks, the mechanics had finished separating the cars. The engine chugged to life and dragged the first seven farther up the line. When it halted, the mechanics got to work on the forward coupling. Sweat dripped from their faces.

"Wasn't sure we'd see you again," Book said. "Thought you might have decided to stay and request a card."

Big eyes blinking, the monster looked back and forth between Book and the courier. Its confusion matched the courier's own.

"Book, what do you mean? Requested what card?"

Book's eyes rolled back and his mouth opened wider. The courier shook him, but all that came was a wordless sigh.

The monster and the patchwork ghost stood beside her, watching. She thought the ghost looked sad, but she wasn't sure. Not being sure made the tears come. She was angry enough to stop them quickly.

She brought the word to mind, saw and felt the shape of it. For months now she had carried Frost's card in the bottom of her satchel, the word at the bottom of her mind. Her undelivered burden. She could hear it as though she'd already spoken it.

*Traitor.*

Once she delivered the word to Book, everyone would know that he had turned against the named. But new questions made her hesitate. Who had left that monster in his car? And why had Book sent Ticket to the Black Square?

People shouted and leapt away as flames swallowed the seventh car entirely. The courier stood to watch the mechanics finish their work just in time. The engine moved again, pulling the front of the train clear. Orphaned on the tracks, the seventh car burned alone.

When the courier turned back, the ghost of Book was standing beside her.

*Trouble.* Book had assigned her the word soon after promoting her from page to courier. She had known that he meant it as a test. That he wanted to give her something for which she wasn't quite prepared.

She had known trouble, though. People talked about trouble all around her, without having a word for it. When they felt trouble they would clench their hands, close their eyes, look away. To deliver *trouble,* the courier knew she would have to be among them. She knew she would have to break the rules.

So she went from town to town, visiting the places where people gathered. The village meeting spots, the eating halls, the stations, taverns, and waterfronts, the chambers of other committees. She listened and she waited. And when someone mentioned how supplies of ghosts were dwindling, or how a monster had been sighted in the forests nearby, the courier whispered the word so quietly, she wasn't sure she'd spoken at all. When a child returned from creche sad and strange, unable to recall the naming songs and still speaking sounds that were not words, the courier whispered again, *trouble.* When a drought came, when sickness spread through town, *trouble.* When an accident at the factory claimed fingers, hands, lives. When a dream got loose and howled in the street. When a ghost went missing, when a well went dry, when a nameless animal butchered chickens in their coop, *trouble.*

Somebody's daughter ran away, and somebody's son was drinking too much. A father coughed blood onto his pillow. An old mother forgot the words for things, forgot the names of her own children. A storm was coming. War was coming, or it had never gone away. We don't have enough naphtha, and winter will be cold. The crops have failed, and we're going to be hungry. *Trouble.*

The courier didn't know where she was when she completed the delivery. Maybe the first time she whispered the word, maybe the last. But that wasn't how it felt. It felt as though she had delivered *trouble* a little at a time, making trouble as she went.

She returned to the train with expired papers. Book was furious. She could have been taken by the watchers, he said. She could have been tracked down by the nameless. She was reckless. She was—

"In *trouble*," she told him. "The word you're looking for is *trouble*."

Her report was vague, and Book stayed angry, because he knew he had to. They needed to make sure the word would stick. Later, when pages delivered the broadsheets with *trouble*, everyone knew the word already.

"Didn't we have that one before?" they said. "Haven't we had it for a long time?"


The ghost of Book looked at the body of the person he had been. New ghosts would sometimes stare at their bodies for days if no one separated them. But the ghost of Book just frowned and patted his belly, as though unhappy with how big it was. Then he turned to watch the flames.

More members of the committee and the crew had joined the crowd around the burning car, but only to watch it burn. Even from this distance, the courier could feel its heat.

The monster touched her arm and said, "Oh."

Walking along the rails came Beryl. She joined the others near the fire, then turned to look into the woods. Her face was in shadow, but the courier knew she could see her. What did she make of the things she saw? The patch-work ghost, the ghost of Book, Ivy unconscious on the ground. And a person who was not a person, tall and skinny and strange, a monster in a too-small page's uniform.

Ivy mumbled and shifted. She would wake soon, the courier knew. And the two calibrationists in their brown suits were walking down the rails, searching for their quarry. For a moment, the courier thought that Beryl might shout to them, might point out the courier and her companions in the trees. Instead, she turned her back on them and stared into the fire.

The courier looked at the ghost of Book. She wanted to hear his voice once more, and not just for what it could tell her. But that part of him was gone now. His ghost squeezed the courier's shoulder and nodded in the direction of the woods, as though to say, *Go, go now.*

She went, and the patchwork ghost went with her, and so did the thing that was not her sister. The night was cold, the forest quiet under a gibbous moon. Autumn had come, and the leaves were a rustling jumble of colors, more colors than they had words for.

# THE
# BLACK
# SQUARE
## SHOW

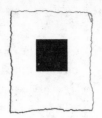

Her father never sent her to creche, never sent her to school. It was her sister who taught her what she needed to know.

It began one winter, shortly after Ticket's eleventh name day, when Ticket told the nameless little girl that it was time to stop playing games of pretend. "*Pretend* is for children in creche," Ticket said. The way she spoke it, the word sounded ugly and shameful.

Ticket had seen enough teaching, she said, to know how teaching was done. She instructed the girl to build a fire in the fireplace. She spread her books over the big table. She put slate and chalk into the girl's hands and said, "You'll need to learn the glyphs. Moon made them long ago. The committees use them, and so do the sayers. They're like words, but without any talking. On other days we'll do numbers, maps, and story. Numbers you already know, but there's more to them than counting. Maps is about what's on the other side of the river and what's on the other side of the woods. Story is just everything that's happened. Story is easy."

This was more than the girl had ever dared hope for. Ticket was talking to her, using words she'd learned in school. The girl hugged herself to keep from shaking. Usually Ticket ignored her. She didn't want to do anything to make her change her mind.

Of all the subjects they studied, story was the girl's favorite. She learned about the wars with the nameless, and about the deeds of the committees, the watchers, and the soldiers of the named. When they talked about story, Ticket made the girl point out where on the maps each story took place. Ticket believed that maps was the most important subject.

But the girl's gaze often wandered to the places where stories never seemed to happen. The empty patches between rail lines, towns, and rivers. The blanks beyond the hills, lakes, and forests of the borders. The named places made one shape, but if she closed her eyes, opened them, then looked at the map *just so*, she could see that all the places *without* a name made a shape of their own.

She pointed to an empty spot east of Hollow. "What's out *there*?" she asked.

Ticket blinked. She looked confused. "There's nothing out there," she said.

"But there has to be something," the girl insisted. "There's something everywhere."

"Not there," Ticket said. "Not until the maps committee adds it to the maps." She gave the girl an odd look. She didn't seem angry, only worried, or maybe confused. She ended lessons early that day.

That was the last time the girl asked questions about the unnamed places, even though she sometimes had to blink away the shape they made. She wondered how the shapes would change when new maps arrived, after the committees added names. They never got new maps for their lessons, though. And a few months later, when Ticket ran away, she took the old maps with her.

Now, fleeing into the dark beyond the flickering light of the burning train car, the courier tried to see those maps in her mind. She knew that the nearest watchtower was behind them, in Brick. How long before her committee could send word back down the line? Before the watchers dispatched a unit to track her? She had until morning, she thought. Maybe midday tomorrow.

She led her ghost and her monster west, their footsteps hushed by pine needles, her ghost's sack of sketchbooks bouncing on his back. The monster stuck close to the courier, startling at the faintest of sounds—at the wind in the trees, at a pinecone kicked up by its own big feet. And then at something moving in the bushes nearby, something sleek and gray, alive and coming toward them fast.

It was the stowaway. The animal must have followed from the train. He drew close, and for a moment the courier thought he might let her pick him up, but when she crouched he bounded ahead. Out here, the stowaway was something different from what he was on the train. Something wild, his eyes electric. Yet he had chosen to come with her.

They trudged on, and two hours later they reached the forest's edge. Near a bend in a stream called the Silver stood a small border town, metal rooftops shining among bright-leafed beech and maple trees. The courier had never been to this town, and she didn't know its name. On the other side of the stream was an unnamed region, a tangled woodland, hazy in the moonlight.

The courier led her ghost and monster through the meadow. The path wound alongside a low stone wall and through a thicket of laurels. Soon they would find a place to sleep. An old barn, maybe, or an unattended shed.

Then, just as they emerged from the trees, a shadow swept over the hills. The courier grabbed the monster and pulled it with her to the dirt. The ghost knelt beside them.

She heard the thing before she saw it, the whine of its engine like the buzzing of a great insect. A flying machine. It came low and fast over the meadow, a dark cudgel in the sky.

Watchers. They had come so quickly. The committee must have kept a signal bird for Brick, must have sent it the moment the fire was out. The watchers had guessed the route she would take.

"Oh, oh," her monster said.

The patchwork ghost took out his sketchbook and began to draw the flying machine.

"Not now," the courier told him. She tugged ghost and monster both into the shelter of the laurels. As the machine descended toward the town, they hurried back up the slope, keeping close to the wall. By the time they reached the forest's edge, the lanterns of a search party were already bobbing toward them over the fields.


Deeper into the forest they went, cutting north. The monster dragged its feet and swayed, whining as it tripped over roots and batted branches from its face. The courier wanted to leave it behind, but if the watchers caught the monster, they would turn it over to the dreams committee hunters, who would use it to track her down. So she took the monster by the arm and pulled it with her through the trees. She felt like the old woman in the Story of the Child Who Went Through the Glass, dragging the child across the countryside.

But this wasn't story, and it wasn't pretend. She had made a monster. She had stolen the patchwork ghost from her committee. The seventh car had burned, and Book was a ghost, and the courier would be blamed. Even if anything remained of the monster that had poisoned him, the courier would be blamed.

She watched the skies for the flying machine, watched the woods for everything else. She felt the stowaway close by, his mind a bright pulse in the dark. She felt him nudging her first one way, then another, taps at the back of her brain like a small cold nose. *Here now—now this way, quick!* Away from the train, the border between them was thinner than ever.

While they ran, morning silvered the edges of the clouds. In time they came to a place that was unnamed and unmapped, hazy in the courier's vision, a deep gully. They picked their way carefully down the slope. The stream below was nameless, but the water was still *water*. The courier drank and filled her canteen.

She and her ghost gathered pine branches and built a shelter among the rocks. The monster climbed in beside the courier and went instantly to sleep, like a shutdown machine. It lay without moving, mouth slightly open, hair tangled in the weeds.

When the courier woke, the monster was still asleep. Outside, the patchwork ghost sat on a rock with an open sketchbook balanced on his leg. She crawled from the shelter to sit beside him. While the ghost sketched the stream below, she looked through the sketchbooks in his sack. She found the one he had retrieved from Book's office and opened it to the page that had caused all the trouble. She wasn't supposed to see this, but what could it matter now?

The divining compartment had no furniture, though a small pillow lay on the floor. Beside it was a rod about three feet in length. On the floor itself—inked or carved into the wood, the courier wasn't sure—were the glyphs used to record every word delivered by the named. She imagined Beryl seated on that pillow with the rod in her hand. Would she point at glyphs to spell known words while seeking the new one?

She flipped through more pages. "You sketched the Black Square's train once," she said.

The ghost looked at her and tilted his head.

"I need to find my sister," she said. "I need to know why Book sent her to the Black Square. Do you know how to find it?"

The ghost seemed to consider, and for a while he watched her search the pages. Then he went back to his work.

The courier gave up and went into the woods, searching for food. She found a handful of edible berries, some roots that might be boiled. The forest was still, more quiet than she liked. No wind moved the branches, and the birds she saw were silent.

She returned to find the monster awake. It stomped barefoot in the stream, swinging its arms and hooting loudly. The patchwork ghost gave the courier a helpless look.

She hurried into the water and grabbed the monster by the arm, dragged it back to shore. "Stupid!" she said. "That was stupid!"

The monster flailed and moaned. Disgusted, the courier let go, and the monster threw itself to the ground and sobbed. The courier searched the skies, saw nothing but thick gray clouds. She covered her face in her hands and sighed, then went to sit beside the monster. She laid their breakfast out on a flat stone.

After a while, she said gently, "I brought food."

The monster remained on the ground, sniffling. The courier ate slowly. She knew there wasn't enough, not even for one, but she wanted to leave enough to share. After some time the monster sat up and examined the pitiful meal. Then, from the pockets of its dress, it drew two crusts of bread and a seed cake. Then a jar of honey, a block of cheese in wax paper, a sprig of parsley, two pears, and a chunk of maple candy.

The courier was stunned. Then she remembered her confrontation with Ivy in the eating car of the Number Twelve the night before. Remembered how the monster had gone ahead as she'd instructed. Alone, the monster had passed through the kitchen car, the storage cars—

"You *stole* these," the courier said.

The monster clapped its hands and grinned, then gestured for the courier to eat. The courier hesitated, but the monster pushed the food toward her and said, "Ah, ah!"

Shaking her head, the courier took a bite from the seed cake. "It's good," she admitted.

The monster looked pleased. It popped a berry in its mouth and swallowed.


With time to think, the courier decided she had been foolish to run straight for the nearest town on the map. The watchers knew every named byway and road. They knew every town, even those on the border.

But Moon had written: *The border is everywhere.* And though the watchers knew the mapped borders, they couldn't know all the inner borders, the un-mapped gray zones like this gully, this stream. The courier closed her eyes and pictured the maps. She saw the shape of the regions between. From now on, she would trace the edges of those shapes. She would walk the borders of the interior.

At sunset they packed their few things and followed the stream. They traveled through the night, moving fast. The ghost, sack slung over his back, showed no sign of wearying. The monster was less frightened now. It saw the courier yawn and tried to do the same, opening its mouth wide and closing it again.

The stream was joined by others. Once, the courier thought she'd lost it, that it had slipped from her mind as nameless things do. But she stopped and held still until she heard its burbling. Soon they were walking over open fields. The air was heavy and still. She saw the ruins of small villages, abandoned since the Silence. The buildings were hard to make out through the fog, harder still to hold in the mind.

Just before dawn, the clouds lifted and the air changed. They were near-ing the Silver again, close to the western border. The waterway was plied by barges. Watchers would be patrolling these shores.

The courier searched the horizon. Trying to find unnamed places was like looking for new directions on a compass. She shook her head and closed her eyes, breathed, tried again.

Suddenly the ghost was standing very near. He pointed, and she saw: a corridor lined with iron structures, towering things like the skeletons of great monsters. They must have served some purpose in the years before something fell from the something tree. Now they rusted in the open sky, and wind whistled through their limbs.

She adjusted her satchel and walked on.

They followed that narrow corridor by night and passed the days in abandoned buildings. A half-ruined barn beside overgrown fields. A squat booth beside a broken dam. A low brick building that smelled of ash and grease.

In one rusting structure, water dripped into pools on a cracked concrete floor. They discovered lockers, and inside them a pair of blue boilersuits. The courier put one on and gave the other to her monster. They fit well enough. Between some derelict machines, the courier built a fire and burned their committee uniforms. The monster murmured wonderingly, clutching its burnt hands. Before they left, the courier plucked the brass buttons from the ashes and put them in her satchel.

They foraged for food, scavenging what they could from the ruins. Sometimes the monster sneaked off without the courier noticing and returned with pockets pull of fresh bread, cheese, dried fruit. She didn't know whether the monster was stealing from the nameless or the named.

"You shouldn't do that," the courier said. "You're going to get caught." But the courier ate anyway, and the monster grinned.

They found paths used only by animals, or they picked their way through pathless wilds. To the courier, it felt like getting lost and staying lost on purpose. It felt like moving in a direction that didn't exist. It made her bones hurt.

The named were supposed to avoid these places. There were stories of children disappearing into the empty places on the maps. But she knew they were on the right track whenever she found the stowaway ahead of them, waiting, its tail a curled invitation.

The courier wondered if the ghost could sense, as she did, the presence of others nearby. The nameless were moving just beyond the edge of her vision. Were they trying to keep out of her way? Or were they watching, following, hunting? She could almost hear their voices in her head. She tried to keep her own thoughts on her feet, her breath, the path ahead. She tried to keep those borders sealed.

. . .

In towns along the spurs and minor rail lines of the westernmost regions of the named—in Nettle and Ingot, Bear and Mirage—the courier went alone, seeking rumors of the Black Square. Dirty in her boilersuit, with her satchel slung over her shoulder, she looked like a traveling laborer. The people tried not to notice her. The mines, ranches, and lumbering concerns of the frontier had workers enough, and ghosts long accustomed to the labor.

In the town of Fir, a woman at the water pump told her that the show had been through some two weeks before. In Plank, a ghost wrangler outpost grown into a village of some two hundred named, she missed the Black Square by only a few days. In Bend, she met two children still giddy from the story of Yarrow, the first dreams committee hunter, performed the evening before.

At night she risked the rails. Like the names committee, the Black Square was bound to its engine. If she moved quickly, she might catch the train in the next town on the line. But the Black Square hadn't performed in Mortar or in Blister. No one had seen it pass through the stations, and those brightly painted cars would be hard to miss.

One night, the courier saw fires on the hills, heard bellowing and gunshots. At a dry goods store, the stock boy told her that a group of soldiers had set up camp just west of town.

"What does the army want out there?" the courier asked.

"Trapping," the stock boy said. "They bring cages from the border a dozen at a time."

The courier remembered all those war machines she and Book had seen on the army train. Each would need to be primed: a monster for every furnace, using techniques her father had perfected.

Another night's hike brought her and her companions to Fold, with its breweries and paper mills, its three bridges of iron. She saw a group of men watching from across a narrow street. One turned and squinted at a notice in a shopfront window. Farther down the street, she found an identical notice pasted to lamppost. When the courier saw what was drawn there, she felt cold. The sketch was not as good as the patchwork ghost's would have been, but her face was still recognizable. The reward was fifteen ghosts, freshly calibrated.

She ran back to her encampment in the woods east of town. The patchwork ghost sat with the stowaway curled in his lap, petting the animal carefully.

"Where is it?" the courier asked. "Where's the monster?"

A buzzing noise rose up from the trees. The ghost stood, and the stowaway leapt from his lap and bounded into the brush. A flying machine emerged over the woods, its engine a thudding roar.

Painted in silver on the cabin's belly was a wide-open eye. The watchers had found her.

She ran with the patchwork ghost to a nameless road. On its cracked gray surface stood the crumbling remains of ancient machines. Vehicles of some kind, most with four wheels but some with more. The courier wove among them, broken glass crunching under her feet, burdock catching at her boiler-suit. The shadow of the flying machine swept over her.

Ghost lenses were meant to reveal unnamed things, but Book had always said that they didn't work as well as the watchers believed. That the only way to see nameless things was through study and focus. But maybe Book had been wrong, or maybe this crew was just better trained. The noise of the engine grew loud overhead, and the courier turned and dashed off the road.

Something burst from the trees in front of her. She cried out as she collided with her monster. The monster's clothes and skin were spotted with sap. It pointed a trembling finger deeper into the woods.

At first the courier saw nothing, only tamarack and ash, and ferns gone brown with the season. Then the yellow eyes of the stowaway opened in a column of light. The animal seemed close, but also miles away. He looked at her and yawned. The monster tugged the courier's sleeve and murmured, pleading. She let it lead the way.

They passed through a rusted iron gate held open by weeds. Beyond was a clearing of high grasses, patches of sun among brambles and vines. Carved stone slabs stood in rows, some pale, some dark; some standing upright, others fallen. The stowaway perched on a block of marble, serene.

The courier had heard of ancient places like these, though few agreed on what their purpose had been. The patchwork ghost moved among the stones, touching the tops of some, crouching to examine others more closely. The courier knelt and pushed aside grass to find ancient glyphs carved into the stone. The glyphs blurred in her vision, made her eyes tear up. When she touched them, they seemed to slide under her fingers. The stowaway reached down to bat playfully at her hands.

Out on the road, watchers debarked from their flying machine. One adjusted his goggles and searched the trees. The courier felt his gaze sweep toward her, then slide past. The watchers moved on up the road, and the flying machine rose back into the sky.

When its sound had faded, the monster touched the courier's shoulder and pointed deeper into the woods. It led her through a gap in the iron fence, then into a dense thicket and down a rocky slope. The ghost and the stowaway followed.

A rusting rail line curved away among the ferns and ivy. Fungus grew from the rotting ties, and nameless plants had sprouted between them. But the courier saw the shine of steel where passing wheels had recently scraped the grime.

"How did you find this?" the courier said.

From one of its pockets, the monster drew a sheet of rough paper. Stamped at its center was a single black square.

The courier had seen notices like this before. They sometimes appeared in the streets of named towns and cities, pasted to walls, slipped under doors, stacked in stations and office entryways. Others showed up in stranger places. Wrapped around loaves of bread. Tucked into shoes and back pockets. Folded among names committee broadsheets. No one knew how the notices were distributed, but everyone knew what they meant: the Black Square Show was coming.

They walked the rails north and west, passing gray marshes, open fields, wooded hills. Ancient structures stood among the trees, and not all were un-inhabited. The courier had escaped the watchers, but others watched her now, she was sure of it. She tried not to notice the lights of their fires, tried not to hear their footsteps on the paths. Was it in one of these nameless villages that the monster had found the Black Square's notice? Was *village* even the word?

At dawn they camped in a nameless gorge. The courier sat with her back against the base of the trestle. She realized that she knew this place. More than a year had passed since she'd come here to make a delivery. Now she spoke the word again, just to hear the familiar sound: *Echo.*

They left at noon, risking the sun. Jawbone was the only settlement of the named for miles around, and the courier wanted to reach it by nightfall.

They tried to keep to the ways in between, but here named places were more numerous, marked on old maps and anchored by story. A rock called the Column, around which some of the first ghost wranglers once maintained a camp. Smoke Bluff, an old lookout station, established long before the watchers had flying machines. Finally they came to Paper Meadow, site of one of the last great battles between the nameless and the named. Here, the pilots of two dozen war machines had fought back monsters that rose in torrents from the nameless forest. The earth was still marked by deep gouges. Hyssop and brown thistle waved between chunks of scorched metal. Hills turned out to be broken war machines, covered now with grass, lichen, and late-blooming flowers.

Clouds moved over the sun, and the day turned damp. The patchwork ghost took the lead, his unbuttoned jacket flapping in the breeze. From the top of a hill, the courier caught sight of Jawbone's high palisades in the broad green basin below.

Jawbone had been built as a military outpost, but now it served as an auction town. A great pavilion stood in its central square, among the offices of brokers and major manufactories. Here the local wrangler operations displayed and sold their captured ghosts. Outside that rich district, Jawbone was a rough border town of leaning shacks and hovels. In crooked alleys and secret warrens, smugglers maintained their caches of nameless herbs and spirits, of wares scavenged from the ruins.

Lights flickered in the watchtower, but most of the town was dark, and few people moved in the streets. The people of Jawbone were gathered in a meadow beyond the rail depot, bonfires blazing. On the tracks stood the brightly painted cars of the Black Square's train.

The sun was just beginning to set. The show would soon begin.


The courier descended into the basin with her ghost and her monster. They picked their way among sumac and tangles of bittersweet. The earth down here was soft and marshy. The courier didn't know where the stowaway had gone. She felt that it was near, but not too near.

They went out among rusting sheds and stacks of lumber, stepping carefully over the rails between freight cars. The courier heard music and laughter. In the meadow, they joined the crowd. Bonfires crackled and sent plumes of sparks toward the moon, a pale splotch behind heavy clouds.

The courier had rarely been among so many people. The smells of mud, wine, sweat, and naphtha mixed in the chill air. The people of Jawbone drank and talked and jostled one another. She overheard a tall, bearded man telling the story of a logging accident. He gestured to the forests north of town as he described cables snapping, logs rolling. Three people had been crushed.

"And the ghosts?" he said. "All three purchased by the concern they'd been working for. All three working those same acres."

The man snorted and spat. His friends shook their heads and barked dismal laughs. They looked at the courier, then at the ghost and the monster. The courier tugged her companions on, moving closer to the Black Square's train.

One car near the front, wider and taller than the others, was illuminated by a row of lamps. Moths circled the flames. The courier remembered what

Ticket had told her of the Black Square, after their father had taken her to see. "It's like story," she'd said. "Except somehow it's really happening. The monsters are there, and they're huge, filling the sky. And when the monsters burn, they burn to ash, right in front of you."

Beryl had also tried to describe the Black Square Show. She'd seen it shortly after becoming a page, when one of the two mechanics who could have been her father got leave from the committee chair.

"Machines of some kind," Beryl had said, and the courier had heard in her voice a mixture of wonder and vexation. "I saw what the machines did, but I don't know how they worked. What I wouldn't give to get a look inside that train."

The engine's bell tolled five times, and the crowd quieted. Parents lifted children onto their shoulders while older children dared one another closer. Brokers snapped for their ghosts to lift them higher in their sedan chairs. A few final murmurs, until the only sounds were the crackling of the fires and the shushing of the wind in the pines.

Then a great whirring noise came from the engine. Its wheels did not turn, but the roof of the big car lifted, and the side facing the crowd swung downward, lowered on heavy chains.

From within the car, a city grew.

Buildings unfolded to tower overhead. When they reached their full height, they stood as though they had always been there. Brick and marble and stone, dirty glass windows, tall doors above scuffed stoops.

The streets stretched into impossible distances. A trick of some kind, the courier thought, like those her ghost used when sketching. A mirage of depth. As for the red light of morning that shone on the walls and windows, those must have been thrown by hidden lamps.

But tricks of light and perspective couldn't explain everything the courier saw. Birds flew across the papery sky. Clouds moved over the sun as it rose from beyond the far hills. Light danced on the river, and the water rippled as though touched by the same wind she felt on her hands and face. The courier blinked, but what she saw didn't change. A hole had opened in the world, and on the other side was a city where the sun was rising.

The city was Whisper, though not as the courier knew it. Scrap piles on street corners, shattered windows. And missing from the scene were structures built in the last two or three hundred years: the spire of the city's watchtower, the army barracks, the restored dome of Whisper Station. This was old Whisper, the city as it was when the first of the named walked its streets—the city as the patchwork ghost had sketched it, months back. In this Whisper, the sayers had not yet taken power or created the committees. The city was an occupied ruin, the one named place in the world. Beyond its borders were no borders at all.

A tall figure, flickering and indistinct in gray robes, approached along the avenue. Whether the figure was a woman or a man, the courier couldn't tell. She was peering into a time before the word *woman*, before *man*. Without those words, the difference was flimsy, a border the named had yet to imagine. How was it that this person seemed to walk toward them from out of the distance, when the car that doubled as stage could only be so deep? Everything the courier had dismissed as trickery was more real now. Her world dimmed as this other world brightened.

The figure passed behind a scrap pile. Scavengers were perched on that pile, and on others nearby. The scavengers watched and listened.

When the figure reemerged, it was no longer flickering. This was Hand, the first namer, face painted with bright green lines. Hand's right hand was a scarred ruin, furrowed, pitted, and gleaming.

Someone approached from the opposite direction, silver robes rustling, arcs of yellow face paint streaked with tears. The courier knew who this was, but she had never imagined the second of the named could be so beautiful.

In the streets of old Whisper, Moon ran to Hand. And while the scavengers listened from their piles of scrap, Moon told Hand about the terrible thing that had happened.


"Three more," said Moon, still weeping. "At sundown breathing, by sunrise gone."

"Three?" said Hand. "Moon, speak the names."

"Sap is one name. That one watched from the roof of the tall gray house. This morning, blood drips from the roof and Sap is gone. Who will watch from the roof now? Who will tell us when something comes from the wilderness?"

"Someone else must watch from the roof. Moon, speak the second name."

"Root is the second name. That one went to the river, to catch fish for the evening meal. Now the river washes blood from the stones, and the one named Root is gone. Who will go to the river now? Who will catch fish for the evening meal?"

"Someone will go to the river, Moon. Speak the third name."

But Moon, yellow face paint streaked with tears, could not speak the third name. Hand held Moon's arm and said gently, "Please. I must hear the name spoken."

Voice breaking, Moon said, "Needle is the third name. That one was counted in bed at sundown. But this morning, on the stones by the well, Needle is a broken thing without breath."

Hand stumbled forward. Moon caught Hand and both were silent for a time, holding each other close.

"The one named Needle might have grown thirsty in the night," Hand said. "Needle knew the way in the dark, knew to go with cup in hand to the well—"

"Only a child," Moon said. "One of twelve."

"Eleven named children now," said Hand.

The scavengers, perched on their scrap piles, muttered to one another about what they had heard, using the words they knew. Swaying, they made of those words a chant that was almost a song.

> *Hand holds Moon.*
> *Moon holds Hand.*
> *Sap gone, Root gone, and Needle gone, too.*

The named at this time were few in number: *ten and ten and ten and three*, according to the records. Hand and Moon had given names to most of those in Whisper—first to the people they brought with them out of the wilderness, then to those drawn by the commotion of words that sounded from the city. Needle was the youngest of them all. In Needle's company, Hand and Moon had divined and delivered *child, smile, cry, gift, carry, hold*. Needle had been like their own child—or maybe Needle was their own child. The records were unclear.

Moon stepped out of Hand's embrace. "We will fight the thing that did this. Track it down and strike it with objects we have sharpened for the purpose."

"But what is the thing?" asked Hand. "One says, *A bird that is not a bird.* Another says, *Something small and quiet that is also large and loud.*"

"You saw it, Hand. Three days past, you saw it."

Hand, eyes closed, tried to see again. "The thing I saw was smoke and wind."

"You saw eyes," said Moon.

"The eyes were black, with the moon in them."

"You saw a talon," said Moon.

"Many talons, sharp and curved."

"And from talon to—"

"Beak, and from beak—"

"To wing, and from wing—"

"It was not a bird, and this is bad divining," said Hand. "The thing changes with each breath, and there is only one in the world."

"You know the whole world?" asked Moon.

"I know we cannot fight what we cannot name."

The courier, watching from the dark, knew what word they needed. The word for a dreamed thing, hateful and hungry, come out of the nameless wilds to punish and devour. *Monster.* The monster might have been drawn to the city by the noise. Something new and strange on the breeze. Or maybe it had been directed there by the nameless who made it.

Whatever brought the thing, nothing in Whisper could sate its hunger. It had taken Sap and Root and the child Needle, and it had taken others before them. There were no committees yet, no dreams committee hunters. The monster would take more if the namers didn't find a way to stop it.

The sun rose over the hills. The courier felt its warmth as the streets and buildings of Whisper glowed in its light.

"I will go and find those who made the bad thing," said Moon. "I will find them, and I will name what they made."

"No," said Hand. "They will take you, Moon, and then I will not have you or Needle. Let us find the word in the stories from before."

It was the old quarrel between Hand and Moon, the one for which the word *quarrel* was divined and delivered. Moon wanted to seek new words in the stuff of the world. Hand wanted to find them by telling and retelling the few stories they knew from before the Silence. Hand had those stories from the oldest of the named—from Bone, Blue, and the other one. Using the new words, those three told Hand what they remembered of the Child Who Went Underground, and the Child Who Flew in a Storm to Another Place, and the Child Who Could Fly and Was a Child Forever. Hand, listening to these stories, divined new words from the listening.

Moon said, "But what if this thing is not from before? What if it was born after something fell from the something tree?"

"Bone, Blue, and the other one, they tell me—"

"Hand, those are not our stories, and the three might remember them wrong."

"The three were here before, and they are here now. They remember more than anyone."

"Will they remember Needle?" asked Moon. "Will they remember the warmth of the child in our arms?"

"Moon, I named Needle. I named Needle and I named you."

"You named me," Moon said. "But you cannot keep me."

Neither spoke for a time. The scavengers chanted:

*Hand named Needle,*
*and Hand named Moon.*
*Needle is gone, but can Hand keep Moon?*

Scarred hand trembling, Hand said, "I can keep you. I am first among the named, and I tell you: do not go."

"I will go for two days, maybe three," said Moon. "If I do not return after three days, will you look for me? Hand, only say that you will look for me."

Moon, in silver robe, yellow lines of paint streaked by tears, waited for Hand to speak. But to speak those words would have been too much like saying, *I agree with you, your way is best.* So Hand said nothing.


The sun went out, and in that darkness the story took a breath. The courier breathed the cool air outside Jawbone again. She felt the warmth of others around her, heard the crackle of the bonfires.

Her ghost and her monster stood close. The ghost was attentive, though he frowned as though he did not quite approve of what he had seen onstage. The courier thought again of his sketch of old Whisper, of a scene like the one the Black Square had just performed, Hand and Moon amid the junk heaps. She wondered whether Book had been right, that the patchwork ghost had seen the Black Square perform this story before.

The monster looked distracted and confused. The courier worried, suddenly, about how it might react to the rest of the story. To seeing Moon among the nameless. To what Moon did to deliver *monster.* Maybe they should keep moving. Maybe she should take her monster's arm and go.

But Whisper had fallen away, and something else was rising in its place. A forest, and beyond the forest a city, and within the city a forest. Beneath the moon walked Moon, following a winding path. And the courier, without thinking, followed Moon back into the story, then into a clearing in those nameless wilds, cradled within the city at the edge of the world.

Here the nameless lay on the soft earth, sleeping and dreaming behind blue masks with narrow eyes. The named had no words for *sleep* or *dream,* yet Moon knew not to disturb them. Across the clearing Moon went, stepping carefully among the sleepers, who were six in number.

Another came into the clearing, big steps on soft moss. This one wore a golden mask, round and huge and shining like the sun. This was the guardian of the dreaming nameless, awake and watchful. The eyes behind the mask blinked slowly.

Moon stood tall and said, "I travel from the city Whisper. I seek—"

But the sun-faced guardian raised one hand, and Moon stopped talking. Those words in the quiet air had caused the others to stir. Gradually they settled again.

For a moment everything was quiet, except for the edge of the world. From the edge of the world came a shushing sound, like someone saying *shhhh, shhhh, quiet now.*

The guardian turned and raised both hands to the forest. From someplace deeper in the trees, two figures emerged. The mouths of their brown masks were fixed in broad grins, and from their chins hung beards of twine and feathers. The taller walked with dainty steps, prancing, almost falling. The other, stooped with age, shuffled jerkily. Both swayed as though drunk, and maybe they were.

They sat beside a stone near the center of the clearing. From a great sack they drew a fistful of glass bottles, a stack of bowls, pouches overflowing with roots and leaves. They worked as one, arms crossing, hands nearly touching as they snatched herbs into a bowl and ground them, cut slivers of root, measured spoonfuls of powders and seeds. From another pouch came an orange flower, which they ground up with the rest. Then a handful of bright black berries, and drops of liquid from three glass bottles. The two stirred and pounded; their masks grinned and grinned.

They divided the stuff into two bowls. They gave one bowl to Moon and the other to the gold-masked guardian. Moon hesitated. But the guardian, with head tilted back and the bowl raised high, poured the stuff through a hole in the mask, drinking every last drop.

The two in brown masks watched and waited. Finally, Moon raised the other bowl and drank in turn. For a time, Moon and the guardian watched each other. Then the bowl slipped from Moon's hand. Moon swayed, stumbled, and fell to the ground.

The guardian nodded to the two in grinning brown masks. They gathered up their bottles, bowls, and pouches, and wandered back into the woods. Then the guardian lay down beside Moon.


Darkness filled the clearing. Moon and the guardian sank into a deeper darkness, as though into the earth itself. Above them were the roots of trees. Down below, a cold blue light.

The six in blue masks rose from that light and formed a circle around the two, as though buoyed by a gentle current. Floating here, Moon knew the thoughts of the nameless, and Moon's thoughts were known to them.

*You came far to find us,* the guardian said, or thought. *And you came farther still to join us in this place below. Why are you here?*

Moon began to tell them of Whisper and its structures. Of the namers' work to repair the old and build anew, with mortar and brick and words for each.

Next the dreamers spoke, their thoughts a chorus, crystalline and cold. They told Moon they knew of Whisper, and of the work of the named. They knew how Hand put one hand into the fire, dislodging the first two words with pain. They knew the noise of words, of the city lousy with them.

The guardian said again, *Why are you here?*

So Moon told the nameless of the creatures that hunted the named, of the living things that were not animals, not *birds* or *fish* or *wolves* or *badgers*, because each was different from every other. *They come to the city from these lands*, Moon told them. *They come from the nameless wilds, maybe all the way from this city at the edge of the world.*

The nameless knew this, too. They told how, soon after Hand's first naming, the nameless had made their first mask, which was the mask of the maskmaker. Others followed, including the blue masks they wore. The masks protected them from words that might describe who they were, what they did. Now they made beasts to aid them in the dark places, to labor and to keep watch.

(The dreamers did not use the word *beast*. They did not use the words *dark* or *labor* or *mask*. They did not use words at all—and the courier, standing in the meadow outside Jawbone, wondered what trick of pretend the players used to make speech seem like thought. She wondered whether it was pretend at all.)

Moon's hands clenched into fists. The waters of the current churned as Moon told the nameless that the beasts did more than labor, more than keep the words away. Moon told of Sap and Root and the child Needle, of all those taken. *With claw and fang and beak and talon, your beasts hunt us, hurt us, break us.*

The waters rippled gently as the nameless considered. Then the guardian told Moon, *We make the beasts, but the beasts do not belong to us.*

Now Moon shook with rage, and the waters churned again. Moon told the nameless that what the beasts did was still their doing. *We cannot fight them, so we are blood on the stones, blood on the riverbank. Will you do nothing to change this?*

The nameless considered again. Moon looked from one dreamer to another and tried to know their minds, but it was the guardian who responded. *The named are changed by words*, that one told Moon. *But the nameless, in turning away from words, are changed by them, too, whether or not we wish to be. We cannot stop the beasts being what they are. If we did, you would only take more from us.*

Moon was silent for a time, and the waters stilled. Then Moon said, *If you will not stop making the beasts, and you will not change the nature of the beasts, will you permit me to witness the making of one?*

The golden mask glowed, then, as though struck by a warm light. The waters grew choppy and strange. Caught in the currents, the dreamers turned in a slow circle while Moon struggled to stay afloat.

The one in the golden mask said, *You would witness the making of a beast because you wish to name it.*

*Yes,* Moon admitted, *I wish to name it. Not just the one, but all of them.*

The guardian raised one hand and floated up, back to the clearing, to waking, leaving Moon behind. The minds of the six dreamers were a storm, a fever. The waters boiled and dragged Moon down, down into that cold blue light. Moon thrashed, trying to escape. *Am I not your guest?* Moon cried. *I trusted you and drank what was offered. Why did you deceive me?*

*To witness the making, you must have a hand in the making,* the dreamers told Moon. *It is the only way. So join us below, and name the creature if you can.*

Moon screamed and struggled upward, trying to wake. *Let me go,* Moon told them, *or more of the named will come for me, for I am second of the named.*

But the dreamers said sadly, *You are second of the named, Moon. But no one will come for you.*

They descended, Moon and the dreamers together.

When light returned, it shone from a dozen candles clustered on one small table. The forest was gone, and so were the roots and currents of the dreaming. Here instead were the walls of a single spare room.

Hand paced the room, troubled. Huddled around the table were the three oldest of the named, born before the Silence, before something fell from the something tree.

"Tell me again," said Hand to Bone, Blue, and the other one, "the Story of the Child Who Went Underground. Was it that same child who took up a weapon and fought the thing in the forest?"

The three sighed, Bone hunched and all in gray, Blue broad and heavy under a pile of blue blankets. The other one, whose name was lost to the records, sat small and shrunken in brown tatters.

"No, no, that was a different child," said Blue from the pile of blue blankets. "The Child Who Went Underground only *heard* the Story of the Child Who Went into the Forest."

"Wrong," Bone snapped, pointing with a bony gray finger. "The Child Who Went Underground never heard that story. You're thinking of the Child Who Went Through the Glass."

"I tell you," croaked the other one, barely visible among brown tatters, "the Child Who Went Underground and the Child Who Went Through the Glass are the same child."

"The same child, but not the same story," said Bone.

"I doubt that," said Blue.

The other one groaned and waved a hand as though to send both Bone and Blue away, but Bone and Blue pretended not to see.

"Never mind which child heard the story," said Hand. "*I* want to hear the Story of the Child Who Went into the Forest. Was the thing in the forest like the things that hunt us now?"

"Maybe," said Bone.

"Yes, very much so," said Blue.

"Not at all," said the other one.

Their memories at odds, the three began to shout over one another, and the air grew strange with the noise of their jumbled words. They looked very tired. Hand looked tired, too. The candles burning on the table were stuck in the grease of the hundred candles they had already burned.

"Please," said Hand, "the *story*."

"And what about Moon?" asked Blue.

"Moon?" said Hand. "What of Moon?"

"Is Moon not second of the named?" Blue said. "How long now since Moon left Whisper and went into the nameless wilds?"

"I do not remember," Hand said. "Two days, maybe three."

Bone tapped the table with long fingers. "Surely someone should go and look for Moon."

"It has been too long," agreed the other one. "Someone should go and look."

"No one will go and look for Moon," said Hand. "I told Moon: *Do not go.* But Moon went. Now it is for Moon to return, or to stay among the nameless and never come back."

The scavengers were seated on their scrap piles, just outside the house. Overhearing the words of Hand, they chanted softly:

> *Moon must return or not return,*
> *Because no one will go and look for Moon.*

Hand lit more candles and stuck them in the grease. The three old ones sighed and settled more deeply into their robes, their blankets, their rags.

"The story now," Hand said, scarred hand gleaming in the candlelight. "And maybe soon we will have the word for the things that hunt us. We are close, don't you think? I think we are very close."

Moon ran. Ran from the nameless, from the dreamers, from the thing the dreamers had made from Moon's own nightmares. Moon ran to Whisper,

robe and hair tearing on branches and briars, hot tears streaking and smudging what remained of the yellow arcs of paint that meant *Moon*.

How long had Moon been gone? The moon was no longer full—yet fuller,
still, than half. Six nights, or maybe seven, but to Moon, it seemed so much
longer, many weeks or more.

The second of the named went alone through Whisper, searching for Hand
as the sun rose over the river. Moon carried in one hand a gift from the nameless. It was a thing from before that needed a name. Some kind of weapon.

In time, Moon came to the house of Bone, Blue, and the other one. The
scavengers crept to the edges of their piles to watch. Moon called Hand's
name, but there was no response. Moon called again, and this time Hand
emerged, blinking in the light.

"Moon," said Hand, "you have returned to Whisper."

"Hand," said Moon, "I have returned."

From inside Bone, Blue, and the other one saw the thing in Moon's hand.
The gift from the nameless, the weapon that needed a name. They began to
moan in fear, because they knew the thing from the old stories, from the world
before the Silence. And they knew what it would mean to name it. The only
way to divine and deliver a name for a weapon was to use it.


The courier's monster was tugging at her sleeve. She brushed its long fingers
away. The Story of Hand and Moon was nearly over, and she wanted to see it
through to the end. Moon had a word to deliver—two words, if the story went
as the courier remembered.

But the monster tugged again, harder this time, forcing the courier to turn.
"What?" she hissed.

The monster pursed its lips and pointed in the direction of the nearest bon-
fire. In its light stood two figures in long coats. Men in black oilcloth, gloved
and hooded, their eyes hidden behind pale silver lenses. Watchers. They were
speaking to the woodcutter who had told the story of the lumbering accident.

The woodcutter met the courier's gaze, and he nodded in her direction. The
watchers turned and started toward her.

The courier grabbed her ghost and her monster and ran with them through
the crowd. She looked to Jawbone and saw a flying machine docked at the
watchtower. It must have arrived while she was caught up in the show. She saw
other watchers in the crowd, weaving among the gathered people, searching
their faces—searching, she knew, for her face.

As she neared the far edge of the crowd, another figure rose up before her.
It was taller by a head than even the tallest in the crowd. The figure was not

a watcher: not a living person at all, but a ghost, its eyes black under a wide-brimmed hat. The ghost saw her and flexed its big pale hands.

The courier turned, but another ghost blocked her way. It was nearly identical to the first, standing just as tall and wearing a similar hat. Both ghosts lunged.

The courier ducked under their arms and ran, drawing curses from audience members as she knocked them aside. The two tall ghosts pursued, forcing the courier, her ghost, and her monster clear of the crowd, out toward the rear of the Black Square's train. She heard the thump of the watchers' boots, saw the flash of their goggles in the dark.

A small, well-dressed man emerged from the crowd. The courier recognized the checkered scarf, the big eyeglasses, the black cane. Sayer Frost raised one hand, and the watchers halted.

Frost's speaker appeared beside him. Smoke wore the same embroidered suit he'd worn the night she met him, the night Rope summoned her from her compartment. Smoke smiled at the courier and beckoned for her to approach.

She hesitated. Did they only want to talk? Maybe they knew the truth of what had happened aboard the Number Twelve. Maybe they'd found the person responsible for the monster that had killed Book.

But the patchwork ghost took her arm. He nodded in the direction of the two tall ghosts that had chased them from the crowd. For the first time, the courier had a clear view of them. They weren't just dressed similarly, they were perfectly identical, though one favored its left leg, the other its right. The courier's breath caught as she realized what they were.

In the ghosts committee ledger they were listed as *the tall one with a crooked step* and *the other tall one with a crooked step*. They were very old, known to the named since the time of the first namers, though some said that the two were even older. That the people they had been—brothers, twins—had worked great wrongs in the years before the Silence. If that was true, it meant they had waited through the long wordless years. Waited with the other ghosts until Moon divined and delivered the word for what they were.

Now people called them the seeker ghosts. They were relentless and cunning, acting always in concert, as though in possession of a single mind. And the sayers lent them out for one purpose only—to serve on deletion committees.

Frost hadn't come with questions or aid. He wasn't checking up on her progress in delivering *traitor*. He was here to remove her from the record of the world forever.

Onstage, the players were trying to finish the show. They still pretended, still spoke the words of the story, but no one was watching anymore. The audience watched the courier instead. What was she going to do next?

Smoke beckoned again. When the courier didn't move, he and Frost exchanged a look. Frost signaled with his cane, and the ghosts resumed their pursuit.

The courier knew what would happen if they were caught. First the monster would be seized and burned—on one of those bonfires this very night, or later, in the furnace of a war machine. The patchwork ghost would be turned over to the ghosts committee and slated for calibration.

As for the courier? To discuss the deleted was itself a crime punishable by deletion. Only a few of the sayers knew what became of the deleted. Those sayers would notify the names committee of her status, and once all references to the courier who delivered *trouble* were expunged, the notice itself would be destroyed. Soon, the namers might wonder whether she had really been among them at all. Even Beryl might wonder—or try hard to forget.

The courier ran. With her ghost and her monster close behind, she scrambled over the rails, between two cars of the train. But on the other side were more watchers, their lenses shining in the dark of the rail yard.

"Oh, oh, oh," the monster said.

The courier saw just one way out. She looked at the patchwork ghost, and she knew the ghost saw it, too.

The Black Square was a territory unto itself, protected by some of the oldest laws of the named. Not even a deletion committee had the authority to cross that border. The courier didn't, either—but the courier was already an outlaw.

The ghost gestured to the walkway between the cars, as though to say: *After you.*

She pulled herself up, the old wood creaking, then reached down to help the monster. It scrambled up beside her, eyes wide. The patchwork ghost tossed up his sack and climbed after it. The walkway groaned under their weight.

The seeker ghosts appeared beneath them, but Smoke shouted for them to stop.

The ghosts froze, and for a moment so did the courier. She saw Frost turn and gaze into the crowd, and the courier knew he was searching for the other members of his committee. Deletion committees consisted always of five members. No authority of the named could stand in the way of a deletion committee, but it could take no significant action—like trespassing upon the Black Square's train—without a majority vote. The seeker ghosts could serve only as nonvoting members, so Frost would have enlisted two other living members from among the committees.

So where were the other two? They had gone to search for her in the streets of Jawbone, maybe, or elsewhere in the depot. Maybe they were closing in on the courier now.

She tried the latch. It lifted easily, but the door was stuck in its frame.

Smoke called, "If you go through there, you'll be beyond our help forever."

She looked from Smoke to Frost. The sayer's eyes were huge behind his thick lenses. In them, she saw something that surprised her: Frost was afraid. Afraid of what she was doing, afraid of what she might do next.

Good.

As one, the courier and her ghost and her monster threw themselves against the door. Smoke shouted, and the seeker ghosts reached for her. But the door burst open, and they tumbled together into the forbidden train of the Black Square Show.

It was nothing like the Number Twelve. Instead of one long corridor, they found a maze of compartments opening one onto the next. The walls looked as though they had been repaired with scrap wood salvaged from wagons, boats, sheds, shacks. Each door was a different height, a different color. The courier threw them shut behind her as they ran.

Most of the compartments were unlit, though naphtha lamps flickered in some. She glimpsed unmade bunks, tables strewn with bottles and plates, chests overflowing with robes, smocks, scarves, trousers. Masks hung from the walls: monstrous faces with great teeth and bulging eyes, mouths like frowning seams, glittering skin. The courier's monster burbled fearfully.

The car had its own monsters—tiny, half-formed things which crawled over the floor and drifted on the breeze. Some were wispy and thin, clumps of creeping dust. Others had almost-fingers, bunches of hair, pale blind eyes, scratching nails. They felt the air with antennae, with whiskered snouts or feathered limbs. On clumsy paws they bumbled away from the courier's steps and slipped through cracks in the walls.

In a large compartment near the front of the car, the courier was confronted with a dozen distorted versions of herself. Mirrors—some tall and short, others wide and narrow—turned slowly on wires bolted to the ceiling. The courier set them spinning as she passed, flooding the room with whirling patches of light. The compartment seemed impossibly long. She should have reached the front of the car already, but no matter how far she went, she couldn't find the next door. Turning, she realized that her ghost and monster were gone. She ran back the way she'd come, searching for a way out.

She found a tall, crooked door, and threw it open. Beyond was darkness, and from the darkness came a cold, stinging wind. The courier drew back. The flashing lights of the mirrors merged and settled before her, glinting like stars, and from those stars came a voice, rasping and strange.

"And what are *you* doing here, my little morsel?"

The courier opened her mouth to say something, but her breath was gone. She fell forward—or the night swelled to engulf her. She was cold everywhere, and all around her the lights blazed. Then the stars faded and went out, and the courier went with them.

She woke on a thin mattress in a large, cluttered room. Sheets of paper lay stacked on tables and desks next to typing machines and ink pots. More paper was scattered over the floor, piled on chairs, balled up and strewn among the other bunks lining the walls. Only the area around a naphtha-burning stove at the center of the car was clear of debris.

Two people stood in the light of the fire. They spoke together quietly. One was a boy who might have celebrated sixteen or seventeen name days. He looked sleepy and annoyed. His thick black hair was a mess, but he wore a fine suit of dark fabric embroidered with whirls of blue and gold. An official from Whisper, she thought, though he was young to be an agent of the sayers.

Beside him stood Hand, first of the named.

The courier shifted and the bed creaked. Dozens of people turned to look at her. Among them were monsters, scavengers, namers of old Whisper in gray and brown robes. They were seated on chairs, on the floor, on other bunks.

The two by the fire stopped talking and came toward her. The boy's suit looked wrong when he moved, hitching and uneven. Hand's scarred hand gleamed in the firelight.

The courier rose from the bed, but her legs gave out and she slid to the floor. When her vision cleared, the two were standing over her. She saw now that Hand wasn't Hand, but a tall, skinny man with short gray hair and bright blue eyes. Flecks of green paint clung to his face, and the scars on his hand were made of wax. He wasn't young, but he was strong; taking her arm, he lifted her swiftly to her feet.

The boy wasn't an official, either. His suit was stitched together from several mismatched pieces of fabric. Pretend clothes. A *costume*: that was the word her committee had delivered. She was surrounded by the players of the Black Square Show.

"Easy," the man said, holding her steady. "The Gardener of Leaves can be tough on stowaways."

*Gardener of Leaves?* The courier followed his gaze to the far corner of the room. There in the darkness loomed a patch of deeper darkness, littered with stars. A monster, a very real one. Human in shape, it wore a heavy purple shawl over its broad shoulders, a floppy purple hat on its head. It was huge and blocky, like something quarried from the night sky. The courier shivered as she remembered falling into that cold. When she spoke, her voice was a dry croak. "It tried to eat me," she said.

"If the Gardener of Leaves had wanted to eat you," the man said, "then *she* wouldn't have spat you back out."

The courier gazed again into those bright pricks of light, and it—she—the Gardener of Leaves—tipped her hat.

The man helped the courier to a chair near the fire. The boy took a pot from the stove and poured her a mug of tea, shoved it roughly into her hands. She smelled the smokiness of fermented draff, felt its tingle in her scalp and at her fingertips. They never had this on the Number Twelve, though she'd tasted it once or twice while out on assignment. She drank, and the warmth spread through her body.

The man bowed. "I am the Gardener of Stones, and I serve as director of our little show." He gestured to the boy. "This is the Six of Trees, one of those who compose the stories we perform."

The words tumbled untethered through the courier's head. *Gardener of Stones, Six of Trees,* a monster called the *Gardener of Leaves.* It was rumored that the players of the Black Square, in the early years of the Silence, had fashioned a system for knowing one another without words. Maybe these titles were what remained.

"The show," she said. "I've never seen anything like it."

The boy snorted. "Do you always ruin things you've never seen before?"

The courier winced. There was something strange about the way the Six of Trees spoke. His words were misshapen, hitching the way his oddly cut clothes hitched, straining against their borders. The sound of them set a pain throbbing behind her eyes.

"Please," the courier said, "I just—"

"You just ran," the Six of Trees said. "Right onto our train, breaking laws older than the word *train*. Why?"

The Gardener of Stones looked uncomfortable, but he let the question stand. The other players had been whispering, but now they were silent, waiting for her to speak.

"I'm looking for someone," the courier said. "A woman named Ticket."

She heard a low growling sound. It came from the Gardener of Leaves, still darkening one corner of the car. Two stars blazed where the monster's eyes might have been.

The Gardener of Stones frowned and ran one hand over his close-cropped gray hair. "There is no one named Ticket aboard this train," he said.

"But she *was* here, wasn't she?" the courier asked. "Maybe you know where she went, where she is now. Please, I need—"

The monster roared. She emerged from the corner, growing taller as she swept across the room. The air went cold at her approach, and the flames in the stove guttered.

"Leaves," said the Gardener of Stones, his voice a warning.

But the Gardener of Leaves ignored him. Cold pricked the courier's skin even through the thickness of her boilersuit. She fell from her chair and scrambled backward over the floor. She heard the stars crackling, heard the low whistle of the wind as the monster crouched over her.

If the courier fell back into that place, she knew she would never make it out again.

She remembered something Book had said, moments before he became a ghost. *Wasn't sure if you'd ever come back,* he'd told the courier's monster, mistaking it for Ticket. *Thought you might have decided to stay and request a card.* The courier still didn't know what that meant, but maybe it was something she could use.

"A card!" she shouted.

The winds shrieked, gathering her up. Cold pierced to her bones. But over the noise, she heard the Gardener of Stones calling for the monster to let her speak. She stole enough breath to shout again, "A card! I request a card!"

The air stilled. The Gardener of Leaves stood back, stars dimming. The monster had heard what she'd said. Everyone in the car had heard. The Gardener of Stones and the Six of Trees looked at each other. The boy was about to say something when the door at the front of the car burst open.

In came the courier's own monster, teeth bared. It knelt beside the courier and wrapped her in its long arms. But the players hardly seemed to notice the monster. They were gazing past it to the open doorway, where the patchwork ghost stood with his sack slung over its shoulder.

With cautious, uncertain steps, the Gardener of Stones went to stand before the ghost. The car was silent as the two stared at each other. Then the Gardener of Stones reached out with both hands—the right still covered in scars of wax—and patted the ghost's shoulders, as though to make sure of something. When he turned, his eyes were bright with tears.

"It's really him," he said. "The record keeper has come back to us."


The players gathered around the ghost. Some touched his arms, his jacket, his hat. A few cried and held one another. A girl still dressed in a gray scavenger's smock tugged at the ghost's sack of sketchbooks, and the ghost opened it so she could look inside. She selected one and flipped through the pages. "Drawings," she said. "So many." She held it up for everyone to see.

Sighs and shouting, then, and laughter too. The Six of Trees frowned, his suit wrinkling as he crossed his arms over his chest, but the Gardener of Stones squeezed the ghost's shoulders again. "I was a young man when you left," he said.

The girl returned the sketchbook to the sack, and the ghost hoisted it over his shoulder and walked through the crowd. The players parted to let him pass, then followed after. The courier went with them, sticking close to the patchwork ghost and tugging her monster along. She felt the Gardener of Leaves watching her, stars pulsing warily.

The next car was more like those of the Number Twelve: a long corridor lit by naphtha lamps, lined with rows of compartment doors. But here the carpet was worn bare in places, and scraps of living draff drifted in the shadows.

The patchwork ghost strode purposefully about halfway down the corridor, opened a door, and entered a small compartment furnished with a plain wooden desk and chair. The ghost, as though perfectly familiar with the place, took matches from the desk drawer and used one to light the lamp. The walls were lined with shelves, and most of the shelves were full of sketchbooks. There must have been hundreds of them.

The patchwork ghost emptied his sack onto the desk and began sorting sketchbooks into gaps on the shelves. Some older volumes he shifted from one shelf to another. Others he paged through before deciding where they should go. His movements were measured and precise. The courier's monster cooed in admiration.

The Six of Trees seemed to notice the monster for the first time. The courier saw him blink his tired-looking eyes, then open them wide in recognition.

"You do know Ticket," the courier said.

He flinched and backed away. "Stones," he said, "we shouldn't keep Frost waiting."

The Gardener of Stones frowned. "We do not answer to Frost," he said. "Nor to any of the sayers, for that matter."

"This woman has trespassed upon the Black Square," said the Six of Trees, his words going stranger and more crooked as his voice grew louder. "She shouldn't even be here. We must give her to Frost before he loses patience."

The noise of his speech made the courier's head throb, but the other players appeared untroubled, and some even murmured their assent. The courier's monster squeezed her arm and pressed itself to her side.

The Gardener of Stones drew himself up to address the crowd. "How many of you first boarded this train without permission?" he said. "How many of you were *fleeing* something when you got here? And how many of you did the Black Square welcome as one of its own, regardless of how you arrived?"

Six set his jaw and said nothing, but the Gardener of Leaves swept forward, stars bristling. "Stones," she said, her voice a cold rasp, "I've had a taste of this one. She's trouble."

*Trouble.* The courier's old word, back for her again. But the Gardener of Stones shook his head. "It doesn't matter what she is. She requested a card." He pulled the courier and her monster with him into the record keeper's compartment. "Six," he said, "tell your Gardener to ready the engine. We leave immediately."

Six looked stunned. The Gardener of Leaves pushed past him, a seething darkness, the cold blowing from her depths in waves. "We are not done talking," she said.

"But my dear," the Gardener of Stones said, "shouldn't you be getting ready for the party?"

The monster shrank a little. "Party?"

"We have so much to celebrate," he said. "The return of the record keeper. The drawing of a new card. What do you think? A case of the stuff we received from Brick last week?"

"I like parties," said the Gardener of Leaves, suddenly meek.

"Good. You get everyone ready. We'll need music, I think. And all the other trappings. For an evening of merriment, yes? The four of us will join you soon." And with that he slammed the door.


The Gardener of Stones stood in place, rubbing his head as he listened to the other players outside, arguing about what to do next. Eventually their chatter receded. Once the corridor was quiet, he sighed and wiped his brow with a handkerchief.

"Why are you helping me?" the courier asked.

"I'm not sure that I am," he said. "I may have appeased Leaves for the moment, but she'll make us both pay in time."

The courier shivered. The compartment was still cold from the monster's breath.

"One hears stories of a fire on the Number Twelve," the Gardener of Stones said, pocketing his handkerchief. "A car burned to its axles. The committee chair a ghost, a courier on the run."

She felt her face grow hot. "I fled in order to save the patchwork ghost from calibration," she said.

"So the record keeper has been with the names committee all this time?"

"Why do you call him that?"

The Gardener gestured to the shelves. "See for yourself," he said.

The ghost was still sorting and shelving sketchbooks as though nothing had happened. The courier ran her fingers over the spines, selected one of the older volumes. Its cover was worn to the boards at the corners and edges. She turned pages and saw drawings of animals and factories, candlesticks, clouds, fences, flowers. People gathered in a market. People seated at a table, laughing and playing cards. People scooping naphtha into the furnace of a great engine. She recognized the precise lines, the steady hand.

"The ghost made all of these," she said.

"The record keeper has been with the Black Square since its beginning," the Gardener said. "Most of our stories are drawn from his sketches."

Thinking of the ghost's drawing of Hand and Moon in old Whisper, the courier said, "Even the story you played tonight?"

The Gardener's expression darkened. "Yes, even that one," he said.

So Book had been wrong about the drawing. The ghost hadn't just seen the story performed. The story was performed because he had seen it. He had been there, in old Whisper. And he had gone uncalibrated for hundreds of years.

"I've had him for almost twenty years," the courier said. "How did you lose him?"

The monster watched, eyes wide, as the Gardener of Stones peeled the false scars from his hand. "We didn't lose him," he said. "Not exactly. Once or twice a century, the ghost leaves the Black Square without warning. He goes searching for new stories, we think, and tries to remember more about the old ones. But he had never been away so long before, and we assumed the worst. If our record keeper had been calibrated, we truly would have lost him—forever."

The courier snapped the sketchbook shut. "Then I have done the Black Square a service in returning him to you," she said. "Now you can help me—"

"I'm not certain you brought the ghost here," the Gardener said, interrupting. "It's more likely that the ghost brought you."

The courier shook her head. She knew why she was here: Book had sent Ticket to the Black Square. But then, Book had started talking about the

Black Square after seeing the patchwork ghost's sketch of Hand and Moon. And the ghost had sketched the Black Square's train as well.

Had all this happened at the ghost's prompting? When they fled from the deletion committee, it was the ghost who had gestured for her to climb aboard . . .

The Gardener of Stones was grinning at her. "I'm right, aren't I?"

The courier ignored him. "Tell me where Ticket went," she said. "It's obvious that she was here."

The Gardener stripped the last of the wax from his hand and dropped it onto the desk. "When you become Black Square, you leave your old stories behind," he said. "You will have the Black Square's protection, but you will not have its assistance in searching for this woman, whoever she is."

"And if I refuse that protection?" she asked.

"I only work with my fellow members of the Black Square. The Gardener of Leaves deals with the stowaways. I will call her back, if you like."

The Gardener of Stones had treated her kindly since she'd come aboard. Now she glimpsed something else in his bright blue eyes, something sharp and cold as a knife's edge.

"Here, let me show you," he said, the warmth returning to his voice. He reached into a pocket beneath his costume and pulled out a small black pouch, and from the pouch he drew a deck of cards. The cards were worn and creased, their backs decorated with a black and gold pattern that reminded the courier of the Number Twelve's engine. He searched through the deck, chose a card, and set it face-up on the desk. She had expected something from the deck for Hand and Moon. A mask, a monster, one of the first words. Instead she saw six identical black shapes, each like a stem topped with three round bulbs.

"They look like trees," she said.

The Gardener nodded, urging her to continue.

"Six of them," she said, understanding. "The man you call the Six of Trees, he . . . he drew this card when he joined the Black Square."

The Gardener looked pleased. He showed her other cards. More shapes, as few as one to a card, as many as ten. The *stones* and *leaves* were red. The *shovels* and *trees* were black. Some cards bore pictures of men and women dressed in heavy clothes and hats, bearing weapons and tools. The four old men were called Beards, the Gardener explained, and the younger men were called Scouts. The four women were the Gardeners. Each Gardener held a different flower in her hand.

"All cards come with their own particular duties," he said. "The Shovels build and maintain the machinery of the show. The *costumes*, the *sets*—we have words for the stuff now. The Trees are responsible for writing the stories we perform. The Gardener of Trees is also our engineer, so the engine, too, is the domain of the Trees."

"And the Leaves?" she asked.

"The Leaves look after the train, and when a performance is underway, they make sure everything and everyone are where they're meant to be. They keep all of us on track."

"With their Gardener acting as sentry," the courier said.

"As I direct the shows, so does she oversee the train itself. We Gardeners have always been authorities and guides. You might think of us as committee chairs."

The worn cards slid smoothly in the Gardener's hands. They moved like living things, like birds flying from branch to branch, always about to take flight or disappear.

"You haven't told me what you and your fellow Stones do," she said.

"Most everyone must take their turn onstage eventually, but we Stones, I'm afraid, are good for very little else." He grinned bashfully, then went on. "The maps committee has its surveyors and cartographers. The namers have their diviners and couriers. Here we have our own titles, except *title* isn't really the word. This is what we have instead of names, and using them helps us to slip more easily into other names—or into a state of namelessness—when we perform. Less to trip up on, you see?"

The courier remembered the scene of Moon among the nameless, how their thoughts had seemed to reach her without sound, without words. So this was part of how it was done: in abandoning their names, the Black Square could communicate over the borders between minds, as she and her stowaway could do.

The Gardener had sorted the cards into two piles on the desk, one large, one small. He patted the smaller pile and said, "Here are the unclaimed cards. To join us, all you have to do is take one."

"So simple?" she said.

The Gardener stopped smiling. "Nothing about your arrival has been simple," he said.

The courier considered the cards. If she drew one, would she keep any of what had brought her here? She wanted to find her sister. She wanted to learn who made the monster that killed Book. She wanted to deliver that word in her satchel. She had been courier, outlaw, trespasser, stowaway. Could she be something else again, and still do what she needed to do?

The Gardener spread the cards in a wide arc. They were about a dozen in number, their backs like gardens of golden plants. The courier wondered if one card or another might call to her. But she heard nothing, felt nothing.

Then, before she knew which card to take—before she knew for certain that she *would* take a card—her monster leaned over the desk and took one for itself.

The monster looked at its card and frowned, turned it for the others to see.

"The Two of Shovels," the Gardener said. "You will labor in the workshop car, turning wood and glue into buildings and trees. Scrap into weapons, paper into sky, paint into stars." He looked concerned. "Do you have any experience with such arts?"

The monster set something on the desk. It was the wax the Gardener had peeled from his hand. While he and the courier were speaking, the monster had molded the wax into the shape of a small animal. Four legs and a tail, tiny triangle ears: a good likeness of the courier's stowaway.

The Gardener leaned down to admire it. "You'll do just fine," he said, and the monster gave him a grin full of wooden teeth.

It was the courier's turn next. She would become Black Square; she had no real choice in the matter. But the Black Square didn't have to know that she would remain the courier. It could make her work the role she drew, but it couldn't stop her from continuing her search for her sister.

She selected a card, turned it over, and immediately felt troubled.

The man on the card resembled the Beards—same whiskery chin, same pointy hat. Other than that, the card looked very unlike the others. No leaves, no trees, no shovels or stones. The man was riding a strange machine, his little feet resting on its pedals. She had seen a machine like that in Hollow, in the junk dealer's warehouse. It had only two wheels, yet it stood upright on a dirt track.

The Gardener of Stones appeared startled. For a moment he said nothing. He cleared his throat and said, "It's been so long since we've seen one."

"One what?" she asked.

He turned the chair from the desk and sat down. "We call it the Rider. There are two, though years will pass before we see either. They don't appear when I go through every card to count them. Even when I turn the pouch inside out just to make sure."

"How is that possible?" the courier asked.

"It's as though they shuffle themselves into the deck a little more deeply. Into a place not everyone can reach." He shook his head as though he didn't entirely believe what he was saying.

The courier wasn't sure she did, either. The image on the card frightened her. She saw malice in the riding man's eyes. The nameless machine looked small under his weight. If it toppled, she thought, he would fall, and something bad would happen.

The car lurched forward, and the courier braced herself against the nearest shelf. The train was leaving Jawbone.

"What does it mean that I drew this?" she asked.

"Different Riders do different things with their time here," he said. "Like everyone else, they usually perform onstage. Unlike everyone else . . . well, it's difficult to explain. I think maybe I'm not supposed to explain. You'll have to figure it out as you go."

The train rolled slowly out of the depot. The courier felt angry, tricked twice over. "I should draw another card."

He shook his head, and her monster imitated the gesture. The Gardener said, "You would always know which card you drew first. The second wouldn't stick. It would be like trying to take a second name."

The patchwork ghost stopped working long enough to give her arm a gentle squeeze. Then he took the sketchbook from her hand and returned it to its shelf.

The train rounded a bend, picked up speed. And there it was, that old velocity, feeling like home even as it stole her away.


Back in the car where the courier had woken, the celebration had already begun. The players of the Black Square had cleared the floor of desks and chairs, moved the stacks of paper to the corners. They drank from chipped mugs and glasses, from jugs, bottles, and jars. Some of the players still wore the masks from their performance, half themselves and half something else. Little monsters scurried everywhere, darting around their dancing feet. Three musicians stood near the blazing stove, playing unnamed instruments. A pipe of dark wood, fitted with bright keys. A thing like an enormous fiddle, mounted upon a peg and taller than the woman who plucked its strings. A drum so big the courier could feel its thunder in her chest.

The Gardener of Stones raised a hand. The players went quiet, and the musicians let their song fall away. Everyone moved closer.

"The record keeper has returned," the Gardener said, "bringing with him the seeds of new stories, of old stories newly revealed. And he brings into our company two new members of the Black Square."

The Gardener urged the monster forward. It swayed shyly and looked at its feet. The Gardener said, "This one is crafty and quiet, with skin like inked paper. This one is the Two of Shovels. This one is Black Square."

The players shouted, and they kept shouting, a great joyful bellow that grew steadily louder. They took turns to keep the shout going. They stomped and clapped, shaking the floorboards, shaking the car till it rocked on the rails. The monster looked at the courier, eyes wide.

Two of the other Shovels came up to greet their new recruit. The monster grinned at them as they squeezed its hands in their own. They were two nearly identical young women, their black hair up in pins, and they smelled of grease, sawdust, paint, and naphtha. The courier thought of Beryl and felt an ache in her chest, felt it quickly burned away by anger.

The Gardener of Stones cleared his throat. He had the players' attention again, but he seemed uncertain. "Rarely are we so lucky as to gain two new members in one day," he said. "The record keeper brought them both, perhaps. And both, perhaps, are needed."

The other players sipped their drinks and waited. The Gardener seemed to have forgotten what he was going to say.

"Well, Stones?" someone called. It was the Gardener of Leaves, her starry bulk looming at the back of the crowd. "Did she draw a card?"

He coughed and said, "She drew a card. And this one—" But he trailed off again, frowning. He couldn't seem to find the words.

The courier stepped forward. "The Rider," she said. "I drew the Rider."

The players said nothing. A few traded nervous looks. The lights inside the Gardener of Leaves grew sharper.

"This one is the Rider," the Gardener of Stones said. "This one is Black Square."

The players remained quiet. Then someone—a tall woman whose long silver hair spilled over the shoulders of her dark green dress—tilted her head back and roared. The others joined her, wailing even louder than before, but they didn't sound joyful this time. Their cries were wild and ragged, almost mournful. They stomped their feet so hard that the courier thought the floorboards would splinter.

When they finally stopped, the courier's ears were ringing. Everyone looked exhausted and stunned. Finally the music struck up again.

"I think that went very well," said the Gardener of Stones.

The silver-haired woman approached with a small jar of spirits in each hand. She gave one to the courier, and the courier saw flecks of yellow paint clinging to the woman's cheeks. She had played the role of Moon that night. The courier realized that this woman was perhaps a year or two younger than she was—her hair had silvered early. She was as beautiful now as she had been onstage.

"The Seven of Stones," the Gardener said. "One of our finest players."

"Or is it our finest?" the woman asked.

"Who can say, Seven, now that new cards have been drawn?"

"Who indeed?" she said, leaning close to the courier. "I suppose that depends on what kind of Rider you are."

"What was the last one like?" the courier asked.

Seven blinked, and the courier glimpsed something behind her breezy performance, something frightened and maybe hurt. But her smile returned quickly. "Oh, they all blur together after a while," she said.

She took a sip from her jar, and the courier did the same. The liquor was strong and strange on her tongue. She coughed.

"These border towns sometimes pay us with the nameless spirits they confiscate from smugglers," Seven said. "It's all rather dreary."

The newness of the word made the courier shiver. *Dreary.* It must have been delivered in the weeks since she'd fled the Number Twelve. It was a word that Book would have liked, she thought. He would have used it to describe her reports.

Seven turned to the Gardener of Stones. "Sadly, we never visit the big cities anymore," she said. "But maybe our Gardener likes living off scraps and contraband."

He gave her a dark look. "You know the law as well as I do," he said.

"But now that the record keeper has returned, we'll have new stories at last," she said. "And new stories require a new audience. Besides, what was it you said? About how we don't answer to the sayers?"

Before the Gardener could respond, Seven took the courier's arm, and her sudden closeness—the warmth of hands against her skin—caused the courier's breath to catch. "I'll show you around," Seven said, and she pulled her away through the crowd.

Most of the players were dancing again. Even the Gardener of Leaves was among them, though she stood to one side, swaying in place while her lights pulsed gently to the music. Plates of food tilted atop typing machines as the train rocked through a bend, and the courier's stomach lurched. The Black Square was going too fast, she thought, given the condition of these cars.

She drank. She saw that her monster was drinking too, beaming at its fellow Shovels. Could the monster become drunk?

"I am sorry for the welcome we gave you," Seven was saying. "But things have been difficult around here."

"Difficult?" the courier asked.

"We hadn't played tonight's story in a very long time. It puts everyone on edge. Most around here won't even call it by name. They call it the Whisper Story instead."

The courier noted that Seven, too, had avoided calling it the Story of Hand

and Moon, and she recalled what Book had told her about the Black Square's
exile to the border towns—about how the sayers had changed law because a
player became a ghost during a performance of that same story.

"But you played it anyway," the courier said.

"Only after *months* of the Six of Trees pushing for it," Seven said wearily.
"He'd written new material, you see."

"So the Gardener of Stones finally gave in?"

Seven laughed. "No, he did not," she said. "Stones remained steadfast
against the idea to the end, but he was outvoted by the other three."

The courier turned and looked for the Six of Trees in the crowd, saw him
standing near the door at the rear of the car. He looked awkward and skinny
in his big awkward suit. Not really a costume, she realized, but something he
must have made for himself. Something he'd patterned on the suits worn by
officials in Whisper. Six's attention was on the courier's monster, which was
dancing with the other shovels. Then the Gardener of Stones drew up to Six
and put one hand on his shoulder.

Seven had stopped walking. Following the courier's gaze, she said, "*This*
should be interesting."

The Gardener of Stones and Six leaned close as they spoke, appearing as
they had when the courier awoke: apart from the others, deep in counsel, like
a committee of two. The courier could hear nothing of what they said, but the
Gardener was clearly trying to reassure the boy. The more they spoke, however, the angrier Six appeared, until finally he pulled away and left the car,
slamming the door behind him.

The Gardener of Stones stood alone at the edge of the crowd, gazing sul-
lenly at his hand—the one he had placed on Six's shoulder, the one that had
earlier born scars of wax. When he looked up, the courier quickly turned away.

"They're a puzzle, those two," Seven said.

"Is the Gardener of Stones his father?"

"In a way," she said. "Stones tries to look after Six, and Six tries not to be
looked after. But the truth is, each can barely manage without the other."

Seven guided the courier to a corner where players sprawled on cushions
and smoked draff from long pipes, their eyes glassy and dreaming. The courier
had already emptied her jar. Someone refilled it with something different,
something that smelled no less strong. For a moment, she imagined herself
back in the common car of the Number Twelve. She caught herself looking
for Beryl.

"It takes some time, getting used to being different people," Seven said.
She was close again, arm brushing the courier's arm, her lips close to the courier's
ear. "For tonight you can just enjoy the company."

A new song started up, and one of the younger players, the girl who had looked inside the patchwork ghost's sack of sketchbooks, began to sing. The courier recognized the words. It was a song about the courier who delivered the words *music* and *dance*. The music grew louder and more frantic, and her monster stomped hard against the floorboards. Some sang along. Others peeled masks from one another's faces and drew close. The courier looked away. It was like watching people undress and become other people at the same time.

The silver-haired Seven of Stones smiled at her, one eyebrow raised.

The courier set down her jar. Somehow, it was empty again, and she knew she shouldn't have another. She headed for the door, plunged through the wild rush of cold air and into the next car. She found herself in a place that was part kitchen, part eating car, part storage area. Three young players were seated around an overturned crate, deep into a game of Monsters and Numbers. They looked up from their piles of dice, maps, and thimbles to watch as the courier stumbled among the stacks of dirty pots. She found water in a basin, drank from a ladle. Refilled it, drank again, then filled her canteen.

The players were still looking at her.

"Where do we sleep?" she asked them.

One shrugged, one pointed toward the front of the train, and the other, ignoring her, picked up his dice and rolled them.

The courier left them to their game. The next car was another maze of cramped compartments. In one, she found a floor covered by heaps of fabric. She fell onto the pile and closed her eyes.

Moments later, her stowaway landed on the fabric beside her. She had known that the animal had come aboard—had felt him nearby, she realized, this whole time—but she was still relieved to see him. The stowaway curled himself against her chest, and she buried her face in his fur as they fell together into the dark.

The courier woke with a headache. Each time the car jounced, she felt it as a thump at the base of her skull. She rolled away from the sunlight streaming in through the car's only window, drew lengths of fabric over her eyes. Then her monster was looming over her, pushing and pulling at her shoulders, cooing with worry.

She sat up. She felt cold and dizzy, and the fabric was a knotted tangle around her, the colors so bright they hurt her eyes. Her stowaway was gone.

Her monster gave her a biscuit. The courier ate, not bothering to ask where the food had come from. The biscuit was warm and buttery, but the monster allowed her only a few bites before it stood and tugged her arm.

Still eating, the courier let the monster guide her up through the train. Players passing in compartments and corridors smiled at the monster. "Morning, Two," one said. Some nodded at the courier, but no one spoke to her. She sipped from her canteen and squinted at the sunlight through the windows.

They came to a car that smelled of sawdust, varnish, and scorched metal. Lumber lay stacked on long shelves, and scrap was gathered into piles. The tiny monsters and bits of living draff that littered the rest of the train were absent from this place.

The center of the car was dominated by a large furnace. It seemed long disused, covered with machine parts, nails, and rags. All around the furnace were worktables, several of them occupied. The courier recognized the two young women from the night before. Sisters, she thought. They worked together, one holding a board while the other sawed. Three other players hammered, glued, and sanded. This had to be the workshop of the Shovels, yet the Shovels seemed so few in number. The noise of their work thumped in the courier's head. The thing they were building lay like an unassembled puzzle near the middle of the car. The courier couldn't tell what it would become.

In a far corner, a small woman stood hunched over the hissing light of her naphtha torch. The monster hummed to get her attention. When she turned and lifted her mask, the courier gasped.

It was Juniper, the farmer who'd built the thing to which the courier delivered *harrow*. The old woman frowned at her from under the shield of her welding mask. She had given the courier the same look over a year ago, when they first saw each other in her barn at the foot of a nameless mountain. So Juniper hadn't been deleted, as the courier had believed. She wasn't a ghost. She was here, aboard the train of the Black Square.

"Juniper . . ."

The others looked up from their work. Juniper's frown deepened, and she raised the torch a little.

"Oh, oh," the monster said, scolding the courier.

One of the two sisters stopped sawing and said, "Rider, this is our Gardener."

Juniper, the Gardener of Shovels. The old woman didn't say anything, only pointed to a paint-spattered table, on which were piled stacks of rough paper, scissors, paint, and brushes. Then she grunted and pulled down her mask.

The courier let the monster lead her to the table and they sat. Her monster cut leaves from the paper and pressed them into the courier's hands. "Ah, ah," it said, and pointed to a pot of green paint.

Now the courier recognized what the puzzle would become. From the wood of other trees, the Shovels were assembling a single tree, and that tree needed leaves.

She glanced once more in Juniper's direction, hoping the old woman would give some sign that she remembered her, but all the courier saw in her mask was the reflection of the sparking naphtha torch.


She worked with the Shovels all day, and that night she helped assemble the tree in the stage car, trunk to limb to branch to twig. Her monster held the ladder while the courier fixed leaves in place. Juniper had stayed behind in the workshop car, but the others were all here, gathered at the base of the tree, calling out advice. By the time the courier was done, her hands were smeared with paint and sticky with glue. The courier thought the tree looked scrawny and strange, but the other Shovels didn't seem concerned. The monster, smiling up at the mostly bare branches, threw one arm over the courier's shoulders.

The brakes sounded. They were arriving at the next border town on the line. Grit, the courier thought—or was it Husk? She'd learned from the sisters, the Four and Nine of Shovels, that the Black Square would be performing the Story of Bird and Shoulder, the first ghost wranglers. The players had played this story before, but they knew more about it now, thanks to the patchwork ghost's sketches.

When the train stopped, the Shovels gathered their things and prepared to head off for the kitchens—they liked to cook and eat together. The monster wanted to go with them, but then it saw the courier lingering.

"Go," she said, but still the monster hesitated. "Really, it's fine," she said, and this time the Two of Shovels grinned and hurried off to join the others.

The courier watched more players arrive, some already in costume. The Gardener of Stones strode briskly onto the stage, turning on his heels, taking it all in. His blue eyes shone in the lights as he inspected the tree. The courier was surprised at how relieved she felt to see him nod in approval.

The Gardener gestured for a group of three children to join him under the tree. "Here, here, and here," he said, showing them where to stand.

The children took their places, then swapped places several times, then held very still as the Gardener knelt and spoke quietly to them. They were dressed in tattered uniforms: not committee uniforms, but something from the time before the Silence. They'd be playing ghosts, the courier realized.

Other players, all dressed in black and dark gray, adjusted the lights in the ceiling, checked the scenery, readied props. These were the Leaves—the ones who kept everyone else on track, the Gardener of Stones had told her. No sign of their own gardener, though the courier doubted she would see that monster unless the monster wished to be seen.

As showtime neared, the car grew busier, and the courier felt a charge in the air. The door at the front of the car swung open, and a huge man stooped to enter. He had a big belly, big ears, and a big sooty beard. His clothes were sooty, too. The man showed no interest in the players. Instead he inspected the machines that raised and lowered the scenery, the stage doors, the roof. He tested connections, tugged at cables, at chains, at his own long beard.

"Enter the Gardener of Trees," someone said. The courier turned to find Seven at her side, dressed in a faded gray suit and cap.

"The Trees write the stories," the courier said.

"Their Gardener is more concerned with his duties as engineer," Seven said. "And he's also our physician, so it's up to him to keep the players running, too." She moved closer and said more quietly, "Listen, I'm sorry about last night. I pounced on you rather quickly, didn't I?"

The courier felt her face grow hot as she remembered Seven's lips close to her ear. "I only left suddenly because I wasn't feeling well," she said.

"And I was feeling a little too well, I think. All those things I said to my own Gardener, for whom I have nothing but respect. I'm in trouble now for sure."

The courier felt a warm thrill go through her at hearing Seven speak that word, *trouble*.

"Oh, but watch this now," she went on. "The stage machines are powered by the engine itself, see? The Gardener of Trees is almost ready."

The bearded man made a few more checks, then turned a wheel mounted to the wall. The boards began to vibrate under their feet. Overhead, ropes glided through pulleys and went taut. At the same moment, a trap door opened near the front of the stage, and from it rose a machine like a great brass beetle, mounted with a dozen tubes of different lengths, each fitted with a glass lens.

A young man with dark eyes and curly dark hair climbed down into a harness behind the machine. He pulled levers and worked a pair of pedals with his feet. The machine was something without a name, the courier thought, something altered and modified many times over the centuries.

"What does it do?" the courier asked.

"Watch," Seven said.

A beam of light shone from one of the lenses, faint at first but then brighter, until the panel at the back of the stage glowed blue. The young man flipped a switch, and a second beam, brighter and more tightly focused than the first, struck the panel near its base. It was the sun, the courier realized, either rising or about to set.

From the stage, the Gardener of Stones called, "An hour or so later, please. And could we have some clouds?"

The man in the harness made adjustments, dimming the lights, reducing the sun to a red glow on the horizon. He slid a pane punched with holes into a slot, and stars shone overhead. At the base of another tube, reels spun, and clouds swept slowly across the sky.

So this was how it was done: the machine provided light for different times of day and night, different qualities of weather, moving clouds. It could probably even make water ripple and birds fly, as she'd seen during the performance at Jawbone. Positioned where it was, the machine would be invisible to the audience. If Beryl were here, the courier thought, she would want to examine it part by mysterious part.

The young man worked quickly and precisely. His movements reminded the courier of the patchwork ghost's. A moment later, she realized why: he wasn't a living man at all.

"A ghost," the courier said.

"Our Scout of Stones." Something changed in Seven's voice, and she sounded even more subdued as she explained, "When he stopped being alive, we kept him on board. Sometimes he plays ghosts, but usually he operates the light machine. Always he serves as a reminder."

The courier watched the ghost work, watched his delicate fingers make small modifications. He would have been no more than eighteen when he stopped being alive.

Seven's eyes were bright with tears.

"A reminder of what?" the courier asked her.

But the Gardener of Stones was clapping for the players' attention. "Five minutes, everyone! We begin in five!"

Seven wiped her eyes with her jacket sleeve. Her costume meant she was playing either Bird or Shoulder, though the courier wasn't sure which. Seven leaned close to her and said, "Careful, Rider. Get too close to the stage, and you'll end up with a part to play."

She hurried off to find her place. All the players were on the move, making final modifications to the set, to their costumes. Meanwhile the soot-covered Gardener of Trees stood stroking his beard, one hand on a great lever that jutted waist-high from the floor. Players walked past him, coming and going, but the big man hardly moved. When he saw the courier looking at him, he winked.

The engine's bell began to ring. On the fifth toll, the Gardener of Trees pulled the lever.

The car went dark. Machinery above and below began to grind and whir, and the front of the car swung open.

From where the courier stood, she could see part of the town outside—the train tracks ran right through the middle of it. Grit, then, and most of Grit's inhabitants had gathered in the narrow street, while others were seated on carts and on nearby porches, balconies, and rooftops. The courier could see their faces in the glow of the stage lights. Some looked wary or bored, others expectant. Then, almost all at once, something in their eyes changed. She saw them leave their town of gray leaning structures and go someplace else. To the place onstage: a quiet meadow bathed in the red light of a setting sun.

In that light, the leaves of the solitary tree didn't look like cut and painted paper. They looked like real leaves on a real tree, and they fluttered in the breeze as leaves should. An aspen, she thought.

Into the meadow walked the vagabonds Bird and Shoulder. The courier knew the Seven of Stones was playing Shoulder, yet she barely recognized her. Her walk was different: loose-limbed yet tired, the walk of a rambler. Even her face seemed changed, her eyes amused yet hungry. Her costume was no longer a costume, just the clothes the vagabond Shoulder woke up in today.

Bird and Shoulder were quarreling, each blaming the other for the nightmares they were having between shifts at the factory. But that quarrel was interrupted by the sight of the three ghosts, who were erecting a tent in the meadow and then taking it down again. The ghosts had probably been at this for a hundred years or more.

This part of the story was new, but the courier could tell what would happen next. The sight of these ghosts would give Bird and Shoulder their idea—the idea they were best remembered for. If the ghosts could perform this repetitive work forever, couldn't they work in a factory just as well? Couldn't they even be made to take Bird's and Shoulder's places, and do the work for them, while they did something else?

The two would succeed in their scheme, though not in the way they planned. Bird and Shoulder were remembered as the first ghost wranglers, but their story ended badly. The courier wanted to watch, wanted to see how it would go—but she made herself turn away.

All day she had painted leaves and pinned them up to dry. She had worked and listened and done everything the other players had asked of her. Now the Black Square was distracted by its own show, and finally no one was watching her.

If the patchwork ghost really had brought her here, it wasn't so she could see the old stories. The others might call her Rider now, but she was still the courier who delivered *snoop*.


Small monsters fled from her footsteps, some stringy and slithering, some scurrying on spider's legs. She peered into a compartment packed with puppet parts, heads and legs and hands all dangling from hooks. In the next she saw rugs, canvas, and burlap piled to the ceiling. Another was packed with miniature houses, trees, factories, trains. Everywhere she looked, a great jumble of pretend. Sayers' robes hung beside monstrous masks. False birds perched on hats and walking sticks. A rowboat laden with bones. Different times and places, fragments of story, things born and things made from dreams. Why had her sister come here?

The stowaway emerged from a shadow with something limp in its jaws. She shuddered as he dropped the small, ratlike monster at the courier's feet. The animal darted away down the corridor.

She followed him to the workshop car, where a sole naphtha lamp flickered on Juniper's workbench. Half-made structures cast strange shadows on the walls. She looked more closely at the great furnace near the middle of the car. It looked much like the one the glassblowers had used in Hollow, though smaller. No fire had burned here in a long time—even the scrap littering its surface was gathering dust. Had the Black Square once made its own glass?

She was about to continue to the next car when a flash of movement drew her to the nearest window. The Gardener of Stones stood in the dark beside the train, his face partially hidden by the upturned collar of a heavy blue coat. What was he doing out there, so far from the performance?

The courier held still while her stowaway stalked the shadows of the car. The Gardener was rubbing his hands together, breathing on them to keep them warm. Every so often he turned from side to side, craning his neck to peer down nearby streets. He was clearly waiting for someone.

Several minutes passed in this way. The Gardener stood in place just outside the window, shifting his weight from side to side, sometimes looking up at the moon, sometimes humming quietly to himself. Suddenly he went quiet and still. The courier followed his gaze to the nearest alleyway and saw someone approaching through the darkness there. The figure stepped partway into the moonlight. They wore a baggy blue shirt tucked into brown pants, and heavy black boots on their feet. Their face remained hidden from sight.

The courier's breath had steamed the glass. Heart thumping, she wiped it with her sleeve, blinked, and looked again. This time she was sure of it: the figure's face was obscured, but not by shadow. By a mask.

She could barely make it out, but the mask seemed triangular in shape, and under its eyes were silver streaks like tears. *It's how they know who they are*, Book had told her of the nameless. He had also said that the Black Square possessed masks of their own for use during their performances, and these she had seen for herself. Was this only one of the players, then, preparing for a part under the Gardener's direction?

No. She sensed that tugging at the back of her mind, that whispering of borderless thought she so often felt when the nameless were near. Could the Gardener of Stones feel it, too?

*Run*, she thought. *Get back onto the train*. But the Gardener of Stones did not run. He stepped forward—and raised one hand in greeting. So he had expected the nameless. This was who he'd been waiting for, here in the shadow of the train, while every named person in Grit, and most every member of the Black Square, was distracted by the show.

The masked figure was not alone—others stood deeper in the alleyway, nearly motionless. The courier stood on her toes, trying to see whether they wore masks of their own.

A loud crash inside the car made the courier jump back from the window. A trapdoor had opened in the floor near the furnace. From it climbed Juniper, a bulky sack slung over her shoulder. She gave the courier a brief glance, kicked the trapdoor shut, and tossed the sack onto her workbench. Inside were bolts and screws and scraps of metal, which she began sorting into piles.

The courier took a few deep breaths, steadying herself. Then she looked out the window again. The Gardener of Stones was gone, and so was the masked figure.

Meanwhile, her stowaway had sauntered up to Juniper's workbench. The courier went to join him there. When the old woman saw her coming, she reached for her welding mask.

The courier said, "The Gardener of Stones—"

"Does his work, and I do mine," Juniper said.

Juniper had avoided her all that day in the workshop. At least now she was talking. If she would not discuss what the courier had just witnessed outside the train, maybe she would speak of something else. Before Juniper could put her welding mask on, the courier said, "I went back to your farm, you know. I thought you'd been taken."

Juniper set her mask down and sighed. She took one of the courier's hands in hers and squeezed it. Her skin was rough as dry wood. "We'll talk," she said. "And then we're never going to talk about any of this again. I like being the Gardener of Shovels. I won't let you take that from me."

From a nearby cabinet, Juniper fetched two jars and a bottle. She uncorked the bottle and poured a finger of dark red liquid into each jar. She put one into the courier's hand. The wine had a rich, fruity smell. Plum, the courier thought.

"Now don't bother me about the Gardener of Stones," Juniper said. "Tell me why you're here."

"Fine. I'm here because I'm looking for someone. My sister."

Juniper sat and the stowaway hopped onto her lap. She stroked the animal as though she'd known him for a long time. "And would this sister look anything like our friend the Two of Shovels?"

"Yes," the courier said. "But shorter, I think, and less—"

"Less like something that crawled out of a bad dream," Juniper said. "I know your sister. She came to my house uninvited, just like you did. And she told me that others would come for me, just like you did. Only this time those others were already on their way."

"A deletion committee," the courier said.

Juniper turned the jar in her hand but didn't drink. "Maybe I should have listened to your warning. If I had, though, I'd still be alone on that farm. Or I'd be another ghost in the factories."

The courier sipped her wine. "What about Ticket?"

"Is that her name? We didn't talk much. She brought me here, told me I'd be safe with these people. And she was right."

The courier had been furious with Book when Juniper vanished, and Book had seemed not to care. Maybe he had cared, though. Maybe he had sent Ticket to rescue the old woman, in secret defiance of the sayers. If so, he had kept it secret from the courier, too.

"Did she come aboard?" she asked.

"Not for long. She brought me to the Gardener of Stones, told him that I'd need a card. I knew she was only using me, but I didn't care."

"Using you how?"

"She needed an excuse to visit the Black Square."

"But why? What did she need here?"

"I don't know, and I don't want to know," Juniper said. She looked suddenly tired. She'd spoken more in these few minutes than she had during the whole of the courier's visit to her farm.

"I have to find her," the courier said.

"You don't," Juniper said. "You're Black Square now, and your sister is part of something else. You're safe here, but only so long as you remain the Rider."

"I don't even know what that means," the courier said.

"Neither do I," Juniper admitted. She smiled. "Might not mean anything. Maybe you get to decide."

The stowaway stretched and reached one paw toward something on Juniper's workbench, a notched shaft. Juniper had been working on it earlier in the day. He batted at the thing but couldn't budge it.

"What *is* that?" the courier asked.

Juniper picked up the shaft and turned it in her hands. She drew a few scraps of metal from her sack and set them in the notches. Now it looked like one of the strange weapons the nameless had wielded in Buckle and in Hollow, and in countless battles with the named. The courier shivered at the memory of glinting blades in an alleyway.

"A prop," the courier said.

But when its blades flashed, it didn't look like a prop. It looked alive with menace.

Juniper selected a metal file and got to work. "Now," she said, "how sharp can I make it before it stops being a prop and starts being the thing it pretends to be? I'm never quite sure."

The courier kept Juniper company while she worked, sweeping sawdust, scraping dried paint from the table and floor. She'd hoped the old woman might say more about Ticket, but she stayed quiet and focused on her work. When the courier left, Juniper only grunted a farewell.

The courier returned to that compartment heaped with fabric for the night, but her stowaway didn't come with her. She slept uneasily, thinking about her sister, and about the Gardener of Stones. Had Ticket come to investigate the director of the Black Square? Could Book have sent her to learn more about his secret dealings with the nameless—or even to help arrange meetings like the one she had witnessed?

When the courier rose from her makeshift mattress the next morning, feeling tired and sore, she went looking for the patchwork ghost. She wanted to sit and talk with him, the way she had aboard the Number Twelve. She wanted to tell him what she'd learned, what she'd seen. The ghost knew the Black Square—he was the show's record keeper, its memory. Maybe he knew more about the Gardener of Stones. Maybe she would discover something among his sketches.

She found the ghost in his compartment, but he wasn't alone. The Six of Trees was seated at the desk with several sketchbooks open before him. His hair was messy, his peculiar suit wrinkled. The patchwork ghost pointed to something in a sketchbook, and Six peered at it carefully, then made notes in a little book of his own. He looked up as the courier came in. "What do you want?" he snapped.

She leaned over the desk. The drawing Six had been scrutinizing was the same one she had brought to Book all those months ago: Hand and Moon in old Whisper.

Six flipped his notebook closed before she could see what he'd written there. "Can't you see we're working?" he said.

The patchwork ghost turned from them and began searching the shelves. Watching him trace his fingers over the spines, it occurred to her that his sketch of the divining compartment—the glyphs on the floor, the pillow, the rod—was on those shelves somewhere. Would that appear in a new performance someday, the committee's carefully guarded secrets revealed?

"The Gardener of Stones told me that the Black Square's stories come from the record keeper," she said.

Six gave her a scornful look. "Stones exaggerates. We Trees do most of the work."

"But his drawings are the beginning, aren't they? How far back do they go? The ghost was there among the first namers, wasn't he? Even before *ghost* was delivered, he was a ghost, watching and listening."

Six looked uneasy.

"Further back," she guessed. "To the something tree, or—"

"I'm not interested in the something tree," he said. "My specialty is old Whisper."

She remembered the city as she'd glimpsed it that night in Jawbone, the worn buildings and broken windows, the junk heaps, the sunlight bright on the river. "You wrote the story I saw," she said.

"You can't have seen much," he said bitterly.

"I'm sorry for what happened," she said. "With Frost and Smoke, I mean. I didn't know they were so close."

"I spent months convincing the Gardeners to stage my version of Hand and Moon. *Months.*" His voice grew strange with his anger, the words twisting on themselves, and she remembered what Seven had told her—that even after Six had convinced three of the Gardeners, Stones had remained set against the idea.

"Can't the Black Square perform it again?" she asked.

"You really have no idea what you've done, do you?" he said. "Everyone was already afraid of that story."

Listening to him made the courier's head throb, but she pushed her discomfort aside. He knew something about her sister. She just had to keep him talking. "Because of what happened that time in Whisper," she said. "When a player became a ghost, and it wasn't pretend. But that was a long time ago."

"Not long enough for people to forget, so we remain exiled to the borders. The Gardener of Stones was convinced that something bad would happen if we tried to perform it again. And now you've proved him right."

"What is he so afraid of?"

"He says he has to protect the Black Square. He says the show is the most important thing, and that's why we can't perform *the Whisper Story.*" He said these last words with contempt—the Six of Trees wasn't one of those who avoided the story's name.

"But you don't believe him?" the courier asked.

"If Stones really wanted to protect us, then he wouldn't have permitted you to join the Black Square."

So this was the truth of why Six resented her, and probably what he and the Gardener of Stones had been arguing about at the party. Stones had taken a risk for her, a big one. But he refused to do the same for the Six of Trees. Why *had* the Gardener protected her? Simply because she'd requested a card? Or because he truly believed the ghost had brought her here for a reason?

"What about the new drawings?" she asked Six. "Have you learned more about old Whisper?"

Six glanced at his notebook. For a moment, she thought he might tell her. But he only said, "It doesn't matter. They won't give me another chance. Not after Jawbone. Not with you here."

His misery was genuine, and the strangeness of his voice made her feel it in her gut. She wondered whether that was the thing that had driven him to take refuge with the Black Square. His peculiar speech would have been considered unacceptable by the named, even dangerous. In creche, and then at school, they would have tried to fix him—would have forced his mouth to shape the words as they were meant to be spoken. And if they couldn't fix him—

Her monster burst into the compartment. Huffing and cooing, it grabbed the courier by the arm and tried to pull her away. The Two of Shovels didn't want them to be late to the workshop car.

Six rose from his chair. "That thing," he snarled. "You brought it here to taunt me, didn't you?"

The Two of Shovels blinked at him. The courier shrugged the monster off and said, "Taunt you? Because the monster looks familiar, is that right? Six, what was Ticket doing here? Tell me."

Realizing he'd said too much, Six swallowed and sat back down. "I guess you did pull the right card," he said.

She didn't know what to say to that. When she didn't reply, Six grinned. "No one's told you, have they?" he said. "They're probably afraid they'll make it true if they say anything."

"Make what true?"

"The last Rider was a great man, but every Rider leaves the Black Square worse than they found it. When people ask what kind of Rider you'll be, what they're really asking is what they should do to protect themselves from you."

She thought of the image on the card, of that big-bearded man on his little wheeled machine. Eventually he would tip over, one way or the other. *Trouble.*

The ghost set another sketchbook on the desk and opened it to a certain page. The courier didn't bother trying to see. She just wanted the ghost to look at her. He hadn't looked at her once since they'd come aboard the Black Square's train. But Six returned to his work, and the record keeper remained at his side.

Maybe the Gardener of Stones had been wrong. Maybe the ghost didn't want her here at all. Her monster tugged her arm again, and this time the courier let it pull her away.

In the workshop car, Juniper assigned her the task of sorting and scrubbing a bucket of rusty bolts. The old woman was the Gardener of Shovels again, and she did nothing to acknowledge their talk of the night before. The courier kept quiet and did her work. By midday, her hands were raw and rust-stained.

She went alone to the kitchen, three cars down, and cooked herself a bowl of cornmeal. She sat on a stool near the window and watched bare trees and muddy fields sweep past. She didn't know where exactly they were going, only that they were someplace on the border—or maybe a little beyond it.

The Seven of Stones appeared beside her. She was dressed in the quilted linen armor of a dreams committee hunter, black with yellow stitching. "There you are," she said.

"Find any monsters?" the courier asked.

"Everywhere I look."

When she didn't respond, Seven leaned down and took the courier's hands in hers. The courier was startled, but she didn't pull away. Seven inspected the rust under her nails. She shook her head. "The Shovels are taking advantage of you," she said.

"And what do you suggest I do with my time?"

Seven threw herself down onto a nearby couch. "Oh, I never make suggestions," she said. "If you don't make suggestions, then you don't have to take them, either."

"But you keep seeking me out," the courier said. "Is it because you're afraid of what I'm doing here?"

Seven bit her lip in an exaggerated way as she thought this over. "You've been talking to the Six of Trees," she decided.

"Well?"

"In some ways, Six is still the frightened kid he was when he first came aboard."

The courier set her bowl aside. "But is he right?"

"No," Seven said, folding her arms over her chest. Then she sighed. "Yes, a little. You wouldn't understand. We haven't had a Rider in almost ten years."

"Six called the last one a great man."

She grimaced. "Six is confused, I think. He just remembers someone who seemed bigger than the safe little world the Gardener of Stones tried to make for him."

"But what was it about the Rider?"

"He was a very talented player," Seven said grudgingly. "The best the Black Square had ever seen, maybe. But he was also the worst thing that ever happened to the show."

"Tell me what he did," the courier said.

Seven seemed to shrink a little, and the courier thought she was seeing a younger version of her: the person she'd been before she drew a card and joined the Black Square. This version of her looked alone and frightened.

"Please," the courier said. "I don't know what I'm supposed to be doing here, but maybe you can help me learn what *not* to do."

Seven sat up and straightened her armored jacket. "I barely remember the last Rider," she said coolly.

"Then why—"

She raised one hand. "You should understand something about that man. He was empty. Hollow. Onstage, he didn't exist at all—or who he was disappeared completely into the roles he played. And offstage, he was a shadow, but not in the way the Gardener of Leaves is a shadow. He was a blankness that moved from place to place. When he wasn't around, it was easy to forget about him. He just slipped from your mind like he'd never been."

The courier felt uneasy. Seven's words described the shape of something familiar in her own mind, something that threatened to slip away even as she tried to grasp it. Her childhood monsters. The dreams committee agents her father had sent for. They had taught her a technique to stop the monsters from taking shape. *Imagine an empty person,* they told her. *Forgettable. A hollow in the shape of a man, without features or a story. Give him everything that frightens you, everything that wants to become a monster.*

She shook it off. The last Rider, unlike the empty man of her dreams, was a real person. "If he was so easy to forget," the courier asked, "then why do you remember him now?"

"I wish I didn't," Seven said. "But I can't forget what he did. And when he left, he took everyone who had studied with him, too. We feel those absences still, along with others he created."

"Players of the Black Square studied with him?"

Seven closed her eyes. "I'm not sure *studied* is the right word. They were *drawn* to him, and he *taught* them. They would gather for hours, even days at a time. I've heard rumors about what went on in those meetings. That they sat together in perfect silence. Eyes closed. Dreaming, maybe, as the nameless dream. But they weren't making monsters. They were remaking themselves."

"Did you know them well?" the courier asked.

"Most of his students were Shovels," Seven said. "A few of the others, too: the Beard of Trees, the Eight of Leaves—no one I knew well. Six wanted to join them, but the Rider wouldn't have him. Because of his voice, or maybe because he was so young. Though Six wasn't the only one he turned away. The Rider didn't want any Stones. We already had our methods, and his were different."

"Which explains why there are so few Shovels with the Black Square now," the courier said. "But why did they leave? What did they learn from him?"

"I don't know, but only a few of the Stones could match their skill. Our Gardener was frightened by what he saw, but also entranced, and he gave the Rider and his students more roles. Others wanted the Rider gone from the train. They believed he was turning the Black Square into something else, something he could control. No one was more certain of it than the Scout of Stones."

"The ghost?"

"He wasn't a ghost then," Seven said, her words breaking a little. "He was very much alive, and I can almost remember the sound of his voice—deeper than you might think, and kind."

The courier saw it again in Seven's eyes, the flash of hurt she'd first caught by the glow of the ghost's light machine.

"Some of the Gardeners agreed with the Scout of Stones," Seven said, talking quickly now. "Trees, who usually thinks of nothing but his engine. And Leaves, who likes being the scariest thing aboard the train. They knew that something was wrong with the Rider. That it would only get worse."

"Can the Black Square expel one of its members?"

"Only if a majority of the Gardeners agree. But the previous Gardener of Shovels—a difficult man with a taste for nameless spirits—belonged to the Rider. And all the Gardener of Stones could think about was our next performance, our biggest of the year. We were to play in Whisper, the night after the sayers recited the law, when the city was full of people from all over the named territories."

"You played Hand and Moon," the courier said, beginning to see how the puzzle fit together.

"Yes," Seven said. "With the Scout of Stones in the role of Hand. And the Rider playing Moon."

The courier recalled the end of the story as she'd seen it performed in Jawbone. Moon back from the nameless wilds, silver robe soiled and torn. In Moon's mind, a word to be delivered. And in Moon's hand, a gift from the nameless. A weapon.

"The Rider didn't use a prop," the courier said. "He used the real thing."

"Want to hear the worst part?" Seven said. "After, we didn't even realize that his ghost was real. So we finished the scene. And the ghost of the Scout of Stones finished the scene, too. It wasn't until the players were speaking their final lines that people in the audience started to scream. They could see blood dripping from the edge of the stage, pooling on the real ground at their feet."

"And the Rider?" the courier asked.

"He escaped in the confusion, and his flock went with him. We sought help from the watchers, but they failed to track them down. I'm not sure they even tried." She held up her hands and added in a different voice, a voice that was part pretend, "And so the sayers rewarded us with exile."

As though in response to Seven's words, the train's whistle sounded its call, long and mournful. Through the window, the courier saw the scattered houses and farms at the edge of another border town. Seven stood abruptly and brushed herself off.

"I'd better get back to rehearsal," she said. "There are monsters in need of hunting."

"Monsters," the courier echoed. "Yes. Good luck."

Seven let out a pained cry. "Never, *ever* say that to a player who's about to perform," she said. "You have to wish for something terrible to happen."

"What? Why?"

"Say that you hope I break a limb. Say it, say it now."

After what Seven had just told her about the last Rider, this seemed strange. But the courier said, "All right. I hope you break your arm. Your left arm."

"Better," Seven said. She smiled and squeezed the courier's shoulder. "You know, I don't keep seeking you out only because I'm afraid of you. Though I am. And it's not just that I always pursue the newest, prettiest thing I see. Though I do. The truth is, I'm glad that a new Rider has come. I think we're overdue for some changes around here."

"What kind of changes?"

Seven gestured to the window. "The view, for example. These border towns all start to look the same after a while."

"You think I can end the Black Square's exile?"

"No," Seven said. "But I think you can make it more interesting."

For the next few days, the courier continued working with the Shovels, sanding, painting, sawing, sewing. She wasn't sure they really wanted her in the workshop car. They tolerated her, she thought, because of Two.

The Shovels adored Two. They patted the monster's back, passed it the tools it needed, told jokes to make it snort. Four and Nine often asked it questions, and when it responded with formless flowing sounds like the burbling of a stream, they nodded as though they understood. As though what the monster said was very interesting, very clever. The sisters and the others must have known the Two of Shovels for what it was: a thing born in dream and made of paper, wood, ink, dust. But they didn't seem to care that it trilled like a bird, that it walked like a child on stilts. Or maybe they liked that it was a constructed thing.

They referred to the monster as *she*, and the courier realized that she was doing this too, when she spoke, and sometimes even in her thoughts. This troubled her. It brought the monster one step closer to being the sister it was not.

At night, she didn't bother pretending to watch the performances. She got right to snooping instead. But each trip through the train was different. Cars she saw one night were gone the next, replaced by others she hadn't seen before.

In the compartments she thought served as pens for goats and chickens, she found the workplace of the Beard of Leaves, the somber man who stamped paper to make the Black Square's notices. Where props and costumes had been stored the night before, she now found barrels of grain and bunches of dried herbs.

She knew this was impossible. At no stop on the line had the Black Square added or removed cars, or shifted their order. Yet the train opened to her like a deck of cards, shuffled and dealt again each night—or closed up like a living thing, quietly working to keep its secrets from her.

On her fifth day aboard, she finished her work with the Shovels early. The train had stopped in Sap, a town on the northern border. With the sun still up, she resumed her search for some sign of what had brought her sister here. After only a few minutes, she found herself in yet another new car, this one full of monsters.

Not real monsters, but suits and props and big weird heads made of paper and fabric, creatures like a forest come to life, like human bodies arranged in nightmare shapes. One monster was made all of brambles and flowers. Others were built on frames that ran the length of the car—giants, maybe fifty feet tall if stood upright. All the monsters were in bad repair.

The courier navigated the maze of leering faces, shining eyes, limbs covered in feathers, fur, and scales, until she found the door. Passing between cars, she caught sight of the Gardener of Stones on the platform. He wore the same blue coat he'd been wearing when she saw him outside the workshop car. The courier threw herself against the door as he glanced back at the train, and she watched him duck around the station, looking like someone who didn't want to be followed.

So she followed him, hopping down to the platform, stepping lightly as she rounded the corner of the small brick building. Last time, in Grit, she had failed to learn the purpose of his meeting with that nameless figure in the dark. She wouldn't let that happen again.

The Gardener of Stones avoided the road and walked through the woods toward town. She followed him uphill among pine trees and sumac, keeping her distance but keeping him in sight. Only once more did he turn to look over his shoulder, and she ducked behind a tree. When he moved on, she followed—out of the woods, between the yards of some rambling old houses, across a street and into a park.

The park was long and narrow. People were gathered around Black Square notices pasted to walls and lampposts. Despite being Black Square now, the courier still didn't know how the notices were delivered in advance of each show.

The Gardener followed a path across the park's narrow middle. The courier took a more winding route, trying to look as though she belonged here. The sun was setting, and the buildings along the park cast long shadows over the grass. The air smelled of mildew and wet leaves.

Across the next street, the Gardener began to move more quickly, and the courier hurried to keep up. Another glance over his shoulder, and then he was gone, ducking between two brick buildings.

When she peered into the alleyway, it was empty and clean, but beyond were ruined structures and old machines—a broken part of town. The shadows moved strangely among the heaps, and the breeze bore strange smells. Something rotting, something burning, something turning to rust. The courier moved closer, slowly now, until she could see the Gardener of Stones again. Then she crouched in the shadows at the end of the alley.

Stones stood alone in a weedy, abandoned lot. A fire burned in a steel drum, its smoke smudging the sun. From a row of low brick structures with sagging roofs, three people emerged. Their masks matched the one she'd seen in Grit several nights before—roughly triangular, with silver lines like tears running down the cheeks. In this light, she could see they were painted a blue so dark it was almost black.

For a long moment, the Gardener of Stones and the three masked nameless stood in silence. Then the Gardener nodded, as though in agreement with something they had said. One of the nameless turned and beckoned, and from the ruins came a dozen more figures. Most looked old, though a few younger men, women, and children walked among them. All were dressed differently, in suits, robes, and dresses, and in loose shirts and trousers of pale colors. Most looked gray and faded; others seemed restless, with a sharp light in their eyes. None wore masks. They were ghosts, all of them.

The courier took a breath and focused. Soon she could hear it: a whispering sound, not in her ears, but in her head. The voices of the nameless, and the Gardener's voice, too.

*So many*, he said of the ghosts.

*But will you take them?* the nameless wanted to know.

A trade of some kind? The courier remembered the others in Grit that night, motionless in the alley behind the masked figure. They might have been ghosts, too. How long had the Gardener of Stones been brokering such deals? The courier wondered what he could offer in exchange for so many ghosts. She wondered what he did with them, and whether the rest of the Black Square knew.

But she must have wondered too loudly, her own thoughts rising above a whisper, because one of the weeping masks turned in her direction. She pressed herself against the wall and held her breath, but already she felt fingers of thought reaching, seeking her out. Those fingers brushed against the border of her mind; she felt their touch like a breath.

*You,* said one of the nameless, without words, without speaking, and they sounded surprised but not unkind. *The dreaming child. Oh, we have heard about you.*


The courier ran, not bothering to be quiet. She burst from the alleyway and nearly collided with a man on the sidewalk. He shouted at her as she passed. Without looking back, the courier crossed the street and plunged into the park.

At the north end, a flying machine had landed. The people who had been talking about the Black Square's notices now whispered and pointed as a company of watchers debarked. With the watchers came several women dressed in rugged canvas trousers, black gloves, and wide-brimmed hats. Some had slender braided ropes slung over their shoulders, others carried weighted nets. Ghost wranglers.

The watchers adjusted their goggles, surveying the area, while the wranglers strode out into the crowd. The courier stopped running—she didn't want to draw their attention—and turned south, away from the flying machine.

She found herself in an open-air market, crowded with people pulling carts of goods to barter. A young girl ladled hot maple sap into tin cups. A man in a threadbare jacket pointed out what he wanted from a shelf of bottles and tins. Some of the vendors saw the watchers and slid drawers under their tables, covered them with burlap. The merchants eyed her suspiciously. She tried not to see what they were hiding.

Beyond the market she cut through an overgrown lot behind more abandoned buildings. Farther south, birds circled taller buildings, their windows dark. She realized that the town of Sap was a small named island in the midst of what had once been a city; the nameless districts were larger and more numerous than the named.

*The dreaming child,* the nameless had called her. Because of the monster she had dreamed? She was known on both sides of the border, then, and nowhere was safe. She ran downhill past quiet structures. Some appeared occupied. She saw well-tended gardens, penned goats and chickens, candlelight flickering behind glass panes. Finally she found the pine wood. She ran hard down the hill, sweating in her boilersuit despite the cold. At the bottom of the slope, where she thought the station should be, she came instead to a pond, the water covered in a dull green film.

She picked her way along the shore, her boots sticking in the mud of the bog. The forest was dark now, and bats swooped back and forth over the still water. On the other side of the pond, she lost her footing and slid down an embankment. Brambles caught at the courier's legs as soil slipped into her boots and under her collar. She brushed herself off and kept going.

Past a stand of sickly pines, she came upon the shining curved rails. She followed them for what seemed like an hour. Then, just when she was certain that she must have gone in the wrong direction, she spotted the crowd up ahead, gathered in the glow of the stage lights. She approached slowly, watching for the shine of lenses in the dark, for blue masks with silver tears, or white masks and gleaming knives.

The last car of the Black Square's train was much like the Number Twelve's—smaller than the other cars and topped with a lookout's cupola. She hauled herself onto the rear deck, found the door unlocked.

Inside was cool and dark, the car crowded with old furniture. Her boots left muddy prints on the floor. Suddenly a patch of deeper darkness loomed up before her. She squinted against a thousand pinpricks of light.

"There you are, my morsel," said the Gardener of Leaves. "But wherever have you been?"

I got lost," the courier said, backing away.

"Lost, my muffin? My cup of molasses? You've been lost since the moment you arrived. Since before you arrived, I think." The stars brightened as the Gardener of Leaves drew closer. Now she could make out the monster's purple shawl, her floppy purple hat. "I see you sneaking about, my fine sweet plum. I see you peeking and peering. And the train gives you answers, but you don't listen. You don't learn."

"Please," the courier said, "I just want—"

"To return to your scheming?" The stars crackled and sparked as though stoked by a strong wind. "Oh, my little spoonful of honey, if you were to disappear right now, no one would mind very much. No one, I think, would go looking."

The courier's back was to the door. She found the knob with one hand. "The Two of Shovels would look for me," she said.

The Gardener hummed. "Just a child, that one. How long ago did you manufacture her? A year? A few months?" She tilted her great blocky head, as though to hear what the courier wasn't saying. "Just weeks, then? What a triumph. Your first, my nice mushy apple? Or maybe you'd had practice?"

The courier wondered what sort of horrible person had dreamed up the Gardener of Leaves. She turned the doorknob but the monster swept closer, crowding her with her bulk. The courier's heart pounded as the cold enveloped her.

She heard something then, and the Gardener of Leaves heard it, too—a scratching sound, faint but very near. They turned to see the patchwork ghost seated on a narrow bed in the corner of the car, sketchbook open on his lap. He was drawing the scene, the stowaway curled up beside him, tail gently flicking. The ghost looked back and forth between them and his sketch as he filled in details.

The Gardener of Leaves took a step back, lights dimming. She tipped her hat, suddenly polite. "Rider," she said. "Record keeper. My apologies for intruding."

"Intruding?" the courier said. "Is that what you call this?"

The monster hesitated, lights paling then brightening again. "Someone should have told you," she said. "This car is reserved for the Rider. It's *yours*, sweet loaf. So you can stop sleeping on that pile of spare fabric. It's very rude."

All at once the stars winked out, and for a moment the courier thought the monster had disappeared. Then the door at the front of the car opened and slammed closed again.

The courier went to the door, found a bolt lock, slid it shut. For a moment she only stood there, body slack against the door, shivering as she breathed. Then she wandered the car, rubbing her hands and trying to get warm. The car was in better repair than its counterpart on the Number Twelve, but it had the same potbellied stove.

She sat beside the patchwork ghost, who was still working on his sketch. His version of the Rider stood tall before a starry patch of darkness. *That* woman looked far braver than the courier had felt. She set her head on the ghost's shoulder and watched, just as she used to do aboard the Number Twelve.

A loud banging on the door startled them both. The stowaway leapt from the mattress and scrambled under the bed.

The courier stood and called, "Who's there?"

From the other side of the door came the thin, fluty voice of the Two of Shovels: "Oh, oh, oh!"

The courier unbolted the door and the monster burst in, grabbing the courier and hugging her hard.

"I'm fine," the courier said, patting Two's back. "Really, I'm *fine*."

The monster let her go. Huffing and tutting, she inspected the car as though for signs of danger. Then she began to organize the furniture, pushing chairs against the walls and turning small tables upright. The courier examined the stove, found the scuttle stocked with naphtha, a bucket of firewood. Found matches on the wall, right where she would have set them. A few minutes later, she had the fire burning brightly.

The ghost, done with his sketch, moved to a chair closer to the light of the flames. The stowaway emerged from under the bed and hopped onto his lap.

When the Two of Shovels was satisfied with the arrangement of the furniture, she settled onto the bed, head at the bottom, big feet on the pillow. Moments later the monster was asleep, mouth open, body still. The bed was narrow. There wouldn't be much room for the courier.

The ghost was carefully petting the stowaway, and the courier could hear the sound of the animal's happy rumbling. She felt something, then—a feeling like the one curled up inside the word *home*—but she quickly pushed it from her mind. The last person who called this place home had made a ghost of a fellow player. Was it here, she wondered, that his flock had gathered to hear his teachings?

The courier stared into the flames, trying not to think. And for a little while it worked, the flames burning the words away. When the train began moving again, she crawled into bed beside the Two of Shovels, pushing her toward the wall. The monster didn't stir, and the courier had almost enough room.

In the night she heard the stowaway's paws hit the floor. She felt them hit, too, as though they were her own hands and feet. A moment later, when the animal left the car through a hole behind an open cupboard door, the courier left with him.

She knew this time that it wasn't a dream. Without trying, she had stowed away with her stowaway, just as she had one summer night aboard the Number Twelve. His senses were her own.

Together they stalked the train, which was even more vast and strange than the courier had imagined. The stowaway could move in ways she could not, leaping through small, in-between places that unfolded and grew as he plunged forward. They passed through compartments like deep caves, tiny rooms behind hidden doors, spaces between the walls where ancient clumps of living draff trudged and muttered, attic spaces where the wind whipped and where monsters like little flour sacks sang wordless songs in the moonlight.

Brisk leaps brought them from one car to the next. They clambered through ducts and open hatches, revealing rooms packed with rambling machines, with crates of dusty costumes, with props of every named thing: books and daggers, hammers and furs, goblets and chairs and chains and jewels. They passed swiftly through a compartment in which a hundred dolls sat in silent counsel, their black eyes gleaming. Another where the air was hot and damp, and where several players lounged, each in their own copper tub. The Seven of Stones was among them; she laughed at something one of the other players said, and the sound of her laughter in their sensitive ears—the scent of her in the warm wet air—momentarily overwhelmed the courier.

Was it the courier's will or the stowaway's that determined their destination? The courier wanted answers to her questions; the stowaway wanted something new. Together they squeezed through a gap in the wall, made friends with the shadows in one corner of a narrow, high-ceilinged compartment that smelled of fermented draff and old paper. A pot of water simmered on the stove. The walls were lined with books and unbound sheafs of paper. The Gardener of Stones was here, pacing back and forth in front of the fire.

But the Gardener wasn't alone. Seated at a table nearby was another man, one who wasn't Black Square. When the courier recognized him, the shock almost sent her tumbling out of the stowaway's mind.

Smoke.

Bristling, the animal remained crouched in shadow as Sayer Frost's speaker sipped from a mug of something hot. The two men were talking quietly. At first the courier heard their words only as the stowaway understood them: a low bubbling shot through with thunks and hisses. In bed beside her monster, she breathed, focused, pressed her mind more fully into that of her host, until the sounds became words.

"One way or another," Smoke was saying, "Frost *will* decide the matter."

The Gardener of Stones frowned. "He asks too much. Smoke, you know the laws are on our side. The Black Square—"

"The Black Square is a curious relic," Smoke said. "It has declined slowly, over the course of a hundred years or more. You shouldn't blame yourself for standing here at the end. But you must accept that the show, like this train, is coming to pieces. No one will notice when it's gone."

"Without the Black Square, there would be no story."

Smoke waved these words away. "Children's games," he said. "Meanwhile, five more attacks since Buckle. This isn't pretend anymore. Gray, this is the worst we've seen since the old days of the war."

*Gray.* That must have been his name, before he became the Gardener of Stones.

"And you believe this woman—"

"She has manufactured monsters," Smoke said. "She made a ghost of her committee chair, set fire to the Number Twelve, stole the property of the namers. We *know* she's connected."

"Connected to what, exactly?"

Smoke looked uncomfortable. "I think you know the one I speak of."

"I do not," the Gardener said lightly.

"The word to describe this person remains undelivered," Smoke said. "But their influence taints everything."

So Frost and Smoke still sought their *traitor*. The courier felt the word pull at the bottom of her mind, a burden grown so familiar she had almost forgotten it was there.

The Gardener looked doubtful. "*Everything?*" he said. "Smoke, that seems too convenient."

"We are sure Buckle was this person's doing. Most of the other attacks as well—maybe all of them. For a while, we suspected Book himself."

"Ridiculous."

"Whoever they are, they're embedded deeply among the named, and yet they remain hidden from us. I would call our runaway courier a likely candidate, but she has been too sloppy, and our enemy is nothing if not careful. But have no doubt: the outlaw you shelter is furthering the enemy's cause. Already the people whisper fearfully of Jawbone, wondering who she is, what she's done, how Frost could let her escape. Gray, we must have her."

"She is Black Square," said the Gardener of Stones. "She drew a card." But the fire in his voice was dwindling.

"In three days," Smoke said, "the sayers will gather in Whisper for the recitation. Frost will speak law on your behalf, if you choose."

The Gardener looked into the fire. "He has never done so before."

"Much has changed since you left."

"I didn't leave. I was forced—"

"More stories," Smoke interrupted, "and stories can be changed. Everything is about to change. Gray, we've found it. The last city of the nameless."

The Gardener held still, keeping his gaze on the fire. The courier saw something in his eyes—a shock of surprise or fear—but when he spoke, his voice was steady. "It's real, then?" he asked.

"The next stage of our plan begins after the recitation. And when Frost acts, the other sayers will fall in line behind him. If he says you should rejoin us, no one will oppose him. You would be a sayer again, Gray. The things you say and do would matter."

"And if I don't turn her over?"

Smoke stood, straightening his embroidered jacket. "Then it won't matter who is and who isn't Black Square, because there will be no Black Square. The laws will be amended to protect the named from every threat. The sayers will speak the show out of being."

The Gardener of Stones stood, his head hanging. Somehow, the courier thought, knowing his name made him seem vulnerable. And seeing that vulnerability, she knew he would accept Frost's deal. To protect the Black Square, to protect his secret dealings with the nameless, to protect himself.

Rage suddenly filled her. It overflowed into the stowaway, filling its body from whiskers to tail. Together they burst snarling from their shadow. Smoke turned, eyes wide as they leapt at him, claws sinking into his flank. They climbed his fine suit and clawed again, more deeply this time, into his throat. Hot blood poured over their paws.

The Gardener backed away, mouth open, eyes wide. Smoke, shrieking, grabbed the animal by his fur and yanked him free. Claws tore flesh and fabric, and some claws broke. Smoke hurled the stowaway across the compartment, where he tumbled into another shadow. The animal's pain was a bright red slash in the dark. The courier fell back, fleeing from the hurt, crashing hard into her own body. She sat up in bed, clutching her hands where she'd felt claws cracking.

Moments later, the train's brakes sounded. Still holding her hand, she stood and went to the window.

The train halted in an abandoned depot where the weeds grew high between the rails. She caught sight of Smoke picking his way over the tracks toward Frost's flying machine, which was anchored to a derelict water tower. The sayer's speaker limped from the wounds she and her stowaway had given him.

She crawled back into bed beside the monster. Later, after the train started moving again, her stowaway returned. He leapt onto the mattress and curled into a ball at her feet. She wanted to pet him, but she knew to leave him be. She could still feel his pain in her own fingers, throbbing deep as the bone. In the window, the moon was low and heavy, chasing the train through clouds sharp as knives.

The courier made preparations to leave. She would go alone this time—no ghost, no monster. They belonged with the Black Square, but she was no longer safe aboard this train. Not with Frost threatening the destruction of the Black Square. Not with a Gardener of Stones who couldn't risk having his secrets exposed.

If she left soon and stuck to the borders, she might have a chance. She could hide until the named forgot her. If what Smoke said was true, then Frost had his war to plan, his attack on the last city of the nameless. Maybe even he would forget about her, in time.

She kept to herself that day, waiting for the train to stop somewhere, anywhere. When the Two of Shovels tried to take her to the workshop car, she resisted until the monster gave up and went alone. She collected some food from the kitchens and a few supplies, tucked them into her satchel. She still had the word Frost had assigned to her, and she had the sketches the patchwork ghost had made long ago of her father, her sister, herself as a child. She considered burning the word in the potbellied stove but decided against it. Maybe it would still prove useful someday. Maybe she or someone else could still deliver it—to that person Smoke had described to the Gardener of Stones, or to someone else.

As for the sketches, she brought them to the compartment of the record keeper. This much of her would remain: the ghost of a shadow of a story. The patchwork ghost watched as she tucked the folded pages into one of his sketchbooks. He looked worried, but the courier couldn't tell if he knew she was fleeing the Black Square or if he just didn't like where she'd chosen to stow his drawings. She left the compartment before she knew which it was.

She looked for her stowaway, thinking she might clean his wounded paws. But she couldn't find the animal anywhere, and anyway she knew better—the stowaway would take care of himself, and if she tried to stick his paws in water, he would reward her with wounds worse than those it had suffered the night before. When she left the train, he might follow her. He might not.

Today she was grateful that the other players ignored her movements through the train, that the train seemed to show no interest in impeding her. She saw Trees working at their typing machines, some in their car full of bunks and chairs and desks, some tucked into other compartments. The Stones she passed were practicing new lines or trading lines from old performances, sayers and maps committee surveyors one moment, soldiers and watchers the next; they roared like monsters, then roared with laughter. She saw Leaves, too, moving ceaselessly about the train in their black and dark gray clothes, speaking quietly to one another as they tidied, took notes, prepared for the next show. Their hushed ways made the courier nervous—how often had one of them been present without her even knowing? She saw no sign of their Gardener, though she knew too well that the monster who guarded the train might be anywhere.

Late in the day, the train shifted onto a siding in a wooded place overlooking an ancient reservoir. The sun was low over the hills. The players debarked and went down to the water. Some built a fire while others brought food and drink from the train's stores. She watched as one of the older children, the Nine of Leaves, led the goats and chickens from their car and let them range among the tall grasses.

Musicians played, and the Two of Shovels was first to dance. Some joined the monster by the fire, the Seven of Stones among them. The courier resisted the urge to go to her, to tell her she was leaving. Whatever she felt for Seven, whatever Seven felt for her—well, they had never figured it out, and none of that would matter now.

Some of the players peeled off their clothes and went into the cold water. The courier watched them floating and remembered *float*, felt that lightness without taking a step. She saw Juniper, the Gardener of Shovels, standing in the shallows with her trousers hiked up over her knees. She didn't see the patchwork ghost. She turned, adjusted her satchel over her shoulder, and headed for the woods.

The Gardener of Trees was waiting for her there, hands tucked into his sooty boilersuit. He was alone; she could outrun him. But when he spoke, his voice was gentler than she had imagined. "Rider," he said, "I've a task for you." He gestured for her to follow and walked off toward the train.

When she hesitated, he turned and said, "I know we haven't spoken. But you can trust me."

Did he know about the meeting between Smoke and the Gardener of Stones? She saw no sign of the watchers, of Frost or his deletion committee. Most other members of the Black Square were down by the water. So she followed the Gardener of Trees out of the woods. She told herself she could sneak away later, after the sun had gone down.

Running his fingers through his beard, the Gardener led her along the tracks, in the direction of the engine. He was a big man with a sure step, his eyes bright in his soot-covered face. He drew up beside the open bay door of a car near the middle of the train. Here a group of Leaves were lowering a heavy machine down onto the tracks of the main line. At first she took it for some piece of stage equipment, but when its wheels met the rails, she saw it for what it was. A handcar.

"I trust you're familiar with the operation of such a vehicle?" the Gardener said.

She had seen them used in rail yards, and on lengths of track between factories in Hollow. She had seen merchants and ghosts committee drovers use them on shorter lines between one town and the next. But she had never used one herself.

The Six of Trees came down out of the car with a sack slung over his shoulder. When he saw the courier he scowled, but before he could speak, the Gardener of Trees said, "Six, you'll explain along the way."

"You're sending me with *her*?"

"Time's wasting," the Gardener said. "Go now, the both of you."

Six was about to say something more, but he stopped himself. He heaved the sack onto the deck, then climbed up after. He looked down at the courier. "Well?" he said.

The courier gazed into the woods on the other side of the tracks. She could still run. No one here would try to stop her. But she was curious now—and Six was annoyed by her presence. She clambered aboard.

Before she was fully standing, Six shoved his end of the beam down, and the handcar lurched forward. The courier staggered as the beam's other end nearly caught her jaw on the upswing. The Leaves, watching from beside the rails, chuckled.

While the courier steadied herself, Six worked the beam alone, and already the little car was rolling faster than she could have gone at a run. The Gardener of Trees, hands in his pockets again, watched them go. Soon they were past the engine of the Black Square and headed over a bridge that crossed a stream fed by the reservoir. She watched the light of the fire fall away into the distance.

"You are going to help, aren't you?" Six said.

She grabbed the beam and pushed hard enough to stagger him. Six clenched his jaw but said nothing. The courier was surprised by how smoothly the handcar rolled over the rails. The air grew cool as the sun began to set. In the dim light she saw bats moving among the trees.

"What if another train comes?" she asked.

"Then we go back as ghosts."

She put her anger into working the beam, thinking that she should have left while she had the chance. She and Six found a rhythm in spite of themselves. The sky darkened, and in the distance she saw lights flickering. The courier recognized this place. It was Nod, the same town where she'd caught up with the Number Twelve after escaping from the nameless in Hollow. Where Beryl had embraced her on the platform, taken her inside, and put her in a warm bath. An ache gripped her chest. She tried to dispel it by working the beam harder.

They passed a weedy marsh, and then a sprawling brick structure, lights shining from the first floor windows. The smell of cold, damp earth mixed with the sour odor of a brewing operation.

"Up here," Six said.

They held the beam steady and let the handcar glide to a halt beside a copse of maple and sumac. Six tossed the canvas sack to the ground, then they both got down and lifted the car off the tracks. It was heavy, but together they managed. They set the car among the sumac, concealed it with leaves and branches. The courier brushed off her hands, feeling pleased at how completely they had hidden the contraption. But when she looked to Six, he said, "You being here is his way of punishing me."

The courier wondered what the Gardener of Trees was punishing him for. Instead of asking, she said, "Maybe I'm the one he's punishing."

Six frowned at that, but he didn't argue.


They walked through the copse and followed a path to the outskirts of the sleepy town, past low gray houses sunk behind bare sycamores. Naphtha lights shone in a few windows.

In the shadow of a brick wall that ran the length of a half-wild park, she stopped and said to Six, "Tell me what we're doing here."

Six looked around. When he saw no one watching, he set down the canvas sack and tugged it open. Inside were stacks of thick paper, each square sheet stamped with a single black square. Notices for the upcoming show.

Six gave the courier a handful of the sheets, took some for himself, and slung the sack over his shoulder. "Time to make our deliveries," he said.

They kept mostly to side streets, avoiding the light from the naphtha lamps. When they passed the first open window, Six tossed a sheet through. They slipped some under doors, pasted others to walls. Some they dropped in the road, let the breeze take them.

The courier thought of how the show would change the place when it arrived, drawing people onto the streets and down past the rail yard, friends coming hand in hand, children shouting, traders pulling carts of food and drink. She felt light on her feet, a secret the town welcomed but kept hidden from itself.

"This is supposed to be a job for the Scout of Leaves," Six said. "But that card hasn't been drawn in years. Lucky us."

He balled up several sheets of paper and stuck them in a bush, making pretend blossoms. The courier caught herself smiling; she stopped before he could see.

On the next street, a group of young men and women emerged from a bar. They walked arm in arm as they sang, with outrageous good cheer, the words of a naming song that was new when the courier was young.

> *Water for the bucket, draff for the bin,*
> *The birds all sing of the season we're in.*

The five of them, laughing as they stumbled, were coming straight toward Six and the courier. Six took her arm and yanked her forward. She gasped, too surprised to resist, as he swung her hard at the wall. She braced herself for the impact, but it never came. Instead, her stomach lurched as she stumbled onto a street that hadn't been there a moment before. She felt as though she'd been turned upside-down, but that the world had turned with her. Six was at her side, still holding her arm as she recovered.

"Where are we?" she whispered.

Six shrugged, and for a moment she thought he was only being difficult. Then she understood. This street didn't have a name. And because it did not have a name, she hadn't even noticed it was here.

Nod was an old town. Like Hollow and Whisper, many of its buildings were built before the Silence. She had seen the nameless warrens of Hollow for herself, and she'd heard rumors that even Whisper had its lost and forgotten corners, but Nod was small in comparison. Could some of its streets have gone unmapped and unnamed after all this time?

Six smiled as he watched her figure it out.

Back on the named street, the singing men and women drew closer. They were only steps away, yet miles seemed to divide them from the place where the courier stood with Six. One woman hesitated and turned. She stopped singing, blinked, and tilted her head, yet seemed unable to focus her eyes on them. Another woman took her hand and pulled her along, and a moment later her voice rejoined the chorus.

The unnamed street was crooked and narrow, and though the ground was level, walking it felt like descending. Eventually the street broadened into a square. Here the air seemed cooler, the stars brighter. The courier heard the shouts of children.

They were playing in a yard behind an iron fence, a group of four or five, chasing one another, hiding behind bushes and trees. On the porch of the old stone house, men and women sat around a table, quiet in the light of several candles. Everyone wore masks, adults and children alike. The children's were bright yellow, and some were decorated with feathers, beads, and colorful stones. The people on the porch all wore different masks: one green, one black and wide, one a dusky silver. One wore a veil of fabric so thin it was hardly a mask at all. Behind it, the courier thought she saw a young woman's smiling face.

The courier's heart was beating fast. She was among the nameless, here in the town of Nod, in a square unknown to the named. But the Six of Trees went close to the gate and nodded to the people on the porch. One nodded back, and another went inside, returning a moment later with a gray cloth bundle.

Six stuck two fingers in his mouth and whistled. The children stopped playing and turned. Some ran straight to him and gathered close around, while another fetched the gray bundle from the figure on the stairs. All seemed excited to see him.

He held up a thick sheaf of papers from the sack and the children took their masks off. The sudden appearance of their faces was more startling to the courier than the masks had been. Two boys and two girls, she thought, or maybe three girls and a boy? The courier couldn't be sure, and she couldn't tell their ages, either. If they had been named, the youngest might have celebrated five name days, the oldest maybe twelve.

They drew new masks from the gray bundle and put them on. These masks were more somber than those they had worn at play: dark gray, with larger holes for eyes and smaller holes for mouths, and fitting more snugly to their faces. Still, the courier could see the children were smiling.

Six gave them the pages, and they divided them among themselves, fewer for the smallest among them. Then they went out through the front gate and padded away over the square. On the porch, the person in the dark green mask struck a match and lit a pipe, the stem of which just fit through the narrow, rectangular mouth. The courier felt everyone there regarding her with quiet interest.

Six tugged her arm, and she went with him into the square.

"Yellow masks for play," she said.

Six tilted his head, considering. "*Play* is probably the word that comes closest."

"And the gray masks," she said. "For delivering those pages? For doing work on behalf of the Black Square?"

"More like sneaking about, keeping hidden. But even more like: *the joy of seeing while going unseen.* If there were words for everything the masks signaled, then those who wore them would have that much less." He sounded bitter as he said this.

"What about these children?" she asked. "What do they get in return?"

"The named pay for our performances in their way. Food, drink, naphtha. The others pay in theirs."

"I've never seen the nameless at the shows," she said.

"Haven't you?" he asked.

She thought back to the performances in Jawbone, in Grit. Had there been a few masked figures, standing at the edge of those crowds? Maybe she *had* glimpsed people there. She could almost see them now, black masks with wide eyes and no mouths at all, ears shaped to cup the sound. Maybe she had let them slip from her mind, just as the singing woman had let the nameless street slip from hers.

Up ahead, the children scattered in near silence. The courier quickly lost sight of them; she couldn't tell whether they had stepped into deeper shadow, onto other nameless streets, or out into the named parts of town. But she understood now how the Black Square's notices might appear wrapped around loaves of bread, inside people's shoes and under their hats, or folded in among names committee broadsheets.

In the light of the nearly full moon, the nameless streets of Nod opened like a series of stage sets. Water dripped from a spout in an empty alley. An animal like her stowaway leapt from an unlighted place and onto a staircase of worn stone. A woman wearing a tall mask edged with curling blue tendrils sat near an open window, humming along to the wordless music from her phonograph. It all moved past her like a dream that would slip away if examined too closely.

Stone sculptures stood on most every street corner, but none were sculptures of people. The courier saw a deer, a tree, a turnip, a hand, a crescent moon. Between the statues and some buildings, as well as between the buildings themselves, the nameless had strung brightly colored cords of fabric. Six saw her looking and said quietly, "The masks aren't the only signs the nameless use to know one another. The sculptures and cords tell more about who they are and about the city itself."

These regions bordered on the named places she knew—Bird Street, Orchard Hill, the market—but they felt *below* rather than *beside*, an underground that was open to the sky. The map of the place grew stranger in her mind, until it started making a new kind of sense.

"How do you know these routes so well?" she asked Six.

For a moment he looked sullen and guarded. Then he said, "Before I was Black Square, I lived for years in places like these."

"Among the nameless?" she asked, failing to keep the surprise from her voice.

"I had a name," he said. "But when I was a boy, I got lost. And then I stayed that way for a long time."

She tried to picture Six as a child, among these masked people. He had been named among the nameless while she had gone nameless among the named. And now they walked the borders together, part of something that belonged to neither.

"You have more questions," Six said. He wasn't warding her off, but inviting her to speak.

"Did you wear a mask?" she asked.

"A few. Not many. Different masks at different times."

They walked on, skirting the named districts. The people there, in that other Nod, almost seemed to see them. A man squinted through a doorway with a naphtha lantern held aloft. Two tired-looking women, walking hand in hand by a culvert, stopped talking as Six and the courier passed, then resumed their quiet conversation a moment later.

The courier began to feel—not happy, but almost comfortable in her hiddenness. Then a patrol of watchers rounded the corner, and she froze.

As the bright beams from their crank-lights swept toward them, Six grabbed her hand and pulled her up a flight of stairs. A moment later they were ducking through the door of some ancient building which she knew appeared on no map of the named. The watchers did not follow, nor did the beams of their lights.

"With their ghost lenses, the watchers see better than most," Six said. "But they still miss most of everything."

The stone walls of the structure stood so high that the courier could barely make out the great vaulted ceiling above.

"What is this place?" she asked.

"I don't know," Six said. "It was built before the Silence, but no one seems to know its purpose. Maybe stories were performed here."

Their footsteps echoed as they walked between rows of benches like the benches in train stations, though these were longer and looked even less comfortable. The courier tried to imagine people seated here. They would have faced all in the same direction. A meeting place of some kind. A place to gather, and maybe to think and speak with others, communicate something—something important, to judge by the grandness of the place. The tall, narrow windows sparkled with brightly colored glass, and the glass formed pictures, of robed men bearing books and weapons, surrounded by birds, by sheep.

"Are there other structures like this?" she asked.

"A few here in Nod, and more in the other old cities. The named have no word for these places, so they don't see them, leaving the nameless to use them as refuges and way stations."

The courier spotted movement toward the back of the great chamber. Three masked figures were seated around a fire that burned in a wide metal basin on the floor. With a start, she realized that she *knew* these masks—the dark blue triangles, the silver lines streaming down the cheeks like tears. They were the same masks worn by those she'd seen with the Gardener of Stones, first in Grit, and then in that empty lot at the ragged edge of Sap.

These nameless, too, had ghosts in their company. They were five in number, faded like print on old paper, though their eyes shone in the firelight.

The Six of Trees held up a handful of the notices and set them on the nearest bench. The masked people did not move or speak, yet the courier felt them acknowledge his offering. And then she felt them turn their minds to her—a whisper on the air, a shiver of recognition. *The dreaming child,* the others had called her, and these three knew her, too.

When Six waved for her to follow, she did not hesitate. She felt the nameless watching as they moved quickly into the dark at the back of the chamber. From there, she followed Six down a long corridor and out through a heavy door. Damp grass under her boots, then firm stone, and at last they were back in the Nod she knew.

"Who were those people?" she asked.

"The living ones, you mean." Six thought for a while, and she worried he might not answer. But finally he said, "There's no word for what they do, but they're something like the ghost wranglers. Or their opposite, maybe. They find ghosts, tend to them, and guide them to places of safety."

The courier thought back to the day before: the secret errand of the Gardener of Stones; the nameless with their weeping masks; a dozen ghosts in a weedy lot. Had they concluded their deal as planned, after she fled?

"Places of safety," the courier repeated. "Safety from the named, you mean."

"From the auctions and the factories," he said. "From the machines that use them for fuel."

She remembered the hum of Frost's flying machine, steady and low, a contented sound. How many ghosts had it consumed that night, so that Frost could present her with a word to deliver? How many more would it devour before the deletion committee stopped hunting her?

They delivered the few remaining notices on their way to the handcar. When she left the last squares of paper on a doorstep at the edge of town, Six nodded, clearly pleased with their night's work. She was pleased, too.

They dragged the handcar out of the underbrush. The sky was dark, but the air was already loud with the speech of birds. Six and the courier took their places and got the handcar moving. In spite of her exhaustion, it felt good to be working the mechanism again, making the wheels turn.

She wanted to ask Six whether he knew about the secret meetings the Gardener of Stones conducted with the nameless. About the ghosts and what he did with them. But to mention Stones might reignite Six's anger, and she didn't want him to close up again. So she risked a different line of inquiry instead. "You never told me why the Gardener of Trees would want to punish you," she said.

"No, I didn't," Six said, though he was smiling.

The strangeness of his voice didn't bother her so much anymore. Something about being out in the open air, maybe. Or maybe she was just getting used to it. "You're still working on the Story of Hand and Moon," she guessed.

"Yes," he said.

"He wants you to leave it alone. The story frightens him."

Six stopped smiling. "It frightens all the Gardeners. Even Leaves."

"Who prefers to be the most frightening thing around," the courier said.

They were almost halfway to the reservoir when the courier saw the sun beginning to rise. A small group of women—woodcutters, maybe hunters—

stopped to watch them pass. Then the women carried on, readjusting the sacks on their shoulders as they crossed the tracks and disappeared into the forest.

Dew shone on the meadows. The courier and Six were silent for a while. Then Six said, "That woman you asked me about. Ticket."

The courier nodded carefully.

"You worked together?" he said. "For the same committee, or—"

"She's my sister."

He took this in. "And the one back on the train?"

"An accident," the courier said, though the word felt cruel.

Six was quiet again. Thinking. The courier could hear the noise of the stream ahead. They would soon reach the bridge, then the train on the other side. This might be her last chance to get the truth from him, but she could only wait for him to speak.

Finally, he did. "Your sister came here, to the Black Square. But you already knew that."

"Yes," she said. "What I'm trying to understand is why she came here in the first place. She brought the woman who drew a card and became the Gardener of Shovels, but I don't think that's all. Ticket wanted something else."

Six hesitated. They were standing on a border, the courier knew, and she was asking him to cross it.

"She came looking for me," he said.

"For you? Why?"

"Because she wanted me to leave the show. She wanted me to work with her instead."

The courier thought of that place to which Book had dispatched her many letters. A sorting room, an in-between place inhabited only by ghosts. "What kind of work?" she asked.

"Scheming, making trouble," Six said. "I seemed useful to her, maybe because of my time among the nameless. Maybe for some other reason. She wouldn't tell me much, and I didn't trust her."

"Do you know where she went?"

"She wore the uniform of a sayer's clerk, so maybe she went back to Whisper. But I don't know. She wears that uniform like a costume. Underneath, she's something different."

"What is she?" the courier asked, though she was afraid of the answer.

"Something dangerous," Six said. "Something even more dangerous than you."

She'd stopped working the lever, was only resting her hands against it as it swung. Six stopped, too, and they let the handcar roll over the bridge and draw up alongside the train, where he pulled the brake.

The Leaves had waited up by the last crackling coals of the fire. They came to meet them, yawning and rubbing their hands, and helped load the handcar back through the open bay door. Their work done, they boarded without a word, and the courier and Six were alone again. He tried to slip away, but she followed him.

"Show me what you found," she said.

"What do you mean?"

"In the record keeper's sketches of old Whisper. You found something, didn't you?"

"It wouldn't mean anything to you," he said.

"I'm the Rider of the Black Square," she said.

"Are you?"

She hesitated, but only for a moment. "Yes."

Six ran a hand through his messy hair. "All right," he said. "Come with me."

They went aboard, and he led her to the record keeper's compartment. The ghost was elsewhere, off making new drawings, maybe. He would have wanted to sketch the reservoir, the bridge, the dam, the people dancing by the fire, the goats and chickens in the grass.

Six took several sketchbooks from the shelves and opened them on the desk. She saw familiar figures and places. Here was Hand, standing among the named of Whisper. Here were those who dug in the scrap heaps, watching, ready to recite what they saw. And here was Moon, returning to Whisper after those weeks in the wilds, clothes ragged, eyes ringed with dark circles.

"The drawings are new," Six said, his voice hushed. "But the story is old."

The courier touched the page. She could almost feel Moon's fury, Moon's grief. Had the patchwork ghost really been there that day? He would have been a gray thing in the ruins, not a person, not alive. But then Moon delivered *ghost*, and like all the other ghosts he became something else, something more.

"Moon returned," the courier said. "Moon found Hand. Moon divined and delivered a word for the weapon, and another for the thing the weapon made."

"That's how the story has always gone," Six agreed. "But first Moon had to find that weapon."

"Moon got it in the wilderness," she said. "A gift from the nameless."

"So the Black Square has always played it," Six said. "But look here." He pointed to the next drawing, and then to the next. His tired eyes had taken on a feverish shine.

The courier saw Moon, back in Whisper now. And she saw that it was here—not in the wilderness—that Moon received the weapon. Not a gift from the nameless, then, but from others. When she saw who had given Moon the weapon, she had to sit down.

She tried to imagine how it might play onstage. Two new scenes.

*Stories can change,* Smoke had told the Gardener of Stones in his compartment the night before. And these two scenes wouldn't just change the story. They would change everything the named understood about what they were and where they had come from. No wonder the Gardeners were afraid. They should all be afraid to play the story this way.

"The Gardener of Stones hid these from me," Six said. "He tried to keep me from writing the story."

"How did you find them?"

"I didn't. The ghost brought them back."

The courier smiled. Of course he did. And that gave her an idea. "Six, how long would it take you to write those new scenes?"

"I've already written them," he said.

"Then make sure you have enough copies for each player who would need one."

"Stones will never agree to stage it," he said. "None of them will."

"I wonder," the courier said.

"If you're thinking about helping me because you think I'll help you find your sister—"

"Maybe I just want to see the Story of Hand and Moon," she said. "I missed the ending last time."

Six shook his head, but she could tell he was trying not to smile. He returned the sketchbooks to the shelves. "It's late," he said.

Through the compartment's one small window, the courier could see the pale pink light of the morning sun on the reservoir. "You're wrong," she said. "It's early."

She left him there in the ghost's compartment and went down the train alone. Two days before the sayers would gather in Whisper to speak law. She knew that Frost would make good on his threat to unspeak the Black Square if they failed to turn her over for deletion. Her satchel was still packed. Most everyone was asleep. She could leave right now, and hours would pass before the other players would notice her absence.

But maybe she didn't have to run. She had a plan now, or the beginnings of one. Was this what it felt like, she wondered—shabby and delirious, grinning under a newly risen sun—to be the Rider of the Black Square, getting ready to make trouble?

Here was the Rider's car, and here was her sleeping monster, half on the bed and half off. Her stowaway lay curled atop the stove, licking his wounded paws. He permitted her to pet him, and she heard his happy rumbling. Good, he was healing. The stove was still warm, though the fire inside had gone out. Two must have lit the fire herself this time.

*Herself.* The courier really had started thinking of her monster this way.

She got into bed and claimed part of the blanket. *Sleep,* that old border word—she needed to wrap it tightly about herself tonight. But sleep did not come easily, and when it did, it was like the nameless streets of Nod, a maze that grew larger the deeper she went. She saw a dozen versions of her sister, each a little different, each a little wrong. Some Tickets wore masks, some stood on porches smoking pipes, some walked hand in hand with other, still stranger sisters.

The courier didn't chase them. She was afraid she would choose the wrong one again—or worse, that one of those Tickets would choose *her,* and lead her down to the place where monsters came from.

She woke late. Her monster was gone, and the train was on the move. She refreshed herself in the compartment with the copper tubs. She was still there when the train stopped again. The Black Square had completed its brief journey into Nod.

On her way back to her car, the courier realized that the train was silent. No one cooking or eating in the kitchen. No Shovels in the workshop car, no Trees at their typing machines, no Stones practicing lines. She didn't even see any Leaves in their suits of black and dark gray, and the Leaves were usually everywhere, keeping an eye on everything.

She was passing between two cars when her monster emerged from the opposite door and grabbed her arm. "Oh!" the monster said, and began to pull her back the way she'd come.

"Two, I am not working with you today," the courier said. "I have too much to do."

But Two shook her head, eyes wide. "Oh, oh, oh!" she said.

Two didn't want her in the workshop car, then. There was something else, something that might explain where everyone had gone. She let the monster lead her up through the train. The sun was setting now. They saw no one else until they came to the costume car. Everyone was here, every Stone, Tree, Leaf, and Shovel, the players all changing into costumes and painting one another's faces.

Through the crowd, Seven spotted the courier and pushed her way closer. "You have to get ready," she said.

"For what?"

"You're performing tonight."

"I am not," the courier said.

"We're playing the Story of the Something Tree," Seven said. "When we play the Something Tree, everyone performs."

The courier turned to Two, but the monster had already left them to help one of the other Shovels.

"I don't have a costume," the courier said, looking down at her wrinkled boilersuit.

"You're fine," Seven said.

"I haven't even seen a script."

"Here." Seven grabbed a stack of bound pages from a nearby shelf and thrust it into the courier's hands.

She barely understood what she saw. The script read like instructions for some complicated dance, or like a poem from the nameless districts of Hollow. "Who am I playing?" she asked.

Seven sighed and took the pages back. "It doesn't matter," she said. "Nobody really knows what they're doing until they get out there."

The courier saw the Six of Trees at the other end of the car. He gave her a helpless smile. Then someone near the door shouted something, and the players started moving toward the stage car.

The crowd swept them into the next car and out onto the stage. The roof and door were already open, and the people of Nod, drawn in by the notices she and Six had delivered, had gathered outside. The stage was dark, but the courier could still see the tree that stood at its center. She gasped.

Unlike the tree of wood and paper she'd helped the Shovels build, this one was made of glass, with a skeleton of iron beams. It rose three, maybe four stories into the air. Hanging from its branches were large glass globes. Despite its size, the tree appeared fragile, like something made to break.

"How—" she said, but Seven was no longer at her side.

The Scout of Stones turned on the light machine, and the tree glowed, a great gnarled crystal. The show had already begun. The players slowly circled the base of the tree. Music rose up, a slow pulsing that seemed to come from the tree itself, and the players matched their motions to the rhythm.

With gesture and movement, the players began to perform the lives of the people from before the Silence. It really was like a dance. The courier tried to find a place among them, but her own body was stiff and uncertain. She kept walking. She tried to remember how pretend had made her feel as a child. She thought of sweat and bug bites, of running with her ghost over the fields, roaring until her throat hurt, then roaring some more. Later, she couldn't have said when it happened, but she soon lost herself in the light of the something tree.

Whole lives played out beneath its branches. Children grew while people traded, fought, embraced, fell. The Children grew older and kissed in the bowers. They grew older still. Some went to sleep among the tree's roots and stayed sleeping. No ghosts grew from their bodies, no monsters from their dreams, but somehow more and more people seemed to fill the stage, turning around that great trunk, and their shadows filled the world.

A brighter light leapt among the branches, then moved from person to person, shifting in color as it swam through the air. Some people tried to climb the tree, reaching as though to grasp the light. Some spun away and hid. A few stood apart from the rest, and there was something strange about these few, something hungry and cruel. When the light came to them, they caught it in their hands and examined it through a pane of glass. The courier thought they might have been the ones who planted the something tree, but if so, they had forgotten how to tend it. While they examined the light, the tree creaked and flickered, sickening.

The music grew loud and strange, like the noise of a machine whose gears have come loose. The light slowed, jerked, flew again. It returned to the tree and divided, clumping like overripe fruit. The people gazed up with mouths open as though to scream, but they made no sound. They stayed that way for a long time. And then something—the light, the fruit—fell from the something tree, and the people fell, too.

One of the glass globes struck the ground and shattered.

At the party after the show, the courier couldn't remember which role she'd played. Had she climbed the something tree, or hidden from its light, or had she examined its light through the glass? She felt she had been all those people and others besides, and also that she'd been the light itself, falling, breaking, going out into nothing and taking every word with it.

"I don't understand how it worked," she said to Seven.

"Neither do I," Seven said. Then, as though to explain, she kissed the courier's face, close to her ear.

The players had gathered in the car of monsters. Lanterns swayed from hooks in the ceiling, and a fire glowed in a little stove. The courier and Seven were seated among the fabric roots of one of the tall, tree-like monsters that stretched from one end of the car to the other.

The courier closed her eyes and breathed, still feeling Seven's kiss just above her jawline.

"We all wrestle with pieces of our stories from before, especially at first," Seven said. "There was someone you spent time with, probably."

"I spent time with a lot of people."

"Oh, of course," Seven said, nudging her and grinning. "But I think there was one in particular."

"Yes," the courier admitted. "But she didn't trust me. And then I had to leave."

"Well, I don't trust you either," Seven said, but she made it sound as though that were a good thing. She leaned against the courier, and the courier descended with her into the silky roots. The threadbare costumes and creaky props had appeared menacing when she'd come through this place alone, in the dark. But in the warm light of the lanterns, the monsters were more like old friends. Even the one that was nothing but a great pile of arms and hands; some players leaned against it as though into an expansive hug.

"Someone needs to repair these monsters," the courier said.

"Not enough Shovels to keep them up," Seven said. "We used to bring them out for battle scenes. Not onstage—they never would have fit. Back then the Black Square performed in fields sometimes. Or in parks and city squares."

The courier tried to picture one of these great beasts lumbering across the meadow outside Jawbone. What if someone had stumbled upon a performance without knowing? They would have been terrified.

Seven nestled more closely against her. The other players drank and smoked their pipes of draff, but there was something subdued about their movements, their speech, even their laughter.

"Everyone is so quiet," the courier said.

"Always quiet after the Something Tree," Seven said. "We can only play that story a few more times."

"Why?"

"The glass fruit. The *somethings*. We have to break one at the end of each performance, and there aren't many left."

The courier could still hear that terrible crash, as well as the completeness of the silence that followed. After, she and Two and a few of the Shovels had helped the Leaves sweep glittering shards from the stage.

"Can't you make replacements?" the courier asked, thinking of that disused furnace in the workshop car.

"Not anymore," she said, sounding bored. The courier knew Seven well enough now to know what that meant. There was something she didn't want to talk about. Something that wasn't boring at all.

"You really don't trust me," the courier said.

Seven got up. "Another round," she said, and she headed off toward the bunk where they kept the bottles of spirits.

The courier took a deep breath. The performance had tired her, drained her of everything but a feeling of warmth for the other players of the Black Square. Her monster was playing cards with the Shovels. The Six of Trees was seated with one of the younger Leaves, showing her how to change the ribbon on a typing machine. The courier closed her eyes, sleepy now, and almost happy—but wasn't something still troubling her? Wasn't something missing?

She sat up with a gasp. An hour since the show had ended, but the train still wasn't moving, and none of the Gardeners were here. Not even Leaves— and the Gardener of Leaves loved parties.

Seven was standing over her, a cup in each hand. The courier got to her feet. "I have to go," she said.

"Do you always leave parties early?"

"Yes, it's just something I do. Where is the compartment of the Gardener of Stones?"

"I don't know. I've never been there."

The courier had been there, once, but only because her stowaway knew how to find it. And she needed to go alone this time. She looked back and forth between the two doors.

"He's up the train," Seven said. "That much I know. What do you want with him?"

"It's like you said the other day," the courier told her. "I'm going to make things more interesting."

"About time," Seven said. And she poured the spirits from the courier's cup into her own.


Walking alone, the courier remembered how it had felt to move with her stowaway through the hidden places. Above, below, and in between. She tried not to fight the train, let it lead instead. She lost track of how many cars she'd passed through—at least a dozen more than she'd thought were part of the train.

And then, in a car of crooked corridors, among doors of different sizes, she heard voices she recognized. She followed the voices to a tall door with flaking gray paint and light shining beneath. She heard a muffled thump, a faint crackling. When she opened the door, all four Gardeners looked up at her.

The Gardener of Stones had just added more wood to the fire in his stove. Juniper, the Gardener of Shovels, was seated at the table with a mug of tea in her hands. Trees stood off to one side, leaning against a bookcase, his beard worried into an unkempt cloud. Leaves was a cold starry shadow in a rocking chair, her purple shawl pulled tightly over her shoulders.

The patchwork ghost was here, too. He sat by the window at the back of the compartment, sketching the scene in his sketchbook. Good, the courier thought. Let him document what she was about to do. Let this be part of the story, whatever happens.

It was the courier who had found this place. But it was the Rider of the Black Square Show who stepped inside, closed the door behind her, and said, "I'm glad you're all still here."

The Gardener of Stones stood. "You weren't invited to this meeting," he said.

"Yet here I am," she said. "Have you come to a decision? About when to turn me over, and where?"

Stones grimaced. "You don't know what you're talking about," he said.

"Stones," said the Gardener of Trees, still tugging his beard, "there's no need to insult her."

The Gardeners were silent, none of them looking at one another. Then Leaves let out a cold sigh which the Rider could feel from across the room. "In fact," Leaves said, "some of us were just saying that we should give you advance warning. Let you get a head start. Some of us were saying that Frost might leave the Black Square alone if he thought you only slipped away in the night."

The Gardener of Shovels looked down at her tea. Juniper had told her that she liked being the Gardener of Shovels, that she wouldn't let the courier take this from her. And for that, the Rider already forgave her.

"I don't think Frost is so kind," she said. "He'll blame the Black Square if I escape, even if I do escape on my own. Which is why the Gardener of Trees prevented me from leaving yesterday."

Trees flinched. "I didn't want you to leave," he said. "But not just because of Frost. I also thought you and Six might find a way to help each other."

"And we might yet," the Rider said. She sat at the table and poured herself a mug of tea from the pot. "In fact, he's already given me an idea."

"Your first, my little corn cob?" Leaves asked.

Ignoring the monster, she said, "You can't let me slip away, but you don't have to turn me over for deletion, either. There is a third option. You can do something Frost will never anticipate."

The monster's lights sharpened with suspicion, but Juniper looked up, curious, and the Gardener of Trees stopped worrying his beard. For a moment, the only sound in the compartment was the scratching of the patchwork ghost's pencil.

Stones crossed his arms over his chest. "Well?" he said.

"The plan is simple," she said. "We play the Story of Hand and Moon. Play it as the Six of Trees has written it, with the new material from the record keeper."

Stones was already shaking his head. "That will only enrage Frost."

"So you've read it," the Rider said.

"We all have," Trees said. "And Stones is right. Performing it won't help us. It won't help you, either."

"But it will reveal to the named who the sayers really are, and what they did to take power."

"It will also lose us any allies we have left among the sayers," Stones said. "It is our duty to preserve the Black Square, not to run it off the rails."

"Even if you give him what he wants," the Rider said, "Frost will destroy the Black Square in time. I'm just his convenient excuse. Next time he won't bother with one."

"She's right about that," Trees said. "The Black Square is the broken door on the border. On every border. If Frost wants it closed, he will find a way."

The courier watched Stones carefully. If he was thinking about his arrangement with the nameless, he did not let it show. "Even if we defy Frost," he said, "law remains law. If we don't find a way to appease him, the sayers will speak the Black Square out of existence. They're already gathering for the next recitation."

"Yes," the Rider said. "Tomorrow night. In Whisper."

Stones and Trees both frowned. But Juniper understood her meaning. "Your plan isn't to perform the Whisper Story out here on the border," she said. "You want to perform it in Whisper."

The Rider held her mug tightly, to keep her hands from shaking. She needed to seem more sure about this than she felt. "Most of the named will already be there for the recitation," she said. "But if they see the Black Square arrive in the city, in defiance of law, they won't go to the saying stone. They'll come to us instead."

The room grew cooler as the Gardener of Leaves leaned forward in her rocking chair, lights gently crackling. "You won't save yourself this way," she said.

"I won't," the Rider said. "And this won't prevent the sayers from unmaking the show. But it might give the Black Square a chance."

"A chance?" said the Gardener of Stones, his voice hard. "A chance for what?"

The courier looked to the patchwork ghost. He had stopped sketching and was watching her now. To him as much as to the others, she said, "A chance to become something else. Something beyond the laws of the sayers. Beyond their control."

The Gardener of Leaves tilted her great blocky head, her eyes two piercing points of light. The monster looked thoughtful, but the Rider had no idea what she could be thinking.

Trees drew close, towering over her, his face grim behind his beard. Would he be the first to vote against her? Tell her to go, to leave the compartment, leave the train while she still could?

"I'm with the Rider," he said, turning to stand beside her. "We should move against the sayers before they move against us."

Juniper set one hand, callused and still grimy from the day's work, flat on the table. "No more running," she agreed. "No more hiding on the border."

The Gardener of Stones shook his head, as though he couldn't believe what he'd heard. "Leaves," he said, "you wanted to give her to Frost the very night she came aboard. Do you intend to give her our train now?"

The Gardener of Leaves tilted back in her rocking chair, and the darkness between her stars took on a warm, orange hue. "I think you had better tell everyone to start rehearsing," she said.

Stones nodded slowly. "Three votes, then, all in favor of the Rider's plan. It's decided: we play the Story of Hand and Moon once more, and we play it in Whisper. But before the Black Square rides against the sayers, in defiance of the sayers' laws, I have one request."

Shovels, mug in hand, turned in her chair to look at him. Trees sat on the table's edge and crossed his arms over his beard. The Rider's heart quickened. She had guessed that Stones would oppose her—but did he have some trick yet to play? The patchwork ghost, as though sensing a change in the air, resumed his sketching.

"My request is this," Stones said. "When we go onstage, risking everything to tell this story—maybe the Black Square's last—I want the Rider there with us under the naphtha lights. And since this is her idea, I believe a role of some significance would be fitting."

The Rider sat up straight. "I can't," she said. "I don't know how."

"How to pretend?" asked Leaves, rocking forward. "Oh, my sweet little apple, I think you do."

"She would make a fine Moon," the Gardener of Stones observed.

Trees looked at her and tugged at his beard. "Yes," he said. "Yes, I can see it."

"Moon," Leaves agreed, her stars sparking with plain delight.

The courier looked to Juniper, hoping she might say something to change their minds. But the old woman only drank down the last of her tea and said, "You have a big day tomorrow, Rider. I think you'd better get some rest."

As though to head off further discussion, the Gardener of Leaves departed quickly, blowing from the room on a cold wind. Trees followed her, looking content, hands thrust into the pockets of his boilersuit. The Gardener of Shovels rose, thanked Stones for the tea, and patted the Rider's shoulder on her way out.

But the woman at the table was no longer the Rider. Whatever courage or foolishness or fever had driven her to haul this plan before the Gardeners was gone. All the courier felt now was a creeping cold, and the certainty that she was very far from home.

"Why?" she asked the Gardener of Stones.

He did not answer, only knelt to stoke the fire. In that flickering light, he looked strange to her, like someone she had never seen before. He was still an old man in loose-fitting brown clothes, but for a moment she thought she glimpsed something older in his eyes, something that was only playing the role of Gray, former sayer of the named, now director of the Black Square Show. When he stood to collect the empty mugs from the table, he was a man again—the man who had just ensnared her in her own trap.

"Why?" she said again. "Why Moon, after what happened the last time a Rider played that part? Do you want to frighten the other players? Turn them all against me?"

The Gardener sighed as he tucked the mugs into a basin on the shelf. Then he put on his heavy blue coat, took a lantern down from a peg, and left the compartment without a word.

The courier stood and went after him. "Where—"

But he'd already started up through the car, quickly rounding the next bend in that twisting corridor. She chased after him, keeping him just in sight through a dozen sharp turns. "Slow down!" she shouted.

She was aware of the patchwork ghost following close behind. She knew that this much corridor should not have fit in a single train car. And already she felt the train moving again, which meant that the Gardener of Trees had found his way back to the engine, had done everything required to spur its machinery into motion.

The maze of corridors stretched in all directions, and time stretched with it. For every ten steps she took, she seemed to advance only one or two, as though the train were leaving her behind as it picked up speed.

The Gardener of Stones was putting more distance between them. "Keep up with me, Rider!" he called. "Keep up if you want to see!"

What she wanted was to grab his coat and shake him. His lantern winked away as he rounded the next bend. She ran harder, but the light gradually faded, and soon she was running in the dark. The Gardener of Stones was gone, the patchwork ghost was gone. She tumbled forward into nothing, a bottomless dark that was colder and more distant from the named world than even the starry expanse of the Gardener of Leaves.

Until finally a door rose up before her. She hurled herself forward, slamming it open—and stumbled out onto the walkway between the cars, nearly colliding with the Gardener of Stones. The patchwork ghost appeared a moment later and shut the door behind them.

The courier leaned against the ghost as she gasped for air. The Gardener of Stones wasn't even out of breath. Raising his voice to be heard over the noise of the engine, he said, "The train keeps this car well hidden. Sometimes not even I am permitted to find it."

He opened the door and led them inside. No corridors here, no compartments, just a wide-open space. Instead of benches, the car was furnished with dozens of cushioned chairs and low-slung couches. Heavy rugs covered the floor, and hung on the walls were paintings of scenes from the old stories: the dreams committee hunter Yarrow, lying wounded in a bower. Moon in exile, making glyphs to record words on paper.

The car was dark, lit only by the moonlight from the windows and the lantern carried by the Gardener of Stones. Yet it was crowded with people, dozens of them. Some sat and dozed while others gathered at the windows to watch the fields and hills of the borderlands gliding past. On one couch, an old woman braided a child's hair. Others danced, played cards, worked on puzzles. Some leaned against one another, some sat alone and stared at nothing in particular. A great many looked up when the courier came in.

Not one of them was alive.


"I know you witnessed my meeting in Sap," the Gardener of Stones said. "Now I want you to see everything, so you understand just how much we risk by returning to Whisper."

Some of the ghosts she recognized from that empty lot, some from the great stone building in Nod. They and the others soon returned to what they'd been doing. Swaying to music only they could hear, fussing with scraps of paper and thread, pacing, studying the pictures on the walls.

"I don't understand," the courier said. "Do you *collect* them?"

"Only long enough to transport them elsewhere."

She walked deeper into the car, and the Gardener followed with his lantern, shining it so she could see. Some of the ghosts might never have been calibrated, so strange were their habits. Others—those who kept perfectly still or only fidgeted—must have been taken from factories, from farms and mines.

"You're smuggling them," the courier said. "Aiding the nameless in their efforts to weaken the named."

"As the named expand their territory, some of the old routes are lost to the nameless," the Gardener said. "For years now, the Black Square has helped fill in the gaps."

The courier thought again of the word Frost had given her. Could she deliver it now, to the Gardener of Stones? He was not the one Frost and Smoke searched for. Only someone aboard the Number Twelve could have told the nameless when to launch their attack at Buckle Station. But the Gardener of

Stones had been a sayer named Gray, and now he smuggled ghosts for the nameless.

The patchwork ghost found a seat among the others and began sketching.

"Where do you take them?" the courier asked.

"To the eastern border, where others who wear the weeping masks will retrieve them and bear them onward, deeper into the nameless territories."

"All to keep them from the named."

The Gardener stopped walking. He looked tired in the pale light from his lantern. "Even with so many gathered here, our work amounts to little. But each ghost we carry over the ghost roads—for that is what we call these hidden ways—is one less for the calibrationists. One less for the furnaces of the machines."

"Like the war machines which Frost plans to send against the last city of the nameless," she said.

The Gardener's eyes went wide with surprise. Then he seemed to understand. "The animal in my compartment that night. It attacked my visitor, its rage almost human." His smile was a mix of wonder and admiration.

The courier drew herself into the light from his lantern. She was aware of the patchwork ghost's gaze, of the hurried scratching of his pencil.

"How many aboard the train know about this?" she said.

"Everyone who would want to know. Everyone, I think, who has tried to find out."

"The other Gardeners?"

"Yes, though Shovels pretends not to notice."

"What about Six?"

Stones looked wary. "The Six of Trees understands the nameless better than anyone aboard this train. He helps make the arrangements."

Her laughter made some of the ghosts turn their heads. "But isn't this the real reason why you vote against his wishes?" she said. "Isn't this what you're protecting when you keep his stories from the stage?"

"I have only ever failed to keep his stories from the stage."

"To protect yourself, then. The namer Gray, still afraid of what Frost might do."

"Afraid, yes," he admitted. "But not for myself. Not for the name I once bore. I have lived many lives, many stories. And when I'm finished here, I'll live others still."

She thought he was talking about the stories performed by the Black Square. Or about his previous life as a sayer of the named. But in the flickering light of the lantern she caught again that *something* in his eyes—something not just old but ancient and terrible—and she wondered.

The Gardener of Stones dropped the lantern to his side; they stood in its light, but his face was in shadow. "No," he said quietly, "the only one I protect by voting against the Six of Trees is the Six of Trees himself."

Many of the ghosts were watching, their eyes like burning coals in the darkness. The courier wanted to get out of there, to run as far from this place as the train would allow. But from the sound of the patchwork ghost's pencil she drew courage enough to say, "Six is something like a son to you, and you a father to him. And it's hard to know when to let a child walk their own road."

Even in the half darkness she could see the bitterness of the Gardener's smile. "There's much you still don't understand," he said. "Six is more important than even he realizes. Did you know it was Book himself who brought him to the Black Square?"

"Book? But why?"

"I don't know the whole story. And besides, Six's story is not mine to tell. Nor is it his, as you well know. For a little while yet, we are still Black Square."

The courier thought of what Six had told her about his time among the nameless. Had Book discovered him somewhere on the border? He must have decided the Black Square was the safest place for him, just as he'd done for Juniper.

The Gardener of Stones raised his lantern and returned to the door. The courier followed. To her relief, she saw that the patchwork ghost followed, too. She would not like for him to remain here among the others, in this car the train kept so well hidden.

The walk from the Gardener's compartment to the car had been difficult, every step a struggle against the train's strange will. Going back took only minutes.

Before he left her, the Gardener said, "Shovels was correct, Rider. You had better get some rest."

The patchwork ghost went with her to her compartment, and her stowaway was waiting for them. The animal sat in the ghost's lap by the fire, and for once the courier had plenty of room in the bed. Her monster must have decided to sleep elsewhere—with the other Shovels, maybe.

Yet the courier slept fitfully, jolting awake every time the train rumbled over a rough patch of rail. She thought of those ghosts, the Black Square's secret cargo. She thought of slipping into Moon's silver robe. She felt she was being dragged through the wilderness by a cruel beast, down into a devouring darkness.

She woke alone at sunrise, choking on draff. She coughed the whole time as she swept the scraps of bad dreaming out the back door. Her head hurt and her bones ached. She was thirsty and cold.

She went unsteadily up through the train, wondering where her monster was, where the stowaway had gone. The players she passed avoided looking at her. The train was moving fast. In the kitchen, dishes rattled in the cupboards.

Seven found her there. "They're saying we'll reach Whisper before sundown," she said. "No time to distribute notices."

"No need," the courier said. "They'll see us coming."

"So this was your plan. To aim the whole show straight at the sayers."

"Isn't this what you wanted? To play the big cities again?"

Seven looked at the floor. "I did want this," she said. "Only now—"

"Now you wish I'd left the Black Square instead."

"I'm a little scared, that's all." She looked up, gave the courier an uncertain smile. "But it's been too long since I've felt *anything* before a show."

They went together to the stage car, where a cold wind was blowing through the gaps around the big doors. The tall car swayed, but Seven's stride was steady as she walked out onto the stage, turning pages of the script. The courier remembered the first time she'd seen Seven, beautiful onstage in the role of Moon. Dangerous and electric. She was still those things, but she also looked smaller, sad and uncertain.

"I didn't ask for this part," the courier said. "You know that, don't you?"

"You think I'm jealous? Don't worry, Rider. I have a different role to play tonight. And you'll make an excellent Moon." She tapped one page of the script. "We'll start with the new scenes."

"I barely know the old ones."

"Right," Seven said. "From the top, then."

She pretended to be Hand while the courier spoke the words written for Moon. They practiced the first lines, and once the courier could recite them without looking, Seven sent her from the stage and told her to return as Moon.

Alone in the dark at the edge of the stage, the courier spoke the words quietly to herself. *Three more. At sundown breathing, in the morning gone.* Then she took a breath and entered. She hurried toward Seven—toward Hand, through the streets of old Whisper—but the car swayed as the train rounded a bend. She tripped and fell at Seven's feet.

Seven helped her up. "The stage won't be moving tonight," she said.

More players arrived while they practiced. The others kept their distance, gathered in small groups to rehearse lines of their own. Some watched the courier's performance and whispered.

"Ignore them," Seven said.

But their presence was worse than an audience of strangers. Again and again, the courier failed to speak her first lines. As a member of the names committee, she had delivered hundreds of words. Now a handful of the oldest words known to the named eluded her. She felt foolish. Beyond helping.

The Gardener of Stones strode out under the lights. He clapped his hands and called for attention, and the Stones gathered around him. Others stood at the edge of the stage, most of the Leaves and Trees, and some of the Shovels as well. The courier's monster was there, her eyes huge in the dim light. The record keeper sat on a barrel with a sketchbook open in his lap.

It was time for a different kind of scene. Part of the show that the Black Square put on for itself. Here, too, the courier knew she was expected to play her part.

"Today we return to Whisper," the Gardener of Stones said. "And tonight we return to *old* Whisper. The last time we played the Story of Hand and Moon, the show was interrupted before we could finish. As for the time before that, you all know how it ended. Some of you were there."

A few of the older players glanced at the Scout of Stones, who was crouched over his light machine, adjusting lenses. The ghost showed no interest in what the Gardener was saying.

"This time, who knows?" he went on. "Maybe we'll finish the show *and* succumb to disaster. Or maybe the sayers will applaud us. Maybe they'll change law in our favor, declare that everyone must throw flowers at our feet and bake us cakes every time we perform."

Some of the players chuckled, and the courier allowed herself a grin. But when the laughter subsided, the Gardener of Stones was facing her. "Rider, do you have anything to say before we begin rehearsing for what might be the final performance of the Black Square?"

Her cue. The players looked tired, curious, frightened. A few, she thought, even seemed hopeful. She tried to think of something encouraging to say, something to make them brave. Then she remembered what Seven had told her about the Black Square's peculiar customs.

"I hope we all break our limbs out there," the courier said.

The players looked startled. Someone at the edge of the stage snorted. Seven caught the courier's eye and shook her head sharply.

The courier cleared her throat. "What I mean is this," she said. "Tonight we tell one of the oldest stories we have, but we tell it new. Whatever our audience thinks of it, the exile of the Black Square will end, and not because of anything the sayers say. It will end because we're ending it ourselves."

No one spoke. Most of them weren't pretending not to be scared, the way Seven was. She hadn't moved them, but she couldn't think of anything else to say. She was scared, too.

The Gardener of Stones grunted. "Some of you already have your parts," he said. "The Rider herself will play Moon. I won't be performing; tonight I will need to serve as director, and not from onstage. So whoever wishes to take the part of Hand, please step forward."

No one moved. The players looked uneasy. Most stared at the floor. The courier looked at Seven, but Seven whispered, "Already told you, I have a different role to play tonight."

Stones turned in place. "Will no one stand as first of the named?"

It was as the courier had feared. When the previous Rider played Moon, he had murdered the Scout of Stones. Why would anyone want to take his place?

"Well," said the Gardener of Stones, looking helpless, "I cannot force anyone to take a part—"

"I'll do it," someone called from the edge of the stage. Everyone turned to look as the Six of Trees stepped forward into the light. He seemed surprised that he'd spoken, but he said, "I'll play Hand."

The Gardener of Stones frowned. "Six, you've never played anyone but ghosts and the silent nameless."

"I can play Hand," he said, though his voice wavered. "I know every word."

The other Stones coughed and shifted on their feet. The courier could guess what they were thinking, because she was thinking it too. How could he speak as the first of the named with his voice, which made words slosh like water from a bucket?

"Writing a story is different from playing it," said the Gardener of Stones. "Six, it won't work."

Six stepped back, his eyes bright with anger as he shrank into his crooked suit.

"Wait," the courier said. "The only story I've performed before today is the Something Tree. If I can play Moon, then surely someone who's been Black Square for most of his life can play Hand."

Stones gave her a furious look. He had told her last night that he voted against Six because he wanted to protect him, and now she pushed for him to appear onstage. Not just as a character in the background, but as Hand, the first namer. Everyone would see him. Everyone would *hear him*. If he floundered or even slipped—

"The Rider is right," Seven said. "We should give him a chance."

Everyone was quiet. The Gardener of Stones was still staring at the courier. *But you have to,* she thought. *You have to let him try, or he'll just go on hating you.*

Finally Stones smiled, his blue eyes bright in the naphtha lights. "Six," he said, "the stage is yours. Let's hear some of those words you know so well."

He left to join the Scout of Stones by the light machine. The other Stones quickly cleared the stage. The courier went to stand beside her monster. Two took her arm and pulled her close as Six stepped out under the lights.

He walked to the center of the stage and faced the closed door, looking lost in that big empty car. He must have seen, as the courier did, that the Gardener of Stones wasn't watching. Instead, he spoke quietly with the ghost about the machine, about lenses, about the brightness of the lights.

Six's lips moved as he recited lines to himself. Then he shook his head and said to no one, "Sorry, sorry," his words barely audible over the noise of the train.

The other players began to whisper. The courier squeezed Two's hand. What had she done? Six was unable to speak. And even if he could speak, the words would come out wrong.

The courier left her monster to stride out onto the stage. She doubted everything. This plan, the show, Six, herself. And with that doubt came the anger she'd felt on her first night aboard the train, when Six had wanted to turn her over to Frost. She summoned all that anger and fear into her body, focused it on Six. He flinched as she drew near.

"Three more," she said to him. The words did not come easily, but it was Moon who spoke them, voice breaking on grief and rage. "At sundown breathing. In the morning gone."

The Gardener of Stones looked up, and the other players were silent. The courier moved even closer to Six, forcing him to face her.

Finally he spoke. "Three?" he asked. His voice was still his own, quiet, fraying under the weight of just one word. For a moment, the courier thought he would stop. Then he swallowed and said more firmly, "Moon, speak the names."

As Moon, she told him the names of those taken by the nameless thing, Sap and Root and Needle. Six's uncertainty steadied her. She would carry them both if she had to. When Six spoke again, his words still teetered, only now he sounded like someone putting new words in a new order, worrying over each even as he gave them breath.

"The one named Needle might have grown thirsty in the night," he said. "Needle knew the way in the dark, knew to go with cup in hand to the well—"

When the Gardener of Stones had played Hand, he had been loud, commanding, unwavering. Six was none of these things. He doubted, he hesitated, he faltered. His Hand didn't want to believe the story his words told. His Hand was trapped and afraid, and the words only made it worse. He was a different Hand, and maybe a truer one.

The other players began to join the courier and Six onstage, taking up their own roles. The Gardener of Stones watched in silence as the Leaves wheeled out the scrap piles, and the scavengers climbed the piles to recite their lines.

*Hand holds Moon. Moon holds Hand. Sap gone, Root gone, and Needle gone, too.*

As the scene went on, Six's voice seemed always about to break, and that made it impossible to ignore. The courier tried not to think about what was happening. She was Moon, whose anger at Hand was her anger at Six, at the Gardener of Stones. At Frost. At her father for the words he would never say, at her sister for leaving her alone with him.

"I will go and find those who made the bad thing," Moon declared. "I will find them, and I will name what they made."

They had nearly reached the end of the scene when one of them spoke a line too soon or the other was late, and the words fell into a jumble. But by then it didn't matter. The players were laughing, amazed. Those who had watched from the edge of the stage began to applaud. The Two of Shovels, swaying on her long legs, wheezed and hooted.

The players were still smiling as they turned to the Gardener of Stones and waited for him to say something. Even the ghost of the Scout of Stones was waiting, watching the stage and the Gardener instead of his machine. Stones ran one hand over his short gray hair. He was beaten, but he looked pleased to have been beaten. "Well, you'd better keep going," he said.

They kept going. They rehearsed that first scene twice more. It wasn't perfect, but on the third try they made it through. The Leaves brought more pieces of the set while the Shovels made repairs, oiled wheels, touched up paint.

They kept going, and things went wrong. Lines forgotten, words spoken out of order, terrible silences. The courier felt she was crossing a narrow bridge above a deep ravine. She was offstage and then on again, trading old Whisper for the costume car, for the forest within a city, for the city beyond the forest. Between scenes, she read and reread her lines. Seven was often close, helping her without saying anything about her performance. Another Black Square custom—the courier saw the sense of it now. She didn't want to know what Seven was thinking.

"What about your own lines?" the courier asked her. "Don't you need to practice?"

"I'll figure them out when the time comes," Seven said.

The engine heaved toward Whisper. The courier and the Six of Trees avoided speaking except as Moon and Hand. Whatever was making this work, they knew better than to discuss it.

The Gardener of Stones pushed them on to the next scene, and then the next—often too soon, the courier thought. She wanted to fix the problems first. There were a lot of them.

Sensing her frustration, Stones took her aside. "It's better to leave it a little rough," he said. "You want to save the perfect performance for when you have an audience."

His voice was gentle. His eyes shone as they did before every show, and maybe more brightly than usual. He had tried to stop Six's story, and now Six was onstage, performing that story. Now they would all have to keep going even if the stage caught fire.

"All right," the courier said, "I trust you," and that seemed to surprise him more than anything.


She didn't know how many hours had passed while they rehearsed, or where they were on the line. But when she felt the train slow, she knew they must have reached the outskirts of the city. The Gardener of Trees sounded the whistle, its three-part voice bright and sharp and a little out of tune. Rehearsal ended suddenly. Stones had said to leave it rough, but it felt too rough, its edges like the pieces of an unfinished puzzle.

From a window in the green car, the courier saw the gleam of Whisper's towers on the horizon. She spotted carriages on the roads. The named were going to Whisper for the recitation of law. They brought goods for market: root vegetables and bottles of wine, jars of honey and jars of pickles. People recognized the train, called to one another, pointed. Lone riders went ahead, probably to spread the news. The delays on the line would let the riders far outpace the engine. Soon everyone would know the show was coming. The sayers would know. Frost would know.

They rode the rails straight into the city. Messenger ghosts moved from door to door, scattering pigeons. On narrow streets, sayers walked in the company of their speakers or rode on sedan chairs borne by ghosts. They scowled at the train, saying nothing.

Among the ancient towers of stone and glass stood smaller buildings of brighter colors. The city was a jumble of past and present, paved with names to every corner. The courier half expected soldiers to come with blockades, but no one tried to stop them.

How many times had the courier walked these streets, first as a page bearing stacks of broadsheets, then as a courier with new words in her satchel? In Whisper she had delivered *clatter, boast, gossip, breeze, shrug*. She saw no pages or couriers now, only members of the other standing committees, cartographers and surveyors of the maps committee, ghosts committee drovers and calibrationists, hunters smoking draff outside the dreams committee's gray quarters, hat brims low over their brows.

The Gardener of Trees signaled the switch ghosts, and the train veered away from Whisper Station and out toward the north end of the city. In fields beside the Other River, merchants and farmers displayed their wares in pavilions and market stalls. Some had come from the farthest cities of the named, and on the river were boats and barges bearing still more people, people who had come to trade, to watch and to listen. Only once each year did the sayers gather to speak law. The named wanted to hear, wanted to remember. They wanted to know how the world had changed.

To the west, the courier could see the ancient quarry, at the bottom of which stood the saying stone, bigger than a boxcar. Book had told her that the quarry magnified the voices of those who spoke from the base of the stone. There, whispering, Moon had delivered *whisper*, and Hand had heard from the very top of the pit.

Now naphtha lanterns were strung overhead, bright colors flashing in the breeze. Men and women stood in clusters on the terraced stone, speakers and ghosts, a few of the sayers come early. They turned to watch the train as it passed.

Another switch sent the train farther north on curving tracks among tall pines, then out over a ridge above another deep pit. This dig site was unconnected to the quarry of the saying stone, though it might once have served part of the same operation. It was deeper and more narrow, and also more wild, overgrown with bittersweet and barberry. Here on the western side, a stream cascaded over the ledge. The train crossed a small steel bridge and halted before a junction.

The Leaves uncoupled the fifth car from the sixth. While the engine bore the front cars toward a wye further up the line, the players turned their attention to the tracks curving down into the ravine, long neglected. They cleared weeds and debris from between the sleepers, checked nails and keys. The Shovels brought tools to fix the worst stretches.

The engine reversed direction on the wye and returned. Someone threw the switch, and the Gardener of Trees reversed down the slope with the tender, the stage car, the green car, the costume car. It inched along, huffing steam. Loose stones fell from the path and ticked down the walls. The players stood and watched the slow descent, unable to do much else.

Finally the engine reached the bottom and pushed the cars into place near the east wall. The players sighed. Some applauded.

The courier stood beside the patchwork ghost, watching him work. In the ghost's sketch, the engine looked too big to fit on the slope. That engine was still in danger of tipping, of breaking the stone with its weight.

Players made trips back and forth between the cars below and those above, for fabric and masks, for food and drink. Some of the Leaves remained on the ridge to guard against snoops. Already a group of children from the market had tried to climb in through an open window of the kitchen car before the Gardener of Leaves chased them off with an icy roar.

The courier thought about the car full of smuggled ghosts. The ghost roads, as Stones had called them, wound their way through nameless territories and borderlands, a route to carry those ghosts to safety. But the Black Square had brought them to the very center of the named world. She hoped the train could keep their car well hidden.

Below, the stage doors remained closed while the players put on costumes and applied paint to their faces in the light of flickering naphtha lamps. The courier watched from the green car as people arrived. They picked their way along the rails or risked steeper paths alongside the waterfall and around ancient, rusted machines. It was as she'd predicted. They were choosing the show over the recitation, crowding the ravine, claiming spots atop boulders and ledges.

Then she heard it, from the direction of the saying stone: a low hum that sent a charge down her spine. The recitation had begun. It reminded her of the nameless insects in the storage car of the Number Twelve, buzzing and alive. They would speak every law ever spoken, beginning with the first—*We are the sayers, and what we say is law*—and proceeding through those governing the committees, the ownership of machines and ghosts, the maintenance of the borders and the army. They would end with new laws, added to clarify matters of trade or committee conduct, to establish authority over recently mapped lands, to regulate the use of each newly named thing, and—if Frost followed through on his threat—to undo the Black Square.

The courier slipped out through a door in the back and found the Six of Trees standing close to the gap between the cars. He still wore his own crooked suit, but his right hand was covered with Hand's burn scars. He raised them to the last rays of sunlight, making the wax glow.

"The sayers started early," he said. He spoke with his own voice, and she was surprised by how much she liked hearing it. She'd grown used to the strangeness, the same way she'd grown used to the small monsters that went everywhere aboard the Black Square's train.

"They probably want to finish in time for the show," she said.

He snorted and dropped his hand to his side. "You actually did it, Rider. You convinced them to play my story."

"It isn't your story," she said. "Not really."

He grinned, but his eyes were sad. "Yet somehow I feel that I owe you."

"You don't owe me, Six. I may have ruined everything."

"You have, just not in the way anyone expected."

"What do you mean?"

"Before you convinced the Gardeners to return to Whisper, most of us assumed you were working for Frost."

She was stunned. "Working for Frost?"

"We thought you murdered the chair of the names committee because Frost wanted him gone," Six said. "We thought the Black Square was next."

Was this what the Gardener of Leaves had believed, when she called the courier *trouble* and demanded she be kicked off the train? How many others had thought this? The Gardener of Stones? Seven?

"But you saw me running from Frost's deletion committee," she said.

"Could have been pretend."

"Pretend," she said, speaking the word as her sister had when they were children, with disdain bordering on disgust. "Of course you would think that. Everything about the Black Square is pretend. No one here can tell the truth."

Six looked hurt. He kicked a stone and it went skittering into a nearby pool. Once the ripples had gone, he said, "I'll tell you something true."

She waited.

"I believe in what you're doing here. But I believed in the last Rider, too. I trusted him, and I wanted to go with him, but he wouldn't have me." His voice twisted around the words.

"You're lucky, then," she said.

"Yes," he agreed, though he sounded uncertain. "Before they left, I told him I could write stories for them. He said they wouldn't be playing that kind of story anymore. I think that means they're still out there, the Rider and his followers. Still performing, in their own way."

"What kind of story would they play?"

"I don't know for sure. But they probably don't look like pretend."

Something flared in the courier's memory—a furnace in the shadow of a great factory, molten glass shining in the dark. And she thought of the similar furnace, cold and dusty, taking up space in the workshop car of the Shovels. "Last night," she said, "Seven told me that we can play the Story of the Something Tree only a few more times."

"Few glass *somethings* left," Six agreed. "But what does that matter? After tonight, we'll probably never play any story again."

"Most of the last Rider's followers were Shovels, right? That's why there are so few Shovels now. Six, were the Rider's followers the ones who made the glass fruit for the something tree?"

"I think they were," he said. "I was just a kid then, but they used to make glass things in their workshop. New branches for the tree, new lenses for the light machine. All of it."

The courier closed her eyes and saw a man with burn scars on his hands working to shape trees, snakes, and flowers from gobs of liquid glass. She saw white masks in dark winding streets, smelled whiskey on hot breath.

"The glassblowers," she said.

"Glassblowers?"

"In Buckle I saw them make ghosts of two dozen people, including three committee pages. I found them again in Hollow, where they tried to make a ghost of me. Frost believes they're nameless soldiers, disguising themselves as glassblowers to hide among the named. But what if he's wrong? What if they're only pretending to be nameless?"

"I don't understand."

"Six, if the Rider and his followers played at being nameless, do you think they could pretend so well, they could dream up real monsters?"

"Yes," he said quietly. "Yes, I think they could."

"I've met them," the courier said. "I've participated in their performances, but I didn't know that's what they were, because they weren't pretend."

Six flexed the fingers of his right hand, stretching the wax scars taut. "The last Rider said something to me, once, when I started writing stories for the Black Square. He said that all the great stories had already been told. That there wouldn't be more until the world changed again."

"And now he's trying to change it himself. Starting with what, a new war between the nameless and the named?"

She couldn't tell whether Six was hearing her. "I need to tell the Gardener of Leaves," he said.

"But the show—"

"I'll be ready," Six said. He hurried away along the rails, up the slope toward the rest of the train. He walked with his hand tucked into his jacket, so the early arrivals wouldn't see the wax scars. The courier tried to picture the child Six had been, a runaway among the nameless. She wondered what he'd run from. She wondered what he'd lost when Book took him from those people and gave him to the Black Square.

Book. His maps and coded notes, his secret meetings. Had Book been searching for the last Rider all along, and for the glassblowers? All evidence of what he'd been doing was gone now, burned up in his compartment, but maybe parts of his operation persisted. Maybe Ticket was still working on his behalf.

For a moment the sun touched the top of the waterfall. The water shone green at the bottom, gold above, and a band of colors arced from the spray. Then the sun was gone and the air grew suddenly cold. The crowd quieted. They knew something would happen soon.

Back in the costume car, a gathering of namers and nameless, of painted faces and bright masks, of scavengers in ragged trappings.

Seven saw the courier and shouted, "There you are!" and ran to her with Moon's silver robe in her hands. With help from the Two of Shovels, she got the courier into costume, then sat her down before a mirror. The monster fetched a tub of yellow face paint and traced the arcs of Moon's markings on the courier's cheeks, her fingertips cool.

When the monster was done, she stepped back and looked at the courier's face in the mirror. "Oh, oh," she said, pleased with her work.

The courier took the monster's hand. "I know I've been hard on you," she said. "But I'm glad you're here. I'm glad you're with me."

The monster blinked her big eyes. For a moment, the courier thought she must not have understood. Then she embraced her so hard, she nearly knocked her from the stool.

"We have to hurry," Seven said. She pried Two off, and the monster's face came away smeared with paint. "I'm sorry," she said, gesturing to her own face. "We'll have to fix it."

"It's perfect," Seven said. "Remember, you've been crying."

She pulled the courier from the chair and away through the green car, then across the stage and into the dark on the other side. The courier still felt cold. The thought of being alone on stage frightened her. She could sense the crowd outside, and it was huge. Waiting to swallow her up.

"What about your costume?" she asked Seven.

"I won't need it until later."

"So you're playing one of the dreamers?" she said, trying to keep her a little longer. "Or the one in the golden mask?"

"I'll see you after the show," Seven said. Before she could walk away, the courier pulled her back and kissed her. Seven took a sharp, startled breath—and the courier was startled, too. She felt Seven exhale slowly and lean closer, and the scent of her was sweet and familiar. They stayed that way for a long moment, no pretend between them.

"I hope you break everything," Seven said.

"I really might," the courier said.

Seven kissed her quickly, then hurried away.

The Scout of Stones was hidden in the floor behind the light machine. The door from the costume car opened and closed as others came and went. The scavengers climbed their scrap heaps. Other players gathered in the dark on the opposite side, but none joined the courier where she stood. The Rider was alone, and as Moon she would enter alone.

The Gardener of Trees appeared at her side, tugging his beard. "You just let me know when you're ready," he said.

"What about everyone else?" she asked. "Shouldn't the Gardener of Stones—"

"The show starts when you want to start, Rider." He put one hand on the lever that would open the stage door.

She closed her eyes and took a deep breath. Moon needed to be angry, so she thought about her sister. All those years ago, Ticket had left her alone with their father, even though she knew about the machines in the cottage, the tests and examinations, the monsters burning in a barrel. Was Ticket's work with Book important enough to excuse her absence all those years?

After Book's car burned, his voiceless ghost had urged the courier to flee. Now she seemed to hear the living Book's voice in her mind.

*Better get out there*, the voice said. *Better get moving.*

"I'm ready," she said to the Gardener of Trees.

He pulled the lever. The doors and roof opened, and the Black Square's machines lifted buildings into the sky. Here was the glow of sunrise, there a flickering gray figure with a burned right hand. Not Six, the courier knew, but a trick of the Scout's light machine. A strip of images passing over a lens made the figure walk across the scenery, as though from a distance and out of a different time, just as another strip made birds fly over the river, and another sent clouds rolling through the sky.

But where was Six? There: crouched behind a scrap heap, his face marked with the green paint that meant *Hand*. When the projected figure reached the heap, it vanished, and Six rose to stand in its place.

The courier walked into the light, and by the time she reached Hand in the streets of old Whisper she was Moon, and Sap and Root were gone, and so was the child Needle, and the paint on Moon's face was smudged by the tears that spilled down her cheeks.

*Hand named Needle, and Hand named Moon.* The people who dug in the scrap heaps chanted, speaking words for what they saw, making story of the story even as it happened. *Needle is gone, but can Hand keep Moon?*

They played the story as everyone knew it. Moon went alone into the wilderness, seeking a word for the thing that had taken Needle. And in the forest in the city at the edge of the world, Moon found the nameless dreaming. The guardian in the golden mask agreed to Moon's request, so Moon slept alongside the dreamers, and was trapped in their monster-making dream.

That scene lasted only minutes, but to the courier, days and nights seemed to pass as the nameless drew from her suffering the breath and body for their creation. And where was Hand? Why didn't the first namer come and drag Moon free of this nightmare? Moon screamed, and the courier screamed, too.

When the lights finally dimmed, she fell to the boards. The players playing the nameless removed their masks. They helped her up, tried to soothe her. She saw their faces, faces she recognized, but she was still afraid. She pushed past them and left the stage.

Onstage, Hand was already pacing in the candlelight, seeking help from Bone, Blue, and the other one. They would talk for a long while before Moon returned to Whisper. She had some time before her next scene. The courier climbed down out of the car, back to where she and Six had spoken before the show.

She took a deep breath of cool air, stretched, shook out her arms. She looked around, almost expecting to find Seven waiting for her. She noticed someone standing in the dark near the ravine wall. Another player, she thought, and she raised one hand in greeting.

The figure came toward her, moving fast. The courier's heart leapt, and she stumbled back toward the door. Then light caught the figure's pale face and red hair. It was Beryl. The courier couldn't speak. Beryl, just as she remembered her, pencil still tucked behind one ear.

Beryl took her arm. "Quick, come with me," she said.

Without thinking, the courier started moving, she and Beryl walking side by side. They had almost reached the ravine wall before the courier stopped and pulled her arm away. "Wait," she said. "Where are we going?"

"I shouldn't have let you leave the Number Twelve alone," Beryl said. "I should have made you stay, or I should have gone with you."

It felt like another dream to have Beryl here with her, in the dark behind the Black Square's train. Was the Number Twelve nearby? Had Book—no, had whoever replaced him as committee chair given her leave to come to Whisper, to the recitation?

"There's still time, if you come now," Beryl said. "Frost is willing to make a deal. We voted, and—"

"Voted?" the courier said. "Who voted?"

"We agreed that I should have this chance to bring you back. The committee voted, and it was unanimous, so I—"

"What committee," the courier said, stepping away.

Beryl blinked. She looked afraid to say the wrong thing.

The courier said it for her. "Frost's deletion committee," she said. "You're part of it. You've been hunting me."

Beryl moved closer, her voice going low. "You needed someone looking out for you," she said. "I'm trying to help."

"So it's you, and Frost, and the seeker ghosts—and who else? Who's the last voting member?"

Beryl glanced to her right, and the courier followed her gaze to the west end of the ravine, where the stream flowed into a grotto. No view of the show from there, so the area was vacant except for one woman standing among the rocks, pale hair shining in the moonlight. Ivy.

The courier choked on a laugh. Ivy, who had hated her for as long as she could remember. Who had probably rushed to Frost the moment she learned he was convening a deletion committee. Ivy knew that Frost would pursue her until she was nothing. Until, like her father, she was something that had never been.

She turned and strode back toward the train. Beryl grabbed her arm again. "Please listen to me," she said. "You won't be safe here anymore."

Through clenched teeth, the courier hissed, "You aren't safe here now."

She stared at Beryl until Beryl let go of her arm. The diviner's eyes shone with tears. Over by the stream, Ivy stood still, though the courier thought she saw her smile. Why had Ivy voted with Beryl? Maybe because she'd known how it would go, and she wanted to give Beryl a chance to fail—to lose whatever influence she had with Frost.

"You should go home," she said to Beryl. "You can't help me. You never could have."

As she walked back to the train, the courier realized that she could no longer hear the recitation of the sayers. They had finished speaking the law. They would be here soon.

As Moon, she ran. Ran from the nameless, and from the thing they had crafted out of Moon's own nightmares, robe and hair tearing on branches and briars. Ran back to Old Whisper, the sun low in the sky, the shadows of the scrap heaps long in the streets.

How long had Moon been away? Six nights, maybe seven. But it seemed like weeks had passed. Now Moon went alone through Whisper, searching for Hand, as everyone expected. Something was different, though. Something only a few members of the audience might have noticed. In this part of the story, Moon usually had something in hand: a weapon, a gift from the nameless. But now Moon's hands were empty. For they had reached the new scene, sketched by the record keeper, written by the Six of Trees, played tonight for the first time.

Those who dug in the scrap heaps saw Moon, and they sang of what they saw.

> *Moon alone in the streets of Whisper.*
> *Moon searches for Hand but does not find Hand.*
> *Moon runs and runs and runs.*

Then the scavengers did something they had never done in any previous performance of the Story of Hand and Moon. They climbed down out of the heaps.

Moon stepped back, startled, and the courier felt the audience startle, too.

The scavengers approached, some bowing, some grinning, some tipping their dirty caps. Their torn and soiled clothes were poorly repaired with bits of wire and thread. Their hands and arms bore scars from sharp things that had cut them in the heaps.

Who were these strange people, appearing in every story of old Whisper, who until now had only kept to the background and chanted what they saw? Scavengers come lately from the wilds, drawn like monsters by the noise of words. The namers had given them names, but they had no talent for naming, nor were they good with machines, nor could they hunt or grow things to eat. So they searched the heaps of stuff from the world long gone, searched for anything that might be worthy of a name.

"Moon returns to Whisper," said one. "Today is a good day!"

"Returned from the nameless lands," said another. "Here to put things right."

"We have been too long without Moon," said a third. "It is a joy to have Moon back again."

Moon tried to get past them, but the scavengers bowed and stepped, stepped and bowed, always in the way.

"How angry you must be with Hand," said one.

*How angry Moon must be,* the others chanted.

"For abandoning you in the wilderness," said the one.

*For leaving Moon alone, all those days and nights.*

Now Moon stood and listened while those who dug in the scrap heaps told what happened while Moon had been away. Told how others had gone to

Hand and asked why the first namer did not search for Moon. How Hand had ignored their questions, ignored the pleas, and remained instead with Bone, Blue, and the other one.

"Finally, Hand could listen to their stories without distraction."

*Finally, Moon was gone.*

"And gone with Moon was the bad idea of naming the world as the world is now."

*Because wasn't it better before? Aren't the stories from before so much better?*

Moon stood silent among those who dug in the heaps. The scavengers raised their eyebrows, daring one another to say more. Then one bowed and stepped closer, holding out an object of shining metal.

"Sometimes we find useful things in the heaps," that one said. "Maybe you will find a use for this? Maybe you will give it a name?"

Moon looked at the thing in the other's hand. A gift. A weapon. It flashed red in the light of the setting sun.


A murmur rose from the audience. They were seeing something they had never seen before. A new part of the story, a new answer to an old question. Where had the weapon come from? Not from the nameless, but from Whisper, from this crew of ragged people. It was an old thing come back again, and they had found it in their heaps of nameless junk.

The audience had begun to understand what would happen, how it would happen. Some might even have guessed who the people of the heaps were, who they would become.

But something else was changing, something outside the story. The courier felt it in the air: a presence like a weight in the sky, bearing down on them. The flying machine descended toward the ravine where the Black Square performed. She knew without having to look whose machine it was.

They might still have time to finish the scene.

As Moon she walked with weapon in hand, coming at last to the house of Bone, Blue, and the other one. They were telling stories in there, stories from the world before the Silence. Moon saw Hand seated at a table where a single candle burned, and the table was covered with melted wax and the tips of blackened wicks. Hand had been listening to the stories for a long time.

When Bone, Blue, and the other one saw Moon in the doorway, they stopped talking.

Hand stood and blinked. "Moon," said Hand, "you came back to Whisper."

"Hand," said Moon, "I came back."

Now Bone, Blue, and the other one saw the thing in Moon's hand, the weapon that needed a name. They recognized it and moaned in fear. It was an old thing come back again.

Hand shushed them and went to Moon. Touched Moon's hair matted with blood and sap. Wiped a flake of ash from Moon's face. Saw Moon's robe torn and soiled.

"Look what they have done," said Hand.

"Yes, look," said Moon, and Hand began to weep.

All the named of Whisper had gathered to watch and listen. They wanted to see what would happen, now that Moon was back.

"Hand," said Moon, "have you found the word for the thing that hunts us? Did you find it in your stories?"

"The three old ones," said Hand, "they know the story of a child who took a weapon into the forest, to hunt a terrible thing. We are close."

"Close," said Moon. "You are so close."

"You went into the forest," said Hand. "And into the city at the edge of the world."

"And into the forest within the city," Moon said. "But you did not come. Not after two days. Not after three."

*Not after four days, not after five,* chanted the scavengers. *Not after six days, not after seven.*

"With the nameless," said Moon, "I made a thing like the beasts that hunt us. I made it from every sad thing in my head."

"Moon," said Hand.

"When I woke," said Moon, "I saw a thing like Needle. Only this thing was wrong. It had Needle's hair but eyes like something else, and feet that were not Needle's feet, and breath like wind in an open door."

"Moon," said Hand, looking up and down the street, "where is this thing now?"

Moon raised both hands, and Hand saw they were blackened with soot. "I made a fire," said Moon. "I used the fire to burn the thing away. The burning took a long time."

"Moon," said Hand, "I told you not to go."

Moon said, "Before I burned the thing, I gave it a name. I delivered a word for all its kind."

"Moon," said Hand, "will you tell me the word?"

Moon told Hand the word, and Hand spoke the word back to Moon, and the scavengers spoke the word to themselves, and so did Bone, Blue, and the other one, and all the rest of the named—everyone who had come to see. They spoke the word to try it out for themselves: *monster.*

"But what is that in your hand?" asked Hand. "Is it something for me to name?"

"It is not for you to name," Moon said, "but you will help me name it."

"Moon," said Hand, "I do not like this. Will you give that thing to me?"

Hand took a step closer, reaching for the weapon. Moon stepped back, and from the weapon came fire, and a noise like thunder in a box. Hand fell. Bone, Blue, and the other one screamed.

And Moon delivered the word: *gun.*

"*Gun,*" said the scavengers, who had given Moon the gun.

Moon dropped the gun to the ground. Blood pooled around Hand's body. From the body stepped a gray dream of the person who had been Hand. The dream of Hand stared at the body of Hand and wondered.

The namers cried out, because of what Moon had done, and also because of the gray thing, the dream of Hand. They saw others, too, standing among them—too many to count. Dreams of the people who had been Sap, and Root, and Needle, and others they did not know. Was there one in a patchwork suit, who watched so carefully, as though to remember every word, every detail? Were there two who stood so close their shoulders touched, very tall, each like the other's reflection?

They had been drawn by the noise, maybe. By the noise of all the people here, and by the noise of the gun. They no longer lived, but they still wanted to see what would happen.

Moon pointed to the thing that had been Hand and said, "That is *ghost.*" Then Moon pointed to another and said, "That is also *ghost.*" Moon pointed to each of them in turn, divining and delivering *ghost,* and the named saw that ghosts were everywhere. The ghosts were more numerous than the living.

Named, the ghosts grew solid, less hazy. One picked up a stone and held it. Another pressed their hands against a windowpane.

The namers gathered close, and in their shushing robes they whispered. Moon stayed apart as the namers spoke of what to do. Finally one of them stepped forward.

"There are things that should be done," said this namer, "and things that should not be done. That is *law.*"

"*Law,*" said the other namers, all except Moon.

"*Law,*" said the rest of the named, who wanted to try it out for themselves. And—

"*Law,*" said those who dug in the scrap heaps. The scavengers climbed down out of their heaps. Instead of chanting the story of what happened, they said something they had never said before, not in any performance of Hand and Moon.

"We are the sayers," they said, "and what we say is *law*."


Sayer Frost's flying machine descended over the crowd. Its searchlight shone into the stage car, erasing the sun from its sky, revealing panels of painted wood everywhere it touched the buildings of old Whisper. Hundreds of ghosts vanished in the glare—most of them tricks of light projected by the light machine.

Six swayed over Hand's body. One of the Leaves had shoved the body onstage when Hand fell. In the dim light, it had been real. Now it was a thing of wood and wire and fabric, but Six was still playing the risen ghost. He seemed stuck.

The courier grabbed his waxy hand. "Six," she said. "Six, it's over."

Six didn't move. The Scout of Stones climbed out of the light machine and came to him. The ghost squeezed Six's hand, met his eyes. Six blinked and looked around.

Those in the audience, shaken so abruptly from the shared dream of the Black Square, rubbed their eyes and lurched as though struck. Already, watchers were moving among them. Some pushed people away from the stage, clearing space for the flying machine.

The machine descended, dropping its anchor line, and the watchers heaved it down. Out from the hatch came Smoke and then Frost. Ivy met them on the ground. She drew close to Smoke—to inform him, the courier guessed, that Beryl's plan had failed—and Frost gazed up into the stage car. When he saw the courier dressed in the torn and filthy robes of Moon, he smiled.

Machines hissed, and the buildings of old Whisper folded back into the car. A moment later, the great stage doors rumbled closed.

Nearly every player of the Black Square had assembled onstage to play the last scene. Still in their costumes, they spoke to one another in frightened whispers. The Gardener of Stones went among them and raised his hands. "To your places now," he said. "Time for the next act."

The whispering stopped and everyone started moving. Most headed for the green car while others went out through the door at the front, toward the engine.

"Next act?" the courier said. "Six, what is he talking about?"

"We're this way." He pulled her with him toward the rear door and others moved to let them through.

Seven was waiting in the green car with the courier's boilersuit. "Take this," she said. "I'm ready for my costume."

"But the show is over," the courier said.

"Is it?" Seven said.

The Two of Shovels pushed through the crowd. She helped the courier out of Moon's ragged silver robe and back into her blue boilersuit. Seven pulled the robe on over her own clothes, then put on a wig of curly dark hair.

"Almost ready," Seven said. She held the courier's head and pressed their faces together, taking the sweat and grime and smudged yellow paint.

"I don't understand," the courier said.

The Gardener of Stones appeared beside Seven and took her arm. "I'm doing what I should have done from the beginning," he said. "I'm turning the Rider of the Black Square over to the deletion committee."

"I'm sorry," Seven said. "We knew you wouldn't have agreed to this plan if we told you about it, so you'll just have to keep up."

Seven did something, then. Held herself more stiffly, stood a little straighter, pressed her lips together *just so*. Now the courier understood the reason for the wig. Seven was no longer Seven—but she wasn't Moon, either. She was the courier in Moon's costume, exhausted from having just performed the Story of Hand and Moon. It made the courier dizzy, standing before this other version of herself.

Seven grinned. "I told you I was the best player in the show," she said.

The courier shook her head. "But—"

"But what good will any of this do?" Seven said, using the courier's voice, asking the question she'd had on her lips.

"It will win us some time," the Gardener said. "Time enough to get the ghosts out of here, if we're lucky. And time enough for *you* to get out of here, Rider, if you hurry."

Six was changing out of his costume, peeling the wax from his hand, trading his gray robe for the blue of the nameless dreamers.

The Gardener of Stones took the courier by the shoulders and said, "Listen to me now. It's just as you said last night. I am not his father, but he is like a son to me. I lost him to the last Rider, and you returned him to me—but now you're taking him away."

"Stones—"

"*Listen.* You were right. I'm letting my child walk his own road. He has another part to play in this, and so do you. Just promise me that you'll look after him."

Six walked up to them, fully costumed. "I'm ready," he said.

The Gardener of Stones kept his eyes on the courier. "Promise me," he said. "Yes," she said. "Yes, I promise."

He nodded, stepped back, and looked over the assembled players. The Two of Shovels wore a blue robe of her own, matching those worn by the ones who had played the nameless dreamers.

"Good," the Gardener said. "I'll see you after the show."

He took Seven's arm and led her to the door.

"Wait," Six said.

The Gardener of Stones turned. Six put his arms around him and held on until the Gardener hugged him back. "You *are* ready," the Gardener said. He patted the boy once and let him go.

Seven looked at the courier, and for a moment she was herself again. In her eyes the courier saw excitement mixed with regret, with longing—and then the Gardener of Stones took her arm again and they both were gone.

Juniper, the Gardener of Shovels, came forward with the courier's satchel. She handed it over, along with a blue robe and mask. "One more scene to play," she said. "Make it good."


They were seven in number, all dressed in identical blue costumes. They left through the back door and slipped out into the crowd, keeping low as they moved away from the train.

"Are you sure about this?" she asked Six. "The Black Square has been your home for so long."

"The Black Square is over," he said. "There's something else I need to do now."

"Then if we both make it out, let's meet at the base of the waterfall. I saw people using a path there before the show."

She could see the Gardener of Stones leading Seven toward the flying machine. Seven struggled as the courier would have struggled, and when the seeker ghosts grabbed her, she shouted with the courier's own voice. The sound hollowed her. Her body was elsewhere, and she was just a blue mask floating through the dark.

A crowd gathered around the flying machine, eager to see who the deletion committee had come for. The Gardener of Stones was speaking to Frost and Ivy, bowing, gesturing to the woman in Moon's costume, maybe trying to make a deal on behalf of the Black Square. When Frost appeared unmoved, the Gardener fell to his knees and clasped his hands together. Overdoing it, the courier thought. But his performance kept the deletion committee distracted from the fact that they had the wrong woman. Frost signaled for the seeker ghosts to take the captive aboard.

Before the ghosts could move, the train whistle blew, monstrously loud between the ravine walls. The engine belched steam as it started along the tracks, pulling its four cars behind. The people still on the slope hurried to clear the way. Many of them cheered it as it passed.

Smoke shouted an order to the nearest watchers, and a half dozen advanced upon the engine. They found it crowded with players of the Black Square, still dressed in the robes of the first named, the masks of the nameless. The watchers dragged one costumed figure from the cab, then another, but others appeared to replace them. Soon the engine was on the slope, and the way was too narrow for the watchers to pursue. One still clung to the engine, but the players pried his fingers loose and sent him tumbling back into the ravine. From the audience came more cheers and shouts of laughter.

Meanwhile, the seeker ghosts dragged their captive toward the hatch of the flying machine. She thrashed and kicked so hard that the wig fell from her head. When the ghosts saw the wig on the ground they dropped her and stepped away, clearly confused.

Smoke, Frost, and Ivy looked back and forth between the woman on the ground and the Gardener of Stones. Seven began to laugh. Smoke bellowed and started after the train, but Frost grabbed his arm and spun him around. He pointed out the players in blue masks with his cane.

Smoke shouted something to the watchers in the audience. They began to close in.

Two squeezed the courier's hand. "Oh," she said.

"Be careful," the courier told her monster—and then their hands parted and the seven of them scattered.

They wove through the crowd, ducking low and moving fast, but the watchers were fast, too. One seized a player and tore off her blue mask. It was the Nine of Shovels, one of the sisters who'd befriended Two. Her roaring laughter joined Seven's. The watcher pushed her aside.

Another masked player careened ahead of the courier, then looped away toward the flying machine with several watchers in tow. Others went in the opposite direction, leading their pursuers into the empty reaches of the ravine.

The courier moved toward the splashing noise of the falls. She found the narrow brook and followed it upstream. She had almost reached the dark rippling pool at the base of the falls when a watcher stepped out from behind a boulder, blocking her way. She turned to run, but another had followed her from the crowd.

She was trapped, but she wasn't alone. Camped near the boulder were a group of men and women who must have watched the show from a distance. They rose to confront the watchers.

"You serve the scrap diggers," one man said to the watchers.

"Scavengers and fakes," said another.

The men got in the watchers' way, tripping one to the ground, tearing the goggles from the other's face. A signal box smashed against the rocks, releasing the bird within. The bird flew up and out of the ravine, making for Whisper as the courier escaped.

Six was waiting for her beside the pool. His mask was in his hand and he was smiling. Downstream, people laughed as the watchers fled toward the tracks. Frost's flying machine rose into the air, its searchlight sweeping over the crowd. People threw rocks and bottles, forcing the machine higher.

The courier removed her mask. "The story worked," she said.

Six's smile faded. "Only on the living," he said.

The courier followed his gaze to the seeker ghosts. The two were coming toward them, and no one dared get in their way.

"This way," Six said. "I saw a path earlier."

The way along the falls was narrow and steep, but it led out of the ravine. They started up, throwing off their robes, tossing their masks aside. Loose stones slid down the slope and splashed into the pool below.

At the top of the ravine wall, the courier emerged with Six into a copse of vine-choked alders. Beyond was the spur they'd taken from the Whisper line. To their left the tracks split, one set of rails leading to where the Black Square's cars awaited their engine, the other veering north toward a line of low gray hills.

From Whisper came flying machines of the watchers, the beams of their searchlights pawing the earth like great fingers. On the rails came other machines, steam speeders to join the hunt.

"If we could move along one of the nameless ways . . ." the courier said.

Six shook his head. "No part of the world is more covered with names."

She could already hear the scrape of boots on the path. The seeker ghosts would soon reach the top.

"So we run," the courier said. "Away, toward the river, find a boat if we can."

Six nodded, though she saw the hopelessness in his eyes. They scrambled over the tracks and were about to run into the meadow beyond when she heard a familiar sound: the rhythmic creaking of the Black Square's handcar. It rounded the bend, its sole operator working hard at the beam. He brought the car to a halt beside them and tipped his hat. It was the patchwork ghost, and perched by his feet was the stowaway. The animal looked up at them and yawned.

They climbed aboard, and Six threw a lever to reverse the handcar's direction. The courier took the other end of the beam, and she and the ghost got the car rolling again. Behind them, first one seeker ghost and then the other came stumbling through the vines at the top of the slope. They spotted the handcar and followed, unhurried yet gaining on them like something out of a bad dream.

The car soon approached the junction. No ghost was there to operate the switch, but a group of audience members standing near the tracks saw the handcar coming. For a moment they froze. Then a woman put a child into someone else's arms and ran to the switch. She threw herself against it, pushing hard. The rails shifted, and the handcar glided onto the northbound track.

They picked up speed around the bend, but the seeker ghosts were still faster. The first to reach them grabbed hold of the deck and vaulted aboard. Six drove his fist into the ghost's belly, but the ghost didn't seem to notice. It caught him up in its arms and began, slowly but relentlessly, to squeeze.

Six groaned as he writhed in the ghost's crushing grasp. The courier imagined ribs cracking, tendons snapping. She screamed and moved toward them, but the second ghost reached for her ankle with one enormous hand. The stowaway hissed and swiped at its face with his claws. Startled, the ghost tripped over the ties and tumbled headlong into the ditch beside the rails.

Meanwhile the patchwork ghost had moved to help Six. With the same precise care he used to sort his sketchbooks, he took both the seeker ghost's arms in his hands and slowly pried them apart.

Six fell choking to the deck. He looked at the courier and gasped, "Keep us moving."

The courier saw why. From the direction of the ravine came the great silver bulk of Frost's flying machine, its searchlight sweeping the rails. Up ahead, the tracks entered a tunnel through the hill—they would have to reach it quickly.

She returned to the beam, but she was working alone. The seeker had the patchwork ghost in its grasp. It pushed him backward as though to break him in half, but the patchwork ghost twisted away. The two moved in a slow dance, deliberate, each anticipating the other's next move as though they had known each other for a long time.

They were still grappling as the handcar rolled into the dark of the tunnel. The soft grind of its machinery echoed in the cool under the hill. The courier heard boots scuffing the deck, then a scrape and a snap, and the thump of something hitting the ground beside the tracks.

A moment later, they emerged from the tunnel and back into the moon-light. The seeker ghost was gone, and so was the patchwork ghost. They had fallen from the handcar together.

The courier pulled the brake.

"We have to keep moving," Six said, still catching his breath.

The courier gazed into the tunnel, waiting for something to move against the light from the other side. But no one appeared, and the tunnel was silent. "He'll come back," she said. "He has to."

"And what if it's the other one who comes out of there?" Six said. "What do we do then?"

She watched and waited. The stowaway brushed itself against her side while Six leaned against the beam. She heard the distant buzz of the flying machine's engine. It would descend upon them soon. But she couldn't leave without the patchwork ghost.

She hopped down off the car. "I'm going back," she said.

Six went after her and grabbed her arm. "They'll take you too."

"Six, I can't leave him."

"You shouldn't call me Six anymore," he said. "The Black Square is ended, and they'll be searching for the players. My name is Thorn."

*Thorn.* That suited him, the courier thought. And she knew that he was trying to distract her, trying to get her to think of anything but her ghost. But it wouldn't work. The flying machine had already appeared over the ridge, its searchlight flashing on the slope. "Thorn," she said, "I'm sorry." She shrugged off his hand and continued toward the tunnel.

A roaring noise from the forest made her pause. She turned to see two beams of light shining through the trees. Something was coming for them, another machine. The courier blinked when she saw what it was: one of those ancient vehicles from the world before the Silence, black and sleek, four wheels turning without rails beneath. There was no word for it.

The machine barreled toward them, then pulled up alongside the tracks, wheels skidding in the dirt. A window slid down, and behind it was noth-ing—a starry nothing in a big floppy hat. The lights inside the Gardener of Leaves twinkled.

The opposite door opened, and someone stood from the pilot's seat. She had dark wavy hair, and even in the dim light the courier could make out the freck-les on her nose and cheeks. She slapped the roof of the vehicle with one hand.

"Well, what are you waiting for?" Ticket said. "Get in."

# THE
# FARTHEST
# BORDER

The nameless machine fell through the night, the roar of its engine flush-ing birds from trees. Ticket shifted gears and worked the pedals hard. Beside her, the Gardener of Leaves held on to her hat through every bump and jounce. The Six of Trees—*Thorn*, the courier reminded herself—sat doubled over in the seat behind the monster, gripping the door handle. He looked like he might be ill. The courier's stowaway was on the seat beside her, ears up.

The Gardener of Leaves turned to face the courier. "Your sister may be the only one alive who knows how to drive this thing, but that doesn't mean she's very good at it."

*Your sister.* The courier could see Ticket's face in a mirror mounted over-head, but she could barely hold the words in her mind.

"Where are we going?" the courier asked.

"Someplace safe," Ticket said.

"One of our *safe houses*," said the Gardener of Leaves, sounding pleased with the phrase.

Ticket glared at her.

"We can't bring them there *and* keep it secret from them," the Gardener said.

"I'm trying to drive," Ticket said. She wrenched the wheel to avoid a hole in the road. The Gardener squeezed her hat more tightly against her head.

Through the rear window, the courier could see Frost's flying machine hovering in the distance, its searchlights lashing the ground. They must have spotted the abandoned handcar by now. Ticket turned the vehicle onto a nar-rower road and accelerated. Branches closed overhead like the ceiling of an-other tunnel, and the flying machine vanished from sight. The courier ran a hand down her stowaway's back, but he remained alert.

"We lost the record keeper to one of the seeker ghosts," she said. "Back in the mountain."

The Gardener of Leaves looked at Ticket, and Ticket's hands tightened on the wheel.

Thorn sat up slowly. "He might have escaped. It was dark in there, and—"

"Imagine if you'd come with us last time," Ticket said to him.

"I couldn't help you then," Thorn said. "I still can't."

The courier looked at him. He turned and faced the window.

Ticket shifted a lever and pushed the machine fast over a rough patch of road. The courier braced herself with one hand against the door as the vehicle rocked and rattled. The underside scraped dirt, and Thorn groaned and bent forward again.

"This is going to be such fun," said the Gardener of Leaves.


They left the dirt roads of the forest for one of the great paved ways of the ancient world. Its surface was smoother, a cracked gray line stretching straight and wide among the trees. Ticket maneuvered the vehicle gently around rusting wrecks. Frost's flying machine was nowhere to be seen.

The courier watched through her window as the landscape changed. They passed lakes, wooded places, dark empty villages. Up front, the monster and Ticket argued about which route to take.

"No shortcuts," Ticket said. "We can't risk it."

*Shortcut* was one of the courier's own deliveries, and hearing her sister speak the word made her shiver.

"But shortcuts are *faster*," the Gardener said.

"We shouldn't even be talking about this."

"I'm going to devour you," the Gardener said mildly.

The courier leaned forward. "How long have you two known each other?" she asked.

Silence from both of them. Then the Gardener said, "Ticket must have been your age then."

"Younger," Ticket said.

"I'm never sure with people who aren't monsters," the monster said.

"You could have told me," the courier said to the Gardener of Leaves. "You could have told me that you knew where she was."

"I didn't trust you then," she said.

"But you trust me now?"

"Some. A little."

The courier looked at Thorn. He shrugged. Having to sit back here with him filled her with a sudden rage. "I hate you," she said to him.

Thorn looked stricken.

"Why don't you tell me these things?" she asked.

"What things?" he asked.

"Things I need to know!"

"Thorn doesn't know anything," Ticket said.

"Thank you," said Thorn, as though he'd been waiting for someone to say this.

Thwarted, the courier kicked the back of Ticket's seat. The stowaway hissed and leapt to the floor.

"Stop that," Ticket said.

She kicked the seat harder.

"Stop!" Ticket said. "You'll make us crash."

The Gardener's lights pulsed a warning, and the courier stopped kicking. She pulled her legs up onto the seat and curled into a ball. She took long, deep breaths to keep herself from crying. She felt young and very small.

Thorn was looking at her, his eyes wide.

"Shut up," she said.

"I didn't—"

"I said shut up!"

Thorn leaned against the door and closed his eyes. The Gardener of Leaves fiddled with the vents. The air was either too hot or too cold, probably because of the icy wind blowing from the monster's depths. The courier looked for the stowaway, but she couldn't see where he had gone. She hoped he hadn't leapt into the Gardener of Leaves.

After a while, Thorn began to snore.

The courier must have slept, too. When she opened her eyes, Thorn's head was on the seat beside her, his messy hair mashed against her thigh. The vehicle had stopped moving, and the front seats were empty.

Outside, morning light glowed red on the broken windows of an abandoned, nameless town. They were parked outside a low brick structure with a sunken roof. The Gardener of Leaves stood just outside the courier's door. The courier got out and watched the monster unscrew a cap from the vehicle's side and lift the spout of a rusty canister to the opening. It gurgled thickly.

"Hardest part of getting this thing to run was making it take naphtha instead of whatever it burned before," the Gardener said. Her lights twinkled merrily. "Luckily we have people who are very good with machines."

"Who?" the courier asked. "Who has people?"

The Gardener's lights dimmed, and she nodded her great blocky head in the direction of the brick structure. "Probably best if you ask Ticket," she said.

The courier strode up to the open doorway. Inside, Ticket stood hunched over a counter. Her face glowed in the amber light from a bulky machine, which seemed to draw power from a loudly clanking engine on the floor. The place reminded the courier of their father's cottage, of the instruments he kept there.

Ticket pressed a button, leaned closer to the machine, and spoke. "Spider to Wolf, can you hear me? Wolf, are you there? The black wind blows to the den. I repeat, the black wind blows to the den."

The words were like those she had seen on Book's scattered papers, arranged to mean something other than what they meant. Ticket repeated them, but the apparatus only whistled and whined in response.

"Ticket," the courier said.

Her sister ignored her. She turned a knob and the whining sharpened, then fell to a wavering thrum. A sound like a human voice rose from the noise, and the courier made out a few words—*the den . . . yellow bird . . . breaking*—but then the voice sank back below the wordless hiss.

"Ticket," the courier said again.

Ticket twisted the knob some more, but it was no use, the voice was gone. She slammed her fist against the counter and kicked the engine at her feet. It coughed smoke and spluttered to a stop. The amber light faded from the machine.

"Where are we?" the courier said.

Ticket stood with both palms on the counter. She looked just like the girl who had taught her numbers, glyphs, maps, and story, only taller and more tired, with one streak of silver in her dark hair. "We're nowhere," she said. "But still far from the nowhere we're supposed to be."

"So this isn't the safe house," the courier said.

"There's nothing safe about this place. Not with the sun coming up and the watchers on the move."

The courier looked outside. She saw no one but the Gardener of Leaves, still standing beside the vehicle. The monster gave her a little wave.

But Ticket still hadn't looked at her. She was wearing the plain gray uniform of a minor functionary of Whisper. A clerk who might have been stationed in the archives, or in a sayer's office. "Ticket," the courier said, "I want to know what's happening. I want to know where we're going, where you came from. What you've been you been doing all these years—"

"I *do not* have time for that," Ticket said. She bundled the machine in burlap and slid it under the counter. Then she dragged the engine into the dark at the back of the room.

The courier followed. "I thought Book was working against the namers, against the named. Was he? Are you?"

Ticket stood and faced her, and the courier saw just how exhausted she was. She'd been piloting that wheeled machine over difficult terrain all night. "You really don't understand how much danger you've put me in, do you?"

"What do you mean?"

"You spoke my name to Frost. When he recruited you."

"He didn't *recruit* me," the courier said.

"You asked him about me, said you wanted to see me. And suddenly everyone in Whisper was wondering why the nameless courier had spoken my name." She tugged her jacket straight. "I can't do the work I need to do with that kind of attention on me."

"Maybe if you or Book had told me what that work is—"

"We had to protect you," Ticket said. "And right now I need to protect all of us from what you've stirred up."

The courier searched her sister's face for some hint of warmth or care but found only stony anger—and a touch of fear. How long had the courier waited and wondered and searched? Now the real Ticket was standing right in front of her, but she seemed farther away than ever.

The air in the room grew colder as the Gardener of Leaves came in and set the canister on a shelf. She frowned at the bundled machine. "Don't see why you bother with that thing when you could just whisper."

"Not now, not another word," Ticket said. She shoved past the Gardener and stormed off toward the vehicle.

"When she could just *whisper*?" the courier asked. "What good would whispering do?"

The monster ignored her question. "I think this was a very good start," she said.


The courier and the monster climbed back into the vehicle. The engine sputtered and popped as Ticket backed it out onto the road. Thorn was awake now.

"Where are we?" he asked.

"Nowhere," the courier said. "Do you think the others are all right? Seven and Two, and the Gardeners, and everyone else? And all those ghosts?"

"I think they got the train out of there while Frost was distracted with us," he said.

Ticket drove them out of town, up steeper and more winding roads. The few ancient vehicles they passed had been dragged into ditches, keeping the route clear. Ticket drove faster, watching the sky as much as the road. The courier checked the rear window. She saw nothing on the move but clouds and birds.

The road leveled off and they drove past barns and farmhouses. Some were ruins, but some appeared inhabited. The Gardener of Leaves, window down so she could rest her elbow on the door, hummed to herself and tapped the roof with one hand. The courier's stowaway lay curled on the seat beside her, dozing. When she let her mind drift close to his, she felt only the faintest ache from his paws: nearly healed. The trees were almost bare now, but the day was bright and warm.

Ticket drove them through another village. The place was quiet and still, but the houses were in good repair. The few people seated on their porches seemed unsurprised to see the vehicle passing.

Ticket drove them over a bridge above a wide stream, then turned into a dirt lot. "We're here," the Gardener said.

They got out and stretched. The stowaway hopped down and chased a rodent into the tall grass at the edge of the lot.

Ticket led them across the road and down a slope toward the stream. Beside it stood a tall, high-peaked wooden structure. The courier smelled food and realized how hungry she was. In a sunken yard, people sat at wooden tables, talking quietly over glasses of beer and plates of bread, cheese, and pickles. A few dogs lay in the sun; they raised their heads to observe the newcomers. Neither the people nor the dogs seemed troubled to see a monster coming through. Inside, in a narrow kitchen, a skinny boy with tattoos of birds and rabbits on his arms chopped mounds of beets. He saw Ticket and nodded.

"Is he still here?" she asked.

The boy gestured with his shiny knife, dripping red juice, to someplace deeper in the building. Ticket straightened her jacket.

The courier followed her down another flight of stairs and past more tables. Sunlight poured into the lower room through tall windows overlooking the stream. The people here looked like farmers, their skin and clothes roughened by sun and weather, soil on their boots and under their nails. Some scribbled in notebooks while others played games with colored stones and bits of living draff or plucked the strings of strange instruments. Small monsters scampered from table to table, tottering, wrestling, stealing scraps.

The courier was sure she had never been here, yet the place felt familiar. The windows overlooking the water, the tall pines on the opposite bank, the little round tables cluttered with glasses and mugs. Then she realized where she'd seen it before—in the patchwork ghost's sketch of Book and Ticket. This was where they had met to trade secrets in the dark.

"What is this place?" she asked the Gardener of Leaves.

"It was a sawmill," the monster said. "But that was a very long time ago. Now it's just what it looks like."

"And what is that?"

The monster shrugged. "A good place to rest and plan. We call it the den."

*The black wind blows to the den,* Ticket had said into that glowing machine. If this was the den, then maybe the black wind was the vehicle that bore them here. And if Ticket was Spider, then who was Wolf?

The monster pulled aside a curtain to reveal a steep flight of stairs. They ascended to a landing, where Ticket knocked a quick pattern against a door. A panel slid open to reveal a pair of dark eyes behind a mask of wood. The eyes narrowed at the courier, the panel slid closed, and the door opened.

Standing before them was a monster. It wasn't wearing a mask—its skin was like the bark of an elm tree. It gazed at the courier with black unblinking eyes.

"They're with me," Ticket said.

"With both of us," the Gardener of Leaves added.

The bark-skinned monster snorted and stepped aside. The courier followed the others into a long room with a high ceiling. A dozen men and women looked up at the newcomers, then looked away again. They stood or sat in small groups, talking quietly. All seemed very tired, and all were in uniform, but few of the uniforms matched. Calibrationists in gray suits sipped tea from tall mugs. A surveyor in brown traveling gear leaned against a wall, polishing her tools with a rag. Two draff haulers in dark green coveralls sat with mugs of beer between them. The courier had never seen members of so many different committees gathered in one place.

Near the back of the room, a bearded man wearing the black coat of a dreams committee hunter sat behind a wide table covered with maps, ledgers, and typewritten pages. The courier looked at the Gardener of Leaves. Here was a man sworn to destroy monsters, yet the Gardener seemed unconcerned. Maybe she had nothing to fear from him. Another monster guarded the door, after all.

The man stood as Ticket approached. The right side of his face was scarred and hollow, as though something had clawed part of it away. He gave Thorn a suspicious look. Then he saw the courier.

"You brought her here?" he growled at Ticket.

"Wolf," Ticket said, "I tried to tell you over the talking machine."

Wolf, the courier thought. So *Wolf* was Wolf—that was just his name. Wolf gestured to a stand in the corner, on which was set a machine identical to the one Ticket had used earlier. "If that thing had worked, then I would have told you not to come. Not with this company."

"She has information we need," Ticket said.

"Then why didn't you simply collect the information?"

"I couldn't leave her," Ticket said. "Wolf, she's my sister."

It was the first time Ticket had used that word since she found them outside Whisper.

Wolf scowled. "Your sister, for whom Frost has convened a deletion committee. Meanwhile, the ghosts committee wants her for interfering with a scheduled calibration. The maps committee suspects that she's been walking uncharted borders. *My* committee hunts the monster she's rumored to have made. And the namers believe that she murdered their committee chair. Have I forgotten anything?"

"Wolf, don't."

"Oh yes," he went on, "last I heard, you yourself—"

"I don't believe that anymore," Ticket said, shaking her head. "There must be someone else. Someone we've missed."

The courier realized what Ticket was saying. "You thought I killed Book," she said.

Ticket looked uncomfortable. "We all did, for a while. But when you moved the Black Square against the sayers, you convinced Shadow otherwise, and Shadow convinced me."

"Shadow?"

The Gardener's stars twinkled. "So I was called, before I drew my card and became Black Square."

"I thought—"

"That monsters can't have names? Don't be silly, honey pot. I was given mine by the same person who dreamed me into being."

The courier stared into the darkness between the monster's lights. Suddenly she knew who had made her. Maybe she had known all along. "Book," she said.

"Ridiculous man," the monster said. "He had to create a whole monster just to deliver one little word."

No wonder Book had always refused to tell her how he'd delivered *shadow*. It was worse, even, than what she had done to deliver *trouble*. The courier said, "Shadow. You remind me of him sometimes."

The monster's stars turned a hazy pink, then faded to pale silver. Shadow had blushed.

Wolf cleared his throat. "Are we done with the introductions? Because before this mess in Whisper, we had stories of a fire aboard the Number Twelve, of Book's body dragged into the woods. If you didn't kill him, courier, Rider—whatever you are—then who did?"

The others were watching now. Not just Ticket and Wolf, but everyone in the room. They had turned from their conversations, shifted in their chairs. Even the bark-skinned monster at the door stood with skinny arms folded, waiting.

"I don't know who killed Book," she said. "I wish I did."

The others grumbled, but Ticket gave her an encouraging nod.

"I'll tell you what I do know," she said. And everyone listened as she described how she'd found Book, alone in his office with a monster like a giant insect. How that monster had already delivered its poison to his heart by the time she arrived. And she told them what Book had been doing just before: burning his notes, his maps, his coded documents.

"Anything he didn't manage to destroy was destroyed when the fire spread and the car burned," she said.

"He was protecting us," Ticket said. "All of us."

Wolf sat down. "The most infuriating man I've ever known," he said. "And probably the finest agent ever to serve this committee."

The courier looked around the room again. Which committee was Wolf referring to, when ghosts, maps, and dreams were all represented?

Ticket was watching her uneasily, maybe guessing her question, but it was Thorn who answered the question. "There's no word for what they are," he said. "Book recruited your sister into their ranks a long time ago. A few months back, they tried to recruit me. When they have to call themselves something, they call themselves the fifth committee."

Wolf shrugged. "We've been around longer than the other four. But who's counting?"

"I thought you didn't know anything," the courier said to Thorn.

"I try not to," he said. "Sometimes I fail miserably."

"So what does this fifth committee do?" she asked.

"Here's what you need to know," Wolf said. "The sayers didn't create the fifth committee, but it exists because of them. We're like their shadow. Closer to them than anything, and most of the time forgotten. Our agents are everywhere. Sometimes we provide the sayers with information they need, and sometimes—"

"Sometimes we don't," Shadow said.

Wolf grimaced. "We strive to maintain a balance," he said. "The last time we failed, two decades of battle followed. By the time the fighting ended, the ghosts outnumbered the living."

The room was silent. A few of those present were old enough to have witnessed that war, or to have fought in it.

Shadow said, "Frost hated the Black Square because he couldn't control it. He hates the fifth committee even more. We've survived this long only because we operate in secret. Very few of the sayers even know we exist. It's hard to speak something out of existence when it was never named in the first place."

Wolf rubbed his face, hand tracing the scars along his cheek and chin. "It's worse than you know, Shadow. They didn't just revoke the Black Square's protections last night. They also named a First Sayer to command the army."

"Frost," Shadow said, and the air around her went cold.

The role of First Sayer was assigned only in times of great peril. It had been some twenty years since the sayers had felt one was needed.

"Have they really found the last city of the nameless?" the courier asked.

Wolf looked uncertain. "Smoke says that Frost knows where it is, but none of our agents can confirm the truth of his claim. We don't even know if such a place exists outside of story."

The courier recalled that day in Book's office when they saw the freight train loaded with new war machines. How they had watched the machines sweep past the window until finally Book drew the curtain. Had Book known, even then, what Frost intended?

Someone knocked on the door, the same pattern that Ticket had used minutes before. Everyone waited as the bark-skinned monster peered through the panel.

"Are we expecting anyone else?" Ticket asked.

"I tried to tell you over the machine, but the signal was too weak," Wolf said.

"Tell me what, Wolf?"

The bark-skinned monster turned from the door, black eyes bright. It looked at Wolf and nodded.

"That the committee chair is coming," he said.

Everyone stood as the monster opened the door. Into the room strode a solitary figure in dusty gray traveling clothes. A ghost, and a very old one, wearing a worn satchel over one shoulder and a gray wool cap like those of the first couriers. The ghost had clear shining eyes, and on the ghost's cheeks were arcs of yellow paint.

Thorn leaned close to the courier and whispered, "Is that—"

"Yes," she said, because she had known the ghost from the moment it appeared. Even without the pale paint on the ghost's cheeks, the courier would have known. It was the ghost of Moon, second of the named.


Wolf stepped aside so Moon could sit. The ghost flipped quickly through the notes and ledgers. Ticket, clearly flustered, began to make her report.

She spoke of what had transpired in Whisper the night before. Of the end of the Black Square, of the changes to law spoken by the sayers, of their ride through the night. The courier saw no surprise or concern on the ghost's face. Finally, Ticket took a deep breath and gestured to the courier. "Moon, this is my sister, formerly a courier of the names committee. She has new information about the recent attacks on the named cities."

Moon looked up and gazed directly at the courier. For a moment, the courier felt as though she were standing at the edge of a ravine, very wide and very deep. She couldn't move, couldn't open her mouth. Everyone was staring.

Then she heard a voice in her mind. It sounded strangely similar to the voice she'd used while playing Moon in the Story of Hand and Moon. And the voice said, *Speak*.

"The glassblowers," she said. "They were once part of the Black Square. And now, I think, they're pretending to be nameless. Pretending so well, they're making real monsters, and using those monsters to—"

Moon raised one hand.

"Start at the beginning," Ticket suggested.

So the courier took a deep breath and remembered herself back aboard the Number Twelve. A cool morning in the month of Stone. Beryl in her bunk beside her, the light shining blue through the curtains that had been her mother's dress. A porter's knock at the door: Book needed to see her.

She could tell from the redness of his eyes that Book had barely slept the night before. Something had kept him up, kept him worried. He slid the new word across his desk to her. *Gob*.

"An easy one for you," he said.

It wasn't the beginning, not really. But she began there, with Book and his assignment that should have been easy, with the furnace beside the factory wall in Hollow, and with those who worked the liquid glass. Then the masked figures in that maze of nameless streets, their blades bright in the moonlight, her escape through a junk dealer's storehouse. She told Moon about Buckle, too, and how Frost believed the attackers to be the same women and men as those in Hollow. She told what she'd learned during her time with the Black Square about the previous Rider and his Shovels. About the glass fruit of the something tree. About the furnace in the workshop car, long unfired.

When she finished, the room was silent. The courier stepped back from the table, though Moon still watched her. Finally, Wolf spoke. "Even if she's right, and these glassblowers were once part of the Black Square, I'm not sure how this helps us. We don't know where they are now."

"We do," someone said. It was the maps committee surveyor. She had finished polishing her tools, and now she was wrapping them in squares of cloth. "They're back in Hollow, or maybe they never left. I saw them three days ago, hawking their trinkets at the market. They seemed desperate to sell what they had."

"Our courier must have interrupted some plan of theirs," Shadow said. "They went into hiding, but now they've picked up where they left off."

The courier looked at Thorn. He had an odd expression on his face. He was thinking about the last Rider, she thought. Did he still believe he was a great man? When Thorn saw her looking, he quickly looked away.

But Moon had seen, too, and the committee chair was watching him.

Ticket cleared her throat. "This is Thorn," she said to Moon. "My last assignment from Book was to retrieve him and bring him to you. But Thorn refused to be retrieved, that time."

The ghost rose and came around the table to stand before him. Thorn was looking at the floor, avoiding Moon's gaze.

"I only came along to make sure the Rider got here safely," he said, nodding at the courier. "I don't know what Book wanted from me, and I don't care."

Moon took Thorn's chin in one hand.

"I can't help you," he said, his words faltering. "I won't."

The courier wondered whether Thorn was hearing that same voice in his head. Tears filled his eyes, and his body began to shake.

"It was just a word," he said. "I only spoke it the one time."

Ticket looked at Wolf, but Wolf shrugged.

"I don't remember it," Thorn said. "I couldn't speak now it even if I wanted to." Tears spilled down his cheeks. Still Moon held his chin and stared. His voice had grown stranger with each word he spoke, and now the sounds he made were hardly words at all. But the courier found she knew him well enough to understand.

"Don't make me remember," he whimpered. "Please don't make me remember."

And then he fell to the floor.


The courier knelt beside Thorn while Ticket propped up his head. Wolf brought a cup of water and tipped it to the boy's lips. Thorn spluttered and pushed the cup away. "I'm fine," he said.

Moon stood over him. Other members of the fifth committee had risen and drawn closer. Thorn looked at them and blinked. Only when he took his hand out of the courier's hand did she realize she'd been holding it.

"Well?" Wolf said.

Thorn sat up, confused. "What did I say?"

"Something about a word," Ticket told him.

His eyes opened wide. "Did I speak it?" He looked up at Moon and blinked. "No, I still don't remember. I couldn't have spoken it."

Moon returned to the table. The ghost sat, loaded a sheet of paper into the typing machine, and began to type.

Ticket took Thorn by the oddly cut lapels of his jacket. "You need to tell me what's going on."

"He needs to rest," the courier said, remembering her promise to the Gardener of Stones. "And he needs something to eat."

Ticket glared at her and was about to argue, but Wolf said, "Your sister is right, Ticket. You've been traveling all night. You should all eat something."

At the table, Moon finished typing and plucked the page from the machine. The ghost folded the single page and wrote something on the back with a pencil. Wolf grunted and went to see. "For you, Moss," he said, holding out the page.

The maps committee surveyor came forward to take it. She unfolded the paper and read carefully. Wolf made a mark in his ledger, then lit a candle and slid it across the table to her. Moss finished reading, then set the paper on fire. When it was nearly consumed, she dropped it into a copper bucket on the floor. Meanwhile, Moon had loaded a fresh sheet of paper and was typing again.

Assignments, the courier realized. The chair of the fifth committee was handing out assignments.

Ticket got Thorn to his feet. "We'll go eat something," she said. "*And* we'll talk."

The bark-skinned monster watched warily as the four passed, then closed the door firmly behind them. The courier could still hear the sound of the typing machine as she helped Thorn downstairs.

In the room overlooking the stream, people were still eating, playing music, tending their stray dreams. They seemed to know nothing of what was happening upstairs, yet they were untroubled by the sight of monsters coming and going from the room. The people of the borderlands were always strange—and this crew, the courier thought, were stranger than most.

Ticket went to the kitchen where the tattooed boy was still preparing food. Shadow waved the courier and Thorn over to an empty table in the corner. The courier recognized it as the same table at which Book and Ticket had been seated when the patchwork ghost had sketched them. A cold shock went through her as she thought again of her ghost falling into the darkness of the tunnel. She needed to look for him. What was she doing here?

"Sit," Shadow said.

Miserable, the courier sat across from Thorn. A minute later, Ticket returned with a board of bread, cheese, fruit, and pickled vegetables. The three ate while the monster watched.

After a while, Ticket said, "So, this word."

Thorn swallowed. "You can ask Shadow about it," he said. "She knows."

"Does she?" Ticket asked, looking at Shadow.

The monster shrugged. "I know that when Book found him living among the nameless, Thorn wanted to go with him to the Number Twelve. Wanted

to join the namers, if you can believe it. Book thought that would be too dangerous, so he hid him among the Black Square instead."

"Too dangerous," Ticket repeated. "Because of a word?"

Shadow leaned back in her chair. "Well, Thorn? Was it because of a word?"

The courier remembered what the Gardener of Stones had told her—that
Six was more important than even he knew. This must be the reason. Whatever Book learned about the boy when he found him. This word.

"We're no longer part of the Black Square," the courier said. "You can tell
us what happened, and you can trust us not to tell anyone else."

Ticket turned to argue, but the courier said quickly, "We are going to listen
to Thorn. And we're going to look after him. That includes keeping his secrets,
if he wants them kept."

"She's right, Ticket," said Shadow. "What the boy tells us doesn't leave this
table."

Ticket, outvoted, leaned back in her chair. "Fine," she said. "Just so long as
he's honest with us. I need to know everything."

Thorn still looked uncertain, but he began. "The word was an accident," he
said. "My father was the only one who heard me speak it."

"Go on," Shadow said.

He took a deep breath. "When I was young, I talked the way I talk now,
only—only more so. I would try to speak words, but the sounds came out all
wrong. Usually they weren't words at all. One time, though, the sounds *did*
mean something. Something we didn't have a word for."

"You're saying that you accidentally divined a word," the courier said. "And
delivered it."

"I don't think it was entirely accidental. I wanted that word, and I wanted
it out of me. Speaking it felt like tearing roots from the ground. But this was
just after my fifth name day, and it's gone now."

"You must remember the thing you were naming," the courier said.

Thorn shook his head. Not denying it, just not wanting to talk.

"Thorn," Ticket said, a warning in her voice.

He closed his eyes and sighed. "There was a ghost," he said carefully. "And
then there wasn't a ghost."

"It was taken by the ghosts committee?" Ticket asked.

"It went away," Thorn said.

"So it was burned, or—"

He slammed his fist on the table. "I told you, it went away!"

People at nearby tables turned to look. Thorn sank down in his chair. Once
the others had gone back to their own meals and conversations, the courier
said quietly, "Thorn, you told us that your father was the only one who heard."

Thorn took several deep breaths. "The ghost was the ghost of my father," he said. "And after I spoke the word, the ghost of my father was gone."

They were quiet for a while. Ticket looked out the window, thinking. Shadow, still leaning back in her chair, hummed to herself. The courier tried to guess what Book had wanted with this word, a word to make a ghost disappear. What would a word like that do, if someone delivered it properly?

The answer, she knew, was the reason Book had hidden him away with the Black Square. This wasn't just any word. It was dangerous. It could change the shape of the world. It was a border word.

"I'm going to see if Moon has an assignment for me," Ticket said. She rose from the table and went swiftly upstairs.

"This is why I didn't want to come," Thorn said. "If Book had wanted me around, he should have brought me with him. Not kept me secret until he needed to use me like some, some—"

"The word you're looking for is *weapon*," said Shadow.

Thorn folded his arms over his stomach and hung his head. Was this what a weapon looked like? Maybe so, the courier thought. A sad thing, unpredictable, dangerous to keep too close.

She felt something then, a familiar buzz at the back of her mind. Prickly, like a burr stuck in the folds of a dress. Her stowaway was trying to get her attention.

"I have to go," she said.

"Where to?" Shadow asked, her voice icy with suspicion.

"I'll be right back." The courier left through the door by the kitchen. She found a path into the woods near the stream. The hum grew louder, until she saw him. Down by the water, her stowaway was rolling on his back in a patch of sunlight.

She stood over the animal and said, "What do you want?"

He rose and drew closer. She felt an electric tingling as he swept his furry body against her leg. Then he leapt into the bushes and was gone.

But he didn't leave the courier alone. A man was approaching from the stream, screwing the cap onto his water flask. When he saw her, he stopped and let out a little yelp. "You startled me," he said, putting one hand to his chest.

He looked familiar. Small dark eyes, small pointed nose, hair like pale frayed rope. But she didn't recognize him until she saw the rope he wore tied around his waist. He was a member of the names committee, the first she'd seen here. The diviner who found names for flying things.

"Rope, what are you doing here?"

"Just received my new assignment," he said. "Now it's back to the Number Twelve before my absence is noted."

"You're part of this? I didn't notice you upstairs."

His smile was bashful, because of course she hadn't noticed him. Even when they lived aboard the same train she had often failed to notice him.

"About what happened back on the Number Twelve," he said. "The ghost, that vote. I'm sorry. It's clear now that Frost was intent on driving a wedge between you and Book. I wish I had understood. I wish I had been able to stop it."

"Book was afraid that his work with the fifth committee would be discovered," she said. "Your work, too, apparently."

Rope scratched the side of his head. "Book recruited me a few years ago. We couldn't trust anyone else, not completely. But he'd planned to bring you in soon, you know."

"Bring me in?" the courier said. "He kept everything hidden from me. Even my sister."

"He thought you belonged with us," Rope insisted. "He told me that you had an important role to play."

"And did he tell you what role that was?"

"This is Book we're talking about," he said, laughing. "Of course he didn't."

They were both quiet a moment. Book had kept too many secrets, she thought. And when he became a ghost, he took those secrets with him. "Rope," she said, "do you know who made the monster I saw in his car that night?"

Rope tucked the water flask into his satchel. "I know you didn't, that much is clear. Wolf believes that Frost arranged it somehow. That he had one of his own agents sneak aboard the train."

"And what do you think?"

"You won't like it," he said.

"Tell me anyway."

He looked at the ground. "I think Book was so full of whiskey and suspicion and guilt that he dreamed the thing up himself. I think Book made the monster that ended him."

The courier thought back to that night. To the way Book had stared wild-eyed into the shadows. *It was waiting for me,* he'd said. But maybe it hadn't been waiting for him in his office. Maybe it had been waiting in his own mind. Long ago, he had made a monster to deliver *shadow.* Could he have made the monster that poisoned him, too?

Rope looked uneasy. "I really can't miss my train," he said.

The courier turned and looked, as though she might spot it among the trees. "Is the Number Twelve near?"

"No. I'll catch the next passenger train from Bottle Station, just down the road. That will get me to Hollow in a few hours. Frost has summoned the namers there."

"Frost? But who's serving as committee chair?"

"Oh," Rope said sadly, "you didn't know. Frost has taken personal control over the committee. But why direct the namers to Hollow, when the last city of the nameless must be somewhere on the border? That's what Moon wants me to learn."

"I'm sorry," the courier said. "I shouldn't have pressed you to tell me your assignment."

"I told you because I trust you. And because I thought you might like to know that one of us is still looking after things back home."

*Home.* He must have seen her wince at the word, because he said quickly, "When all this is over, I think the committee would be lucky to have you back." Hesitantly, he added, "Any message you'd like me to pass along to—"

"No."

"Right," he said. "Well, I'm glad you found your way here. The den is probably the safest place in the world for you. If you want my advice, you'll stay right here as long as you can."

He turned and continued along the path, up to the road, calm and unhurried. No wonder Book had recruited him. He must have come and gone from the Number Twelve dozens of times without anyone noticing. And the fifth committee needed people who were easy not to notice, easy to forget.

She took the path to the stream. She couldn't bring herself to return to the den, not yet. Under the bridge, the water poured foaming down a series of low falls. Farther down, it swirled in deep pools, then rounded a bend behind a stand of pines.

She sat among the rocks and listened to the water. She wanted her stowaway to return. She wanted the feel of something warm beside her. And she was surprised by how much she missed Two, now that her real sister was nearby. The courier was closer to that version of her sister than she was to the one who'd brought her here.

She knew that Rope's advice was sound. She also knew she couldn't take it. Safe as this place was, she didn't have time to linger. She had to find the patchwork ghost.

The air grew suddenly cold. She looked up, expecting clouds, but the sky was clear.

"There you are," Shadow said. The monster's stars were dim in the bright light. She stood with her hands on her hips. "I was starting to think you'd sneaked off."

"I might still," the courier said, getting to her feet. "There's nothing more I can do here."

"I can't let you leave, my dumpling," the monster said. "Not when I still need to hear the rest of your story."

"What story?"

Shadow's voice was a low growl. "Back upstairs, you told us what happened to Book the night of the fire, but you didn't say enough about what came before. Why was Book so convinced that Frost had beaten him, I wonder?"

The courier took a step back, sending loose stones skittering into the water.

"Oh, I know about Frost's late-night visit to the Number Twelve. And I know you met with the sayer aboard his flying machine. What happened there to turn you against your old friend?"

"Nothing!" the courier said. "That isn't what happened."

The monster's lights flashed, and she tilted her great bulky head. She was looking at the courier's satchel. Without thinking, the courier had moved her hand to it.

"Something in there, maybe?" Shadow said. "Something Frost gave you?"

The courier was stuck between the eddying pools of the stream and Shadow's colder depths. The monster drew closer.

"A word," the courier admitted. "He gave me a word to deliver."

"So many new words today. And what kind of word is this?"

"Frost believed that someone aboard the Number Twelve was working with the nameless. Pretending to serve the committee while trying to destroy it. I was supposed to find that person and deliver the word to them. Name what they are by naming their crime."

"And you failed."

The courier swallowed. "Yes."

Shadow sighed, shrinking a little. "Good," she said.

"Good?"

She lowered herself slowly onto a rock close to the water. "If you'd succeeded, you would have handed Frost the means to take power even sooner."

"I don't understand."

The monster patted the spot beside her. After a moment's hesitation, the courier sat.

Shadow said, "Frost bends people to his way of thinking by keeping them afraid. Afraid of the nameless, afraid of monsters, afraid of everything they don't understand. Fear is the fuel his deletionist agenda runs on."

"He made Book afraid of me," the courier agreed. "And he made me suspect Book."

Shadow grunted. "What he really needed from you was proof that the fear was justified. Imagine if you had produced this person he sought. Every committee chair would have panicked, wondering who in their own ranks was working to destroy them. And they all would have thrown their full support behind Frost."

"But when I dreamed up a monster, and stole the patchwork ghost, and ran from the Number Twelve, I made myself into the person he needed."

"You also made him chase you," Shadow said. "That slowed him down, and the Black Square slowed him further. The sayers have given him his army, but thanks to last night's performance, the sayers are losing the trust of the named. With the exception of the namers, the standing committees remain independent, and Moon is ready to move against him. He'll be desperate now."

"Which is why I have to leave," the courier said. "I have to find the patchwork ghost while he's distracted, while there's still time."

"Losing the record keeper is a terrible thing, and not just for you. But you can't save him. Not without confronting Frost—and to put yourself in Frost's way would jeopardize Moon's plans."

"Moon can make new plans."

Shadow heaved a huge sigh, stars sparking then fading again. "Sometimes I wish I hadn't spat you back out that night I caught you on my train," she said.

The courier tensed.

"I'm not going to eat you," Shadow assured her. "But I do wish you would talk to your sister."

"Shadow, she hates me."

"I didn't say she *likes* you, my plum. But there's no telling when you'll see each other again."

"I don't understand why you care about this."

"Maybe because Book cared about it," Shadow said. "Or maybe because he didn't care enough. Or maybe I just think our chances against Frost are better if the two of you can work together. Ticket needs you, you know. She can't say it, but she does."

The courier looked up at the safe house. Light flickered in an upper window as another set of orders burned. She wondered if Frost would even bother having her ghost calibrated, when he might burn him instead. Like Frost's flying machine, the war machines didn't run on common naphtha. They ran on ghosts. And if Frost's army really was moving against the last city of the nameless, they were going to need a lot of fuel.

"I'll talk to my sister," the courier said. "And then I'm leaving."


They found Ticket in the dirt lot, crouched beside her vehicle. In the light of day the courier saw the many scratches in the black paint, the rusted metal beneath. One side of the vehicle was raised on a jack, and the bark-skinned monster was below, banging at something with a hammer.

When Ticket saw the courier and Shadow approach, she nodded but stayed crouched. "Should have a smoother ride once we're done with these modifications," she said.

The bark-skinned monster made a sound that was almost a laugh.

"Once we're done with these *repairs*," Ticket corrected herself. "I may have pushed it a little hard last night."

"And yet you seemed so calm," Shadow said, and the courier wished, not for the first time, that they had a word for this—for saying one thing but meaning the opposite.

The bark-skinned monster pointed at one of the wrenches spread by her feet. Ticket handed it over. If Beryl were here, the courier thought, she would have loved to watch this monster at work. She'd be down there with her, full of questions as they rooted through the guts of this ancient machine. And Beryl *could* have come with her, she reminded herself. But she had joined the deletion committee, trusting Frost instead of trusting her.

Shadow nudged the courier with her elbow. She said to Ticket, "So you have your new assignment?"

"I can't talk about it," Ticket said.

"I don't expect you to," she said. "I just came to let you know that I'm going."

Ticket looked up. "Going? Where will you go?"

"I have to find the patchwork ghost. I can't leave him to be calibrated or burned."

Ticket stood and brushed herself off, looked at the tree line. "It'll be dark soon," she said. "It's too dangerous to leave now."

"You seem to prefer traveling at night," the courier said. "I can camp outside Bottle, then catch the first train in the morning."

"There's a place for you here. I'll show you as soon as we're done."

The bark-skinned monster was pointing at another wrench. Before Ticket could move to help, Shadow said, "You two go ahead. I can take it from here."

Shadow hunkered down beside the vehicle, and the courier followed Ticket back to the den. Instead of entering by the kitchen, they circled around the back and went through a door down near the stream. Inside, shelves along the walls were stuffed with gear and supplies. Coils of rope, rucksacks, shovels and pickaxes, tarpaulins, tents, canteens. And hanging from pegs were uniforms—at least one for every division of every committee. The courier paused when she spotted a courier's uniform.

"Sometimes we have to be other people," Ticket said. "I've never worn that one, though."

The courier ran one hand over the dark green wool, over the old wooden buttons. "These should be made of brass," she said.

Ticket waved her deeper into the building. The next room had one broad window with a view of the bridge over the stream. Narrow bunks lined the walls. The place was cramped, but also clean and cool.

"How many places like this does your committee have?" the courier asked.

"Four or five," Ticket said. "There used to be more. We keep our safe houses near the borders, and when the borders move, we have to move with them. Not this one, though. This one has been here since the beginning."

"But don't you work in Whisper?"

Ticket hesitated. "Most of the time, yes."

"I once visited the place where Book sent my letters," the courier said. "But it was just an office of the messengers."

"Officially I work for the messengers," Ticket said. "I direct the ghosts and signal birds, which makes me privy to a lot of information. I read most of your letters right there in that office you saw."

"But you never wrote back," the courier said.

"That would have been too risky," Ticket said. "We had to keep you safe."

The courier felt the old anger welling up in her, and before she could stop herself, she said, "Then how could you leave me there? How could you leave me, when you knew what he was doing?"

A moment passed before she saw Ticket understand what she was talking about. Their father and his experiments, the machines in his cottage, the cold metal table.

"Book came for you, didn't he?" Ticket said.

"But you didn't."

"I don't think you understand how difficult this work is." Ticket looked suddenly tired. "Being two different people at once isn't the same as pretend. There's no word for what I am, for what I do. And anything that makes me too much of one person or the other is dangerous. For me and for you."

The courier turned away. She felt tired, too. Even her anger made her tired. She could imagine herself doing as Rope suggested, slipping into one of those bunks and sleeping for hours, for days. It would feel good to disappear for a while, to let the burbling of the stream and the cool breeze from the window wash the dreams from her head.

"I'm glad you kept writing those letters," Ticket said. "They were more important than you know."

"Important enough to ignore for ten years." She knew she sounded like a child, but she didn't care.

"I didn't ignore them," Ticket insisted. "I read every one. And thanks to you, I remembered what I would have forgotten."

"Lock," the courier said. It felt strange to speak his name aloud after so many years. "I should have let us both forget."

"No," Ticket said. She put one hand on the courier's arm. "Your letters kept him in my mind—kept him in Book's mind, too. And because we remembered—" She stopped, hesitating on the border of her committee's secrets.

The courier turned to face her. "Book said something about you, you know. Just before he became a ghost."

Ticket looked worried and a little suspicious. The courier had to be careful. She wanted to know what Ticket had been about to say, but she didn't want to tell her about Two, or about who Two looked like. Not yet.

"He said he'd waited to hear from you," she said. "He thought you might have joined the Black Square."

Ticket snorted. "He knew I'd never do that."

"He seemed worried. Maybe even hurt. He was expecting a report."

Ticket's jaw tightened as she fought down some feeling. "I couldn't report back because I was on an assignment for Moon. It was urgent."

"Something about Lock?" the courier asked.

Ticket started to shake her head, but she gave in. "Yes. I used a messenger ghost to infiltrate Frost's office and retrieve some files."

"What did they say?"

"The sayer couldn't forget Lock either," she said. "He couldn't stop thinking about that deletion. Not in all that time."

"But why?"

Ticket sighed and sat on one of the bunks. "For years we had something like peace with the nameless," she said. "But they resumed their attacks suddenly just after Frost came for our father—around the time when Book brought you aboard the Number Twelve. Watchers were being cut down by assassins in white masks. Small monsters lured hunters into ambushes. And everywhere the fifth committee went, we heard whispers of a new threat."

"The glassblowers," the courier said, sitting down across from Ticket.

"It seems so. But Frost was convinced that it all went back to our father. That Lock had somehow unleashed these attacks against the named. That he'd sent someone—a person who could move undetected between the nameless and the named—to destroy the sayers and the committees."

The courier felt it again, that weight she carried everywhere, the undelivered word. *Traitor.*

"But why would Frost think that?" she asked. "All our father's work was done on behalf of the named."

"Maybe so," Ticket said. "But he kept you nameless, and he kept you secret for all those years. Frost became convinced that Lock had other secrets, too. Secrets his deletion committee missed when they took the place apart."

The courier remembered how it had been that day. The books from before the Silence piled and burned in the yard. Her father's equipment loaded onto the flying machine, his notes collected into boxes. She had been terrified but also grateful. *Here I am. I've been here all this time.*

"After I left," Ticket said, "did you ever see him with anyone else? Anyone you didn't know?"

The courier shook her head. "There was no one like that."

Her sister seemed disappointed, but she sighed as though relieved of a burden.

"Wait," the courier said, remembering. "There was one group of people. But they couldn't have had anything to do with the attacks."

"A group of people? Who were they?"

"Dreams committee agents," the courier said. "After you left, my dreams got worse and worse. Lock must have realized that it was more than he could handle alone. If one of those monsters had escaped, or—"

"Wait, you're sure they were from the dreams committee?"

"The hunters go after monsters, and these people—they try to stop monsters from happening in the first place," the courier said. "They taught me techniques to stop making monsters."

Ticket leaned closer, interested. The courier closed her eyes. She had never tried to describe the experience of those peculiar nights and days. Never put it into words—not in her letters to Ticket, not to Beryl, not even to the patchwork ghost.

"There were certain ways to breathe," she said. "Ways to keep my mind clear. They tied a piece of rope around my wrist, so I would feel it and remember I was dreaming. And when I did, I was supposed to dream of something—an empty person. Except it was more like a hollow, bottomless thing in the shape of a person. Every thought that might become a nightmare, I just gave to him. That way, none of the nightmares could escape."

"And these people?" Ticket asked. "What were they like?"

"They were kind," the courier said. "They looked after me for days, and I felt safe with them. But I don't remember any of their names, or which division of the dreams committee they represented. But you must know something about them."

For a moment Ticket considered this silently. Then she slowly shook her head. "There is no such division of the dreams committee," she said. "There never has been."

"Some temporary subcommittee, then," the courier said. "Formed under special circumstances."

"The fifth committee would have known about it. *I* would have known about it." Ticket's voice was hushed and flat; she was trying to sound calm. "Those people weren't with the dreams committee. I don't think they represented any power of the named."

The courier felt suddenly cold. Her father had invited them into their home; they had guided her, helped her build borders around her mind. But she couldn't remember their voices. She couldn't remember a single word they'd spoken. If they hadn't come from one of the committees, then where *had* they come from?

"I don't remember their names," the courier said, "because they didn't have any. And our father was the one who sent for them. Ticket, he was working with the nameless."

"Maybe Frost was right," Ticket said. "Maybe it began with Lock, with our family."

For a moment they sat without speaking, and the only sound was the babbling of the stream outside. Finally the courier said, "But if Frost is right, then what does this have to do with the glassblowers? They aren't truly nameless—they're only very good at pretending."

It had something to do with the last Rider, she thought. Had he been among the nameless her father sent for? Or had those nameless dispatched the Rider to the Black Square, seeking recruits?

"There's another piece of the puzzle," Ticket agreed. "Something we're still missing."


The door by the stream opened, and they heard the approach of heavy boots. Wolf appeared in the doorway, arms crossed over his chest, a scowl pulling the scars on his face taut. "So he isn't with you either?" he said.

Ticket stood. "What's happened?"

"It's the boy, Thorn. He's gone, along with that word he can't seem to remember."

The courier's heart raced. When she'd left the table upstairs, she'd told Thorn she would be right back. She shouldn't have left him alone.

"Shadow?" Ticket asked.

"Slipped past her somehow," Wolf said. "But I think I know where he's gone. He was upstairs when news came in through the talking machine. The Black Square made it out of Whisper last night, and the train was seen headed toward Hollow this morning."

Something about that was wrong. Thorn had chosen to leave the Black Square. When they fled together in matching costumes, he'd told her: *There's something else I need to do now.*

Only she and Moon had seen the look on Thorn's face when he learned that the glassblowers were in Hollow. He wasn't going back to the Black Square. He was seeking the Rider and his followers.

"I need to talk to Moon," the courier said.

"Moon will be gone by now," Ticket said. "Everyone has their orders."

The courier went to the window. Sure enough, the ghost was up on the road, headed for the bridge over the stream. In that faded gray uniform, with a worn satchel slung over one shoulder, Moon looked like a courier who had been out on delivery for hundreds of years.

The courier pushed past Wolf and Ticket, ran outside, and followed the path up to the road. She heard the others following, heard Ticket call for her, but she didn't stop.

When she got to the bridge, Moon had just reached the other side. The ghost turned at the sound of the courier's approach. Seeing those bright gray eyes fixed on her, she had to steady herself with one hand on the balustrade.

"Moon," she said. "I've been following your orders for most of my life. I've worked so hard, and I've delivered so many words."

Moon blinked, clearly startled. The courier drew closer. Now that she'd started talking, she found she couldn't stop. "I read every word you wrote down. I wore a uniform like yours, and I was good at being a courier. I delivered *shortcut* and *trouble* and *moth* and *echo*."

She glanced back, saw Wolf and Ticket nearing the bridge. Wolf looked angry. To her surprise, Ticket put one hand on his shoulder and made him wait. Moon was waiting, too, with that stillness peculiar to ghosts.

"I've worked for you, I've delivered words for the world as it is. For a while I *was* you. I spoke the first words among the first namers, in old Whisper. I went with you into the nameless wilds, to the city at the edge of the world. I received the gift of a weapon, and I still feel its weight in my hand. I took your exile as my own. But for a long time, all I really wanted was to find my sister. I thought that if I named every part of the world, then eventually I could name the part that kept her from me. But now I've found her, and it's not enough."

Moon's gray eyes were unreadable.

"Book believed that I had a role to play," the courier said. "Now I know the truth of who he was and what he did for you, and it frightens me. But whatever happens next, I'm going to be part of it. I don't need to join your committee. But I'm not stopping here, and I think you should know that."

Moon smiled, then, and put a hand to the courier's cheek. The ghost's fingertips were cool. The courier closed her eyes and heard that voice in her head, the one that was either Moon's voice or her own voice, speaking as Moon.

And this time the voice spoke three words: *Courier, deliver yourself.*

When the courier opened her eyes, Moon was holding something out to her. A folded sheet of paper. Had Moon typed something up in advance? An assignment for her, just in case?

She took the paper and unfolded it. At first, what she saw made no sense to her. Then she understood.

Moon turned and continued over the bridge. A minute later, the ghost disappeared around a bend in the road.

The courier folded her assignment and walked in the opposite direction. She said nothing to Wolf and Ticket as she passed them, trusting they would follow. When she reached the door to the den, Shadow and the bark-skinned monster were just returning from the empty lot. They saw her and followed, too.

*Good,* the courier thought. Let them all see.

She went through the bar and upstairs to the meeting room. The agents of the fifth committee who remained were talking and drinking. They quieted as the courier entered, and watched as she strode across the room to the table.

The candle had burned low. The courier kept the paper folded as she held it to the flame.

What Moon had given her wasn't an assignment. Not really. The ghost had typed up nothing in advance. The paper bore no words, no instructions, no orders at all. It was blank. But no one else knew that. The chair of the fifth committee was letting her choose her own path.

*Courier, deliver yourself.*

The others watched as the paper burned. By the time the courier dropped the ashes into the bucket, she knew what she was going to do.

Shadow was a blotch of roving stars in the dimly lit supply room. Other agents had taken much of the equipment; the monster worked to organize what remained. She grumbled to herself while the courier and Ticket browsed the uniforms. If Shadow had an opinion, she was keeping it to herself.

The courier held up the dark green uniform of a names committee courier to the light of the naphtha lamp. It looked almost exactly like the one she had burned in a derelict factory. That seemed so long ago, but it had only been about two weeks.

"Too familiar?" Ticket asked.

"I need something to help me go *unrecognized*," the courier said.

"This one, then." Ticket held up the black coat of a dreams committee hunter.

The courier tugged the lapels, straightening the coat on its hanger. Most people feared the hunters; just touching the fabric felt dangerous. It might be good to walk the streets of Hollow in a coat like that, dark and sleek as a raven's wing. But what if she crossed paths with someone who needed her to track and kill a monster? Worse, what if she encountered another hunter? They were few in number. They probably all knew each another.

"Better not," the courier said. "Wolf is angry enough already."

Upstairs, he had quietly seethed at Moon's decision, but he and Ticket had both seen the ghost put that sheet of paper into the courier's hand. He couldn't argue against letting her go.

"Are you sure about any of this?" Ticket asked. "You know you can refuse the assignment Moon gave you."

"I'm going," she said. "I have to find Thorn."

She had told Ticket that this was her assignment from Moon—and the courier did plan to pursue Thorn. She had promised Gray to look after him, and the boy needed her help. But that wasn't the whole reason.

Thorn had gone looking for the glassblowers, she was sure of it. And she, too, was determined to find them. She had to know the truth of the last Rider—and the truth of the glassblowers' connection to her father, if there was one.

Besides, Rope had told her that the Number Twelve was in Hollow, that Frost had taken control of the train. And wherever Frost was, that's where the patchwork ghost would be.

"Let me bring you to Hollow myself," Ticket said. "I know the roads between here and the city. I can get you there fast."

Shadow nudged a box deeper onto the shelf, making tools clank. "Even faster with a shortcut," she said.

"There's a shortcut to Hollow?" the courier asked.

"Not yet," Shadow said.

"*Shadow*," Ticket said, a warning in her voice.

Shadow shrugged and started filling another crate, stars glittering with amusement.

"Shortcuts again," the courier said. "That's one of my words, you know. Why do you keep arguing about it?"

"I know all your deliveries," Ticket said. "Whenever I get a new broadside, I try to guess which words are yours before Book can tell me. I'm usually right."

The courier was startled. She had always wondered whether her sister read her letters, but it never occurred to her that she might be following her deliveries. Something shifted in her chest and she felt tears coming to her eyes. To stop them, she reached for another uniform.

"This one," she said, holding up the plain gray coveralls of a draff hauler.

"That's almost exactly what you're wearing now," Ticket said.

"It's perfect," the courier said. No one would wonder why a draff hauler would be walking the ragged back ways of Hollow. They would only think she was there to collect another bin of material for the refineries.

Ticket said, "I'm proud of you, you know. What you did, chasing after Moon that way. It was like something out of story."

The courier knew she should want this, want for her sister to be proud of her. But the cold anger returned, sticking in her throat and keeping her from saying anything at all. Ticket—sensing this, maybe—returned the black coat of the dreams committee hunter to its place on the racks.

"I'm going to check on Wolf," she said. "And then we should probably get some rest."

After Ticket was gone, the courier sat with the uniform folded in her lap. Shadow started humming. She was rolling up sleeping bags and bundling them with straps and buckles. The courier knew she'd been listening, but she didn't want to talk about her sister.

"Tell me what you know about the Shovels," she said to the monster. "The ones who left with the last Rider."

"A boring lot. Arrived together, drew their cards together, left together without a proper goodbye. I never liked them." Shadow set down another sleeping bag. "Is that the real reason why Moon is sending you to Hollow? To chase them down?"

"You were right when you told me that Frost's agenda runs on fear," the courier said. "And no one has made the people of the named territories more afraid than the glassblowers have."

"What does Moon expect you to do about them?"

"I've encountered them twice before," she said. "I know them, and they know me. So I'm the one who has the best chance of learning the nature of their scheme."

"I hope that's as far as it goes. Those are dangerous people."

"You called them boring."

"The most dangerous people usually are," Shadow said.

The courier squeezed the fabric of the uniform. "The first time I saw them, they could have made a ghost of me, but they didn't. The second time I saw them, they tried to hunt me down, but I got away. Both times, the borders between us were ragged and thin."

"How so?"

"When I'm around them, I feel their thoughts like whispers under my skin. They pretend so well at being nameless that they drag me into the story they're playing, whether or not I want to play along."

Shadow sat on a storage trunk and sighed a cold sigh. "The Black Square is ended, and all the old rules are changed," she said. "So I'll tell you who they were, before they drew their cards."

"You said they came together."

"With Gray, the Gardener of Stones," Shadow said. "They were sayers, once, all of them. Their circle stood opposed to Frost, so Frost engineered their expulsion. They were so lost, and so sad. Every word they'd spoken for decades had been law, and now their words meant so little. They could barely speak, let alone pretend. They were blank slates. No wonder the Rider saw an opportunity."

"They must have hated Frost," the courier said. "They must *still* hate him. Is that why they're doing this? Making monsters, murdering people, pretending to be nameless?"

"If so, they're idiots," Shadow said. "They're helping Frost more than they're hurting him."

"Then whatever they're doing now will only help Frost even more. I need to find out what it is."

"Because Moon needs to know," Shadow reminded her.

The courier was too tired to keep up the act, almost too tired to speak. She looked into the next room and was grateful to see that her stowaway was lying curled on a bunk near the window. He had already chosen where they would sleep.

"Shadow, do you think he has a chance? The patchwork ghost, I mean."

Shadow slumped forward, stars dimming. "About as good a chance as any of us, I suppose."

When the courier slept, her thoughts were not much slowed. In her dreams she walked the winding streets of Hollow. Music from one of Book's old phonograph records floated down from an open window, and the shadows bristled with blades and insect wings. At the same time, she was aware of her sister asleep in one of the other bunks. It was like when they were children: her sister snoring gently, she too worried to give herself to sleep. If she wasn't careful, they'd wake to a room full of draff, or worse.

So she left her dream of Hollow and reached for the sharp little fire of her stowaway's mind. He had left the bed to navigate another labyrinth, the dark in-between spaces of the safe house. She went with him to the bar, empty now, where they padded past sheets of moonlight. He was tracking the rich red scent of some rodent. She crouched with him under a table, waiting for his chance to pounce, but his prey must have noticed him, because it failed to appear.

When they got bored, they searched for someplace else to be. At the back of the kitchen, a narrow flight of stairs curved upward. Silently her stowaway climbed, emerging between two shelves at the back of the meeting room.

Here, a few lanterns still flickered. Wolf was seated at the table with papers spread out before him. He examined maps, made notes in his ledger. Strange, that a hunter of monsters seemed to care so much about paperwork.

Stranger still, the bark-skinned monster was with him. She stirred the bucket of burned orders with a stick, then carried the bucket to an open window and emptied the ashes into the wind. Neither monster nor hunter seemed to notice the stowaway.

Wolf tapped his pencil, thinking. The bark-skinned monster went to stand behind him. Then, to the courier's amazement, she wrapped both arms around him and pressed her face against his neck. Wolf set down his pencil and put his hand over the monster's hand where it clutched his shoulder. "I know," he said.

Wolf tilted his head back, and the monster pulled him away from his work. She ran one hand over his old wound. The courier, back in her bed, nearly startled awake as the monster pressed her rough lips to Wolf's. The dreams committee hunter rose in his seat, drawn upward by the kiss. Her hands, like two bunches of twigs, were on his chest, under his coat, pulling at his shirt.

The stowaway's attention was elsewhere. He tugged at the courier's mind, wanting her to hear something. His ears were very good. She heard it—someone outside, weeping at the door to the den. The door creaked open, and the weeping grew louder as the intruder moved through the building.

The stowaway leapt into the light, growling and hissing. Startled, the monster pulled herself from Wolf's embrace, and Wolf leapt to his feet. The weeping was loud enough now that they could hear it, too.

The monster ran for the door. Just before she reached it, the door burst inward, tearing the deadbolt from the wall.

Through it came the courier's own monster, the Two of Shovels. Her hair was in tangles, her clothes dirty and torn, her eyes feverish. She barreled into the room, long fingers clawing at the air, shrieking like something freshly torn from a nightmare.

The courier threw off the covers and sat up, heart beating hard enough to hurt. Was it only a dream? No, she could hear the wailing with her own ears.

She'd thought her monster had escaped with the rest of the Black Square, but somehow she had found her way to the den. The courier jumped from bed, grabbed her satchel, and ran from the room. Her sister called after her, but she kept moving. She had worn the draff hauler uniform to bed. Some part of her had known to be ready—though she couldn't have imagined this.

In the meeting room, she found the bark-skinned monster grappling with Two. Wolf stood a few paces back, scowling.

"Two?" the courier said.

Both monsters froze. Then Two broke free and ran to the courier, wrapped her in her long arms. Every part of that strange, tall body was shaking. The monster burbled in her ear, trying to tell her something.

"Two, I don't understand," she said, realizing only now, so far from the Black Square, that *Two* had become the monster's name.

She held her at arm's length. The monster was still wearing her costume from the night before, though the blue robe was dirty and torn, and her mask was gone. How had she come all this way, and so quickly?

Still burbling, the monster pawed at the courier's arms. She stopped when Ticket came into the room. The two looked at each other, and the courier saw them recognize the similarities, the differences.

"Oh," the monster said.

Ticket, whispering as though afraid to let the monster hear, said to the courier, "This is what you made? *This* is your monster?"

"Oh, oh," Two said, her eyes very wide.

"I dreamed I found you," the courier told Ticket. "Only it wasn't you."

"No, it wasn't," Ticket said.

Two began to pull the courier toward the door. Gentle at first, then more insistent.

"Two, stop," the courier said. "You're safe here."

The monster shook her head and pulled harder.

"Wait," Wolf said. He had been watching in silence all this time, but now he grabbed Two by the shoulders and pulled her close. Two blinked, trembling, as Wolf stared into her enormous eyes.

"You're wrong," he said to the courier. "She isn't safe here. None of us are."

Two shook harder and started mumbling again. Wolf let her go, and the courier caught her as she stumbled.

Ticket said, "Wolf, what's going on?"

"She's been a captive of the dreams committee. Of someone like me. And if she escaped from someone like me, then she didn't really escape."

The courier recalled what she knew about the dreams committee, about its hunters. When they caught a monster, they rarely destroyed it right away. A pile of ashes was useless, but a living monster could be used to track the person who had dreamed it.

"We have to go," Ticket said. "Now."

Before anyone could move, one of the windows smashed inward and a woman swung through, landing crouched amid the broken glass. She had long black hair and a long black coat. From the window, a light brighter than daylight stabbed into the room. A flying machine hovered out there, its engine thrumming.

The bark-skinned monster roared and charged at her, arms outstretched as though to push her back out the window.

"No!" Wolf shouted.

The woman rose and flung something, a weapon of braided cords and metal weights. The cords wound themselves around the monster's legs, and she fell to the floorboards like a toppled woodpile. Wolf threw a knife and the woman spun, batting it aside with her coat. When she stopped, her gun was drawn and aimed at Wolf.

Soldiers came up the stairs, boots pounding. No watchers this time, no threat of deletion. They had come with rifles and bullets.

The courier pulled Two toward the hidden stairs to the kitchen. A pair of soldiers were close behind, boots crunching broken glass. They raised their rifles, but Ticket moved to block them.

The courier screamed. She could already feel the blasts that would crumple her sister and leave a ghost where she stood. But before the soldiers could fire, Ticket raised her hand and spoke a single word.

*Fall.*

Her voice was her own, but it was something else besides. The room went silent, as though that one word had punched a hole in the air and drained out the sound. *Fall* was a very old word, yet Ticket had spoken as though it were something new—as though she were a courier making a delivery.

*Fall,* Ticket said, and the soldiers fell.

They cried out as broken glass pierced their knees and hands. A rifle clattered over the floor. Ticket snatched it up and backed away.

The courier hesitated at the top of the narrow stairs, trying to understand what she had just seen—what she had just *heard*.

The dreams committee hunter stared in horror at the soldiers, at the blood pouring over broken glass. The bark-skinned monster grabbed her leg and tried to pull her down. The hunter kicked her away and turned the gun on her. Then came another word.

*Burn.*

It was Wolf who spoke this time, his voice a booming command. In an instant, the gun in the woman's hand glowed red and flame burst from the grip and between her fingers. She gasped and dropped it to the floor.

More soldiers poured into the room. "Run!" Wolf shouted.

He spoke that word like any other, but it was enough to send the courier and Two and Ticket all stumbling down the narrow stairs to the kitchen and out into the cool, unquiet night.

They headed for Ticket's vehicle, but more soldiers were gathered in the lot. The vehicle was bathed in light from the flying machine.

Ticket pulled them down the path toward the stream. They had almost reached the bank when two more soldiers emerged from the underbrush, one in front of them, one behind.

*Stop,* Ticket commanded. Her voice lacked some of its earlier power, but the soldier blocking their way held still, his eyes wide. The other soldier barely hesitated. He knocked the rifle from Ticket's hands before she could raise it, then gestured for the three of them to move back up the path.

Ticket took a sharp breath. She was pale, and her hands shook from the exertion of what she'd done.

"Move!" the soldier said, waving his gun. He was young and scared, and that made the courier nervous. They started back up the slope. They were almost at the top when the soldier suddenly lost his footing. He fell forward as though off the edge of a cliff, vanishing in an instant.

In the place where the soldier had been, Shadow stood and put her hat on.

"I'll leave him in the woods somewhere," Shadow said. "He'll wake up cold and lost but otherwise in fine health. Minus the gun, of course."

The courier wanted to hug Shadow, but she didn't know if that was possible. Ticket was still catching her breath.

"Hurry now," Shadow told her. "You're the only one who can get her to Hollow."

"The soldiers have the vehicle surrounded," Ticket said.

"And so?" Shadow said.

"We'll have to take a shortcut."

"Finally," Shadow said.

From the top floor of the building came the sound of gunfire. The courier looked up and saw smoke billowing from the broken window.

"I'll help Wolf," Shadow said. "Whisper if you need me."

*Whisper, shortcut.* The courier thought she was beginning to understand what those words meant to Shadow and Ticket. She followed Ticket down the path past the unmoving soldier, alongside the stream and into the woods, with Two trailing close behind. Ticket's steps were steadier now, but she still looked pale.

"What you did back there," the courier said. "It took a lot out of you."

"We call it spelling," Ticket said. "It feels a little like lining up the glyphs in your mind, then—"

"Delivering the word," the courier said. "Or delivering it again."

"We can't do it with just any word. We have to spend weeks or months learning each one, making it part of who we are. None of us have studied more than a few dozen."

"And you've studied *fall* and *stop*. And *whisper*, I'm guessing."

Ticket looked annoyed for a moment—at Shadow, the courier knew, for saying too much. "*Whisper* is an old one," she said. "Everyone learns *whisper*."

"Is this something Book could do?"

"Book was terrible at it. I think his training as a namer interfered. That's part of why we have so few members among your committee."

"Are there others besides Rope?" the courier asked.

"Rope," Ticket said, as though just remembering him. "Yes, but only one in my time. A young page named Thumb."

The courier remembered a boy with ink on his hands, stuffing broadsides into his satchel. His first assignment in the field had been at Buckle. His first and last.

Two, sensing something, squeezed the courier's arm and said, "Oh, oh." The courier patted the monster, trying to reassure her.

Ticket watched all this, troubled. "When did you—" She didn't seem to know how to finish the question.

"Just before the fire that burned Book's office," she said. "Just before I had to run."

The courier's stowaway had caught up with them. He brushed himself against the courier's legs, then against Two's. Two knelt and petted him carefully.

"We have to keep moving," Ticket said sharply, and marched on ahead.

Two looked worried. Weeks ago, the monster had stepped into the hole that Ticket had left in the courier's life. All together, they were like a puzzle with too many pieces. Ticket seemed angry, maybe disgusted. No one wanted to meet a monstrous version of themselves.

The courier squeezed Two's hand and pulled her along, going quietly among the pines. The wind moved high overhead and made a shushing sound, and the needles were soft under their feet.

Ticket rubbed her temples with her fingertips. "We're close," she said. She looked the way Beryl sometimes did after a long day in the compartments of the divining cars.

"I don't know what you're planning," the courier said. "But are you sure this is something you can do?"

"What's the most number of words you've delivered in a day?" Ticket asked.

"Four," the courier said. "I delivered two on the Number Twelve, one in the town where we were stopped, and one in Book's office, right after he gave me the assignment. He was furious."

"If you can do four, then I can manage three." The competitive glint in her eyes was something the courier remembered from races to the top of the hill outside Stem, from games of Hand and Moon. "In fact, I can do five or six if I need to. Maybe more."

"I'm sure you can. Just don't make me carry you out of here."

Ticket stopped and patted her pocket. She looked suddenly afraid. "A compass," she said. "I need a compass."

The courier fetched hers from her satchel and gave it to her.

Ticket sighed as she cradled it in her hands. "This makes it easier." She walked with the compass held out before her, turning left, then right. "A little farther this way."

"Where are we going?"

"I've been thinking about those lessons I gave you when we were kids," Ticket said. "Some of the things I taught you, I taught you wrong. Back then,

I thought the unnamed parts of the world were only waiting to be mapped and named."

"Aren't they?"

"Nothing on the other side of the border waits in place. Not even the shape of the land is certain. Only once something is named does it stay put. We aren't rediscovering the world from before the Silence. We're making a new one as we name it, choosing its shape as we go."

Ticket stopped in a clearing. On the far side, the trees were older, the forest darker and more dense. "There," she said.

"What?" the courier asked.

Ticket swayed on her feet, took a deep breath. "A *shortcut*," she said.

The courier felt the air change. A warm breeze carried an oily smell into the clearing. And she heard something through the trees: the churning of great machines.

"That sounds like—"

"Hollow," Ticket said. "It's just through those trees and down the hill. And now it always has been."

"What do you mean, it always has been?"

"I couldn't have done this before without risking the secret of the den's location. But since it's been discovered, the den may as well be here, close to Hollow."

"But Hollow is hours away by train."

"The train's been going the long way around," Ticket said.

The courier rubbed her forehead. The change wasn't just happening in the world—it was happening in her memories, too. Hadn't she been hearing the sound of machines since they first entered the forest? And hadn't she glimpsed the lights of the city through the trees?

"I told you I know your words well," Ticket said. Suddenly her eyes fluttered shut, and she fell back against a tree trunk. The courier and Two both steadied her.

Ticket opened her eyes and looked back and forth between them. She seemed confused. The courier got the canteen from her satchel and unscrewed the cap. Ticket sipped, some of the water dribbling down her chin. "I'm fine," she said. "You should go."

"And leave you here?"

"I have to return to the others, and then I have an assignment of my own." She gave Two a strange look. "This one can go with you."

"Safer for all of us, I think, if I keep her close," the courier said.

"*Her*," Ticket repeated. "I was gone so long, of course you had to replace me."

The courier was stunned to realize that her sister wasn't angry or disgusted. She was jealous.

Ticket took Two's arm. "Listen to me," she said. "She's our sister, and you need to protect her. Do you understand?"

At the word *sister,* Two's eyes opened wide. She nodded, very serious.

"Good," Ticket said. She brushed them off and stood on her own, steady again, or doing a good job of pretending. She held out the compass.

"Keep it," the courier said, closing Ticket's fingers over its face. "You might need to find your way back to me."

Ticket nodded and put the compass in her pocket.

The stowaway was already moving through the trees toward Hollow, drawn by the smells on the air. The courier and Two followed him across the clearing and into the pines. She looked back to see Ticket hurrying along the path toward the safe house. She had only just found her sister, and now she was gone again.

The trees thinned as they walked. Soon she stood with her monster alongside a rail line, crowded on both sides by crumbling brick buildings. She took Two's papery hand and pulled her alongside the tracks, into the city. The smoke from the factories reached all the way to the clouds, orange in the light of the rising sun.

The city around them was beginning to wake. The courier and Two stuck to side streets and alleyways. Merchants entered shops through back doors, their keys jangling. Naphtha lights flickered from workers' compounds. Through wide warehouse doors came ghosts bearing crates for waiting tramcars. All moved in the shadows of the greater factories, which never slept at all.

They passed draff haulers who emptied bins into ghost-drawn carts. The courier avoided their eyes and tried to look like she was on her way to an assignment of her own. She had pulled off Two's torn robe—the boilersuit she wore beneath was dirty, but that would only help the monster blend in.

Two turned at every new sound: a flock of pigeons taking flight, a girl pulling a fruit cart with one creaking wheel, the bubbling and sizzling from a busy eatery kitchen. Meanwhile, the courier felt a wild, almost too sweet joy rising in her chest. The joy wasn't hers—it came from her stowaway as he bounded from shadow to ledge to windowsill to rooftop. *Stay close,* she thought, but he ignored her and wandered in ever widening circles.

The courier knew only one person in Hollow who could help her find the glassblowers. And that person, last time she'd seen him, had told her to forget they'd ever met.

She didn't know the exact location of the junk dealer's warehouse. Last time she found it, she'd been fleeing the glassblowers while they played at being white-masked nameless, and she'd left by way of an underground river. So she headed toward those nameless parts of the city where she'd first become lost, hoping to spot anything that seemed familiar.

The city's watchers were numerous. Worse, platoons of soldiers had joined the patrols, staking out intersections in groups of three or four. In the broader boulevards, war machines walked among the soldiers. They were lizard-like scouts, the smallest of the machines she had seen from Book's office that day long ago. But they didn't seem small now, each half as long as a train car, their heads reaching as high as second-story windows. In the belly of each machine, she knew, a pilot sat at the controls, negotiating with the spirit of the monster that had burned in its furnace during the priming process. Most people gave the machines a wide berth while pretending not to notice them, though some children pointed or even followed to see where they would go. Two wanted to do the same; the courier had to pull her away.

They took a winding route, skirting the edges of the nameless districts. She spotted a courier standing alongside a maps committee scout, the pair guarded by two soldiers. They were consulting a map, comparing it to the road they walked. Was this why Frost had brought the Number Twelve to Hollow? To try again to name and map these elusive parts of the city? If so, he must have learned of something valuable within, something worth summoning the bulk of the army along with the entirety of the names committee.

From a side street came several soldiers with a dozen captives, hands tied behind their backs. The captives wore the bright colors favored by the poets and musicians who made their homes in the nameless districts. Some were bruised and bleeding from cuts on their heads. One plump young man, balding above his great nest of curly yellow hair, saw Two and grinned, recognizing her for what she was. The courier quickly dragged her monster away—

Only to be stopped by a tall, brisk man with a thick mustache and a clipboard. He was dressed in the brown uniform of a ghosts committee drover. At his signal, two columns of ghosts marched forward, blocking the intersection she'd meant to cross.

The courier pulled Two back. The ghosts' expressions were blank, their eyes dull. They shuffled by, short and tall, wearing the faces of the young and the old. They were dusty and gray and coated in soot. The hands and arms of some were scorched, probably from having been made to work too close to the furnaces.

The courier looked for another way forward, but a crowd had already begun to form, and among them were watchers and soldiers. She faced forward and waited, holding Two close.

Minutes passed, and still the columns of ghosts marched on. The drover, consulting his clipboard, looked pleased with the orderliness of the procession. The courier peered around the corner. A few blocks away, soldiers guided the ghosts up ramps and into the waiting cars of an army supply train.

Fuel, the courier realized. The ghosts would be used as fuel.

She steadied herself with one hand against the cool brick wall. The ghosts were only ghosts, and ghosts are never afraid. That's what her father had told her, that's what everyone said. So why did she feel so afraid for them? The ghosts walked as though sleeping, and so they would walk into the fires when the war machines required them. In her mind, the patchwork ghost fell again from the handcar, into the dark of the tunnel. He did not cry out. He barely made a sound as he landed.

On the other side of the columns, others waited for the ghosts to pass. Living factory workers, clean shaven, their belts hung with polished tools. Two draff haulers with ghosts of their own. A man with a white mustache wearing a fine blue suit, checking his pocket watch. And still the ghosts kept coming.

"Oh, oh," her monster said quietly, tugging the courier's sleeve.

She turned to see a familiar figure in a courier's uniform. It was Ivy. She looked tired and pale, her usually perfectly combed hair in tangles. With her came the seeker ghosts, taller than anyone in the crowd, their broad hats shading their eyes from the morning sun. None of them seemed to have spotted the courier or her monster. Not yet.

"We have to go," the courier whispered.

"Mm," said Two in agreement.

They approached the first column of ghosts. The drover took no notice of them; he had gone to the corner to watch the progress of those nearer to the train. When the courier saw a gap between one ghost and the next, she dashed forward, pulling Two with her. They cleared the first column, but collided with a ghost in the second.

The ghost stopped and looked at her. It was the ghost of a woman in a sooty blue dress. The courier thought she saw something familiar in that woman's sad eyes, in the shape of her nose and chin.

Two stumbled, bouncing off another ghost, and that ghost knocked down several more. Those in the rear kept marching, tumbling into those ahead of them. Soon ghosts in both columns were falling, dropping into heaps. Others turned down side streets or walked in small circles.

The drover saw the commotion and shouted. The courier couldn't make out his words. She couldn't move. She could only stare at the ghost in the sooty blue dress—and the ghost stared back. She didn't know the woman, of this she was certain. So why couldn't she look away? What was she looking for?

Her monster grabbed her and pulled her from the intersection.

The drover screamed for them to stop, for someone to stop them. But the man with the white mustache only dropped his pocket watch and stared with his mouth open, and the draff haulers were busy trying to keep their own ghosts from getting mixed up with those bound for the boxcars. Soldiers and watchers emerged from the crowd, but were quickly tangled up among the ghosts.

The courier saw Ivy recognize her, saw the exhaustion in her eyes replaced by cold fury. The seeker ghosts saw her, too. They strode forward, shoving other ghosts out of the way.

The ghost of the woman in the sooty blue dress remained in the intersection, serene amid the confusion, watching the courier go.


The courier tried not to think as she ran. The seeker ghosts knew her now, and they knew how she thought. She plunged with her monster down the narrowest streets she could find, seeking the nameless zone. She felt it around the next corner, on the other side of an overgrown lot, at the bottom of a flight of stairs—but by the time she arrived, it always seemed farther still.

"Oh, oh, oh," said Two, miserable.

Somehow the courier had led them in a circle. The engine of the army train was just ahead. So, too, were Ivy and the seekers. No, it was worse than that: only one ghost was with Ivy. Which meant the other was somewhere else, unseen and drawing closer.

The courier pulled Two into the nearest side street, where they pressed themselves against the wall between two refuse bins. She closed her eyes and breathed, trying to focus. How had she crossed over the last time? A warm night, whiskey in her belly, the starless sky close overhead. The factories booming and the ground humming under her feet, the sharp scent of naphtha on the breeze. A pang of hunger, a wrong turn. Then music from an open window, and suddenly the shadows had gone strange.

She heard footsteps drawing near, heard Two fretting beside her. But she didn't open her eyes, because with her eyes closed, she could *see*. She saw a man with a round face, stubble on cheeks and chin. He sat hunched, eyes narrowed, peering at her. It was the junk dealer.

She was looking through the eyes of her stowaway, and the junk dealer was looking back. "Is that you in there?" he asked.

She wanted to cry out, to ask for help, but her stowaway only let out a mournful *mew*. The man reached out one hand, and the stowaway pushed the top of his furry head against his palm.

"Well, you may as well join us," he said. Then he leaned close to the stowaway's ear and whispered one word, not to the animal, but to her: *Remember*.

And she did remember. Not the city she'd walked, but the one her stowaway knew. Hollow as a patchwork of light and shadow, a puzzle made of smells, of breezes stroking whiskers and fur. How many times had the animal been here? One time or a dozen, it didn't matter. What he knew, he knew with his body, as a map of wordless sensations.

The courier gasped and opened her eyes. Two was still beside her, crouched between the refuse bins, shaking and afraid. One of the seeker ghosts neared the corner, boots clomping out of rhythm. The other approached from the opposite direction—the courier couldn't hear his footsteps, but she could see his long shadow sliding along the bricks.

But she saw other things, too—things her eyes had missed just moments before. She saw the way the city folded in on itself. Saw how it might be tugged apart, like a ball of yarn under a set of claws.

She squeezed Two's hand. "You have to trust me," she whispered.

The monster, eyes wide, nodded slowly.

The courier stood, pulled Two from their hiding place, and hurled her at the opposite wall. Two squawked and stumbled, but the bricks of the wall were the bricks of a street; a street that was very far away, yet separated from this one by only a few steps.

"Oh," Two said, looking at her feet.

The seeker ghosts appeared at the edges of the courier's vision. She stepped out from between the bins, let them see her. She wanted them to see her, wanted the chase. Maybe she had come back to her body with too much of her stowaway in her brain. She didn't care. If she had to run, she would run because she wanted to, and because she was fast. She wanted the ghosts to know they could not catch her.

They closed in, limping but strangely quick, a dream knitting itself up around her. They flexed their big hands and something shone in their eyes—the closest these two could come to smiling.

The courier stepped forward over the border.

She looked back to see Ivy appear beside the ghosts, her hands on her knees, out of breath. She looked in the courier's direction, and her eyes were blank. The courier had the uncomfortable feeling of gazing out from the other side of a mirror. Ivy turned from her and began to pace, searching the ground while the ghosts ran their hands along the brick walls.

The courier's mind was more fully her own again, and she knew the ghosts would find their way through soon. She took Two's arm and together they fled deeper into the nameless districts of Hollow.

Here on the underside of the world the named places were close but just out of reach, bright streets full of words and movement. She thought she could have returned if she needed to, but for the moment it was easier to stay here, on this side of the border.

She guided her monster onward, remembering her stowaway's route as she followed it. The animal had gone places where they could not follow, traversing gutters and rooftops, bounding over balconies, slipping behind drains and narrower ways, but she knew these streets now, from her stowaway's memories and then from her own. Soon they put the named parts of the city far behind them. The neighborhoods of the nameless opened wider, filling space, no longer confined to edges and corners, to crooked fingers wedged between the buildings and avenues of that other city.

Something was different, though. Something had changed since the courier last came here. That time she had glimpsed figures through windows, heard music, seen movement on the streets and along the walkways. Now everything was still. No movement, no sound except those that reached them from the named city—the rumble of the war machines, and the deeper, rhythmic thudding of the factories.

Her monster looked worried.

"We're almost there," the courier assured her.

She found the door through which the junk dealer had snatched her that night long ago. Around the next corner was the overgrown lot. The plants were taller than before, ferns up to her waist, burdock high as her shoulders, towering mullein. The barges in the canal were loaded high with crates.

They found a gap in the fence and followed a worn track toward the building, past a cart stacked with boxes. The great sliding door of the warehouse stood open.

Two stopped walking. "Oh, oh," she said, suddenly panicked.

The courier took her hand. "It's all right," she said. "I know this place."

Two shook her head: that was beside the point. The courier realized why. She had pulled the monster out of a dream that looked like this warehouse, and *that* warehouse had been a frightening, terrible place—a place from which she had needed rescue.

"I have to go in there," the courier said. "Do you want to wait?"

Two looked unhappily around the weedy lot.

"Come with me, then. I'll look after you, the way you're always looking after me." Guessing at the nature of the monster's fear, the courier added, "And
I won't abandon you there. When I leave, you'll leave with me."

Two still seemed frightened, but she nodded. She held the courier's hand
tightly as they passed through the great door.

Like the streets outside, the warehouse was changed. Here was the junk
dealer's office—the desk and chair, the flickering naphtha lamp—and here
were rows upon rows of shelves, reaching back into darkness as far as the courier
could see. But most of the shelves were empty. All that remained of the dealer's nameless goods were scraps and rags.

Her stowaway appeared from among the shelves, light on his paws. He
swept his warm body against her shins, rumbling his approval. When she bent
to pet him, he moved just out of reach and flopped onto his side.

The courier stood straight as the junk dealer approached from the same
part of the warehouse. He still wore his gray cap and his rumpled blue shirt,
but the silk robe was gone. Slung over his shoulder was a bulky sack, buckled
tight. He looked tired.

The courier said, "I'm sorry. I know I've broken our deal by coming here."

"You could have done worse to me," the junk dealer said. His voice was
just as gentle as she remembered, but now it was edged with something else—
exhaustion, or maybe fear.

"What happened? Where are your wares?"

The junk dealer set the sack down at his feet. "You've seen what's happening in this city. The soldiers and their weapons. The namers and cartographers.
Most everyone has fled deeper into the nameless territories."

She glanced back at the barges. She had thought they were waiting to be
unloaded, but now she understood that the junk dealer had just loaded them.
"You're fleeing, too," she said.

"I work the border, and the border is moving. I have to move with it, thanks
to your committee."

"I'm not sure it's my committee anymore," the courier said.

"Isn't it? You've traveled a strange route, and in strange company, but in
the end, aren't you still out on assignment? Aren't you still trying to make
a delivery?" He saw the courier's surprise and smiled. "A lot of people come
through my doors, courier. Some of them close to the sayers—some with unusual offers. So I learn things, whether or not I want to. Isn't that why you're
here? For information?"

"Yes," the courier said. "But I have nothing to trade."

The junk dealer picked up his sack and went to stand in the doorway. He
looked for something out in the shadowy lot, and when he found it the courier

sensed it, too: by the gate, a presence like a questioning breeze. The junk dealer sniffed the air. "They'll be here soon," he said.

"Who?" the courier asked, ready to grab her monster and run.

He turned to face her, and she saw it this time, just for an instant—the fear in his eyes. A hungry, crackling fear, like fire climbing a wall. "Quickly, courier of the names committee. Tell me why you're here."

"The glassblowers," she said. "The ones who chased me to your door that night. I need to know where they are."

"Do you?" he said.

"I know *who* they are. They were sayers, once, enemies of Frost, then players of the Black Square. And I know what they've done to the named, the trouble it's caused for the nameless. I have to find them before they do something worse."

The junk dealer considered. "I think we can help each other," he said. "You may not have anything to trade, but there's something you can take." He opened his sack and drew out a zippered leather case. "I can't risk keeping this any longer."

"What is it?"

The junk dealer opened the case and showed her. Inside were a dozen glass tubes of dark liquid, stoppered with cork. "I don't care what you do with the stuff," he said. "Save it, pour it out onto the street. Deliver it to those you call the glassblowers, if you like. Their supply must be running low. Maybe they'll even barter with you for it."

The courier ran one hand over the tubes. The liquid swirled where her fingertips brushed the glass. She recalled a trip into the forest at night, figures in brown grinning masks swaying as they mixed powders and crushed herbs, poured liquids from glass bottles. This wasn't one of her own memories. It was one of Moon's.

"Drugs," she said. "These are the drugs the nameless use to dream their monsters."

The junk dealer closed the case and thrust it into her hands. "Take it, and I'll tell you what you want to know."

"You've been providing this stuff to the glassblowers," she said.

He glanced out the door. The courier saw something move in the shadows, like an animal darting along the fence.

"They're here," the junk dealer said. "They are more lenient than the named when it comes to people of my profession, but this they will not forgive. I can't have it here when they arrive. And you can't be here, either."

She took the case. It was small, but it felt heavy in her hands. When she put it in her satchel, the junk dealer let out a long breath. "Walk alongside the canal," he said, "but go the opposite way this time. That will bring you to an old rail line. It emerges from a tunnel, crosses a bridge. Follow it over the bridge, and then keep going."

"For how long?"

"Go until you can't go any farther," he said. "You'll know when you've arrived."

More movement outside. This time the courier saw three figures in coarse brown clothes approaching through the weeds. They wore masks of plain wood, edges rough and uneven, with large round holes for eyes, crooked gaps for mouths.

"Quickly now," the junk dealer said to the courier. "You'll have to take the other door."

"Who are they?" she asked. Their masks looked heavy and uncomfortable, held together by bulky spikes.

"Wood masks for judgment," he said. "Remember: the tunnel, the canal, the bridge. And most importantly, don't let my visitors find you."

The three figures were waiting outside, a dozen paces from the door. In the weeds around their feet the shadows seemed alive, boiling with menace. The stowaway hissed and backed away.

"What about you?" the courier asked.

"Go," the junk dealer said. "Whatever happens, you will not see me again."

The three nameless figures did not move or speak, but the courier heard a faint whispering at the back of her skull as the junk dealer went to stand before them. Their deliberations had begun. Meanwhile the shadowy forms among the weeds—monstrous cousins of the monster Shadow, maybe—slithered closer.

Another hiss, but not from the stowaway. It was Two, tugging the courier's arm, trying to pull her back from the door. Her monster was right, she thought, to be afraid of those other monsters, those masks. She was afraid, too.

Yet she hesitated. Twice this man had come to her aid. What would become of the junk dealer now, if the nameless ruled against him? Would they let their monsters crush the breath from his lungs or drag him away to some dark and nameless place to be devoured?

He held still as the snakes of shadow entwined his ankles. The whispering of the nameless grew louder as they worked through their case. They disagreed on some points, but gradually the conflicts were settled and the streams converged, three minds becoming one. Then they were ready to deliver their judgment.

The snakes rose up the junk dealer's legs in anticipation, and a groan of fear escaped his lips. His hands were in fists at his sides—not to fight, only to steel himself for what would come next. The smoky coils tightened.

*No*, the courier thought.

And the nameless heard.

The snakes twitched as though scenting the air, and the three wooden masks turned in her direction. The junk dealer turned, too. When he saw her, he closed his eyes and hung his head. Twice he had saved her—and twice she had defied him.

The stowaway growled low as the nameless approached the doorway. The courier saw the eyes behind those masks, saw them see and *recognize* her.

*You*, they said without words. *The dreaming child.*

That was what the nameless in Sap had called her. Now nameless minds sought hers with questioning tendrils. She felt Two's fingers squeeze her arm harder, and the courier remembered her promise to look after her. They would need to run, and soon. But she had questions of her own.

*Why do you call me that?* she demanded. *I am no child. Is it because I dreamed this monster?*

The nameless seemed to notice Two for the first time. *No*, they told her. *Not that one.*

The others, then. The dozens she had made when she was young, those biting and scratching creatures in the dark corners of her room. But if the nameless knew about those monsters, did they know the people who taught her how to stop making them?

*Who were they?* she asked. *I thought they were agents of the dreams committee, but they were yours all along, weren't they?*

The nameless considered this but kept their thoughts guarded. They were not in the habit of answering questions. Their masks meant something different.

The junk dealer looked at her again and shook his head. He was afraid the nameless would discover the contraband hidden in her satchel. And, she realized with a shock, he was even more afraid for her. His concern surprised and touched her. Maybe she could still save him—and maybe she could save herself in the process.

*You should reconsider your judgment,* she told the nameless.

Shock opened their thoughts, and the air vibrated with anger. *We do not need—*

*You need him,* she insisted. *He can help you.*

The snakes shimmered and seethed, sharing in the rage of those who'd created them. But she had won something from her gambit: the judges hesitated, their thoughts wrinkled by doubt.

The courier pressed on. *Conflict is coming between the nameless and the named. Your people flee over the borders, and this man knows the borders. Battle lines are forming, and he knows how both sides operate. Why give up the chance to keep him on yours?*

The junk dealer looked back and forth between the courier and the judges. He understood what they were discussing well enough, though as the judges deliberated again she saw in his eyes more curiosity than hope. A long moment passed, during which the monstrous ropes of smoke flexed impatiently.

Then one of the judges gestured, and a single snake unwound itself from the junk dealer's legs. The courier let out a sigh—they had listened, they had understood, they were letting him go. But the snake did not return to the grass. Instead it shot through the door, straight toward her.

She had time to take only one step backward. Two was quicker, however. She got in front of the courier and brought her foot down hard. The other monster writhed under her boot, nearly slipping away, but Two was already crouched, already grasping it with both hands and holding tight. "Oh, oh!" she said.

Another snake flung itself toward them. This time it was the stowaway who pounced. The animal snatched the monster in its claws, and the monster wrapped its body around the stowaway's middle. Both went still, the stowaway's jaws ready to tear, the monster's coils constricting. Neither would win that fight. And now all three of the monsters of the nameless were bound, one to the junk dealer, one to Two, and one to the stowaway.

Two looked up at the courier. "Oh!" she said again, and the courier knew she meant the same thing she could read in the junk dealer's eyes. They wanted her to run, to get out of there.

But she had promised Two they would leave this place together. She would not abandon anyone else.

*Stop this,* she said to the nameless. *I have more important matters before me.*

She felt their scorn like the sting of a whip. What could be more important than their judgment, which would determine whether any of them would leave this place?

*There are others,* she told them. *Glassblowers who pretend to be nameless, the source of all this trouble. I need to find them.*

*Not our concern,* came their reply. *The glassblowers are not ours.*

So they knew of the glassblowers, knew they were named who wore the masks of the nameless. *But they pretend to be you as they kill the named,* she insisted. *If not for them, the army of the sayers wouldn't be searching these streets. You could have stopped this long ago.*

The judges repeated, *They are not ours.*

"I am not yours, either," the courier said, speaking the words aloud this time. The tendrils of smoke shuddered, and the nameless closed their eyes and breathed as though to fight off a wave of nausea. Even the junk dealer seemed momentarily stunned.

*I am not yours,* she said again, silently this time, willing them to understand. *And if you won't stop those who cause so much destruction, then I must do it myself.*

The three conferred again, keeping their thoughts walled off from her. Her stowaway growled and struggled against the monster, rolling with it once over the floor, pinning it again with his hind legs. Finally, the judges turned back to her. They gestured to their monsters and the monsters wriggled, trying to return. Two let hers go, and after a moment the stowaway did the same—resisting, the courier knew, the urge to chase and pounce again. Two stood straight, and the courier realized that she was often slouching: when she drew herself up to her full height she stood over six feet tall.

*You may leave,* the nameless told them. *But our business is not concluded.*

"It certainly isn't," she mumbled, loud enough for them to hear. But the junk dealer was still immobilized by the monster wrapped around his legs. *What about him?*

*We will conclude our proceedings when you leave.*

The junk dealer nodded to her, mouthed the word he had spoken earlier: *Go.* In spite of his circumstances, he didn't seem so helpless now. His eyes had brightened, and he looked like someone with something to bargain.

The courier forced herself not to run to the door, and Two strode calmly at her side. But once they were back on the street, they both moved faster, and this time the stowaway stayed close.

The junk dealer's directions took them past a boatyard, empty except for a few rusting wrecks. Up ahead she saw the rail bridge, its tall struts flaking green paint over the waters of the canal. The tunnel from which the tracks emerged was lightless and choked by ropy vines. It led in the direction of the factories at the heart of the city. The courier wondered whether the other end was still open, ignored and unseen by generations of the named. A cool wind blew from the dark. It felt bad to turn her back on it.

She crossed the bridge slowly, taking care with each step, feeling for weak points in the decking. Two followed close behind, mumbling to herself. The stowaway bounded across quickly—he did not like to linger over the water.

They followed the tracks past ancient mills, their tall windows dark, whole walls collapsed into mounds of brick. Beyond were smaller structures separated by empty lots and ruins. To one side of the tracks, lakes of dark sludge and heaps of slag stretched into the distance. Flakes of ash blew on the breeze and smoke rose from bright pools of muck, the waste of Hollow's refineries. No one lived out here, nameless or named.

"Oh," Two said sadly.

The tracks traced a wide arc through the ruins. Nothing moved on the rails, no birds flew overhead. The courier would have preferred the streets to this open sky, but she recalled the junk dealer's warning and kept to the rails.

She shielded her eyes as a hot wind blew dust out of the ruins. Her monster coughed and spluttered. A hundred paces ahead, the tracks joined a dozen others in a broad switchyard. When the dust cleared, the courier saw beyond it an enormous brick structure with a domed roof, where all the many rail lines ended. A roundhouse. From a louver at the top of the dome, a thin line of black smoke rose into the sky.

The roundhouse appeared better maintained than the other structures in the area. So this was where the glassblowers kept themselves hidden. Walking toward it, she felt a hot rage bubbling up inside of her. These people had terrified and deceived her. They had plotted her death while welcoming her to drink with them. They had murdered the pages Paw, Wheel, and Thumb, along with dozens, maybe hundreds of others.

"Two," she said, "you should wait here. You won't be safe inside."

"Hmf," she said, offended.

So together they picked their way through the maze of the switchyard, which narrowed as each set of rails joined the next. Eventually only two sets remained. These passed through a tall arched opening in the roundhouse.

"Not that way," the courier said to Two.

They circled the structure until they found a smaller door half-hidden behind crates of glass bottles. When the courier opened it, she heard a low buzzing sound, warm and alive. It was the sound she'd heard that day in the storage car of the Number Twelve—the nameless insects humming in their papery hive. The sound vibrated through her body, a warning and an invitation.

She opened the door. The stowaway slipped through first, and the courier and Two followed him into the dark.

The interior was vast. Light shone through the smoke at the peak of the domed ceiling, through gaps in the slate tiles. Pigeons roosted among the beams. Between the iron columns that supported the roof, a dozen lengths of track extended from the turntable at the center of the building, like spokes of a wheel. On some of these tracks, ancient engines stood rusting.

The courier kept close to the wall, but her stowaway bounded off toward a fire burning in a steel drum. Around it, worn rugs lay over the brick floor. The courier saw makeshift living quarters: leaning tables and chairs, bunks built against the curving wall, cabinets, a chipped washbasin.

Beyond were racks of robes, smocks, coats, and suits, piles of boots and shoes. And hanging from lines strung between the steel supports were masks, dozens of them, all different shapes and colors in sets of three or seven or twelve. Most the courier didn't recognize—tall ovals of green, thick orange masks marked with white handprints, purple veils strung with shining beads. Others she knew. She saw sleek masks of dark gray, like those the children of Nod had worn when they delivered notices for the Black Square. And bright in the firelight, pale with narrow slits for mouths, the white masks of the nameless warriors.

Two was sniffing the air. The courier smelled it, too—grease and fire and something worse, like draff gone sour. The smell came from the center of the roundhouse. As the courier's eyes adjusted, she saw that the turntable was covered by a lumpy heap of glittering muck. This was the source of the smoke she'd seen from outside—it rose from a chimney embedded in the heap and billowed up to the louver above.

She drew closer. The heap was composed mostly of machine parts: wheels and pistons, pipes and rivets and curved sheets of iron. But they floated in a thick mass of liquid glass, which moved as though alive, rolling, twisting, fitting pieces together.

A monster. The glassblowers were dreaming it into being. They lay scattered over the turntable on thick blankets, their heads close to the heap. On their faces were blue masks, the masks of the dreaming nameless. Their chests rose and fell with the slow rhythm of deep slumber.

The courier circled the turntable, stepping over tracks as she passed workbenches covered with tools. Two followed, her quiet complaints mingling with the warble of pigeons overhead. The courier counted eight sleeping figures. They must have collected parts from the abandoned engines and piled them here, then immersed them in molten glass. The fire in the furnace roared as the monster's gleaming bulk rose and fell. Even from this distance, she could feel the heat of its rattling breath.

"Oh!" Two said, pointing at one of the sleeping figures, one who wore no mask over his face. It was Thorn.

The courier crouched at his side. His face was bruised, his wrists and ankles bound with wire. The courier shook him, and he moaned quietly. He was hot to the touch, his clothes soaked with sweat. She hissed his name into his ear, but he didn't wake.

When the courier looked up, Two was holding a large pair of cutters. She must have fetched them from one of the workbenches. The courier shifted Thorn onto his side and Two sheared the wires. Thorn's eyes fluttered open, but he didn't seem to see her.

"Thorn," the courier said, as loudly as she dared. His eyes closed again. Drugged, she thought.

She took his arms and Two got his legs. Together they lifted him, but they'd gone only a few steps when Thorn began to gasp. The farther they got from the monstrous heap on the turntable, the more he struggled for breath. Before they could leave the turntable, the other sleepers began to stir. Their minds were overlapping territories; the courier couldn't wake Thorn without waking them all.

"Back, back," the courier hissed, and they returned Thorn to his place near the monster. The boy's breathing calmed, and the others were still again.

As the courier watched, the monster continued to take shape. Somehow it was both monster and machine, with curved sheets of metal forming a torso that was also a boiler. It had four legs, and it had wheels on those legs, and the wheels rested upon the rails, forged to their dimensions.

Thorn was sweating, moaning in his sleep. If she couldn't wake him, she would have to go in after him. She took the junk dealer's case from her satchel and opened it on her lap. The liquid inside the glass tubes swirled darkly.

"Oh!" said Two, disapproving.

"I have to get Thorn out," the courier said. "And I have to stop them from finishing that *thing*."

Wringing her hands, Two looked at the monster in its cocoon of liquid glass. The courier reached up to take one of her big hands in hers. "I need you to watch over me," she said. "To protect me while I sleep. Can you do that?"

Two pulled her hand away, pouting through her fear. But the courier didn't have time to argue. She took a glass tube from the case, unscrewed the cap, and drank its contents in one gulp. It tasted like bitter smoke. Burbling with alarm, Two knelt beside her, hands fluttering over the courier's throat and chest and belly, as though she might somehow coax the stuff back out of her body.

For a moment, the courier thought she would vomit, but she took a deep breath and kept it down. As Moon, she had consumed the same drug or something like it among the nameless dreamers in the forest. It surprised her how this, too, felt like pretend. She set the case on the floor. She lay back with her satchel as a pillow and stared at the smoke winding through the louver in the ceiling far above. As her body went warm, and her skin tingled, she wondered how the smoke knew where to go. Her monster was beside her, stroking her hair, which meant she could close her eyes now.

When she opened them, the moon had taken the place of the louver. It was bright and full, and the dome of the roundhouse was the dome of the sky. The hundreds of holes in the roof were stars.

The courier sat up and shivered. She was alone on the shore of a canal. Dark shapes moved on the water—barges piled high with ghosts and misshapen glass figurines. The barges moved without pilots. They knocked into one another as they floated downstream, spilling ghosts and glass into the water. The ghosts sank with the glass into the black current.

She stood and walked alongside the canal through the empty city. The houses, mills, and factories were a hollow, lightless jumble. Her stowaway emerged from the shadows and brushed his tail against her ankles. Part of the dream, she thought, until she felt the familiar warmth of the animal's mind thrumming alongside her own. He must have fallen asleep on the bunk and come here with her, dreaming his way through the same strange city. She was glad.

Her stowaway darted along the path beside the canal. Up ahead, a stone building towered over the water. It was topped with ornate spires, and its windows were pictures made of colored glass. A blazing red light shone from its open door, out onto the canal, where ghosts loaded crates onto the barge docked there. A warm breeze blew from within. The courier followed it inside.

Here was the glassblowers' workshop, the one she had visited in Hollow long ago, but everything grown to fill the vast interior of the nameless structure. Massive tables dominated the room, and the tables were covered with more monstrous glass figurines. At the back, the furnace stretched to the ceiling, its firebox nearly overflowing with crackling blue coals.

The glassblowers were still at work, using tongs to tug fresh gobs of glass into strange animal shapes. Even in this shared dream they wore the blue masks of the dreaming nameless. They took no notice of the courier.

She picked up one of the figurines and turned it in her hand. First it looked like torn tree roots, then like a lizard, then like a steam engine. Pieces of the monster outside. Additions, facets, revisions.

Her stowaway slipped deeper into the building. The courier followed him to the furnace, where one glassblower fed the fire with chunks of naphtha. No, not a glassblower—it was Thorn in his poorly cut gray suit. Over his face was a heavy iron mask. He worked clumsily, burning himself again and again. The mask muffled his screams.

The courier grabbed the mask with both hands. At first Thorn panicked and backed away, but she reassured him with one hand against the back of his neck. Thorn held still while she found and loosened the buckles holding it in place. When the mask fell away, he blinked at her as though he'd just woken up.

"I was a child again," he said. "I was waiting for my father to come home."

"Thorn, what were you thinking, coming here by yourself?"

He frowned, clearly confused. Then he seemed to remember. "I thought the nameless of Hollow would see me if I came alone. I knew I would need their help."

"So you didn't come here to join the glassblowers?"

"Join them?" he said. "No, I want to stop them."

Somehow, in this dark and cluttered dream they shared, the courier knew he spoke the truth. "But what happened?" she asked. "Did you find the nameless?"

He looked at the shovel in his hands as though noticing it for the first time. "The last thing I remember, I was stepping off the train and onto the platform." He touched the back of his head. "I think someone hit me. They must have knocked me out."

"Did you meet someone named Rope aboard the train? He's a member of the fifth committee, and a names committee diviner. He wears a rope for a belt."

Thorn squeezed his eyes shut. "I don't remember anyone like that."

But of course he wouldn't, even if he'd seen Rope. The courier usually forgot about Rope the moment he left her sight.

"Who is he?" Thorn asked.

A suspicion was forming in her mind, but she wasn't sure enough to speak it or even think it through—not here, in this dream that wasn't her own, with the minds of others so close. "I found some of the true nameless myself," she said. "Or they found me. They wore bulky wooden masks held together with spikes."

"I know them," Thorn said. "They can help us. We have to—"

"I tried," she said. "They refused me."

"They know me, though. I can convince them to come with us. To see what's happening here."

"Then we need to leave now," she said.

The untended fire had burned down fast, and the room was dim and cold. The colored glass in the windows shone like ice. The courier took Thorn's hand and led him toward the door. Only now did she see that her stowaway was gone—and so were the glassblowers.

"Hurry," she said.

But when she turned, Thorn was gone, and the hand she held was made of glass. She screamed and dropped it. The hand shattered, broken fingers skittering over the floor.

Gloved hands closed around her arms and legs, and masked faces loomed up all around. The glassblowers dragged her outside and carried her down to the canal, where a full barge waited. Before she could scream again, two ghosts came forward with another eyeless, mouthless mask of iron and fitted it over her face.


"Another dream," her father told her. "I need you to stay awake now. I need you to keep your breath nice and even." He spoke as he always did when he was disappointed in her, each word pronounced with great care.

The courier was a girl again. She lay on a cold, hard surface with a nest of wires fitted over her head while her father peered at his blinking instrument panels. He adjusted dials, watched needles rise and fall, hummed to himself.

"Lock," she said.

Eyes still on the needles, he said, "What I need you to do now is to think of something very, very sad."

The courier laughed until tears stung her eyes. She hated being in this place. But what she hated even more was how happy she felt to be home. She knew that her ghost was outside, waiting for her to start their next game of pretend. Later, maybe, her sister would give her another lesson in maps or numbers or story. Or had Ticket already gone, already left her here?

She tried to sit up, but her father put one hand to her chest and pressed her back down.

"We don't want to have to start over," he said.

No, she didn't want to start over. But here she was, back where she began. That was very sad, wasn't it? Was it sad enough for him?

"Interesting," her father said, making notes.

She looked around the room. Something was different about the cottage. The back wall, where her father usually hung his coat and hat—and where her own yellow coat had a hook of its own—was missing. At first she saw nothing there at all, but when she blinked and worked hard to focus her eyes she could make out a vast, dimly lit place. She saw dozens of train tracks there, pointing from a circle in the center like rays from the sun. Why did that place seem so familiar?

The roundhouse, where the glassblowers had their hideout. Even now she could see them sleeping on the turntable. She saw Thorn, too, and her own slumbering body, and Two crouched beside her, looking scared.

And there was the new monster, almost fully formed. Steam rose from the chimney on its back, and the boiler swelled with breath. But it was still so hungry. It had to be fed. She was feeding it, and so were the others. It ate and ate and ate.

"They wanted me to forget about you," she said to her father. Lock said nothing, only checked his needles and his notes. "For years I thought you were deleted only because of what you're doing now. Because of me. Your nameless secret."

Lock turned to her and frowned. He adjusted the wires on her head. "Focus now," he said.

"But I decided to remember," she went on. "Forgetting would have been too much like forgiving. They would have to delete me to make this go away."

Her father set down his notes and turned back to her. He seemed to really see her, then, for the first time since she'd appeared in his cottage.

"What about your sister?" he asked. "Can you make yourself forget how she hurt you?"

"No," she said, and she felt the monster lapping at the fire of her anger. "But I think I can forgive her. What could she have done, even if she'd stayed? She was a child, too."

The courier felt the dream change as she claimed it. It wasn't good, it wasn't happy. But it was hers. She was still helping the glassblowers to make the monster, but she worked with a different material now.

"Those people you brought to help me with my dreams," she said. "They weren't from any committee of the named. Why did you bring them here? What did they want with me?"

Her father frowned and shook his head. He was a dream, and he knew only what she knew, nothing more. Still, she had to try.

"The last Rider," she said. "Was he one of them? Did he work with the nameless before he joined the Black Square?"

Still he said nothing. The courier sat up and removed the nest of wires from her head. Her father didn't try to stop her. There were tears in his eyes. "It was my fault," he said. "Only mine."

She knew he'd said it because it was her dream, and because that was what she wanted him to say. But she needed more.

"Tell me," she said. "Tell me what you did."

He wiped the tears from his face. "I think you know," he said. "Remember what our visitors taught you."

They taught her to know when she was sleeping, with that rope around her wrist as a reminder. Taught her to keep the worst of her thoughts from escaping over the border. The dreaming child.

"But it wasn't just about keeping the dreams from escaping," her father said. "Think what you did with those thoughts."

She was only talking to herself. Lock wasn't Lock, he was part of her own mind, a mirage of memory and knowledge and guesswork. But maybe that mirage was right.

"The empty person," she said. "That hollow thing in the shape of a man."

"Go on," her father said. "What was he?"

"He was nothing. But I gave him all those thoughts, everything that frightened me. Just like Moon did in that forest long ago. Just like I did when I made Two. And just like I'm doing now for the monster in the roundhouse." She gripped the edge of the table with both hands. "Is that what you're saying? That the nameless tricked me into making a monster?"

Her father said nothing, but she felt she knew the answer now. All those years ago, the nameless had taught her how to stop making monsters—but first they'd shown her how to make just one more. The nameless in their wooden masks had given her the same answer, when she'd asked them if they called her the dreaming child because she'd made Two. *No*, they had said. *Not that one.*

She must have dreamed up something terrible, that first time. And where was her first monster now? What had it done?

"I have to go," she told her father. "I have to wake up."

"Just a moment," Lock said. He fished something out of his shirt pocket and gave it to her. It was a small brass key.

"What's this?"

"Something you think you might need," he said.

She squeezed the key in her hand. He was right, she thought. She might need this, though she didn't know why.

She got down off the examination table. She was the courier again, and no longer a little girl. But the little girl was still close—*Here I am, I've been here all this time*—and she was coming with her.

As she passed through the cottage door, she looked back to see her father hunched over his instrument panels. He continued scratching notes into his notebook, studying nothing.

She squeezed the key as she walked, learning its notches and ridges. The brass grew warm in her hand as she went looking for Thorn. He was probably back in his own dream, a captive again.

She took the path down past the briars and around the pond to the forest. The trees were taller and older than she remembered, the forest darker. She found the clearing she had sometimes visited as a child, the ground lumped with tangles of dry grass. At the center of the clearing stood a tall brass bed, with pillows and sheets and a thick knitted blanket, yellow and red and orange.

Had this been here when she was a child? She recalled something ancient, partly sunk into the dirt, something made of metal that might have been brass—but there was no word *brass* then, so she couldn't be sure. The bed might have been dragged into the woods and abandoned during the confusion of the Silence, or maybe sometime before.

She felt Thorn's dream at the edges of her own. Its echoes came to her through the trees, moans of pain and fear, and with it the rusty stench of blood. She had to cross that border somehow.

A crashing noise came from the cottage. Someone was toppling equipment, overturning furniture. The courier smelled the sharp smokiness of burnt naphtha, just how it was the day Frost came with his deletion committee. But it wasn't Frost who came for her now. The glassblowers must have realized she'd escaped.

She crawled into the bed, burrowing under the sheets, pulling the covers to her chin. A cool breeze rustled the leaves and made the branches shake. She drew the covers up over her eyes and sank deep into the mattress, falling into the dream below the dream. She was standing beside another bed, in a little room with one small window.

It was early morning, or very late in the day. A stout, square-faced man lay in the bed, wounds on his chest, throat, and arms. The sheets were soaked with blood. His eyes were closed and his mouth was open. His tongue looked dry behind his crooked teeth.

A skinny boy stood beside the bed. He could have celebrated no more than four or five name days. Thorn. The courier put a hand on his shoulder.

"Fathers," she said.

"You've come too soon," the child Thorn said. "He's still alive."

The courier looked down and saw that she now wore the white uniform of a ghosts committee collector. The man on the bed clutched his side and groaned. His wound seeped, and a small gray crescent emerged from between his fingers. It was a sharp-edged length of iron.

"The machine at the factory broke," Thorn said. "Pieces got stuck in him."

The boy used a pair of tongs to pull the metal free of the wound. His father screamed. Thorn dropped the piece of metal into a box beside the bed.

The courier saw that the box had no bottom. The whole of the roundhouse was there—it was like looking down through the smoke louver. The monster was directly below, rumbling.

"You don't have to do this," she said to Thorn.

But he was already pulling another chunk of metal from his father's leg. The man screamed again. Thorn dropped the piece of metal into the box.

"I don't want him to be a ghost," Thorn said.

"Everyone becomes a ghost eventually." The courier wasn't sure if she'd said that, or if it was something the ghost collector had said long ago. The air was growing warmer, and she smelled naphtha. The glassblowers were coming.

"You aren't supposed to be here," Thorn told her. "I don't know the word yet."

"Do you find words for things sometimes?" the courier asked.

"I get words wrong, and sometimes they turn out to be the right words for something else."

An iron pin glinted from a gash in the injured man's chest. Thorn went to grab it with the tongs, but the courier stopped him. "Don't," she said. "Focus on the word instead."

She needed to get them both out of here. To escape the roundhouse. To bring Thorn to the nameless judges and try again to win their help. But the dream was nearing the moment when Thorn would divine and deliver his border word, the one that made a ghost go away. Maybe here he could remember.

The air was hot and hard to breathe. The courier felt the glassblowers seeking her, felt their rage. They would tear her apart, burn her, melt her down—

Thorn's father stirred. He saw the pin in his chest. "Get it out!" he screamed. Thorn reached with the tongs.

"Thorn, try to remember," the courier said.

"How can I remember something that hasn't happened yet?"

"All this has *already* happened."

A blue-masked figure crawled in through the window. Another came through the door, and a third emerged from under the bed. Thorn stepped back.

"Out, out!" his father screamed.

The glassblowers closed in. Thorn swung his tongs, but one of them grabbed his wrist and twisted the tool from his hand. The courier shouted and punched at them, but the glassblowers were too strong—this was their dream now. One held her arms, another grabbed her hair and tilted her head back. The third approached with a steaming iron ladle and tipped it to her lips. She screamed as her mouth filled with molten glass.


The courier woke on her feet. Two glassblowers flanked her, holding her up, keeping her in place. She coughed and spat hot liquid.

Not glass. It was a searing, pungent mixture that went like lightning through her veins, jolting her from sleep into wild waking.

A piercing sound stung her ears. Two lay pinned to the floor nearby, wailing as a blue-masked glassblower ground one knee into the monster's back. She squirmed, eyes rolling with panic.

The courier reached for her, but her captors wrenched her away. She shook her head, blinking the last scraps of Thorn's dream from her eyes. Looming before her was the round face of a golden sun. Its rays glittered as it danced toward her, and its eyes were great black pits. Behind the sun's gold grinning mouth were grinning red lips.

The man removed his mask and gave a little bow. The courier recognized him—it was the older glassblower who had shared his whiskey in their workshop, the night she delivered *gob*.

Thorn coughed and groaned. The courier turned to see him still on the turntable, struggling to sit up. "Gardener," he said, and the courier understood his meaning. This man had been the Gardener of Shovels, when he was with the Black Square.

"You can both call me Glue," he said. "That was the name assigned to me by your committee, courier. Though I've not had the opportunity to use it for quite some time."

The other glassblowers were still waking up, helping one another to their feet and passing around a steaming mug of the wakeful brew. They gave none to Thorn, who could barely keep his eyes open. The courier stood a dozen paces away from where she'd laid down to sleep. Two must have seen the glassblowers stirring and tried to carry her out of the roundhouse. But the old man, playing the role of Guardian to his sleepers, had been there to stop her. "You saw us arrive," she said. "You let me join your dreaming."

"We've known you had potential since the first time we saw you," Glue said. "And we were right! All our previous efforts were frail little creatures.

You witnessed that mess in Buckle. But this one is something different, I think. We couldn't have done it without you. You and our Six of Trees."

The courier turned again, gazing past Thorn to the great hulking beast they had helped to construct. It lay dozing upon the tracks, bigger than any engine the courier had seen, bigger even than the Number Twelve. Its head, resting between the rails, resembled that of a lizard, but its snout was short and stubby, and it had pointy, leathery ears. With each drowsy breath, the monster's bulk swelled. Steam trickled from its nostrils, and its body was covered in heavy scales of dark glass. Its tail lay curled to one side, itself the length of a train car. Its powerful limbs were tucked almost daintily under its body. It looked more animal than machine, but pieces scavenged from the old engines were unmistakable. Smoke puffed from the chimney that rose between its shoulders, and its limbs were lined with wheels and pistons.

The newly wakened glassblowers walked slowly around the monster, inspecting the results of their work. They didn't speak, but the courier sensed satisfaction in the way they leaned back to take in the sight.

"The army of the named will destroy that thing," the courier said.

Glue clicked his tongue. "Haven't you heard? Frost leads his army against the last city of the nameless. By the time they return to Hollow, they'll be too late."

Two wailed, still pinned to the floor.

"Let her up," the courier said.

The glassblowers ignored her. Thorn had crawled from the turntable to lie with his back against one of the steel support columns. The glassblowers ignored him, too. A few brought a cartful of naphtha from the other end of the roundhouse. They dumped it directly onto the tracks, a few feet from the monster's snout.

The courier watched the monster's flanks expand with each breath, watched its claws flex. If it followed the tracks she'd taken here, over the canal, through that old tunnel, it might reach the named part of the city in minutes.

"People will be hurt," she said.

"People *will* be hurt," Glue agreed. "But at least their ghosts won't be put to work in the factories. There will be no factories left."

The monster's nostrils twitched and its eyes opened to slits. The four glassblowers tending to it took several steps back. The monster stretched, whipping its tail from side to side. Then it stood, extending its legs and neck so its head rose up into the dome. A dozen pigeons abandoned their roosts to flee through the louver. The monster watched them go, eyes blinking lazily. The courier recognized those eyes, huge and round and golden. They looked like her stowaway's eyes.

The monster lowered itself back onto the rails and yawned, revealing rows of sharp iron teeth. It sniffed the naphtha, licked the pile with its great glassy tongue, then tore a chunk from the mass with its teeth. It ate carefully, letting nothing fall from its jaws. A rumbling filled the air as fuel tumbled down the monster's throat and into its firebox.

"Water," Glue commanded.

The glassblowers brought a big steel basin. The monster was seated upright now, but it showed no interest in the water.

"Closer," Glue said. "Push it closer."

The glassblowers looked at one another, hesitating before kneeling to nudge the basin forward. They kept as far from the monster as they could, and the water sloshed. The sound made the monster stand suddenly, and the glassblowers stumbled backward, one tripping over a rail before scrambling away. The monster's eyes flashed, and the courier recognized that expression from her stowaway. It wanted to chase, to pounce. The monster resisted the urge, though, and bent its head to drink, long tongue flicking. Steam hissed from its chimney.

The old man sighed. He had been more nervous than the courier realized. She said to him, "All this for the sake of some performance your Rider has scripted for you?"

Glue looked hurt. "This isn't pretend," he said. "We fight to free the ghosts of the named."

The courier thought of the ghost in the sooty blue dress, marched from factory to boxcar, fuel for the battle to come. She thought of her patchwork ghost, imagined his sketches burning with him.

"No, for you it's just another show," she said. "Ghosts are about to burn because you sent the named to war. The monsters, the killings—none of this is for the nameless, or for the ghosts. All you want is to humiliate Frost, just as he humiliated you when he stripped you of your titles."

Glue's hands tightened on the mask, cracking the face of the golden sun. "Is that what your Gardener of Stones told you? Gray is a coward, hiding in the Black Square, lost in his little stories. And what is the Black Square now?" Glue spat on the floor. "He could be helping us change the world. Once the sayers learn that Frost can't protect them, they'll welcome us back."

"And when Hollow has burned and the last city of the nameless fallen, is that when you'll change the world?" the courier said. "Or when the destruction is over, and you have your seat at the saying stone again, will you order ghosts to rebuild it all just as it was?"

A bird flew in through the open door of the roundhouse and landed on the back of a nearby chair. Glue looked relieved. Eagerly, he removed the small tube secured to one of the bird's legs. A messenger bird, the courier realized.

Glue uncapped the tube, removed the roll of paper, and read quickly. He turned to face the other glassblowers. "Ready yourselves," he called. "Our Rider will be with us soon."

The glassblowers who had tended to the monster removed their masks and drew gray robes on over their boilersuits. In war stories, the nameless used strange weapons—long hooks and blades, staffs equipped with pulleys and ropes—to tame monsters, to climb and crack open the machines of the named. These false nameless armed themselves with similar weapons before putting on their new masks, white for war.

The messenger bird still sat perched on the back of the chair, black eyes blinking. The courier thought of the birds in the dovecote Rope had built in the last car of the Number Twelve. She thought of the care with which he had looked after his flock.

When Thorn told her that someone must have knocked him unconscious as he debarked at Hollow Station that morning, she had begun to suspect something about Rope. Now, free of the dream, she was certain of it. She started to laugh.

"Does this amuse you?" Glue asked.

"Your Rider," the courier said, still laughing. "Your Rider is Rope."

Glue regarded her cautiously. "Our Rider has had many names," he said. The care with which he chose his words told the courier she was right.

Frost had tasked her with finding someone who walked among the namers but operated in the places between. Someone whose movements might have gone unnoticed. Someone who could have alerted the nameless—these false nameless, it turned out—to the Number Twelve's schedule.

And Smoke, meeting in secret with the Gardener of Stones aboard the Black Square's train, had described someone deeply embedded among the named, too close for them to see.

Rope. Kind to everyone, even to her. A namer and a member of the Fifth Committee, privy to Book's secrets, yet so dull and unremarkable he was almost invisible. Rope must have stolen a look at the schedule all those months ago, then sent a messenger bird to arrange the attack at Buckle. He had probably sent another bird to Brick, alerting the watchers there, the night she'd fled from the train. And yesterday he would have spotted Thorn on the train from Bottle and guessed his intentions, would have turned him over to the glassblowers before quickly slipping back to the Number Twelve.

The courier spoke loudly enough for all the glassblowers to hear. "If Rope is the one whose story you're playing, then I pity you." She felt as though she were onstage again, performing for her audience. But she had to choose her words carefully, because this wasn't pretend. "He must have told you your attacks would shake Frost's grip on power. But all you've done is help him bring the other sayers in line."

"Frost is off chasing stories," Glue said, to her and to the others. "The real threat is here, poised to strike at the largest city of the named."

"Your little show is the best tool Frost has," she said. "The more afraid you make the named, the quicker they are to obey him."

The old man slapped her hard across the face. She tasted blood and smiled; she was fully awake now. The glassblowers still gripped her arms tightly, but she could sense their doubt. The one on Two's back looked up at Glue, as though for an answer to what the courier had said. The courier recognized the blind, milky-white eye of the woman who had watched her from beside the furnace that night in Hollow.

Two flailed and nearly knocked the mask from her captor's face. She snarled and bent the monster's arms behind her back.

The courier clenched her fists. She felt something sharp digging into the palm of her right hand. It had been there all this time, warm and jagged, but she'd dismissed it as a lingering scrap of dream. And it was that—but it was also something more: the brass key her father had given her.

The courier turned. The monster had finished drinking. It was staring straight at her now, its eyes golden moons in the dark.

How had the key come with her from the dream? Maybe she had been able to shape it from the scrap, because maybe it wasn't just a key. It was a piece of the monster—a piece she'd kept apart from the rest, kept for herself without the others knowing.

The white-masked glassblowers carried from the shadows of the roundhouse what looked like a large lidless crate. They strode up alongside the monster, and this time they didn't hesitate. Something about the masks helped them commit to their roles. One of them motioned the monster lower, and to the courier's surprise it obeyed, settling onto the rails. They heaved the object up onto the monster's back.

It watched, curious, as they ran straps under its belly and fastened buckles. A rope ladder hung from one side. Not a crate, but a litter for the glassblowers to ride in.

"We could have helped you, courier," Glue said. "We will be sayers again. We will cast out Frost and unspeak the deletion committees. We would have been your friends—that's what I wanted. But those were the hopes of a foolish old man. The others were right. We should have made a ghost of you while you slept."

"Oh, oh," said Two. Her voice was weak now, and she no longer struggled.

Glue reached into the open front of his boilersuit and pulled out a gun. He gazed at the weapon with something like awe. "The Rider entrusted me with this," he said. "It's the same gun he used onstage in Whisper, our last night with the Black Square. But he had it for a long time before that. Do you know what he told me? That this is the gun to which Moon delivered the word *gun*. The gun Moon used to shoot Hand. Is that true, or just another story?" He aimed it at the courier. "Doesn't matter, really."

The courier closed her eyes and breathed, squeezing the key in her hand. And she found, more easily than she'd expected, the churning heat of the monster's mind.

*Help me,* she thought. *I need you to help me.*

She heard the monster snort as though in response, heard it rumble as it shifted its bulk. When she opened her eyes, Glue still held the gun, but he was looking past her. She turned to see the monster on its feet. It shook forcefully, sending a white-masked glassblower flying from the ladder on its side.

Thorn looked back and forth between the monster and the courier. He seemed to understand some part of what was happening. He rose shakily to his feet.

"Get that thing under control," Glue called.

The courier squeezed the key more tightly. *Hurry!* she thought. And the monster padded swiftly toward her, glass scales clacking. Glue turned his gun on the monster.

The blue-masked glassblowers backed away, pulling the courier with them. She brought the heel of her boot down hard on the left one's shin; he groaned and loosened his grip. She twisted free of the other, then ran at Two's captor, driving into her with one shoulder. They both went sprawling over the floor.

She heard gunshots and looked up. Glue screamed as he fired again and again. The monster didn't seem to notice. It batted him aside with one great paw, and he arced flailing through the air and landed against the rails with a dull *crack*. His body lay still on the sleepers.

The white-masked glassblowers were up again, running after the monster, waving their arms. The courier felt her connection to its mind weaken as they gentled it with their own thoughts, urging *calm, easy now, easy.* Glue had not helped make the monster, only acted as guardian while the others dreamed. But they outnumbered her, and they were shutting her out. She could only watch as the glassblowers led the monster back to the tracks.

The three still in blue masks were up again, closing in on the courier and

Two, their eyes bright with anger. But all the glassblowers froze at the sight of something at the edge of the turntable, blocking their monster's route. It was a small gray smudge, its eyes two shining chips of gold. The stowaway.

Seeing it, the monster tensed its limbs and made a new sound, low and deep and dangerous: a bottled roar. It flattened its ears and arched its back as the stowaway padded forward. The animal planted his paws on the ties and growled.

The monster's eyes widened at the sound. It crouched and growled louder. The glassblowers took several steps back.

The stowaway seemed to double in size as his fur stood on end. He still looked tiny next to the monster, but the monster responded as though he were the biggest thing in the world. It arched its back higher and steam shot from its valves. The stowaway didn't back down. Their growling grew louder, each overtaking the other in waves.

The courier wasn't sure which of them moved first. Both were suddenly leaping and rolling, a storm of clattering glass scales, flying fur, and flashing gold eyes. The stowaway was a gray blur darting between the monster's limbs, through clouds of steam. The monster leapt, froze, circled, and leapt again. It crashed into one of the old engines, sent it toppling in a cloud of rust and dirt. For a moment the courier lost sight of the stowaway. Then it leapt clear of the debris and landed atop another engine. With a screeching bellow, the monster charged and sent the engine spinning. It struck one of the iron columns, bending it. Dust rained from the ceiling.

The glassblowers were still trying to control the monster, but they were panicking, shouting, failing to maintain their roles as silent nameless. And the monster's brain was a blazing furnace—everything that drew close was instantly burned away.

The blue-masked glassblowers moved for cover, and the courier ran toward Thorn. He was already up and headed for the door at the back of the round-house. But Two grabbed the courier and pulled her in the opposite direction, just as a section of the roof crashed down in front of them.

The stowaway dashed from side to side, leading the monster in a wild dance. The monster spun and swiped another column, cracking it in two. A great beam tumbled from the ceiling, followed by an avalanche of slate tile. The glassblowers scattered.

The courier ran for the arched doorway with Two at her side. The stowaway burst past them, and the monster came careening after. The courier felt its heat as it passed, and she felt something of its mind, too: not angry, not scared, but brimming with an eager, untamable joy.

The courier emerged just in time to see the two beasts disappear among the ruins. Then the building collapsed behind her, the rest of the roof falling in one great mass, pulling most of the circular wall down with it, engulfing her in a cloud of red dust. She ran, coughing and blinking as she stumbled over debris and railway ties.

Someone tall was moving toward her through the dust. Two, she thought, and reached for her. The figure grabbed her and hauled her into the air, carried her away from the rubble and out of the dust.

It wasn't Two. The gait was uneven, the grip so strong it hurt. The courier screamed and pounded her fists against the broad back, but she may as well have been punching a steel drum. It was one of the seeker ghosts, and she was his prisoner.

The ghost swung her down off his shoulder as though to dash her head against the ground, but someone else caught her—his twin. One ghost had her by the ankles, the other by the wrists, and together they carried her to an empty mining cart that stood alone on the tracks.

Ivy was waiting there, exhausted and disheveled but smiling.

"Ivy, please listen—"

She touched the courier's lips, shushing her. Her finger came away with blood on it. The courier was still bleeding from where Glue had hit her.

Ivy smiled. "I'm not supposed to hurt you," she said. "But how will anyone know?"

She punched the courier hard in the mouth. Her teeth broke skin and her mouth filled with blood. She writhed in the ghosts' grasp as they swung her once, twice, then up and into the mining cart. She struck her head against the rim and fell down, down into a darkness where no words could follow.

She woke with head pounding, limbs aching. Her ankles and wrists were bound to the rigid chair upon which she sat. She blinked, trying to focus. The room seemed familiar, though she was certain she had never been here before. A door to her right was guarded by two watchers. To her left was a broad window, through which she could see brick walls and city streets sliding past. She heard the slow, steady clacking of rolling stock. Not a room, then, but a compartment. She was aboard a train.

Sayer Frost sat behind a plain desk at the front of the car, his attention on the plate of food in front of him. Judging from the rich smell, the sayer was eating the roasted flesh of an animal. Smoke and Ivy were seated near the window. Wandering restlessly over the rug between them and Frost's desk was—the courier blinked again—the ghost of a pig.

"Our guest is awake," Smoke observed.

The watchers at the door stood a little straighter. Smoke rose from his chair and went to stand before the courier while Frost continued eating.

"You will have to pardon the sayer while he finishes his meal," Smoke said.

"He prefers to eat while the ghost of the animal persists. Having it present, he says, improves the flavor. Are you hungry?"

The courier tasted blood in her mouth and her stomach turned. She said nothing.

"I am sorry for the tightness of the bonds," Smoke said to her. "Bad enough that you have suffered such injuries. Our seekers are not usually so clumsy." He looked at Ivy.

"She was difficult to keep hold of," Ivy said.

"Indeed, and just as difficult to find. With all that running, she must be thirsty. If you would, please?"

Ivy hesitated, then rose and poured a glass of water from a carafe. She brought it to the courier and raised it to her lips. The courier sipped. She *was* thirsty, but instead of swallowing, she spat the water in Ivy's face.

Ivy blinked, flung the rest of the water onto the floor, and raised the glass as though to strike her. The courier did not turn away.

Smoke made a little sound of disapproval.

Ivy took a deep breath, returned to her seat by the window, and set the glass on the table. She wiped her face with her sleeve.

Smoke turned a chair and sat facing the courier. He gave her a thoughtful look. "That was rude," he said. "We are people of words. Yet the extremes to which you've pushed us these last several weeks—it's all rather embarrassing, don't you think?"

"How's your throat?" she asked.

His hand went to the dark blue scarf around his neck, which she knew he wore to hide the injury her stowaway had given him—the injury *she* and her stowaway had given him, with their claws.

"I don't know what you mean," he said.

The courier tried to snort, but instead she coughed, and the coughing hurt. She wondered where Two was, whether Thorn had made it out of the round-house alive. She couldn't ask without the risk of giving them away.

"Where is Beryl?" she said.

"Beryl remains aboard, though her future with the namers is uncertain."

"She remains aboard," the courier repeated.

"Ah," said Smoke. "You don't know where we are. It's because this car is new, a replacement for the one you burned. Not an exact copy, but close enough. We are riding the Number Twelve out of Hollow and into nameless territory."

Smoke leaned forward, eyes suddenly bright. "Now here is a puzzle for you, courier. We call it the Number Twelve, even as stock comes and goes from the train. How many cars would have to be replaced before we would have to stop calling it the Number Twelve? Before it became something different enough to require a new name?"

He sat back in his chair and raised one finger. "You will say that so long as the engine remains in place, the train it pulls remains the Number Twelve. And yet our puzzle persists, because parts of the engine wear out all the time, and these are replaced by new parts. After hundreds of years of service, little of the original remains. And when the engine has changed entirely, piece by piece? Is it still the Number Twelve?"

Smoke looked sad. "Maybe there is no answer. Maybe that is what makes it a good puzzle. I am just a man who has lived more than half of his years, and now the strangest things keep me up at night." He sighed. "Our little committee has changed, too. Beryl has left, and I have taken her place. A somewhat irregular arrangement. But then, our work is nearly concluded."

The courier strained against the bonds. She felt the gaze of the watchers. Their ghost lens goggles flashed. They wore heavy batons at their sides.

Frost set down his cutlery and wiped his chin with a napkin. One of the watchers opened the door and gestured for someone to enter.

The courier shivered when she saw who it was: Book. Smoke pointed to Frost's empty plate and said, "Take that away."

"Book?" the courier said.

It was only the ghost of him, of course, and the ghost didn't look at her. He went to the desk, picked up the plate, and turned to go.

"Book," the courier pleaded.

The ghost hesitated a moment but still didn't look at her. Had he been calibrated? No, the courier saw the light of Book's mind still shining behind the ghost's eyes. He hadn't been calibrated. He was only ashamed.

The ghost was almost through the door when Frost tapped his desk. Book turned, and Smoke pointed at the ghost of the pig, which had settled onto the rug, looking worried.

"This too," Smoke said.

Book took up the rope tied around the pig's middle. After a few tugs, it rose and went with him out the door. The watcher closed the door behind them. Through all this, Ivy seemed uncomfortable. She stared out the window rather than look at the ghost of her former committee chair.

Frost was gazing at the courier with the hint of a grin on his lips. Keeping Book's ghost was something he was savoring, just as he'd savored the cooked flesh.

The courier looked away, focusing her attention on Ivy. "Who is committee chair now? Have you even called a vote?"

Ivy didn't turn from the window.

Smoke said, "A vote will be called in due course. Given all that's happened, and given the task before us, the namers require special guidance and direction. That is why Sayer Frost generously devotes his time to the restoration of this committee."

The courier twisted her wrists, looking for some weak point in the bindings, but they held firm. "I found your glassblowers," she said.

"So we've heard. And why did you seek them out after all this time, I wonder."

"To join them," Ivy said.

"I was trying to *stop* them," the courier said. "Listen to me. They aren't nameless. They're only pretending."

"Oh?" said Smoke. "Their attack on Buckle seemed real enough, as do the other monsters they've made. But Ivy tells us that the glassblowers are unlikely to have survived the collapse of their hideout. Still, watchers are patrolling the area."

"Watchers won't be enough," the courier said. "The glassblowers have built a new monster, worse than anything we've seen before. It was made to destroy Hollow. It could make ghosts of hundreds, maybe thousands of people."

Smoke, one eyebrow raised, turned to look at Frost. The sayer gave no response that the courier could read, but Smoke pursed his lips and nodded. "Such stories," he said. "Really, courier, you spent too much time with the Black Square."

"This is not pretend," the courier said.

"The sayer understands what's happening here," Smoke said. "As does Ivy. She was correct when she said that you sought out the glassblowers because you wished to join them. You serve them now—and all the nameless who wish us harm—by trying to frighten us from our mission."

"What mission?" the courier said.

Smoke's smile was patient. "It's just as the old stories say. A forest, and beyond the forest a city, and in the city—well, you know how it goes. We ride to the last city of the nameless, to erase the last of everything we cannot name."

The courier leaned forward and looked directly at Frost. "That assignment you gave me?" she said. "I never stopped working on it, you know."

Frost's expression did not change.

"The man you asked me to find was the previous Rider of the Black Square," she said. "He murdered another player onstage, then fled the show with his followers, who became the glassblowers. The watchers never found him because he started playing a new role. He joined the namers and got close to Book, earning his trust. He became the diviner who finds names for flying things, and he's been using the committee's signal birds to communicate with the glassblowers all this time. He told them to attack Buckle, and likely planned their other attacks as well. He must have dreamed up the monster that killed Book. I don't know his real name, or if he ever had one. But the name he uses now is Rope."

For the first time, Ivy looked concerned. Before she could say anything, Smoke said, "More stories. More pretend."

"Check the train, then," the courier said. "See if he's still on board. I think you'll find that he's vanished. The glassblowers were expecting him."

Frost slammed his fist on the table. Smoke and Ivy jumped. The sayer's eyes were bright with anger.

"It seems it's time," Smoke said to Ivy.

Ivy rose and collected her satchel, which had been hanging from the back of her chair. No, that was not her satchel, but the courier's own, with Frost's word still in it.

The courier laughed. "This is how you planned it, isn't it, Frost? That word was always meant to be delivered to me."

"Not at all," Smoke said. "You've done much good work in service of the named. The names committee relieved of its false chair. The Black Square's corruption ended. The so-called fifth committee scattered and on the run." He tilted his head, as though just realizing something. "Failing to deliver that word might be the best work you've ever done. So much has been gained as a result."

He signaled to the watchers. One undid the bindings from her ankles and wrists, the other pulled her to her feet.

"Deleting me won't stop the monster from destroying Hollow," the courier said.

"But you aren't being deleted," Smoke said. "You should have listened to Beryl when she came to you in Whisper. Don't you see? You're like the train that's had every car and every piece of its engine changed. What do we call you now? Courier? Rider? Agent of the fifth committee? But you are none of those things, so you need to become something else—and another title won't be enough. You need a name."

Ivy was smiling again. "And lucky us," she said. "They've asked me to pick one for you."


With Ivy walking ahead, the watchers escorted the courier down the train. They passed the door to her own compartment, and she wondered if someone else was living there now. Through windows and between cars, she caught glimpses of the old part of the city just east of the factories, where artisans still worked the ancient forges and machine shops that had powered the city's fast rise in the years after its naming. This wasn't far from the glass-blowers' workshop, where she'd gone to deliver *gob*. Would the monster destroy this neighborhood on its way to the city's heart? It might already be on its way.

She saw few of the namers. Most were probably in their compartments, preparing for what lay ahead, though a few sat in the eating car alongside surveyors and cartographers, reviewing fragmentary charts of the city with new sections sketched into the gaps. They would all be expected to deliver names to the regions beyond the border while they marched alongside the soldiers. As the courier passed, only a few glanced up, and those who looked didn't seem to recognize her.

In the storage car, the courier said, "Ivy, everything I said back there is true. You could check to see if I'm right. If Rope isn't aboard the train—"

"I'll look into Rope after this is over," Ivy said.

"Please, this won't end with some victory over the nameless. It will end with Hollow burning."

Ivy spun to face the courier, and the watchers halted. The shelves creaked around them as the train rumbled forward. Ivy said, "I saw that new monster when it ran from the roundhouse."

"You saw it? Ivy, why didn't you tell the sayer?"

"The dreams committee hunters will handle it—if it moves on Hollow at all. Chances are it will just flee deeper into nameless territory."

"No, Ivy, that thing was built for destruction."

"And how are you so sure, I wonder? Could it be that you had a hand in making it?"

"Ivy, I know you, and I know you want to fight the way your grandmother did. But that monster—"

Ivy took a step closer. "What I *want* is to finish cleaning up the mess you've made and get Frost off our train. But that won't happen until he has his war and we have a new committee chair."

"Then call a vote—"

"There won't be a vote. Smoke says that Frost will name the next chair himself."

"And you expect him to choose you," the courier said. "Ivy, together we can still—"

"*Together*? Nothing you're part of can come to any good. That's been the problem with you from the start."

She turned and led them onward. The courier could think of nothing more to say.

In the ghost car, all the ghosts were still, as though they'd just been calibrated. They didn't fiddle with their buttons or shoelaces. Their puzzles of rope, wood, and metal lay ignored on the seats beside them.

Everything went dark as the train entered the tunnel. The watchers held the courier's arms more tightly, as though she might slip away into the shadows.

In the last car of the train, a small, brisk woman was lighting naphtha lamps. She wore the plain brown uniform of a ghosts committee calibrationist. When she saw Ivy, she pocketed her matches and said, "Finally. I've had everything ready for nearly an hour now."

Seated at a low table was the patchwork ghost. The courier tried to run to him, but the watchers held her in check.

"Ghost," the courier said. "Oh, ghost."

The patchwork ghost looked sad to see her. His patches were faded, his eyes sunk in shadow. The watchers sat the courier in the opposite chair and redid the bindings around her ankles and wrists. Then one went to guard the door while the other stood at the courier's side. Rope's signal birds warbled in their roost overhead.

The calibrationist grunted as she lifted a bucket of water onto the table, setting it directly in front of the ghost.

Ivy stood over the courier. "You've given names to how many people?" she asked. "Hundreds, I would think."

The courier looked around the car, past Ivy, searching for a way out. The door at the back could be unbolted, or the hatch in the roof of the dovecote. But the train was still moving, and even if she weren't bound to her chair, the watchers would easily overpower her.

"We can make this just as easy as one of those deliveries," Ivy went on. "Easier, even. There must be some names you like. Names you wanted when you were a child, maybe? You could have your pick."

When the courier didn't answer, Ivy sighed. She lifted the courier's chin and looked into her eyes. "How about Paper?" she said.

The courier closed her eyes and turned her head. Ivy was good. Paper was one of the first names she'd wanted, back when she would still ask her father to take her to see the names committee.

"It's a good name," Ivy said, leaning against the table. Not unkindly, she added, "I think it suits you. Try it out, at least? Say it back to me."

The courier kept her eyes closed, kept her breathing even. She tried not to think about the word.

"Paper," Ivy said again.

The courier shook her head, thought of a dozen other words to crowd out the one. *Sky, lid, stem, bridge, tin, mint, purple, bulb.*

"Serving with a deletion committee," Ivy said, the warmth gone from her voice, "I've learned things they don't tell us here on the Number Twelve."

The courier opened her eyes. The patchwork ghost was watching her. The calibrationist stood directly behind him, and she was rolling up her sleeves.

"This is Spool," Ivy said. "You recognize her uniform, of course. Spool, would you please tell our guest about the calibration process?"

Spool gave the courier a bland smile as she gathered up her brown, shoulder-length hair and tied it back with a piece of twine. "It's simpler than most people imagine," she said. "But a demonstration is probably best."

She placed one hand on the patchwork ghost's chest and set the other against the back of his head. Then, leaning forward, she pressed his head down into the bucket, submerging his face in the water. The patchwork ghost did not resist.

"Ghosts don't breathe," Spool said. "That's how it is, not being alive anymore. But new ghosts, you see, they still have too much of their lives left in them. Usually you'll find them stuck on some familiar task, repeating it over and over. Hanging clothes on a line and taking them down again. Sweeping a clean floor. Patrolling a forest border like they're still with the army. Useless. As for the old ghosts, they pick up habits and ideas from too much time among the living. Oh, the trouble they can cause. I've seen ghosts that start fires. Ghosts carving shapes into wood. Ghosts who fill their pockets with pebbles. Living people stuff. Just no good for ghosts at all."

A spasm went through the patchwork ghost. He put both hands on the table and pushed, but Spool held him down.

"Now this ghost," she said, "this ghost is unusual. It's like a new ghost *and* an old ghost at the same time. It has strange new habits, and it's still walking around with some of its old life in its head. How long has it been kept hidden from my committee? A very long time I think, and most recently by your old committee chair. That's a bad thing to do. A ghost like this, oh, it might seem useful because it can do useful things. But it's confused, and it might confuse other ghosts."

The ghost tensed and began slapping the table with his hands.

"Please stop," the courier said.

"But I'm not doing anything to hurt it, not really," Spool said. "A ghost doesn't have to breathe. *Can't* breathe—not even this old ghost. See, all you have to do is remind them that they aren't alive. That's it. That's how calibration works. There are lots of ways to do it. Some of the new ways make it so you don't even have to be in the same room. Imagine that. Me, I prefer the old methods. Simple and direct. And very effective."

The ghost slapped the table harder, then pushed with both hands, trying to lift his head out of the bucket. The calibrationist held him there. "Poor dear," she said. "See, it's only confused. The ghost doesn't need to breathe, but knowing that it *couldn't* breathe even if it wanted to has got it upset. Awful to see them this way."

The ghost was slamming the table with his fists now. He tried again to rise, but Spool said, "Ah, ah, there now," and leaned hard against him.

"Please stop," the courier said. "Please, please stop."

Spool looked to Ivy, and Ivy nodded. The calibrationist seemed disappointed as she lifted the ghost's head from the bucket. His eyes were wide, blind with panic. He opened and closed his mouth as though desperate to breathe, but he did not draw a breath.

Ivy snapped her fingers to get the courier's attention. "My first offer was generous. Don't make the mistake of turning down the next one."

"You have to stop this, Ivy. The patchwork ghost is important to the committee's work. Let's go to Frost now. You can tell him—"

"Dirt," Ivy said. "Dirt, I need you to focus."

The courier shuddered.

"Dirt," Ivy said again. "A fine name, don't you think? What would we do without dirt? We need it to walk on, to build on. We can bury things in it, secrets and seeds. Dirt under our feet, wherever we go."

The patchwork ghost seemed to remember where he was and what was happening. He shook his head at the courier, urging her not to give in.

The courier steadied her breath. She thought of her own words this time, strong in her mind, *brass* and *switchback, burdock, echo, walnut, mustard—*

"*Dirt.* Say it back to me, Dirt. Tell me your name."

The courier pushed Ivy's voice far away. She made it small, distant, a sound without meaning. But it grew clear and close again when it said sadly, "Spool, you may resume."

Spool plunged the patchwork ghost's head back into the water. The ghost held still, and Spool said, "There we are, not fighting so much this time." She sounded disappointed.

The courier's eyes burned with tears. "Please don't do this," she said.

Ivy tucked a lock of pale hair behind her ear. "We don't have to, Dirt. You can make us stop. You just need to take a name." She bent down so her face was level with the courier's. "Say it. Say it back to me."

The ghost was beginning to panic again. It held the rim of the bucket with both hands and pushed. Spool tightened her grip and said brightly, "Easy now."

"Please," the courier said.

"*Please, please, please,*" Ivy said, mocking her. "Maybe that should be your name?"

The courier turned away and tried not to listen, but she could still hear the ghost struggling. The table swayed and water sloshed. Ivy said into the courier's ear, "It's because you think you're better than the rest of us, isn't it? The nameless courier, Book's favorite. She can deliver anything, and it's all just so easy for her."

The ghost thrashed and his chair scraped the floor. "Almost there now," Spool said.

The courier shouted to him, "You are the record keeper! Remember! You are the record keeper and you are my friend!"

The ghost stilled, and for a moment the courier thought he was gone. Then he began to struggle again.

Ivy gazed directly into the courier's eyes. She shook her head and grinned. "Of course," she said. "Why didn't I think of it sooner?"

The grin faded as she closed her eyes. The courier recognized that look. It was the look of a courier about to make a delivery. She could hear the word coming from a distance, like thunder, even before it passed Ivy's lips.

"Trouble," Ivy said.

The courier inhaled sharply. *Trouble* was already part of her, in her blood and in her bones. Ivy had seen it there, drawn it out, echoed it back to her. It was already almost her name. For years she had been the courier who delivered *trouble*. Now she felt the warmth of the word, felt it filling her, *trouble*. It was good and right and she wanted it, wanted to be claimed by it even as she claimed it as her own.

She screamed, a frightened animal sound, tearing from her throat. She pushed the word back and said to the ghost, "You are the record keeper. You keep the record. You are my friend, the patchwork ghost, and you keep the record."

Ivy stroked the courier's hair and said quietly, almost tenderly, "Trouble, Trouble, Trouble. Talk to me, Trouble. Tell me your name and this will be over."

The courier screamed again, but with less force this time. Ivy caressed her as she cried, with her hand and with the word, *trouble, trouble*, and the courier wanted so badly to give in.

"Ghost," she said, her voice quiet and raw. "Ghost."

But the ghost was still, all struggle gone. Spool lifted his head from the bucket and water streamed down his face and onto his suit, which had faded to gray. The ghost's eyes were empty.


The door burst open. The watcher posted there raised his baton, then lowered it again. Standing in the doorway was a ghost from the ghost car. The courier recognized her as the short ghost with one arm. She was good with machines, and she often assisted the mechanics when the engine needed repairing. A favorite of Beryl's. The ghost took a few steps into the car and stood before the watcher as though she belonged here.

Behind her came the big ghost with gray eyes. Then another, the bald smiling ghost. Moments ago, they had all seemed calibrated. Now they seemed almost alive.

"What are you doing?" Ivy said to the watcher. "Get them out of here."

Grudgingly, as though corralling ghosts was beneath him, he spread his arms and shooed them toward the door. But as he came within reach, the two taller ghosts grabbed his arms and the short ghost with one arm drove herself against his chest, turning him from the doorway and pressing him against the wall.

He bellowed, suddenly afraid. The other watcher drew his baton and moved to help. But before he could do anything, Beryl came charging in, a big wrench gripped in both hands, her long red hair unpinned and wild. She swung at him, and he stumbled back to avoid the blow.

After Beryl came the monster Two, who scurried over to the table while the diviner and the watcher circled each other. Ivy backed away, eyes wide with confusion and terror. Two knelt beside the courier and began cutting the cords around her wrists with a pocket knife.

"Cease!" Spool cried. "Desist!"

As though drawn by the sound of her voice, three more ghosts streamed into the car and ran straight for Spool. "Desist!" she shouted again. The ghosts grabbed her and lifted her into the air. Ivy watched, mouth open, as they carried the calibrationist through the door at the back of the car and hurled her from the train.

The watcher pinned to the wall was shouting and struggling, but the ghosts held him in place, unyielding, almost structural—a cage of limbs. The other watcher kept his baton held high as Beryl swung her wrench again and again. She lost her balance and he charged forward, slamming into her.

Beryl cried out and grabbed the watcher, bringing him down with her. The baton slipped from his grasp and went rolling over the floor.

The courier strained at the cords around her wrists, desperate to help, but Two was still sawing with her knife. Ivy grabbed a naphtha lamp off the table and swung it at the monster. The glass shattered and flames spilled down Two's arm. Two dropped the knife and slapped at the burning naphtha, but the fire only spread faster, quickly engulfing the wood and paper and dream stuff of her body.

The courier screamed and pulled harder, and the bonds on her wrists snapped. She grabbed the knife and started cutting the cords on her ankles. Ivy backed away and watched, eyes wide and shining, as Two burned with a white-hot flame, papery skin peeling away in sheaves.

From the moment his head came out of the bucket, the patchwork ghost had remained perfectly still, water dripping from his face. Now he blinked and seemed to see again. He saw the courier bound to her chair, saw Beryl grappling with the watcher, saw the monster burning. He stood and sent his chair tumbling. He grabbed the bucket of water and poured it over Two. The water hissed, steam mingling with black smoke as the smell of burnt naphtha and wet paper filled the air.

Two was scorched and charred, diminished, parts of her burned away completely. She lifted her arms. The fingers of her right hand were like bones, and her left wrist ended in a blackened stub. Two looked surprised and a little sad. "Oh," she said. "Oh, oh."

The courier heard a loud *thunk* and turned to see Beryl getting to her feet, breathing hard, wrench still clutched in her hand. The watcher lay at her feet, unconscious. She started toward Ivy.

Ivy backed away, shaking her head. Her mouth was moving, but no sound escaped her lips. The ghosts had returned from the deck at the back of the car, but Ivy didn't see them until she'd backed into their arms.

The ghosts lifted her and carried her away. She clutched at the doorframe, and for a moment they couldn't budge her. Then they pushed together with such force that they all tumbled together off the deck. Ivy made no sound as she vanished with the ghosts into the dark of the tunnel.


The train emerged into the midday sun and started across the bridge over the canal. It would reach the roundhouse soon.

Beryl dropped her wrench and took the knife from the courier's hand, used it to finish cutting the cord around her ankles. The courier kicked the scraps away, then went to her monster and touched her gently. "Two, I'm sorry."

Two's grin was lopsided, her face scorched. Beryl removed her own jacket and placed it over Two's shoulders, covering the worst of the damage.

The monster patted the fabric and her grin grew larger. She liked the new clothes.

"She must have followed Ivy and the seeker ghosts back to the train after they captured you," Beryl said. "Somehow she knew to look for me."

"I'm surprised you didn't turn her over to Frost." Beryl looked hurt, but before she could say anything, the courier asked, "How did you do that with the ghosts? I thought they'd all been calibrated."

"I needed them to seem that way, so Spool would overlook them. I've been getting them ready since I returned to the train last night."

Three of the ghosts still held the watcher against the wall. He was breathing and his eyes were open, but his body had gone limp and he seemed unaware of what was happening around him.

The courier went to the patchwork ghost. She put her arms around him and said, "I thought you were gone."

To her surprise, the ghost hugged her back, and she could tell at once something was different about him. Heat radiated from his body as though a fire had been set in his core.

"Ghost?" she said, backing away. He squeezed her arm reassuringly, but even his hand was warm.

Beryl touched his forehead. "Strange," she said.

"What's happening to him?"

"I don't know. He resisted the calibration, but I think the effort must have cost him."

A heady mix of gratitude, anger, and fear brought hot tears to the courier's eyes.

"I'm sorry I couldn't get here sooner," Beryl said. "Frost has watchers posted everywhere." Quietly, she said, "Did Ivy—"

"No," the courier said quickly, before she was sure. She thought through all the names Ivy had tried to give her. *Trouble* hitched and almost caught, then fell with the others like leaves from a tree. "No, she didn't name me. I'm sorry to disappoint you."

"I'm not disappointed," Beryl said. "I came for you, didn't I?"

"In Jawbone, you mean? And then in Whisper?"

Beryl looked at the floor. Her hands were balled into fists. "I was trying to help you," she said.

"Help me? By joining a deletion committee assigned to hunt me down?"

"I thought I could protect you. That I could convince the others not to"— she paused, struggling to find the words—"not to complete their task if you agreed to take a name."

"And when you called the vote to calibrate my ghost?"

"I was wrong," Beryl said. "I should have trusted you. And I know you won't forgive me now, but I really do want to help. Here." She reached behind her back and removed something she'd had tucked into her belt: the patchwork ghost's sketchbook. He grabbed it eagerly, sat at the table, and wiped water away with his sleeve. With a pencil from his jacket pocket, he began to draw the scene, beginning with the watcher sprawled beside the stove.

"The others are going to come looking for us," the courier said.

"You'll be gone before they get here," Beryl said. She climbed the ladder into the dovecote, opened the hatch to release two of the birds. She was halfway back down when the train's brakes sounded. The courier went to the window, saw the ruins she and Two had walked among only hours before.

"The chief engineer is a friend to us both, and an enemy to Frost," she explained.

"You know the chief engineer?"

"Remember the ghost we saw in the cab that day we ran over the roofs of the cars?"

"Yes," the courier said. "The same one helped me free the patchwork ghost on the night of the fire. You're saying that the chief engineer—"

"Is a ghost, yes. A ghost who's been working the engine of the Number Twelve for a long time."

The train had almost come to a halt. The courier put her hand on the patchwork ghost's shoulder. "You'll have to finish that later," she said.

"Do you have someplace to go?" Beryl asked.

The courier checked her pocket and was relieved to find the brass key still there. "Here's what you need to know," she said. "The people who tried to kill me in Hollow have made a new monster, worse than anything we've seen before. And I helped make it. I could say that I did it against my will, but that wouldn't be entirely true."

Beryl flinched.

"It felt *good*, Beryl. Bad at first, but by the end it felt good to dream what I dreamed, and to make a monster of that dream. And now, because I helped make it, I might be able to stop it. So that's where we're going. To hunt down a monster."

Beryl took a deep breath and nodded. "That makes sense," she said, though she sounded like she was trying to convince herself.

"What about you?" the courier asked. "Will you still be safe here, after this?"

"Not entirely," Beryl said. "But I'm not working alone."

The train had nearly come to a halt. The courier ushered Two and the patchwork ghost out onto the deck. The ghost climbed down the ladder first, and Two followed.

"We might not see each other again," Beryl said.

The courier thought of a dozen things she might say, but she left them unspoken and climbed down after the others.

The courier led the way past abandoned buildings and broken masonry. She kept one eye on her ghost. Some of his patches were bright again, others still faded and gray. His eyes were feverish, and he clenched and unclenched his hands as he strode forward. Two was also changed; one of her legs no longer worked as well as the other, but she hopped along undaunted.

The courier stopped in the shadow of a crumbling brick building. She squeezed the key and breathed. The metal grew warm in her hand, then so hot it almost burned. The thrumming engine of the monster's mind was still close.

She led them into a zone of narrow streets, broken cranes, empty warehouses. A warm breeze blew dust and scraps of paper through the ruins. Ahead, five streets converged at a circle. At its center was an overgrown garden, weeds and late-blooming flowers spilling over broken pavement.

Two pointed to the garden and burbled excitedly. The courier saw it, too: a section of rusted fence, along with most of an ancient fountain, torn from the ground and dragged onto the street. The monster had come this way. A trail of dirt and uprooted flowers led down another street toward a large, dark pond.

Before they could follow the trail, several figures emerged from between two buildings to stand in their way.

The glassblowers were only four in number now, still wearing their white masks, still armed with the strange, cruel weapons of the nameless. Their clothes were torn and coated in dust, their masks chipped and cracked.

With them came the diviner who found words for flying things. Even though the courier had known he would be here, she still struggled for a moment to remember exactly who he was. She fixed him in her mind: short bristly hair, a length of rope tied around his waist.

"Rope," she said. "You always seem to know where I'll be."

"I've watched you carefully over the years," he said. "I suppose I've come to know how you think. And now we both want the same thing—to find that monster. You know where it is, don't you?"

"I'm not going to help you," the courier said.

"But my friends have worked hard for this moment. I don't want to see them disappointed. I don't think you want to disappoint them, either."

Rope's voice was mild, as always, but his meaning was clear. She could sense the rage behind those white masks. Four of their number—Glue and the three glassblowers who'd still been wearing blue masks when the roof fell—were gone now, ghosts in the rubble of the roundhouse. Those who still lived wanted to hurt her.

"I know what they stand to gain from this," the courier said. "But I don't see why you're helping them."

"I'm here for the story, of course," Rope said. "The end of peace, the fall of two great cities. Finally the storm breaks. Finally something *happens*."

"I don't believe you," the courier said.

"But this is what I've been working for from the start. Who do you think divined that word for Frost? The one you've still failed to deliver? Maybe you could deliver it now."

That shouldn't have surprised her. Diviners often had to work outside their specialties. But that meant Frost—or more likely Smoke, working on the sayer's behalf—had sought out Rope and assigned him the task of divining *traitor*. Maybe Smoke had sensed Rope's peculiar qualities, and believed their secret would be safe with the diviner everyone forgot. He could not have realized that they were asking their traitor to divine the word for what he was.

How pleased Rope must have been. And how happy he would be now, if she delivered the word to him. It would make a good end for his story. The courier gritted her teeth and said nothing.

"Well, the word doesn't matter," Rope said, though he was clearly disappointed. "You'll be remembered for something far greater. You made the monster that will break Hollow."

"Which monster do you mean?" she asked.

For the first time, Rope seemed confused. "You know the one," he said.

"But do you?" she insisted. "Do you mean the monster we made in the roundhouse today? Or the one I made as a child?"

Rope blinked. He must have known the truth, of course, as well as she did. But maybe he had pretended so well that he'd forgotten. Buried it beneath his other roles.

*A blankness that moved from place to place.* That was how the Seven of Stones had described the last Rider, and it described Rope very well. It also described the monster the courier had been tricked into making, all those years ago. A hollow thing, an emptiness in the shape of a man. A piece of rope tied around her wrist.

He looked nervous now. Maybe he was starting to remember what he was: a monster created by a frightened little girl.

"Enough words," he said. "I don't understand why or how, but you have some special connection to that monster. Lead us to it, or you'll leave here a ghost." He turned his bland smile on Two. "And we'll finish burning this wretched mistake from the world."

Two roared and ran at him. The courier shouted for her to stop, but even with her bad leg Two was fast. Rope didn't move. One of the glassblowers unslung a weighted net from his shoulder and flung it over Two. She fell screeching at Rope's feet.

At his signal, another glassblower lit a naphtha torch and brought the flame close.

"Stop," the courier said.

Rope raised one hand and the glassblower halted. Two held still as the fire flickered just inches from her face.

"If you're ready now?" Rope said.

The courier looked in the direction the monster had gone, down the street that led to the pond. There was nothing remarkable about the street—like the others leading from the circle, it was lined with old row houses, with trees and creeping vines. Yet something felt different about it, in a way she recognized. The shadows, she thought, were *less empty*.

So the glassblowers weren't the only ones who had pursued her through the nameless districts of Hollow. Good, she thought. Maybe now they could conclude their business together.

"Just don't hurt her," she said to Rope. "I'll show you the way. See these tracks?"

He strode forward, saw the dirt and uprooted flowers, and nodded. "Please lead on."

The glassblower lifted Two and slung her over his shoulder like a bundle of twigs. He kept the naphtha torch burning.

The courier squeezed the key in her hand and led them downhill toward the pond. The patchwork ghost walked calmly at her side. She could hear Two's furious burbling as she bounced against the glassblower's back.

A cool breeze blew up from the water, sending dry leaves skittering over the street. The courier kept her eyes straight ahead. She felt Rope and the glassblowers watching her, ready to pounce if she tried to escape. But she wanted them with her, wanted them close.

They were halfway to the pond when she saw movement at the edges of her vision, something flitting among the roots and vines. Then bulkier shapes rose up as though climbing stairs out of the earth. Her scalp tingled at the sound of a wordless whispering which she heard without hearing and could almost understand.

A figure in a heavy wooden mask stepped out onto the street in front of them, and the shadows followed. The courier turned to look back up the slope. Rope and the glassblowers saw what she saw: a second figure standing between them and the way they'd come. A third appeared from a vine-choked alleyway.

Masses of living darkness writhed at their feet. Each wore coarse brown clothes and rough masks held together with metal spikes. Wood masks for judgment.

*This one's mine,* the courier said without speaking. *But he can be yours if you want him—the others, too. A gift from the dreaming child.*

The whispering grew louder as the nameless deliberated. It didn't take them long this time. Ropey strands of shadow snaked over the pavement, quickly surrounding the glassblowers.

They swung their blades, but the tendrils avoided the blows. The one carrying Two threw his burning naphtha torch; the shadows caught it and flung it away. Then the tendrils closed in.

They coiled around the glassblowers' ankles and snaked up their legs, wrapping themselves tightly around their bodies. They slithered up their arms and pried open their fingers, forcing the weapons from their hands. The glassblowers' screams were cut short by the tendrils that slipped under their masks. Their eyes were left uncovered, though—the courier saw them widen with fear as the monsters lifted them from the ground. They grasped for vines and the trunks of trees, but the monsters pulled them swiftly into the shadows from which they had emerged.

Two lay on the ground, spluttering as she freed herself from the net. The courier and the patchwork ghost helped her up.

Rope raised one hand to the nameless. "I understand," he said. "They were no longer needed. They've served their purpose to the nameless. You've done the right thing. The best thing."

The whispering resumed. More tendrils slithered forward to encircle Rope. They tapped his ankles and hovered close as though scenting him.

"They would only have been in the way," Rope went on. "We have our monster, and the army of the named has left Hollow unguarded. We have everything we need."

The whispering grew louder yet somehow remained a whisper. The tendrils twined up Rope's legs. He did not scream or try to bat them away.

"I still require the courier," he said. "You understand, don't you? The beast listens to her. There's the matter of Hollow, and the battle ahead, and all the battles still to come. What a story we'll have to tell."

The tendrils tugged at Rope's middle, gently at first, then with real force. They twisted him open, his upper half turning like the lid off a jar. The courier stared in shocked silence as the tendrils probed and weighed what they held.

Rope was still speaking. "I'm glad you're finally here," he said calmly. "I've been working such a long time, and I've been so alone. Sometimes I forgot who I was. Did you know that I learned to dream? By accident, of course. I didn't like that at all."

The tendrils took him apart, piece by piece. There was no blood, no snap-ping of bones. Rope was hollow, a rubbery white shell with nothing inside. She saw past the last Rider, the diviner who found names for flying things, to what he really was—the connection she'd been searching for between her family and the glassblowers. The nameless agents her father had invited into their home had used her young mind as a workshop in which to build their perfect monster—a monster that could forget what it was, even as it set about the long, monstrous work of reviving a war.

Rope turned his eyes on the courier. "I did try to divine a name for the insects that stung you," he said. "Really, I tried. That's how I ended up making one of my own."

She'd guessed that Rope had made the flying monster that killed Book, but now she could tell he had made it out of fear, loneliness, and confusion. A monster's first dream, and he had used it to make a monster. She pictured him sneaking into Book's office, abandoning his creation in some dark corner of the compartment.

Both Rope's legs and one of his arms were on the ground. The tendrils worked at what remained, burrowing through the empty spaces to take him apart from within.

"So alone," he said. "I think that's why I forgot. It was easier to be someone else. But I always remembered again. Of course I had a lot to do."

Rope's other arm fell, and then the tendrils pried his head from his body. They dropped it to the pavement, where it lay flat and still among the other pieces.

The whispering had ceased. The three nameless looked at the courier, but she had nothing more to say, with words or without. Neither, it seemed, did the nameless. They withdrew with their monsters into the shadows.

"Oh," Two said. She stood looking down at the empty uniform, still cinched with a length of rope.


Thorn came running down from the circle. When the courier had last seen him, he'd been sleepy and clumsy, still struggling to shake off the effects of the nameless drug the glassblowers had given him. Now his eyes were clear. He seemed to have escaped the roundhouse unscathed.

"You changed their minds," she said.

"You already had, when you spoke with them earlier. They let you go and followed, hoping to draw out the monster you'd made."

"Did they always know what he was?"

"I only understand parts of the story," Thorn said. "Years ago, there was a group of outlaw nameless who wanted a new war against the named. But after the last conflict all the nameless were forbidden from dreaming up monsters like those that had fought the war machines. So this group came up with something different to get around the rule."

"Something worse," the courier said. "Because he could blend in, and because he could use words against the named."

"Words and stories," Thorn agreed. "The outlaw nameless were never caught, never judged."

"Because they didn't make the monster themselves," the courier said. "They used the dreams of a nameless girl who'd been raised by the named."

"Is that how Rope knew where you were?"

"Today, and maybe yesterday, too," she said. "And it might be why he joined the names committee. Monsters always return to the people who made them."

That left just one thing the courier didn't know. Had her father understood what the nameless were doing? Was it part of the deal he'd made with them? Or had he been tricked, as she was? She would never learn the truth. Even if she could dream her father again, he wouldn't be able to give her an answer.

While they walked, the courier explained what had happened aboard the Number Twelve. How Two had received her burns, why the patchwork ghost seemed different now. The key grew hotter and hotter, until it almost burned her hand. They were very close. She led the others toward a boathouse on the pond. A few flecks of gray paint clung to its ancient walls, and the ceiling was partially collapsed.

Outside the door, Thorn said, "I feel it, too."

"I don't know what the monster will do when it sees us," she said. "It knows us, but we have to be ready for anything."

Two burbled quietly, but she didn't seem afraid. The patchwork ghost looked eager to proceed. So the courier went inside, and the others followed. At the far end of the structure, a huge door stood open to the pond. A pair of rails ran through the middle of the floor and down into the water. Stowed to either side were about a dozen small boats, some crushed beneath fallen sections of the roof.

The monster lay curled in a shaft of sunlight, eyes lidded as it released small puffs of smoke with each sleepy breath. It was not fully asleep, only dozing. As the courier approached, she saw its eyes shift and its great steel claws flex.

Curled up against the warmth of the monster's belly was her stowaway, also dozing. The animal saw her and yawned, and the monster yawned, too.

She imagined them fighting and chasing their way through those empty neighborhoods, yowling, screeching, battling around every corner and down every street. They must have tired each other out. They were friends now.

"Oh!" said Two, and the courier thought she sounded jealous.

The two beasts rose and stretched. Then the stowaway padded forward, brushed against the courier's leg, and permitted her to lift him in her arms. Thorn reached one hand in the air. The monster bent down, sniffed his hand, and pressed the side of its face against his open palm. He stroked the great glass scales on the monster's cheek, and from deep in its belly came a satisfied rumble.

Steam rose from the monster's chimney as it lapped water from the pond. When it had finished refilling the tank in its belly, it joined the others on the street. The monster seemed happy for the company, but the courier knew it was far from tame. She felt a warm buzz of familiarity between the monster and herself. But she still gripped the key tightly in her hand, just in case.

They returned the way they had come. The courier and Thorn weren't talking about what they were doing, but she suspected he felt the same way she did. The two of them—along with the stowaway—had all helped make this creature, and now it was their responsibility. But what were they going to *do* with it?

They passed what remained of Rope, the pieces of him already disappearing under leaves. The monster gave the uniform a sniff and walked on. It was more interested in the stowaway, watching with half-lidded eyes as the animal batted at insects among the tangled shrubs that crowded the side of the street. Two kept some distance, her remaining hand thrust into a pocket of the jacket Beryl had given her. She watched the monster and mumbled to herself, quickly looking away whenever it shifted its enormous head in her direction.

The patchwork ghost looked around at their companions with an expression the courier recognized: he would draw this scene as soon as he could.

In time they came to the tracks by the canal. By then she had come to a decision.

"Here's what I'm going to do," she said. "I'm going to follow the Number Twelve to the last city of the nameless. None of you have to come with me. None of you should, probably, because if you join me, you'll be what I am."

"Which is what, exactly?" Thorn asked.

Moon had told her: *Courier, deliver yourself.* She put one hand on her satchel. She didn't need to see the word, because she knew it as though she'd spoken it a hundred times. Yet when she made the delivery, it still sounded new and strange.

Two burbled quietly, and Thorn blinked. He repeated the word back to her, trying it out for himself. "Traitor," he said.

Two came forward and took the courier's arm in her singed fingers. She cooed admiringly. It was the first time the monster had heard a word delivered. The patchwork ghost looked pleased.

"Traitor, traitor, traitor," Thorn said to each of them in turn. He nodded at the stowaway and said again, "Traitor," then saluted the monster he'd helped to make: "Traitor."

The monster huffed once and stepped onto the tracks. Steam sighed from the chimney as the beast settled onto its haunches, wheels snug on the rails. It crouched with its back to the named part of Hollow.

The courier lifted her stowaway into her arms and climbed up into the litter. Two came next, and then the patchwork ghost, and finally Thorn. There was plenty of room for all of them. They waited for something to happen, for the monster to move. It yawned a great smoky yawn but remained stationary. The courier wasn't sure what to do. She leaned over the edge of the litter, and the monster turned one big, golden eye toward her, then slowly opened its huge mouth.

The courier felt the key pulsing gently in her pocket. Was the key keeping her safe, granting her some measure of power over the beast? Maybe that was only in her head. In any case, the key didn't belong to her. It had come from her dream of her father, but it was still part of the monster.

She tossed the key to the monster, who caught it in its mouth and swallowed it down. Satisfied, it faced forward, drew a deep breath, and held it. The pistons on its forearms began to move. Slowly at first, but accelerating quickly, the monster rolled out among the ruins.

The stowaway pawed open the courier's satchel and crawled inside. She patted his warm body through the fabric.

"What is it?" Thorn asked her.

She realized she was smiling. "This reminds me of one of the stories from before the Silence," she said. "You know the one. The Story of the Child who Flew in a Storm to Another Place."

Thorn looked troubled. "But this is nothing like that story," he said.

"Don't you see it? I'm the child who flew in a storm." She cradled her satchel. "And here is the animal who rides in a basket. The ghost is the person made of metal, and Two is the person made of straw."

"That would make me the animal who's always afraid. But I'm not afraid."

"Not anymore, maybe," she said.

Thorn still looked doubtful. "What about our monster? There's nothing like that in the story."

"Of course there is," the courier said. She reached forward to pat the scales at the base of the monster's neck. "Our monster is the storm."

The monster picked up speed as it roared toward the ruins of the round-house, where only hours before it had been born from the dreaming of many sleepers. It didn't spare the place a glance as it steamed past the switch-yard. The monster glided without a judder past crumbling brick structures, heaps of rusting machine parts, stands of bare twisted trees.

Deeper into the empty districts of unnamed Hollow they plunged, past slag pits and pools of bright blue waste. The stink was sharp and strangely sweet. It didn't seem to bother the monster, which breathed deeply and kept its furnace running hot.

"I think Two likes the new monster," Thorn said.

Two's shyness was gone. At the front of the litter, she patted the monster and murmured, urging it faster. It rumbled happily in response, stretching its legs as it zoomed down straightaways, leaning into the curves. Smoke rose from its chimney in a thick black plume.

"I think the new monster likes her, too," the courier said to Thorn.

The patchwork ghost drew frantically. He was like another engine, his body throwing off heat of its own. The courier watched him complete a sketch of Two looking over her shoulder at the monster, followed by one of the courier climbing aboard with the stowaway. The next showed the monster engine as it appeared from the litter, eager and joyful, shining like a jewel in the cool afternoon light. In the picture, it was drawing close to a train.

The courier looked up and saw the last car of the Number Twelve ahead. She had thought the namers might reach their destination first, but here they were in front of her, moving fast but not nearly as fast as their monster.

Thorn shouted over the engine's roar, "Shouldn't we be slowing down?"

The courier leaned over the side of the litter and called to the monster, "That train up ahead!" The monster heard, but pretended it hadn't. It was an unruly child, brimming with new power.

"Can you do something?" the courier asked Two.

Two seemed to notice the Number Twelve for the first time. She began rapping the monster's neck and scolding it, "Oh, oh, oh!"

Still the monster charged forward. They were just five car lengths away now. In seconds they would collide with the little car at the rear of the train.

Four, three. The courier held on with both hands. And then, just before impact, the monster leapt from the rails. Legs extended, it landed with a jolt and hit the ground running. Couriers and committee pages turned to look out the windows, eyes widening.

The monster wasn't as fast on all fours as it was on wheels, but it still moved at several times the speed of the Number Twelve. A minute later, they were out ahead of the engine. The monster leapt back onto the tracks, folding its legs and dropping its wheels to the rails.

"Do you think they noticed us?" Thorn said.

As though in answer, steam shot from the base of the monster's chimney, sounding a shrieking trill: the monster had a whistle. Two laughed as it released one blast after another, trumpeting its joy.

They entered an older part of the city, small buildings huddled close along curving, hilly streets. The committees of the named had long assumed that Hollow contained only a few unnamed pockets within its borders, peculiar neighborhoods where artists, runaways, and other malcontents lived alongside those nameless—probably considered odd among their own people—who gleaned some thrill from spoken words. Now the courier saw that the nameless districts of the city were sprawling, maybe bigger than the Hollow she knew.

This Hollow featured the same strange sculptures and brightly dyed cords the courier had seen in Nod, that night she and Thorn delivered notices for the Black Square. But the place seemed abandoned. Tramcars stood frozen on the tracks, their doors left open. A green mask lay broken on the street.

Sensing her unease, the stowaway squirmed in the courier's satchel. She let it out before it could growl. The animal paced for a while, then settled near the front of the litter, close to the heat from the engine.

Up ahead they spotted another plume of smoke on the horizon, and soon the monster was closing in on another train. This one was slower, a freight train. The courier held to the litter's edge, ready for the monster's next leap. When the moment came, it felt more like gliding—the beast hopped just high enough to stretch its legs and run with its belly close to ground, barely losing any speed.

The beast was learning control, the courier thought—just as it raised its head to let out an exultant bellow.

At the sound, the windows of the last car of the train flew open, and a half dozen soldiers peered out. At first they did nothing, frozen by the sight of the monstrous machine. Then they raised their rifles.

"Move!" the courier shouted. She and Thorn crouched, Two cried out wordlessly. This time the monster listened, veering away as shots rang out.

Several struck the monster's flank, one with a loud cracking sound. The stow-away was up on all fours, eyes wide with panic.

More shots followed, but the monster put a row of buildings between itself and the soldiers. It thundered down a city street, gouging the road with its massive claws as it picked up speed. The courier leaned over the side of the litter, spotted a broken scale high on the monster's left haunch.

"What are those soldiers protecting?" Thorn asked.

The courier recognized the boxcars: she and Two had seen drovers loading them with ghosts. Those the Black Square had saved were so few by comparison. "Fuel for the war machines," she said.

"Then we could stop them right here," Thorn said. "Cut the army off from its supply."

The army's machines would already be fully fueled, but here was their reserve. Without it, the attack on the last city of the nameless wouldn't last long.

She called to Two, "Can you get us up alongside the engine?"

Two looked worried, but she nodded and leaned against the monster's neck. She burbled quietly, and the monster's great eyes shifted as it listened. The courier still felt hints of the monster's thoughts at the boundaries of her own, but the bond between the two dreamed creatures was stronger.

The monster turned and dashed between buildings, back toward the train. Just behind the tender was another military car, armored and bristling with guns. "The train is guarded front and back," she said.

More shots rang out, forcing the courier and Thorn down again. The monster roared, smoke and steam erupting from between its jaws. Two patted its neck and spoke gently, urging it to keep its distance.

"We can try to overtake them," the courier said. "Block the track, or destroy it if we have to."

"It might work," Thorn said. "But the monster would have to move even faster, and maintain that speed for a long time."

The courier knew what he wasn't saying. They didn't know how long they had before the monster's engine ran out of fuel. It had no tender, no reserve supply. The glassblowers had probably expected it to consume whatever naphtha it found while laying waste to Hollow.

The patchwork ghost rose suddenly to his feet. For the first time since they'd climbed aboard, he had stopped drawing. Now he gazed thoughtfully at the freight train. The courier stood to face him. "What is it?" she asked.

The ghost pointed to the cars near the middle of the train, but all she saw was boxcar after boxcar.

"I don't understand."

The ghost patted his own chest with an open palm, then pointed to the train again. He wanted to go aboard.

"It's too dangerous," the courier said. "They have guns. They'll capture you, they'll—"

The ghost took her hand and placed it on his chest. The heat was almost more than she could bear. He was burning away from the inside. She gasped and pulled her hand away, shook her head. Everything was moving too fast.

The ghost gestured again. Up ahead, the track shifted into a long leftward curve. When the train reached that point, the soldiers at the front and back wouldn't be able to see the middle cars. That was their chance.

"Oh," said Two, worried.

"Do it," the courier told her. "Quickly. We don't have much time."

Under Two's direction, the monster fell back a dozen car lengths. When the train shifted into the curve, Two gave a little shout and the monster swept in close. Both military cars were out of sight.

"Can he really help them?" Thorn said. "He's the record keeper. He's only supposed to record the story."

But the patchwork ghost had played a part in most everything that had happened. He had sketched the divining compartment and Book's meeting with Ticket, guided her to the Black Square, helped them escape on the hand-car. "I don't know if he can help them," the courier admitted. "But he's always been part of the story."

The monster kept a steady pace, edging closer until its claws were kicking up ballast from beside the track. The courier helped the ghost up onto the low wall of the litter. He reached across the gap and pulled the lever to open the boxcar door; it slid open with a clattering rumble. The ghosts inside stepped back.

The courier touched the patchwork ghost's arm. "Promise me I'll see you on the other side," she said.

The ghost gave her a look, kind yet resolved. It was the same look he used to give her at the ends of those long summer days, many years before, when she'd wanted their games of pretend to go on forever. But eventually her father would call for her, and the woods beyond the field would grow dark. The ghost had always known when it was time to go home.

He leapt from the litter. His long arms and legs flailed as he sailed through the air, but he landed on his feet, and the other ghosts caught him.

When he was steady he turned and looked back at the courier. A dull pain lodged itself in her chest. They had only just been reunited, and now she was abandoning him again. How could she let him go alone?

Then she caught a flash of movement at the edge of her vision—the stow-away was bounding past her. In an instant he had sprung onto the litter's edge, then across the gap and into the boxcar. He landed nimbly at the patchwork ghost's feet and crooked his tail.

The stowaway must have felt the courier's anguish as his own; he had gone in her stead. The ghost knelt to run one hand along the animal's back.

A blast of gunfire sounded from near the engine. The train was coming out of the curve and the soldiers could see them again. "Oh!" Two shouted. The monster veered away, and the ghost's bright patches vanished from sight, but not before more bullets found their target.

The gunfire faded into the distance as the monster galloped through a garden between tall tenements, huffing thick masses of smoke from its chimney. It emerged onto a street at the top of a ridge and halted.

The view beyond stretched far to the east. The freight train descended through neighborhoods of brick and stone houses, spires and elevated tramways. Lengths of bright fabric were pulled taut between the buildings, and statues of animals, flowers, hands, hats, and shovels stood on the corners. The train crossed a bridge and vanished into a wooded place, thick with fog.

Could this be the way the living Moon had come, all those hundreds of years ago? The second of the named had traveled from Whisper, years before Hollow was named and expanded; this whole area would have seemed, to Moon, like another part of the unmapped wilderness. The courier thought of Seven in the role of Moon, walking the nameless wilds in search of the word *monster*. She thought of herself in that role, the dream drawing her down to the place where monsters were made. And she thought of the ghost of Moon, and imagined the three of them—the courier and Seven and Moon—walking hand in hand in hand, deep into the fog.

The monster was still catching its breath, furnace crackling low. It heaved a smoky sigh and settled onto the street. Something was wrong. Two, fretting quietly, climbed down out of the litter, and the courier followed.

The monster blinked mournfully as it watched them approach. Two, all fear and shyness gone, put one hand under the monster's chin and patted its snout with the other. The monster sighed again, relaxing into her touch.

The courier spotted the wound. At the base of the monster's neck, one scale was missing, and a few around it were cracked. She moved in for a closer look. Where the scale had been she saw exposed skin, gray and leathery. The area looked irritated and raw, but she found no bullet wound, no tear in the hide. And the other scales, though damaged, were holding.

She returned to Two. "Nothing serious, I think," she said. "It should be able to keep going."

Two looked suddenly furious. "Oh!" she said.

"We'll be more careful," the courier assured her. She looked up into the monster's eyes, huge and sad. "Of course it's a little scared, it's never seen guns before, and—"

"Oh!" Two said again, and stomped one foot. She turned her attention back to the monster, stroking its cheek and singing quietly, "Oh, oh, oh . . ."

The courier shivered when she realized what Two was doing. Book had named Shadow when he delivered *shadow,* and the Black Square, collectively and maybe without meaning to, had given Two her name. But this was, she thought, probably the first time a monster had named another monster.

"You're calling it Oh?" the courier asked.

Two glowered. "Erm!" she said—not a word, and not a sound the courier had heard her make before, but one she understood.

"Sorry," the courier said. "Her. You're calling *her* Oh."

Two nodded, satisfied.

The courier looked up at the monster. "Oh, do you think you can carry on?"

Hearing the courier speak her name, something changed in the monster's eyes. They were sharper and more focused. She was, the courier thought, a little less wild than she had been minutes before. But she also looked glad and eager, and steam rose from her nostrils.

Two patted the monster proudly. The courier left them and climbed back into the cab.

"Is it all right?" Thorn asked.

"More than all right," she told him. "But *it* is *she,* and her name is Oh."


That creature of smoke and thunder carried them down the slope toward the forest. Near the bridge, Oh found the rails and mounted them, wheels clacking into place. Her pistons churned and her whistle sounded bright and clear. The opening in the trees seemed to spread wider, like a great pale mouth opening to consume them, the track its silvery tongue. A moment later, the city was gone.

The forest was cool and quiet, a maze of trunks and tangled limbs, of rocky slopes and ancient paths winding through the fog. Birds flew from branch to branch, specks of red and blue in a gray world. The courier smelled damp earth and rotting leaves, and the sharp smoky scent of Oh's burning naphtha.

None of this fit with the maps the courier knew. To the east of Hollow should be nothing but scrubland and patchy forests. A few small towns connected by paths and dirt roads, and beyond that the eastern border, where the maps ended and the nameless lands began.

But here was a place folded up inside the world the courier knew. Ticket had said that some lessons she'd given her when they were children were wrong; the maps were wrong, too. East of Hollow, the named had spent centuries going the long way around, and for centuries this place remained hidden, a patchwork borderland just outside the largest city of the named.

The courier turned at the sound of screeching, followed by a crash. The noise echoed among the trees. Through the fog she glimpsed a river, and floating on the river was a barge. Hundreds of people were onboard, their masks brighter and more colorful than the birds.

"The nameless of Hollow," Thorn said. "They're fleeing by boat."

Another whining screech, and this time the courier spotted the source of the noise. On the riverbank stood a war machine, a ghost-burner outfitted for battle. It might have been among the unfired machines she'd seen from Book's office the year before. This one was much changed, however. It had been fed a monster, primed with its spirit.

The machine stood on four long, spindly legs, and its body was segmented, stretched tall. Its armor plating had taken on a greenish tint, and its folded forearms were fine-toothed blades. A mantis. It had just used its arms to cut down a tree and drop it into the river, blocking the path of the barge. The people on the barge were scrambling, pushing against the tree with long poles.

The mantis was not alone. Three smaller war machines, slithering like great armored lizards, pursued along the riverbank. One darted out into the water. It snatched a pole in its jaws and snapped it in two.

"They're going to be slaughtered," the courier said. "Two—"

But Two was already urging Oh to change course, and the monster needed little encouragement. She leapt from the rails and charged down the slope, dodging around rocks and trees. As they neared the river, she let out a furious roar.

The mantis stopped and turned. It had just begun cutting another tree; now it withdrew its blades and held them in a defensive stance. The pilot was seated behind thick glass panes within the head; the courier saw his eyes widen as Oh closed in.

She had known, even when she saw the monster half-formed on the tracks of the roundhouse, that the glassblowers were building something that could stand up to the war machines of the named. She had known the monster's burning rage and her powerful thirst for destruction—she'd supplied some of her own rage to that dreaming, and so had Thorn. Still, the courier did not know until this moment the depth of Oh's ferocity.

She leapt at the machine, still roaring. The mantis pivoted, swinging its blades, but Oh quickly had one arm in her claws, the other in her jaws. With a quick jerk, she broke the first arm and yanked the second from its socket. The pilot, screaming, spun his machine and fled.

Oh was faster. She bounded once, twice, then clamped her jaws around the machine's middle. She lifted the mantis into the air and shook it so its legs and broken arm flailed, then hurled it against the rocks. Its firebox cracked and flames poured out; the pilot scrambled from the thing's head.

The monster was about to pounce on him, but Two shouted to direct her attention upstream. One of the lizard machines had seized the barge with its teeth and was dragging it onto the bank. The barge's engine smoked as its propeller churned and spluttered. People leapt into the water as the other lizards advanced, tails whipping. One machine trampled people in the shallows, and the other machine snatched a silver-masked figure its jaws. Even from this distance, the courier could hear the horrible sound of cracking bones.

The pilots were seated in small cabs just behind the lizards' bulbous heads; the courier could see them pulling levers, turning wheels. They did not direct the lizards' every movement, but were in constant negotiation with the monstrous spirits of the machines. Still, their intentions were clear. They would destroy the barge, killing any nameless who resisted. That would give other soldiers time to move in and capture those who remained.

Three white-masked warriors emerged from the panicking crowd and surrounded the nearest machine. It dropped the silver-masked figure to the deck and wriggled backward, startled. The nameless warriors bore staffs mounted with hooked blades, and near the base of each staff was a spool of cable. They moved quickly, unreeling the cables as they circled the machine.

The glassblowers, in their masks and costumes, had captured something of the nameless warriors' menace, but none of their grace. These three did not run so much as dance around their adversary, a whirl of white and silver. When the lizard snapped at them, they looped its jaws shut. When it tried to back away, they pulled the lines taut.

As the snared lizard struggled, another pilot directed his machine toward the nameless. The white-masked warriors stood firm, blades up, but were forced to let their cables go slack. The snared machine began to slip free as the other reared up, ready to strike.

Oh charged, spitting steam as she leapt the fallen tree. The machine shot forward to meet her, baring long steel fangs, so fast the courier screamed. But Oh was ready; she grabbed the lizard just behind its head and held tight with her claws. The lizard's jaws snapped furiously, inching closer. Oh brought up her left foreleg and drew the wheels hard across the lizard machine's throat, slashing it open. She twisted the head free and threw it into the river. The body of the machine slumped into the mud, its pilot trapped.

The three nameless warriors pulled their lines taut again, pinning the other machine to the ground. Then they threw themselves upon it, prying armor plates free with their hooked blades. Still the machine thrashed. One warrior stabbed through the window into the cab, piercing the pilot's chest. The others drove their blades deep into the guts of the machine, jamming the bonelike linkages, snapping chains. Finally the machine lay still.

The last remaining pilot fled, directing his lizard to ford the river. When it reached the opposite bank, it crawled away among the reeds.

The courier closed her eyes and breathed, trying to slow her pounding heart. The air stank of naphtha, of blood, of the sickly-sweet fumes from the war machines' engines. Her stomach turned. That was the smell of burning ghosts.

Below, three new ghosts had risen to their feet. Each stood staring at their own bodies: the pilot in his dismantled machine, the two masked figures on the deck of the barge. Meanwhile, the nameless were helping one another out of the river. Among them was one man without a mask. He stomped up from the mud and straightened his gray cap. When he saw the courier, he shook his head and grinned.

The courier said, "You told me I'd never see you again."

"I think I'll stop trying to guess what you'll do next," the junk dealer said.

Three more barges rounded the bend in the river, each packed full of masked passengers. The courier recognized them as the same barges she had seen moored in the canal behind the junk dealer's warehouse that morning. Then they had been stacked high with his wares; now they carried people.

"After you intervened, the judges offered me a deal," the junk dealer explained. "All the nameless of Hollow, all who remain. I have to get them to the other side of the forest."

"You're bringing them to their last city," the courier said.

He made no reply.

"You won't make it," Thorn called down. "The army of the named is on the move, and they have stronger machines than these."

"The lizards were mere scouts, dispatched to patrol the river," the junk dealer agreed. "But so long as none report back to their commanders, we might slip through." He gazed across the river, to the place where the last lizard machine had just vanished among the trees.

The courier understood what he was asking of them. "Two," she said, "do you think Oh can catch it?"

Two's smile was answer enough. Thorn looked worried, though. He called down to the junk dealer, "Do you have any spare fuel?"

The junk dealer consulted briefly—silently—with three green-masked figures who were tending to the engine, then returned with a small heap of naphtha in a wooden cart. Oh looked up, nostrils flaring at the scent.

"I'm sorry we can't spare more," the junk dealer said. He held the cart steady as the monster eagerly devoured its contents. The courier felt the eyes of the nameless on her and on the monster she'd helped make. They must have thought it strange, this creature that was part machine, part nightmare.

While Oh ate, three figures in pale suits climbed down out of the barge. The courier knew their masks: dark blue triangles with silver streaks beneath the eyes. They went to the new ghosts—not just their own, but the pilot's, too. They touched each in turn and guided them gently onto the barge.

When Oh was done eating, Two got her attention and pointed out the path across the river. To the courier's surprise, Oh nodded. She stepped carefully into the shallows, then leapt out into the water. Her scales rippled as she paddled with all four paws, head held high.

The courier looked back to see the junk dealer return to his barge. All four craft were on the move again by the time Oh crashed through the reeds and into the marshy lowland beyond.


The tracks of the lizard machine were marked plainly in the soft earth. The monster stomped through muddy pools and over grassy mounds, trampling shrubs, sending water birds screeching into the air. Soon they passed back into a dense wood, the air dark and cool, broken branches signaling the way.

They found the lizard curled in the shadow of a hemlock tree. When the pilot realized he'd been spotted, he directed his machine deeper into the trees, slipping through the underbrush.

Thick smoke poured from Oh's chimney as she charged after him, claws raking the earth. The lizard machine was smaller and nimbler. It darted from side to side, leading Oh on a twisting, turning chase. It dove into a gulley, then reappeared in a maple grove. The monster wheeled and went after it.

"She'll never catch it if she follows its every move," the courier said.

Two seemed to understand. She patted Oh's neck and pointed the way forward, over the gully. The monster grunted her assent and leapt the gap. Beyond the maples, she came within a boxcar's length of the machine before it shot off in another direction. Instead of trying to follow its course, Oh maintained her speed and cut a wide arc through the trees. When their paths crossed again, Oh was so close that she might have snatched the machine by its tail. Instead she barreled onward, unrelenting—maybe even enjoying the chase as she herded the machine and its pilot away from the denser parts of the woods.

The soil grew sandier, the grasses taller, the trees shorter and more sparse.

The lizard machine moved faster but had fewer places to hide. They skirted marshes and leapt small streams. Finally, in the valley between two sandy hills, Oh pounced and pinned the machine to the ground.

It squirmed under her weight, trying to free itself, the whine of its machinery growing in volume until it sounded like a scream. The monster dug in with her claws and tore the lizard in two.

Its pilot pulled himself from the cab, out onto the sand. He rolled and raised his hands, but not in surrender. The courier heard the blast before she saw his pistol.

Oh brought one foot down on the soldier, crushing him where he lay. Thorn clutched his shoulder and staggered backward, dropping soundlessly into the back of the litter.

The courier knelt beside him. She looked for the wound, but all she saw was blood oozing from between his fingers.

"It's worse when it isn't pretend," he said.

With the knife from her satchel, the courier cut the left sleeve off her boilersuit. Thorn winced as she wrapped it tight around the wound. Seconds later, the blue fabric was stained dark red. Blood dripped down Thorn's arm and onto the floor of the litter.

"We have to go back to the nameless," the courier said to Two. "He needs a real bandage and proper care."

Thorn grabbed her arm. "We have to keep going," he hissed.

Two looked back and forth between them, worrying the stub of her left arm with what remained of her fingers. Oh turned, her long neck stretching as she sniffed the air.

"Don't you hear it?" Thorn said.

"Hear what?" the courier asked.

"Listen," Thorn said.

The courier heard the tick-ticking of the lizard machine's furnace as it cooled. She heard the fire burning in Oh's belly. And then she heard something else, something almost indistinguishable from the rush of blood in her ears. The sound swelled, shushing and hissing, then crashed and fell away and swelled again, marking a strange rhythm. The courier had never heard anything like it.

She stood. Two and Oh were staring at her, waiting. "All right," she said. "Bring us a little farther out."


Oh carried them over rolling sandy hills, past gnarled trees and tangles of tough-looking shrubs. To the north was the river, widening between the hills, its banks grassy—that was the way the barges would come. The sun was a pale splotch at their backs, and thick gray clouds were massing overhead.

The courier felt a change in the air, a cool wind mixing with the heat coming off their monster's engine. The breeze was damp. She licked her lips and tasted salt. Then, from the top of the next hill, they saw it. The courier stared until her eyes began to water. She blinked and looked again, trying to understand.

"Help me up," Thorn said. "I want to see."

She looped an arm under his uninjured shoulder and pulled him to his feet, and they leaned side by side against the litter. The ground ahead was sand, all sand—until it gave way to a vast gray *something*. The something reared up at them, frothing as it clawed at the sand, then dragged itself back to itself. It stretched away under the clouds forever, heaving and rolling as far as she could see.

Water, she realized, when she saw where the river joined it. It was water. But the word *water* wasn't enough to describe this, and neither was *lake*. What to call a lake as wide as the sky? Birds bobbed on its surface. Birds flew above and dove into it. Birds walked on the sand and were birds beside it.

"The edge of the world," Thorn said.

Is that what this was? The sound of all that water rushing, cresting, crashing, falling—that was a sound to swallow time and turn it into something else, something bottomless. Standing this close, she thought she didn't need words at all. What good were words in a place like this?

"Ah," said Two. She pointed north with her scorched hand. Nestled against the shore was a city. Not a big city, not so sprawling as Hollow, but its spires reached higher, so high they looked lonely up there in the fog.

The sculptures that stood among them were enormous: sculptures of fish and birds, of hammers, picks, and shovels, of human eyes and ears. The statues were in ill repair, some crumbling, some rusted or grown over with vines. *Beyond the forest, a city.* It stood on the border between water and land, though much of it was claimed by water. The far end was entirely submerged, with streets that ended in lapping waves. Farther out, the tops of buildings and a few statues peeked above the surface. All the buildings were dark, but the city was not abandoned. Clusters of pale lights shone through the mist—encampments of some kind, maybe.

Farther north and several miles inland, the rail line emerged from the forest and crossed a broad scrubland on its way into the city. There, among the gnarled trees and low-growing shrubs, the army of the named was gathering. Machines unloaded machines from flatcars while soldiers arranged themselves into columns. The Number Twelve was near the back of the line, and the courier could just make out the uniforms of the namers.

In a switchyard, the army shunted cars onto sidings. Rolling forward through the yard was the freight train, the one full of ghosts from Hollow.

The courier must have a made a sound, because Thorn put one hand on her back and said, "He's all right."

She didn't know if that was true, but she couldn't bear the thought that Thorn was wrong. "We still need to turn around," she said. "We have to find someone who can look after that wound."

"Then bring me down there, into the city," he said.

The courier began to protest—they had no idea who lived down there, or whether they would welcome guests such as themselves—but Thorn said, "Someone needs to warn them about what's coming. The army from one direction, their own people from the other. They have to be ready."

The courier looked back to the river to check for the barges, though she knew they would still be plying that narrow, winding course through the forest for hours yet. By the time they arrived, the army might already have captured the city in which they planned to seek refuge.

"He's right," the courier said to Two. "Let's go."

Two let out an urgent yelp, and Oh charged north toward the city. She crossed the river over an old bridge, then descended toward the water, kicking up sand as she went. Thorn's voice had been steady, but now his body sagged. The courier caught him and eased him back into a corner of the litter.

"Let me know when we get there," Thorn said. He closed his eyes.


All along the ragged, restless edge of the world, the endless green swells gathered ridges of white from the gray curve of the horizon. It was almost a comfort, the courier thought, how small it made her feel.

Oh brought them into the outskirts of the city. Sand had drifted onto the streets and up to the doors of dark brick houses. Faces peered from some windows, and figures sat or stood on the stoops. Others milled about on the sidewalks, shuffling slowly from corner to corner. The people of the city were not nameless, as the courier had expected. They were all ghosts. Dozens in every building and dozens more on the street, some nodding and waving to one another as the living might do.

Like the buildings themselves, most of the ghosts were faded and frayed, as though the salty winds were slowly wearing them away. The courier saw ghosts reading books, a ghost combing another ghost's hair, ghosts rolling marbles in the dirt, ghosts seated on rooftops with views of the water. Most ignored the monster and her passengers, though a few turned to watch as Oh strode past.

Up ahead, a cluster of lights shone through the mist. As they drew closer, the courier saw hundreds of candles burning in a sprawling wooded place. The candles were set in lanterns, on rocks, around the bases of statues. Paths wound over hills and among the trees, skirting streams and small ponds. Meadows opened between the more densely wooded areas.

*And within the city, a forest.*

The place was thick with ghosts. Most were seated cross-legged in the grass, while others sat on benches or with their backs against the trees. A few of the living were here, too. Three nameless sat on a little hill with ghosts gathered close around. A fourth walked the paths between the stones, sticking new candles in puddles of wax left by the old. All wore blue triangular masks with silvery streams of tears—the masks of ghost tenders. None of them looked up at Oh's approach.

Thorn was awake again, leaning against the side of the litter. The courier said to him, "Is this where they bring all the ghosts? Here, to this city on the edge of the world?"

"The Black Square never transports ghosts farther than the outskirts of Hollow," he said. "But this must be the place where the ghost roads end." He looked tired and pale, almost a ghost himself.

"We'll keep going," she said. "Do physicians of the nameless wear certain masks?"

Thorn ignored the question. "I need to get down there," he said.

"Thorn, no."

"They can help me," he said.

"They help *ghosts*."

"They'll know where to take me, maybe."

The courier hesitated. But Thorn was weakening quickly; the corner where he'd been resting was slick with blood. So she nodded to Two, and Two patted Oh's neck gently. The big monster crouched low. The courier climbed down first, then helped Thorn to the ground. He kept one arm over her shoulders as she walked him up the hill.

The three nameless were gathered around a low stone slab, upon which many candles burned. Seated close to the candles was a ghost, more tattered and faded than all the others, just a wisp of gray floating over the grass. The courier could not have said whether it was the ghost of a man or a woman. The person the ghost had been might have lived in the time of Hand and

Moon, before the words *woman* and *man* were divined and delivered. The courier sensed a powerful and desperate want in the brightness of the ghost's eyes.

The nameless held very still, as though waiting for something to happen. Slowly, the ghost reached one hand out toward a candle flame. Another inch or two, and the ghost would catch fire and burn like a sheet of paper.

The ghost *wanted* to stop being a ghost.

The blue-masked nameless did not nudge the ghost's hand forward—only waited, gave the ghost space. Others nearby were watching. The masked figure who kept the candles lit paused on the path. The courier heard, in the distance, waves crashing against the city's streets. How many of the ghosts out there wanted this? How long would it take for each to find their way to the flame?

For a moment longer, the faded gray ghost held one hand a finger's width from that flickering light. Then the ghost drew back.

Thorn slumped against the courier. She heard a tapping sound; it was his blood dripping onto the grass. Finally, two of the nameless rose and approached. They saw the blood. One examined the roughly tied bandage. The courier felt an exchange of thoughts between Thorn and the masked figures. In a moment, they had come to some kind of decision. The nameless reached to take him.

"Thorn?"

The masked figures looked at her, alarmed, and Thorn shook his head. Not because he didn't want to go with them, but because they should not use words, not here. She swallowed back everything else she wanted to say—the reminders to warn the nameless about the army and the refugees, the command that he find a proper physician, that he *survive*—and she let the nameless carry him away.

They set him down among the ghosts. He lay on his back and closed his eyes, breathing slowly. One of the ghost tenders returned to the candle-covered slab. The other walked down the path and out onto the street, disappearing among the buildings. That one, the courier thought, had better be going for help.

The other nameless had all returned to their work, the one setting candles and lighting them, the other two keeping vigil. Slowly, the ghost reached toward the flame again.

Oh bore them quickly back through the streets of the city. The courier and Two were silent as they rode. Sometimes, in empty spaces between the buildings, they glimpsed more clusters of burning candles in smaller wooded places. The courier wondered how many ghosts would touch their fingers to those consuming lights before the end of the day.

Frost had no idea what his army was marching toward. Not a city of warriors prepared to defend their people. Not a city of monsters ready to meet him on the battlefield. This was a city of ghosts—of undefended riches. Of hands to work the factories, of fuel to power their machines. For years, this city had been filling with ghosts, many smuggled out of the named territories by the nameless and the Black Square. Frost would seize them, more than replacing years of lost property. He would return to the named a hero.

"Hurry," the courier whispered to Two. Two urged Oh through the streets, and they soon emerged back onto the sandy hills.

The army was already advancing. At the front were the war machines, maybe fifty of them. She saw some lizard scouts and fast-moving mantises like those they had encountered in the forest. Most, though, were the bearlike brutes, some walking on all fours, others on their hind legs, many with naphtha throwers mounted to their arms.

Standing higher than all the others were the three command vehicles. On the army's right flank, a spiderlike machine walked on tall, spindly legs. Opposite was a thing like a beetle the size of a building, with mandibles as long as trees. In the middle was the lead machine, shaped like a great tortoise, a cannon mounted to its armored shell.

Soldiers marched among the machines, guided by detachments of watchers. Three flying machines drifted overhead, serving as the army's eyes. Taking up the rear was the Number Twelve.

The sight of the army seemed to awaken some monstrous instinct in Oh's burning heart. Steam shot from her mouth and smoke rose from her chimney in a thick plume. Suddenly she was running over the hills, roaring so fiercely that sparks flew from her mouth. It took both Two and the courier screaming and pounding at her neck to convince her to stop in a low valley, out of sight of the flying machines.

When the roaring of the monster's furnace had leveled off, the courier said to Two, "Keep her steady, and let me know if there's trouble. There's something I need to do."

Two grunted her assent, and the courier sat cross-legged on the floor of the litter. In the warmth from Oh's furnace, she breathed, emptying her mind as she'd taught herself to do as a child, pushing away every fear that might become a monster. There were almost too many: Thorn bleeding in that place of ghosts; Beryl in the midst of Frost's army; Seven and the rest of the Black Square broken and captured. . . . She let each thought go until only one remained. In the perfect borderless quiet, she sought the mind of her stowaway.

At first, she found only darkness. More fears floated up. Had he been lost to the forest? Caught by soldiers and killed?

No, she felt him. He was there with the army, but he was hiding. The courier dove deeper through the in-between places, found him hunkered in the dark. He seemed happy to have been found by her. His mind was full of sound and movement and light; she pressed her face to it, pressed her eyes behind his eyes, her hands down into his paws.

She felt the dirt under his paws, felt whiskers brushing tall grass, smelled the sickly, stinging ghost smoke in the air. The stowaway was crouched under a rail car watching people do what people did: moving things, shouting, telling ghosts what to do.

Drovers unloaded the ghosts from boxcars and directed them over the switchyard in columns. The ghosts shuffled along between the rails or stumbled over the sleepers. They smelled dusty, like rags left to dry in the sun. Most were gray and ragged, but she glimpsed among them a bright splotch of color. The patchwork ghost was being marched with the others toward the machines, machines that would soon require more fuel.

She urged the stowaway closer. He kept to the dark under the cars while the stupid booted feet of the living clomped past, then sprang out into the switchyard and wove among the nearly soundless feet of the ghosts, drawing closer to the one with the brightly colored patches. That's when he and the courier felt the heat coming off him: except it wasn't just the one ghost anymore. From every ghost nearby—all those who had been with him in that boxcar, maybe—came a dazzling warmth.

There was something else strange about these ghosts, something the courier didn't think she could have seen with her own eyes. They moved differently, their steps more certain, their bodies tensed. The patchwork ghost had changed them, and he was still changing others, laying one hand briefly on the backs and shoulders of those he passed.

The warm ghosts still obeyed the drovers, and they walked in straight lines. They still followed the machines that would require them as fuel. But they no longer stumbled over the rails and the sleepers. Instead, they looked at one another like people who shared a secret. The patchwork ghost was preparing them for something, maybe to escape. But he would need more time to reach them all.

Something dragged her from the stowaway's mind, and she gasped as she tumbled back into her own.

.    .    .

Two was crouched directly in front of her, shaking her awake—and Oh was on the move again. The big monster went slower than before, taking a round-about route, keeping to the low places among the hills. But she clearly intended to put herself between the army and the city on the shore.

"Oh, oh," Two said, scolding her, but Oh pretended not to hear.

"I think we have to let her do this," the courier said.

Two's eyes widened.

"The patchwork ghost is up to something. If he succeeds, the whole army will fall apart, because he's taking their fuel away. But he needs more time."

Two looked unhappy.

"We could send Oh ahead without us, if you're scared," the courier said.

"Oh!" Two said, and stamped one foot, which was the response the courier had expected.

"Then we'll go with her," she said. "Try to keep her clear of the greatest threats. But we'll have to be ready to let her—"

"Nn," Two said, her glare a warning.

"To let her be a *monster*," the courier finished.

In spite of her height, Two looked so much like a child that the courier wanted to grab her, pull her from the litter, and hide her among these hills. Oh craned her neck to look at them, and she seemed to understand some of what had been said. She snorted a puff of smoke from her nostrils, and Two grinned. Everyone was in agreement.

They came down out of the hills and into an abandoned village west of the city. About a hundred leaning houses stood clustered around the rails. Gulls perched atop caving rooftops, watching the monster come bounding into town.

The war machines were drawing closer, bulbous shapes under a cloud of dust. Two of the flying machines circled over that cloud, but one was coming toward them—its crew had probably spotted Oh.

Oh drew up to the tracks by a depot near the village center. She turned twice around the rails, then sighed as she settled her wheels onto them.

Two leaned forward, pressed her cheek against Oh's, and spoke into the other monster's ear. The courier could just make out the sounds. Not words, only gentle hisses and whispers, yet the monster seemed to understand. She set her jaw, great gold eyes shining in the sun, and turned to face the army.

"Ready?" the courier asked.

Two pursed her lips and nodded. A rumbling vibration went through Oh's body, and the litter shook. The monster took a deep breath and her wheels began to turn.

*Please don't do what you're about to do.*

The courier yelped and spun in place. She and Two were alone in the litter, but she thought she'd heard her sister's voice. It was as though she were standing beside her, speaking low. "Ticket?"

*Don't,* Ticket said again. *I'll be right there.*

This time she could almost feel Ticket's breath on her ear. And suddenly she understood. *Whisper.* Ticket had whispered to her.

Two stared at the courier, confused and worried.

"Wait," she said. "We can't go yet."

Oh grumbled and hissed as her wheels stopped turning. She turned her big head to look at the courier, who held up both hands, urging stillness.

Then, from around the nearest street corner, a black machine came roaring. Two screamed. Oh leapt from the tracks and crouched, growling, ready to spring. But it wasn't a war machine. It was Ticket's ancient vehicle, covered in mud, engine whining, all four wheels kicking up dirt. It skidded to a halt beside the tracks. Ticket stepped out of the driver's seat, and Shadow emerged from the opposite side.

The courier jumped down from the litter and ran to her sister. As they embraced, the courier was surprised to feel tears coming to her eyes. She was even more surprised to see that Ticket was crying, too. Ticket stepped back and wiped her face with the back of her sleeve.

"I saw you charging through the valley," Ticket said. "I thought you'd reach the army before I could catch you."

Two murmured to Oh, calming her as best she could.

"What *is* that thing?" Ticket asked.

"She's called Oh," the courier said. "Two named her."

Two climbed down from the litter to stand near the rails. She tugged at the jacket Beryl had given her, flashing the brass buttons of the names committee.

Shadow's stars flashed. "So you're naming things now," she said, and Two looked at the ground, grinning bashfully.

"I'm glad you're all right," the courier said. "What about the others?"

"Wolf has his own assignment," Ticket said. "He made it out alive, but—"

"The den burned," Shadow said, her lights crackling red.

"And Wolf's companion?" the courier asked. "That other monster—"

"We searched the rubble. Found no trace of her."

"Shadow, I'm—"

"No time," Shadow said, brushing past her. Her red stars darkened, until they could hardly be seen. Oh watched warily as she approached. Shadow leaned first one way, then the other, sizing the monster up. "The glassblowers did this?"

"I helped," the courier admitted. "So did Thorn."

"And that animal who's always following you, from the look of it," Shadow observed. She slowly raised one hand into the air. Oh pulled back, then lowered her head and sniffed.

"She's magnificent," Shadow said, stars lightening, going gold. "I've never seen anything like her."

"Isn't that how it is with monsters?" the courier asked.

Shadow circled Oh, taking in her pistons and wheels, the chimney atop her furnace. "She's something more different still. Fire will undo us, but this one runs with a belly full of the stuff. The named made war machines to kill monsters. This is a monster built to kill machines."

Oh huffed proudly, sending a little cloud of smoke from her nostrils.

"That may be true," Ticket said. "But charging straight at the army isn't a very good plan. What were you thinking?"

Before the courier could respond, Shadow said, "Ticket, your sister is a fighter. That's something you should probably get used to."

"I'd still like to know why—"

"The patchwork ghost is back there," the courier said. "He rode in on the fuel train. I think he's trying to get the ghosts away from the army, but he needs more time."

"Oh, oh," said Two, pointing.

The flying machine was drawing closer, and so was something on the rails—something small but fast. A handcar. Its operators were very tall, and they wore identical, big-brimmed hats.

"Won't they ever stop coming for me?" the courier asked.

"The seeker ghosts have never failed to catch someone," Ticket said. "I don't think they know how to stop."

"I'll take care of those two," Shadow said, her stars glinting sharply. "The rest of you, get the ghost the time he needs."

Ticket looked back and forth between Oh and her own vehicle—that old competitive edge. Grinning, the courier said, "I think ours is faster."

"Fine," Ticket said. "But we're doing this my way. We come at them from the side, target one of those command machines."

The courier looked out over the massed army. "We'll never get there in time," she said, "not even with Oh."

Now Ticket was smiling, too. "We'll get there," she said.

. . .

At first the courier was worried about bringing someone new aboard. But after sniffing Ticket briefly, the monster gave an enthusiastic grunt—pleased, maybe, to meet someone so much like Two. Oh needed more convincing to leave the rails and abandon her head-on assault, but once they were moving again, north out of the village and into the scrubland, she bounded with obvious glee through the cool salty wind.

Ticket laughed, amazed and thrilled in spite of her exhaustion. She put her hand on Two's shoulder. "Thank you," she said.

Two looked confused.

"I asked you to watch after our sister. I thought she'd be a ghost by the next time I saw her, but here she is. Here *we* are, all three of us."

"Ticket?" the courier said, suddenly worried, because this didn't sound much like Ticket.

"I'm very tired," she admitted, "and we've lost so much. Our most important safe house. One of our best agents. Maybe more than one—Wolf is broken, or he will be once he has time to slow down. But I still have you."

"Ticket—"

"Let me say this, before I convince myself not to. You were right. I should have replied to your letters. But I was so ashamed of leaving you, and the easier thing was to bury the shame under silence. I'm sorry."

The courier's eyes were hot with tears. Through the years of the Silence, the world had convulsed and twisted, and her family had a silence of its own. How many words would it take to crack it apart?

"You were a child when you left," the courier said. "It wasn't your fault."

She held Ticket as she cried, and for a moment she felt like the big sister—the one she'd had sometimes, the one she wanted always. The old anger was still inside her, but it was diminished, changing into something else. Something she didn't have a word for yet.

Ticket pulled away. "I'm glad you had your patchwork ghost," she said. "And that animal. And Two, and this new monster." She started laughing.

"I make the strangest friends," the courier said.

"So do I." Ticket looked back toward the village. The courier could see the handcar of the seeker ghosts gliding among the buildings, down to where Shadow waited for them. Even off the rails, she thought Oh would be able to outrun them, but could anyone truly stop them? Shadow had told the courier nothing about her plan.

A buzzing sound drew the courier's gaze to the sky. The flying machine was following, slower but steady.

"Quick, down that way," Ticket said, pointing to a marshy area of low-growing trees.

Two didn't have to tell Oh to change course this time. Oh plunged among the trees. Two laughed as the monster ran splashing through the shallows. The courier knew what Ticket would do next, even before she saw the compass in her hand. Somehow, the four of them were of one mind. Not as the courier and her stowaway were—more like leaves on the same wind. Because the courier had made Two and helped make Oh. Because Two was like Ticket, and Ticket was the courier's sister. Because Oh and Two were good at being monsters together.

"Up there," Ticket said. "A *shortcut*."

At first the courier thought the spelling hadn't worked. A moment ago, they'd been surrounded by trees and water, and they were surrounded by trees and water now. Oh seemed to sense something, though. She scented the air, climbed from the water, and cautiously climbed the slope. Only then did the courier see what had changed.

Columns of soldiers marched by in front of them, so close she could make out some of their faces. Ticket had brought them right up to the army's flank yet kept them hidden. It had seemed not to work only because it was so easy for her this time, here in this nameless land, with nothing set down except the words for *grass, water, trees, marsh*. . . . Already she felt her memory shifting to fit the shape of the land.

"We don't have long," Ticket said. "That flying machine will be crewed by some of the more experienced watchers. They have their ghost lenses, and they know how to let their minds see past what their eyes are telling them. They'll find the shortcut soon."

The army continued to advance, war machines trundling along between squadrons of foot soldiers. From here, the courier no longer had a view of the village they'd left behind, but Shadow and the seeker ghosts must surely have found each other by now.

A restless grumble sounded from Oh's furnace. She was building up a head of steam and she wanted to *move*.

"Ah?" Two asked.

"Not yet," the courier said.

Long minutes passed as soldiers and machines went by. Oh's rumbling grew deeper. Eventually the vanguard reached the shore, and stopped in confused awe as the first pilots and soldiers saw the expanse of water beyond. Most behind them halted, while other pushed their way forward, trying to see.

War machines jostled each other as they parted to let the nearest command machine heave its great beetle-like body through. The commander within was no doubt eager to regain control over the troops. The machine looked even bigger up close, its black armor plates gleaming, its legs like the struts of a bridge. Its mandibles opened and closed as it swung its massive head from side to side.

Oh's growl spread from her engine to every part of her body, and soon she was shaking so hard that her glass scales rattled. Two looked at the courier, and the courier looked at Ticket. Ticket grasped the litter's edge with both hands, closed her eyes, nodded.

"Now," the courier said.

Oh flew as though she'd been fired from a cannon. Three leaps brought her clear of the trees, and the fourth took her over the first column of soldiers. Those in the next column scattered. They must have felt her heat and heard the rage in her screech, but they could not have understood what they were seeing.

Oh's mind was someplace far away now. The courier was glad that the monster was on her side.

Two war machines moved to block their path, a pair of bearlike brutes. One was covered in long spikes; the other had hatchet blades for hands. When the first charged, Oh leapt again and landed in front of the second. She grabbed it by the middle, and its hatchet hands flailed uselessly. Oh hurled it into the spiked machine and both careened into the trees, breaking apart as they rolled.

Oh had barely slowed down. She was closing in on the beetle, gnashing her teeth, ready to go for its throat. The beetle flexed its mandibles, each nearly as long as Oh herself. They looked strong enough to crack her like a bottle.

"Bring us around the other side!" Ticket shouted.

Two cried Oh's name and the monster went low, dashing between the command machine's legs as other machines circled and the mandibles closed on empty air. Oh spun and slashed at its belly from below, but her claws only scraped against its metal plates The nearby soldiers had recovered and were closing ranks.

"This one's too armored," Ticket said. "Quickly!" She took the courier's hand, then closed her eyes and breathed, just as the courier would have done before making a delivery. The world went quiet, and into that quiet, Ticket spoke a single word.

*Float.*

She spoke it as the courier had first spoken it, in a pond covered in yellow maple leaves, her body shivering in the cold. The courier shivered again as Oh and Two fell away beneath her. There was the courier's shadow, no longer touching her feet. And there was Two, staring up at them, mouth open as the courier and Ticket soared upward.

When they set down on the command machine's back, the courier let herself breathe again. From up here, she could see the Number Twelve halted on the rails. The names committee couriers had debarked. Soldiers escorted them over the scrubland, alongside the huge mass of ghosts.

The courier widened her stance against the rocking of the machine. It reminded her of running with Beryl over the cars of the Number Twelve. But this machine's back was curved, and there was nothing to grab onto if she slipped.

She spun at a loud clanging noise. A dozen paces away, near the middle of the beetle's back, a hatch had opened and a soldier was climbing out, rifle in one hand.

"*Trouble!*" Ticket shouted.

The soldier's jacket caught on the hatch, just as the beetle took a rocking step. He jerked back, tumbled down over the machine's side, screamed as he fell.

Ticket sank to one knee, catching her breath, and the courier knelt beside her.

"You really do know my deliveries," the courier said.

"I try not to use *trouble* often. I never know exactly what it's going to do."

The courier helped her back to her feet, and together they ran for the hatch. A short ladder brought them down into a long corridor with a curved ceiling. The air inside was hot, and it smelled of burning ghosts.

They ran through the beetle's abdomen and into the control chamber at the top of the thorax. An officer stood peering into a scope, turning it as though searching for something—for Oh, probably. More soldiers, three of them, sat or stood around him. Ticket walked forward.

"Ticket," the courier hissed, but the soldiers had already seen her. They raised their weapons, and the officer stepped back from the scope.

"*Sleep,*" Ticket told them.

The officer opened his mouth as though to protest or to issue a command, but his eyes fluttered shut first. He and the other soldiers collapsed to the floor.

The courier felt the word like a warm blanket and nearly succumbed as well, but she fought to stay awake. Ticket faltered, and the courier caught her. She shook her, spoke her name. Ticket was breathing, but she would not stir. She had pushed too hard and snared herself in her own spelling.

An explosion outside rocked the machine. The courier set Ticket gently on the floor, headed for the stairs at the top of the chamber, and climbed into the beetle's head. The pilot was seated between the glass domes of its eyes.

To the machine's right, the vast bulk of the army proceeded down out of the scrubland. To the left, the courier saw that endless expanse of water. The last city of the nameless was directly ahead, a few miles down the shore. And right in front of the beetle was a leaping, snarling whirl of destruction.

All around Oh, ruined machines smoked and burned. She was tearing another brute to pieces with her claws and teeth. Flames burst from the wreck as she ruptured its furnace. Another approached from behind—she sent it sprawling with a swipe of her tail. She leapt, got its body in her jaws, and shook it as it pounded at her sides with both fists. The body snapped and the machine's arms went limp. Even from up here, the courier could hear Two's squeals of delight.

The pilot of the beetle was covered in sweat, muttering to himself as he worked pedals and levers, negotiating with the monster in the bones of the machine. It seemed to be resisting him, but he finally overpowered it and the machine lurched forward.

Two looked over her shoulder and screamed as the great mandibles closed around Oh's middle.

"No!" the courier shouted.

The pilot turned, eyes wide. She grabbed him and tried to pull him from his seat, but he held to the controls. Oh writhed and twisted as the machine lifted her into the air. Two, bent over the side of the litter, beat her one fist uselessly against the mandible. The courier could hear glass scales cracking. If Oh's furnace was breached, the fire would burn them both away.

The courier punched the pilot in the face, and he slumped sideways in the chair. She pushed him to the floor, where he lay sprawled.

The mandibles opened and dropped Oh to the sand. She landed hard amid the fragments of her own scales.

Without a pilot, the spirit of the monster used to prime the beetle machine was making the decisions. With a thundering blast of steam, it descended upon Oh—then pivoted at the last moment to snatch up the nearest mantis, swiftly crushing it.

The other machines halted, their pilots clearly stunned. The beetle drew closer, catching a brute under its foot, sweeping three others aside. The machines broke open and burned, explosions rocking the beetle, rattling the great glass circles of its eyes in their frames. Oh rose slowly and shook her head. Two was back on her feet, patting the monster's neck.

"Watch out!"

The courier turned at the sound of her sister's voice. She stood leaning against the railing at the bottom of the stairs, pointing at the pilot. He was up on his knees and reaching for the controls. As the courier fought him back, the beetle swung to the right, bringing into view the great armored dome of the tortoise machine at the army's center. It was gazing at them with shiny black eyes.

"What have you done?" the pilot said—to the courier or to the monster inside the machine, she wasn't sure.

The tortoise aimed its cannon directly at the beetle. Fire flashed from its muzzle, and the world went sidewise as the courier fell into darkness.

She woke in the sand, with sand in her mouth and in her eyes, sand under the collar of her coveralls. Ticket was on her knees beside her, breathing hard. She must have dragged the courier clear of the wreckage. They were two dozen paces from the beetle, which lay on its side, legs twitching like strange bare trees. A grinding noise from deep in its innards grew steadily louder.

The courier spat sand from her mouth and wiped her eyes, gagging on the sickly fumes from the wreckage. She smelled burning ghost as she sat up, tasted metal in her mouth.

Ticket leaned against her, exhausted. How much spelling had she done to get them out of there? The army of the named was before them, and behind them was the burning machine, and beyond that was the edge of the world. Soldiers closed in, their rifles raised.

Then the ground shook as Oh came galloping over. The soldiers hesitated; they had seen what the monster was capable of. Oh crouched and swung her tail, and the soldiers fell back, clutching their rifles to their chests.

"Ah!" Two shouted, gesturing with her spindly hand. As soon as the courier and Ticket had clambered up into the litter, Oh sped away. She ran through the smoking wreckage of the machines she and the beetle had destroyed. Several brutes and mantises tried to block her escape, but Oh zipped around them. Soon she was out ahead of the army, charging along the shore. A few gunshots rang out, but none found their mark.

Ticket stood at the back of the litter, holding on with both hands. "I can't see the ghosts," she said. "Did they escape?"

All the courier could see was smoke and fire, and soldiers scrambling among the war machines. She put one hand on Two's shoulder and said, "Can you get us a better view?"

Two murmured something to Oh, and the big monster veered from the water and up into the sandy hills. A dark oily substance seeped from the wounds on her sides, and the courier heard a dry stuttering from her engine, but Oh's gait remained steady.

Below, the army of the named was regrouping. The surviving war machines, some three dozen in number, arranged themselves at the fore. The tortoise-shaped command vehicle lumbered toward the water, filling the gap left by the downed beetle. The spider, its long legs almost dainty on the sand, shifted closer to the center. Then all the machines resumed their advance, with the soldiers forming columns behind them.

Moving quickly up through the ranks were the couriers of the names committee. Seeing them, the courier felt more strongly than ever that she had become something else, something not like them at all. Still, she knew what task lay ahead of them. No members of her old committee had ever walked the city's streets or seen those who resided there. But one of the couriers would succeed in naming it eventually, with a word that fit well enough—and once the city was named, the army's invasion would be that much easier.

"Oh!" said Two, pointing farther north.

The courier looked, and a cold, helpless feeling trickled down through her body. The great gray mass of ghosts were still held captive, still being marched forward by drovers and soldiers.

Ticket put one arm around her. Their gambit had slowed the army down. They had destroyed one of the three command vehicles and a dozen other machines. But it wasn't enough, and now Oh was injured, Ticket was exhausted, and their presence was known.

The flying machine came buzzing after them, finally making up for their shortcut. The courier searched the sky for the other two. One flew west toward the sun, which was red and swollen above the trees. Its signal lights flashed, and the courier saw what its crew had spotted. The junk dealer's barges had floated clear of the forest. The barges might reach the city before the army of the named did, but once there, they would be captured with the rest.

The third flying machine hovered over the city itself. This one, too, was signaling, probably to inform Frost and his generals of the great wealth of ghosts awaiting them.

More lights flickered in the city—the ghost tenders' candles, the blue and gold lanterns over the streets. And there was something else, something moving at the city's outskirts. The courier stood straight, trying to see. Oh had noticed, too; she bounded to the other side of the hill, bringing the city more fully into view.

Huge shapes passed in and out of the light from the lanterns. Slowly the shapes drew closer, emerging from between the buildings and out onto the sand. They were monsters taller than the tallest war machines, like shaggy trees but upside-down, silver eyes shining from tangles of roots on their heads. The courier counted three, four, five of them, each with arms hanging nearly to the ground, long claws glinting at the ends of their great grasping fingers.

Among the giants came smaller shapes, stranger still, no two alike. A rolling ball of thorns. A thing like a walking pile of crates. A tall man covered from head to toe in nettles and flowers. Something made of hands that walked on its hands, felt its way with its hands, gestured menacingly with many long fingers.

The courier had been wrong—the city was not defenseless. The monsters had been slow to wake, or blue-masked dreamers had only just finished dreaming them. But they were here now, and though the courier had made a monster of her own—though she rode atop another she'd helped to dream—the sight made her shiver. These monsters were massive, their strangeness terrible. With them came nameless fighters, masks white for war. They were only a dozen in number, accompanied by monster handlers in gray cloth veils. Leading the force was a tall figure in gray and red robes, antlered mask spattered with dark red splotches.

Oh reared back and roared, black smoke billowing from her chimney, and Two let loose a howl of recognition. The monsters of the nameless responded with a chorus of shrieks and gibbers and wails. From the five giants came a low droning, like waves from other waters: dark and deep, to drown out the noise of the distant machines.

The flying machines' signaling turned frantic, and the army of the named halted. Even from up here, the courier could see the reactions—first confusion, then dread—among the soldiers. Some of the war machines pivoted as their pilots looked at one another. The named outnumbered their enemy many times over, but these were monsters straight out of story, bred in nightmares and built for battle.

Ticket shaded her eyes with one hand and squinted into the wind. "Look," she said, her voice somber.

Signal flags rose over the surviving command machines. The soldiers and war machines remained stationary, but the ghosts were on the move again, urged forward by drovers. The sight of the monsters must have spooked the commanders. Even if they had the advantage, they would need to prepare for a longer fight. The war machines were going to refuel.

"Oh, oh!" Two shouted, and Oh snorted in agreement.

The courier knew what they were thinking. By the time the monsters reached the machines, the majority of the ghosts would be consumed. But Oh was closer and much faster. She could get there in time.

"They'll see us coming," the courier said, gesturing to the flying machine above them. "Their guns will tear us apart before we reach them."

"Nn!" Two said sharply, arms folded over her chest.

"It's too dangerous," the courier insisted. "They'll be ready for us this time." Even as the courier said this, she felt a rumbling under her feet. Oh was building up a head of steam.

Ticket must have felt it, too. "You can't stop them," she said to the courier. "And I don't think you should try."

Two turned as though to argue, then realized what Ticket had said. "Ah!" she exclaimed, triumphant.

Before the courier could respond, Ticket said, "I don't know if we'll make it out, but we *can* surprise them one more time." Ticket's smile did little to hide her exhaustion, but the courier knew what that smile meant: arguing would only embolden her. Anyway, wasn't this what she really wanted? To ride with her sisters, her monsters, down along the edge of the world, until the world could no longer hold them?

Still, she had to ask. "Ticket, how many spellings have you already worked today?"

"Same as always," Ticket said. "One less than the day requires."

Oh kept her long, scaly body close to its shadow as she ran. The sand whirled around her, forming a cloud that mixed with the smoke from her chimney. She sounded her whistle, quietly at first, then louder and louder, like a kettle coming to boil.

The flying machine had no chance of keeping up, but the army could not fail to see her coming. When rifle fire started, Oh wove from side to side, seeming to gather speed and fury from each burst; her roar was louder than all the guns combined.

Two laughed gleefully as Oh brought them closer to the front line. Soldiers scrambled around the war machines, slamming furnace doors closed, waving back drovers and their ghosts.

The tortoise machine's cannon swiveled toward them, and the courier shouted. Oh sprang from the blast, but the impact pelted them with sand and sent the monster sliding. They emerged from the smoke to another barrage of rifle fire. Most of the bullets struck the ground as Oh leapt and dodged, but a few found their target. The courier kept her head down, wincing with each loud *crack,* knowing it meant another broken scale, another chance at a killing blow.

She looked at Ticket, and Ticket nodded. It would have to be now.

She turned from the courier, held a cupped hand beside her mouth, and leaned forward as though to whisper into someone's ear. The courier felt the spelling but she did not hear the words Ticket spoke. She thought she could guess who her sister whispered to. A moment later, she knew she was right.

Down the line, one of the brutes burst into flame. The machine stumbled forward and fell, its furnace cracking open with a screech. In the light from the explosion the courier saw him whirling among the machines, the hunter in his black coat, readying more fire. Wolf's eyes were red, his scarred face contorted with rage.

Other members of the fifth committee emerged from the army's ranks to join him. The courier recognized the surveyor Moss, but most she had never seen before—ghosts committee drovers, maps committee scouts, at least one other hunter. Some must have hidden themselves among the troops weeks or even months before, performing the duties expected of them, waiting for their moment. The courier couldn't hear the words they spelled, but she could see the effects. As Wolf set a mantis ablaze, another fell to pieces as though every bolt and rivet had been plucked from its frame. A brute sat down and held its head in its hands, swaying as though drunk. Two lizard scouts stood motionless, joints frozen. Pilots all along the front line abandoned their machines and ran.

Ticket's eyes were unfocused, her face ashen. She opened her mouth as though to ask a question, but no words came. Too many spellings, the courier thought. Her voice was gone. It was as though the Silence had reclaimed it.

"How long will you be this way?" the courier asked, steadying her.

Ticket shrugged and shook her head sadly: a long time, maybe. Two crouched beside them, cooing as she patted Ticket's hair with her singed hand.

"I've got her," the courier said. "Oh needs you now."

To the courier's surprise, Two embraced them both with her long, skinny arms. "I," she said.

That was unexpected. "You?"

Two drew back and nodded seriously. "I, Oh, I," she said.

The courier wasn't sure what that meant, but the monster's confidence was encouraging. Two rose and patted Oh's neck. Oh responded with a satisfied huff, then turned and crouched. With the pilots distracted by the fifth committee, this was her chance. Oh growled deeply and sprang toward the nearest machines.

A pair of mantises saw her coming and held their blade arms wide, poised to strike. Oh didn't slow down. When one of the machines lunged, she ducked and caught its arm in her jaws, dragging the machine to the ground as she bounded past. Before the mantis could swing its other blade, Oh hurled the machine down the line. Mantises and brutes scrambled clear as its long limbs cracked and flew from its body.

The courier heard that sound from Oh's engine again—a stuttering like a dry cough. The monster stumbled and the other mantis caught her with its blade, cracking scales along her haunch. Oh bellowed and spun, sweeping the machine's legs with her tail. Then she was on top of it, tearing at its silvery skin with her claws.

Ticket, still leaning against the courier, pointed to the south, where the great ragged host of monsters neared the midpoint between the city and the army of the named. They had to keep the machines busy a few minutes longer.

Drovers were leading the ghosts away from the front line as the rest of the war machines mobilized. In the face of Oh's ferocity, none of them could refuel. The dozen or so pilots who managed to evade the fifth committee's spellings were coming for Oh instead.

She crouched and snarled, daring them closer. The first to move was a brute armed with a naphtha thrower. Oh dodged the blast, pivoting to keep her passengers clear of the flames, then grabbed the weapon and turned it back upon the machine, miring it in fire.

Next three lizards attacked in unison. Oh snatched the first in her jaws and shook it, snapping its neck with a loud pop. The second she pinned to the sand, where it writhed and snapped. While Oh was distracted, the third sank its teeth into her right hind leg. Oh kicked and twisted, but the machine held tight.

Another brute thundered toward her. This one bore no weapons but its claws, and instead of trying to break Oh's armor, it wrapped both arms around her neck to grapple her. Oh shook and backed away; the courier heard that coughing sound again, a rough spluttering. The brute still clung to her, squeezing harder, and the smoke from the monster's chimney went pale and thin.

The brute's pilot jammed his controls, opened the hatch, and scrambled out of his machine. The lizard on Oh's hind leg released its grip and ran. All the war machines were backing away now, and the courier soon saw why. The tortoise had tilted its great shell forward—the better to strike so close a target.

The courier shouted, "Two, we have to get her out of here!"

"Oh, oh!" Two said, but Oh was stuck in place. The monster and the pilotless machine were a pair of frozen dance partners. As the cannon fired, Oh howled and heaved the machine's rigid bulk around, shielding herself from the brunt of the blast. Fire filled the courier's vision, and the explosion spun the world, water over sand over sky.


The courier clung to Ticket; they hit the ground together and rolled. Oh landed with a crash down by the waves, scales and machine parts rattling. The courier looked up in time to see the monster heave a sigh and then lie still amid the wreckage of the brute. She was bleeding from a dozen wounds, and her flesh was scorched. What had become of Two, the courier could not tell.

Wolf and the fifth committee agents fought on, but they were surrounded by machines, and several agents knelt in the sand, voices broken. Each blast of flame Wolf spelled was weaker than the last.

The courier and Ticket rose. Ticket's bottom lip was bleeding, and they both were covered in scrapes and burns. Maybe they had worse injuries—the courier wasn't sure. But it might not matter, because the machines were closing in, cutting them off from Oh and from the fifth committee. The sisters held each other. When they agreed to ride a monster into battle, the courier thought, they had both known it would probably end this way.

From between the nearest machines, dozens of figures came running. Soldiers, the courier thought—until she recognized their blue wool uniforms, brass buttons gleaming.

The couriers of the names committee crowded close to the sisters. With them came diviners and pages and the ghosts from the ghosts car, along with much of the Number Twelve's crew. They stood facing the machines, arm in arm, defiant. The courier knew all these people, and a few she could call friends, but many more of them had feared and resented her since she'd first come aboard the train. Yet here they were, her committee, gathering to protect her.

Beryl pushed her way through to the courier's side. She was out of breath, strands of red hair sprung loose from the mass she'd pinned up with her pencil.

"What are you doing?" the courier said.

"They brought us here to name the city," Beryl said, "but we can't name anything if we're ghosts."

"If you live, they'll call you traitors."

Beryl frowned and mouthed the word silently to herself, trying to understand.

"It's what Rope was, among other things," the courier said. "It's what I am now. What you'll be if you don't do what Frost wants."

The other namers had heard. They spoke the word quietly to themselves and to one another. *Traitor.* They seemed to like the sound of it.

"Too late," Beryl said.

Three mantis machines drew closer, swinging their bladed arms. One of the pilots shouted for the namers to move, but the committee only tightened the circle. The pilots looked baffled. Beryl was right. They could threaten the names committee, but they would not make ghosts of its members—not without new orders from Frost.

Those orders might come soon, she thought. The courier stared into the eyes of the tortoise machine, knowing he was probably up there, staring down at her. If so, he could also see the monsters of the nameless coming for him. He had to make his decision quickly; every delay brought the opposing army closer.

The tortoise's cannon remained pointed at Oh, who still lay slumped by the water. She heaved a dry cough, and another thin puff of smoke rose from her chimney. Two stood beside her, cradling her great head and crying. The courier hadn't known that she'd dreamed her up with tears to cry. They streaked down her papery cheeks, inky gray.

The war machines kept their distance, waiting for the tortoise to fire. Oh shifted and tried to rise, but her legs shook and she fell back to the sand. Her scales had lost their shine, and so had her eyes. She was injured, but even worse, she was out of fuel.

Ticket squeezed the courier tighter. Because she couldn't speak, the courier thought, and because she wanted to make sure her little sister didn't do something stupid.

Two patted Oh's face, coaxing her forward, pulling at her jaw, even scolding her. Her insistent burbling seemed to be having some effect: Oh looked sad, but some of the brightness was returning to her golden eyes.

Because, the courier realized, Two wasn't trying to make Oh stand. She had a different idea, and Oh had finally given in. The big monster rose up on her front legs, just a little, and opened her mouth wide.

"No," the courier said. "Oh no, no, no." She started toward them—and now Ticket did have to hold her back. The courier screamed as she struggled to break free. Two must have heard, because she turned and smiled. Then she leaned forward, putting herself within reach of Oh's jaws. Dutifully, almost gently, Oh snatched Two up with her teeth, tilted back her head, and swallowed her whole.


The tortoise fired its cannon just as Oh began to move. The explosion caught her and flipped her forward through the air. She hit the ground and tumbled, smashing the litter. Sand rained down from above. The courier felt it in her hair, heard it hiss against Oh's glass scales and against the metal skin of nearby machines.

For a moment, Oh was motionless except for the wheels spinning on her legs. Then she rose to her feet and shook the splintered litter from her back, sending broken scales flying. Her eyes were bright. A steady stream of smoke rose from her chimney. She stretched, raised her head, and opened her mouth wide.

Oh's roar was a grinding, piercing obliteration, a sound that meant *grief, rage, hunger, fire*. When it ended, she barreled directly at the tortoise.

Two brutes moved to block her way. Both stood upright on their hind legs, tall as two-story buildings. One gripped a mass of hooks and chains in its claws, the other a baton lined with spikes. The monster slowed, and she and the machines regarded one another. For a moment the courier could hear the waves again.

Oh drew a breath so deep it made her sides swell and set her scales rattling. Steam rose from her nostrils and sparks flew from between her teeth. Then, when the war machines were only steps away, she opened her jaws wide.

From her core, Oh loosed an exhalation of fire. It struck the machines with force enough to send them sprawling. The machines writhed, trying to stand, but Oh stood over them, her flames going from orange to blue. Both fell to heaps of smoking slag.

New signal flags rose over the command machines, orders from Frost and his generals. The remainder of the half-fueled squadron around the tortoise staggered forward to arrest Oh's charge. The machines surrounding the names committee broke off in pursuit of Oh, and a unit of soldiers poured in to take their place. They grabbed the namers one and two at a time, wrenching them from the circle, dragging them away. They struck with the butts of their rifles, threw couriers and crew to the ground. The sound of screams joined the hiss of waves and the screech of claws tearing metal.

Below it all, the droning of the giants grew louder as the monsters approached. The courier could feel it through the ground, and she knew the soldiers could feel it, too. They were near to panic. Soon one of them would open fire—and after one fired, others would, too.

"You have to stop this," the courier said to Beryl. "You have to get them out of here."

Beryl shouted for the namers to run, to fall back toward the hills. Some tried. Others attempted to retrieve their fellow committee members from the soldiers, only to be seized themselves. The spider machine advanced, long legs picking its way over the melee, its great fangs flexing.

Oh would not save them. The courier felt the monster's mind blazing, felt her fury focused to a red-hot point as she broke and burned machines between her and the tortoise. The fifth committee was nearly silent—what spellings they had left would be no help. The monstrous droning filled the silence they left. Many of the namers turned to flee, and the soldiers, shaking with fear, raised their rifles.

Then the soldiers stumbled forward, falling to the ground as something struck them from behind. It was a flood of ghosts, the army's fuel supply returning to the front line, but not to serve as fuel. They swarmed the foot soldiers, knocking them over and holding them down, pulling rifles from their hands. Other ghosts climbed war machines and dragged pilots from their compartments, threw them screaming to the sand.

The ghosts were deliberate, silent, relentless. They poured over the army in waves.

Through the crowd of gray, the courier glimpsed a flash of brightly colored patches. He was there, the patchwork ghost, directing their movements. He waved for a group of dozens to charge in defense of the fifth committee agents. Others he dispatched in the direction of the spider machine.

All this time, the courier had thought he planned only to free the ghosts, lead them away from the army and out into the nameless wilderness. But she had underestimated him again. The patchwork ghost was leading them into battle.

The stowaway walked at his side. The animal brushed up against his leg, and the ghost paused to pet him. He looked up and saw the courier. Then another wave of ghosts rushed past, and he was gone.


The footsteps of the giants grew louder, along with the wild burbles, howls, and shrieks of the smaller monsters. The ghosts had overrun the great bulk of the army, immobilizing most of the soldiers. The enormous spider machine wobbled as ghosts climbed its tall legs and pulled bolts from the joints. Oh was picking apart the last of the machines guarding the tortoise.

But she hadn't reached the tortoise yet. It fired its cannon again, this time at the monsters of the nameless. The shell exploded against the chest of one of the giants, and it burst into flames. The monster kept walking as fire engulfed the rootlike tangles of its head and spread down its long, outstretched arms. The silver eyes flashed, then went dark. The giant fell, its claws digging into the sand.

The tortoise would not have time to fire again. Oh clambered onto one of the last brutes and leapt from its shoulders, mouth open wide. She caught the tortoise's neck in her jaws. The great machine veered and stumbled, crushing smaller machines underfoot as it tried to shake Oh loose. Oh bit down harder and pried armored plates with her claws, fire pouring from between her teeth. Signal flags waved desperately, and a flying machine emerged from a hatch in the shell. It flitted away as Oh tore open the great metal neck and dragged the tortoise down.

Everywhere across the battlefield, soldiers grappled with ghosts while war machines burned around them. Many more machines stood slumped, the last of their fuel consumed. Oh leapt from the toppled tortoise to chase the few that remained upright.

The monsters of the nameless thundered closer, their shadows long in the red light of the setting sun. With them came the warriors in their white masks, their leader appearing taller with every passing moment, arms spread wide, antlers rising into the sky. Watching them, the courier felt unsteady on her feet. Ticket and the namers felt it, too. They crowded close together, held one another as the earth shook. This was no longer like seeing something out of story. They had fallen *into* story, and the story was old and very dangerous. All the monsters were giants now, the tallest of them brushing the clouds. They were creatures of storm and darkness, devouring the air, wreathed in lightning. The warriors charged, and the antlered mask of their commander pierced the sky.

The remaining war machines turned and ran, stumbling as they fled. Oh knocked a brute to the ground, tore it open with her claws. Another she caught with her fiery breath, sending the pilot scrambling from the cabin before its furnace burst.

The spider lay in pieces now; the ghosts had disconnected its legs. Other machines fell as they ran out of fuel; Oh barreled off in pursuit of those which had escaped over the hills and back into the scrubland. Soldiers ran with them, scattering to avoid being trampled. Soon nothing remained on the sand but ghosts and monsters and smoking ruins. The army of the named was broken.


Still the nameless and their monsters advanced, but something had changed. They seemed smaller as they drew near, and their horrible noise quieted. As they approached the courier and the namers, they did not look so frightening anymore. They looked threadbare and old. Creaky, poorly put together. Diminished.

The masked warriors, too, were less threatening, their weapons shabby and dull. Their commander approached the courier, Beryl, and Ticket. He removed his antlered mask.

It was Gray, the Gardener of Stones.

White masks lifted one by one, revealing faces the courier knew from the Black Square. She recognized a few of the shovels, some of the stones. Seven was among them; she rushed toward the courier, laughing, and threw her arms around her neck.

"The monsters," the courier said, still dazed. "They were huge. I felt the earth shaking."

"It's almost as though you've learned nothing about pretend," Seven said.

Players of the Black Square stepped out from behind the legs of the giants, and the monster handlers pulled back their gray veils. Leaves, most of them. The players used long poles, ropes, and pulleys to lower the giants to the ground. The operators of the smaller monsters threw off the contraptions they wore over their bodies: the mass of stuffed fabric hands, the suit covered in nettles and flowers, the great ball of thorns.

And now the courier remembered. The night before the Black Square returned to Whisper, she and Seven had gathered with others in a car full of monsters. Props, costumes, enormous pieces of pretend—they hadn't been put to use in a long time, Seven had told her. Now here they were again, dusty and worn and ramshackle, and with one last performance behind them.

Some of the players had flutes and droning pipes—the sources of all the noise. They wiped their sweating brows and embraced one another. The ghost of the Scout of Stones set down the enormous drum he'd been beating for the giants' footsteps.

Thorn crawled out of the monster made of crates. He looked very pale, and for a moment the courier thought that he, too, was a ghost. But he was smiling as he approached. His shoulder was bandaged.

"The nameless brought me to the Black Square's train, where the Gardener of Trees patched me up," he explained. "They made it to the city."

"You should be resting still," said the Gardener of Trees. He had been the monster made of nettles and flowers. Petals still clung to his beard.

A small figure in the gray robe of a monster handler pushed through the crowd. It was Juniper, the Gardener of Shovels. The old woman took both the courier's hands in her own. "So now we know what kind of Rider you are," she said.

The courier turned at the buzzing sound of a flying machine, the same one that had evacuated from the tortoise. It landed amid the nearby wreckage. From its hatch climbed Smoke, and with him came Frost, leaning on his cane. As they approached, the speaker clapped loudly and steadily. The sayer's face was red, his eyes bulging with fury.

"A fine show," Smoke said, still clapping. "I've never seen anything like it."

Gray bowed but kept his eyes on the speaker. Wolf and the other members of the fifth committee drew up behind Frost and Smoke, surrounding them.

"And now," Smoke went on, "for the sake of your performance, for your pretty hour of pretend, our people are left defenseless. How many more will be slaughtered by the nameless? How many of their ghosts will be smuggled here, to this desolate place, where they serve no use to anyone?"

The courier spotted two tall figures at the edge of the crowd: the seeker ghosts. They circled the fifth committee and the namers, approaching from either side like pincers. When Ticket saw them, she let out a mournful whimper. Shadow had seemed so sure she could beat them, but here they were. She wondered what they had done to overcome the monster, whether they had already burned her.

Gray ignored Smoke and said directly to Frost, "You have failed. Your army is gone, and there is nothing pretend about that. The sayers will turn their backs on you now. Frost, you spoke the Black Square out of existence. So who will you blame, I wonder, when the story of this day is told?"

The seeker ghosts drew closer to the courier, but Frost moved first. He crouched to pick up a pistol one of the soldiers had dropped. For the first time since the courier had met him, Smoke seemed surprised by what his sayer was doing. He quickly masked his confusion with more words. "The named will know of your treachery here. Not just yours, Gray, but that of the names committee. There will be a purge. Mass deletions, if necessary. The other sayers . . ."

He trailed off, because Frost was striding ahead, cane in one hand, gun in the other, ignoring Gray and his speaker both. The sayer's expression was usually cool, his eyes unreadable except for the certainty that everything they saw was beneath him, and therefore incapable of causing him harm. Now the courier could read his eyes plainly, and all she saw there was rage.

He pointed the gun at her.

Seven screamed. Beryl lunged for Frost, and Ticket tried to push the courier out of the sayer's way. Frost spoke one word.

*No.*

His voice was small and cold, a flake of ice in the salty air. The courier felt the word through her whole body. It froze her in place.

*No,* Frost said again. The speech of the sayers was not unlike spelling. Their words gave shape to the world, so they spoke only in concert, and only after months of careful deliberation and coordination among their speakers in the offices and galleries of Whisper. When the sayers spoke, they spoke law.

But what was the word *no,* spoken as law? A negation, a force to snuff out action and thought. Beryl stood in place, arms limp. Thorn fell to his knees. Ticket's mouth was open, but she could not speak. Not even the seeker ghosts moved.

Smoke looked horrified. He tried to say something, tried to reclaim his place as the speaker's voice, but *No,* Frost told him, and Smoke gagged. Wolf managed to take a step forward, his blackened hands clenched as though to spell more fire. *No,* the sayer said, spitting the word like an angry child, beyond consoling, beyond reason. His voice went higher and louder with each repetition, twisting the word, strangling it, *no no no no no*.

He aimed the gun at the courier's heart and fired.

But while all else was still, Gray had moved to stand in front of her. Maybe some fragment of his old power as a sayer granted him the strength to move, if only long enough to take that single step.

His antlered mask cracked down the middle and fell from his hands in two pieces. *No* was the only thing keeping him standing now, the courier thought. Finally he moved one hand far enough to feel his chest. Only then, with the blood bright on his fingertips, could he crumple to the sand.

No one else moved; no one could. Frost threw the gun to the ground and pointed at the courier with his walking stick, a signal to the seeker ghosts.

They closed in around her, their eyes black in the fading light. One took her arms and held them. The other slipped his big hands around her neck.

The courier could still see Ticket, her every muscle tensed, her jaw rigid, her eyes bright with desperation. She saw Thorn, staring up at her in terror and shame, unable to stand. She saw Beryl and Seven, still as statues, though behind their eyes she knew they were screaming. She felt sorry they would have to see this. She wondered if they would still seem so beautiful to her when she was a ghost. She thought: *I haven't even introduced them.*

The hands on her throat tightened, and her vision dimmed. In the darkness she saw flashes of light. The flashes sparked and spun in the shadow the seeker ghosts made together on the sand. That shadow, she realized, did not belong to them. It was packed with stars, and the stars were moving.

One moment, Sayer Frost stood atop the glittering darkness. The next, he was stumbling backward, sinking as though into thick mud. He flailed his arms, and the walking stick flew from his hand. When the seeker ghosts realized what was happening, they let go of the courier and tried to back away. But the shadow was everywhere they stepped. Together with Frost, they plunged into the sky below, into Shadow.

The courier staggered, gasping for air. Shadow stood and caught her, and the courier could still see Frost and the seeker ghosts shrinking as they fell. They vanished amid the stars in the monster's depths.

She must have sneaked up on the seeker ghosts, not to fight them, but to disguise herself. She had followed them as close as one could follow, waited for the ghosts to bring her to Frost so she could devour the man who had undone Book and unspoken the Black Square, who had turned the fear of the named into an engine of destruction.

Ticket threw her arms around Shadow and the courier. The courier felt her sister's hot tears on one side of her face and Shadow's icy cold on the other. Then Beryl was there, hand on the courier's head, looking at her neck.

"I'm fine," she said, though it hurt to breathe. "What about Gray?"

He lay on his back beside the broken mask. Seven was cradling his head in her lap. Thorn knelt beside him and held one of his hands in his own. Gray coughed, and blood spattered his lips.

"Help," Thorn said. "Someone please help."

The Gardener of Trees joined Thorn at Gray's side. He peeled the robe back from Gray's wound and said, "Water." One of the Leaves brought him a canteen, but as soon as he washed the blood away, more blood came. The Gardener of Trees shook his head.

"Six," Gray said. "*Thorn*. It's your help I need."

"I'm here," Thorn said.

"That word of yours, Thorn. It's time."

Thorn went rigid. "I can't do that," he said. "Please don't make me do that."

"None of these ghosts want to be ghosts," Gray said. Speaking was causing him pain, yet his voice was full and clear, the words carrying as though he were back onstage. "Not the ghosts on the battlefield. Not those in that city there, waiting hundreds of years to touch their hands to the fire. Your father did not want to be a ghost, Thorn, and neither do I."

The ghosts that had come from the factories of Hollow were gathering. They ringed the living, hundreds of them, maybe a thousand. And they were joined by others from the city. The courier recognized some that had arrived with the Black Square, those she had seen in the train's most secret car. Ghosts from the Number Twelve—the short ghost with one arm, the big ghost with gray eyes—still stood among the namers. All the ghosts seemed to know that something important was happening. They wanted to see.

"I can't," Thorn said. "I don't even know how."

Seven stroked Gray's hair gently. He saw the courier and beckoned her closer. "They'll just come back," he said, his voice weakening. "Another army needing more fuel. The ghost wranglers, the factories. Please, courier. I need this to matter."

She knew what Gray was asking, knew why he called her *courier* and not *Rider*. He wanted her to make the delivery. But how could she deliver a word that only Thorn knew?

Then she remembered that first day on the run from the watchers, beside a nameless stream. She had opened the patchwork ghost's sketchbook to find his drawing of the divining compartment. Glyphs etched into the floor, a rod to point with.

"You're sure?" she asked Gray.

"I told you," he said. "I've lived other lives, and I'll live others still. Help me finish this role, won't you?"

She didn't know whether what he said was true, but she knew he wasn't pretending. Gray believed what he said.

The courier took up Frost's walking stick. She found an empty square of sand and marked it, in three broad arcs, with every glyph used by the named. It was a crude version of what she had seen in the sketch, but maybe it would do.

Beryl stood beside her, watching. When the courier was finished, she gave her the walking stick. "Show him," she said.

Beryl seemed confused, then doubtful. "He's had no training. He isn't even a member of the committee."

"He's already divined the word once. He just needs to remember."

Beryl turned to look at the other namers, as though challenging them to stop her. No one moved or spoke. So she gestured to Thorn, and the boy rose to join them before the glyphs.

"Your dream in the roundhouse," the courier said. "You were about to speak the word, weren't you?"

"It feels far away now," he said.

Beryl put the walking stick into his hands. "Use this to bring it closer."

Thorn looked at the stick, then at the glyphs.

"This is similar to what we use on the Number Twelve," Beryl said. "You just have to choose the glyphs. Pretend you already know the word, and the word will come to you."

Thorn held out the walking stick and breathed. He pointed to one glyph, then another. Then he stopped and shook his head. "Are you sure we should do this?" he asked the courier. "You know what will happen."

She looked to the ghosts. They were crowded close, their eyes bright and eager—like the eyes of the living just before she made a delivery. Two ghosts stood closer than the rest. The ghost of the Scout of Stones, who would have been operating the light machine if this were a scene from a story. And the ghost of Moon, who must have arrived with the rest of the fifth committee. Both were watching intently. The courier did not hear Moon's voice this time, but somehow she knew the ghost's mind. Gray was right. This was what they wanted.

Thorn sensed it, too. He knelt in the sand and resumed his divining, but the walking stick trembled in his hand. He froze between glyphs. "I can't," he said.

Beryl got down beside him. "Everyone thinks the naming songs are for children," she said. "Each a separate little rhyme to help them remember the words. But the truth is, they're all one song. And to find a word, you just have to finish the next part of the song."

"But I don't know where to start."

"Start with anything. Start with words you know. Start with something you can see."

Thorn looked up. Hundreds of pairs of eyes looked back. "The ghosts are quiet," he said.

"Good," said Beryl. "The ghosts are quiet. Now keep going."

"The ghosts are quiet, gone is their breath."

Beryl gave him an encouraging nod.

"The ghosts are quiet, gone is the breath. The heart—" He shook his head.

"Almost there," Beryl said. "The ghosts are quiet, gone is the breath."

"The heart counts the numbers from birth until—"

"Now the glyphs," Beryl said.

Gray's breathing grew ragged. Everyone else watched without a sound. The players of the Black Square, the namers, the agents of the fifth committee. Even Smoke, who took a handkerchief from his pocket and wiped his forehead. And the ghosts—hundreds upon hundreds of ghosts. They were all watching. But Thorn couldn't move.

Moon came forward and knelt on his other side. The ghost placed one hand beside his on the stick, and Beryl did the same. Thorn and Beryl and Moon closed their eyes. Slowly, the walking stick began to move, sweeping over the glyphs as though to clear the air above them. It went in circles before coming to rest over the first glyph. Then it moved with greater force, circling and swaying until the stick—or the three of them together, or the word itself—chose the next.

The courier watched, already sounding out the new word in her mind. When the walking stick stopped for the last time, she knew they had it right.

Thorn bent forward and pressed his forehead to the sand, exhausted. Beryl leaned against him, and Moon placed one hand on his back.

To the courier, Beryl said, "Can you—?"

She was already hurrying to Gray. Seven stroked his face as he drew another rattling breath. The three other gardeners, Shadow, Juniper, and the Gardener of Trees, stood over him. The courier knelt and took his hand. He blinked up at her, his eyes glassy. The ghost of Gray, in spite of him, was beginning to take shape—and that was the rest of what she needed.

·  ·  ·

She delivered *death*. Gray was just alive enough to hear; he smiled as his body settled more deeply into the sand. The almost ghost of him shone with a brief pale light, and the wind carried the light away.

The other players of the Black Square spoke the word, trying it out for themselves. So did the agents of the fifth committee, and so did Smoke. The namers spoke the word, and the pages looked at one another, because they knew it would have to go on the next broadsheet. A border word, their first in ages.

The ghosts could not speak the word, but they heard it spoken. One by one, and then dozens at a time, the ghosts glowed and then winked out. Some smiled as they left, some closed their eyes. Some opened their arms as though to catch the wind. Seven stood and reached for the ghost of the Scout of Stones; he took her hand, and then he was gone.

The ghosts from the Number Twelve were also going away. Some held one another's hands as they drifted apart. And from among them came the haggard ghost with blue eyes, the chief engineer of the Number Twelve. That night in the reference car, the courier hadn't noticed the engineer's right hand. Now she saw that it was covered in scars from a terrible burn, as though it had once been held to a blazing fire.

The ghost went to Moon, and Moon stood. The two of them—Hand and Moon, first and second of the named—reached for each other. Their fingers shone where they touched, and the rest of them followed, light mingling before it faded.

Another ghost stepped forward, big but quick on his feet, grinning as though he had something clever to say.

"Oh, Book," Shadow said.

The ghost of Book drew close to the courier and held out his hands. She laughed when she realized what he was doing. She put her right hand in his, rested her left on his hip. They danced a few circles over the sand.

Shadow danced with them, her feet to Book's feet, her body swaying over the ground, playing the role of his shadow but adding flourishes of her own. The courier wondered whether this was how it had been when Book dreamed her up, when he delivered *shadow* and gave Shadow her name.

The courier moved close enough to rest her head against Book's shoulder as they turned. Then he was gone, and the courier and Shadow stood with only the wind between them.

The courier looked around. A few ghosts remained, but she didn't see the one she was looking for. Beryl and Ticket and Seven were looking, too.

"I don't know," Shadow said. "Maybe he's already gone."

The courier ran out onto the battlefield. A few soldiers still wandered among the burning machines. And everywhere ghosts flickered and went out—but the patchwork ghost was nowhere to be seen.

She sat on the ground, closed her eyes, and breathed. She searched for the stowaway's mind and found it, a glow like a beacon up among the sandy hills. She pressed herself closer, merged her senses with his.

Together they lay curled in the patchwork ghost's lap. The ghost was trying to finish a sketch. They stretched and pushed their head against his arm until he set his pencil aside and ran one hand down their back. The courier was soothed by that feeling, warm and unsayable, which came rumbling up as though from the heart of the world.

The ghost looked down and the courier knew, just before the wind took him, that he saw her there behind the stowaway's eyes. They landed with all four paws on the sand.

# THE
# NAMED
# WORLD

[art tk]

That night, around the fire they built just beyond the reach of the waves, Beryl divined the word *sea* and the courier delivered it. They knew the word wouldn't be enough. They could have thrown a hundred names into the sea, and the sea would have swallowed each and gone unchanged by them.

There were other fires on the sand, and people moved from one to the next, saying hello. The players of the Black Square, the namers, the agents of the fifth committee. Even a few pilots and soldiers, who had deserted the army rather than return on trains to the named territories, sat huddled around the flames.

Oh had returned from hunting the last of the machines, her fury gone or drawn deep into her churning heart. She accompanied some namers to the Number Twelve, and they came back with food and water, and with a bin of naphtha for her. Shadow and Thorn went into the city, to the Black Square's train, for instruments and bottles of spirits. When he returned, Thorn said to the courier, "The refugees from Hollow are there. They're lighting fires of their own, finding places to sleep."

"And the ghosts?"

"Gone, all of them."

The courier could see the lights in the city multiplying. In the opposite direction, machines still burned in the dark.

The players of the Black Square built a pyre for Gray, their Gardener of Stones, just beyond the reach of the waves. The gibbous moon painted a silver road over the sea while the body burned. When the waves drew close, sand and bubbles glittered like jewels in the firelight.

Shadow had taken the Black Square's deck of cards from Gray's pocket, and the courier asked to see them. Gray had told her that the Rider cards hid themselves from sight, but she found both quickly. She remembered how he had made the cards dance between his hands like living things.

"I think he tricked me," she said to Shadow. "I think he made sure I'd take that card."

"Maybe," Shadow said. "Or maybe Gray tricked himself, because he knew what we needed, even though it frightened him. I'm sorry he can't be here for the party."

People were already singing and playing music. Their voices grew louder as the skies darkened, and the first bouts of laughter shivered the air like new words. A lot of people had died, and their ghosts were gone. There would be more fires, more songs. The living would stay up late.

Wolf was restless. Instead of sitting by any fire, he went around collecting chunks of driftwood and adding them to the flames. When the courier's wandering path crossed his, they acknowledged each other but did not speak. She could feel his grief, dark and smoldering—no words were needed, and none were wanted.

The courier found Beryl and Seven sitting together. Beryl was holding Seven's hands and rocking back and forth with laughter, her red hair wild and completely undone. The courier's heart started beating very quickly. She didn't know who to sit beside, so she stayed standing, across the fire from them both.

Beryl noticed the courier and said, "Seven was just showing me how good she is at being you."

"I don't—"

"I don't know what to think of this," Seven said, which was what the courier had been about to say. Seven held herself a little stiffly, speaking each word with almost too much care.

Beryl's laughter grew louder. "You see?"

"Is that really what I sound like?" the courier asked.

"That is exactly what you sound like," Beryl said. "Come here."

The two moved apart so the courier could sit between them. They kept talking, and the courier's heart beat too fast for a while longer. Beryl told stories about growing up on the Number Twelve—about playing with the other committee children in depots, sneaking ghosts from their car and hiding them from the adults, making their own broadsheets with the printing machine.

Seven talked about the Black Square, and she talked about who she had been before the Black Square—something she'd never done while she and the courier rode the train together. She had been raised in a little border town called Knife, she said, and by the time of her seventh name day she'd been bored of it for as long as she could remember. Bored of the stream that ran behind the house, bored of the wranglers passing through with shackled ghosts, bored of the bells that rang every time someone saw or thought they saw a monster in the woods outside of town. She was even bored of her name.

She didn't tell them what name their committee had given her, but she told them how easy it had been to run away, to ride the rails until she found the Black Square. The moment she'd sneaked aboard, however, the Gardener of Leaves caught her, spat her out in the woods, and told her to scram. She had sneaked aboard twice more, and only after she was caught the third time did the Gardener of Stones finally set her before a dozen facedown cards.

The courier leaned back and listened, her elbows in the cool sand and her legs folded close to the fire, and for a while she felt happy. But there was something she needed to do before she got too tired. Neither of the other women seemed to notice when she rose and slipped away into the dark.

Her stowaway found her and brushed against her legs to let her know he was there. Together they went into the sandy hills, up to where the tall grasses grew. The moon was bright enough that she quickly found what she was looking for. While the stowaway stalked among the grasses, the courier sat and opened the patchwork ghost's sketchbook to the last page.

The moon had moved a quarter of the way across the sky by the time Ticket found her. The courier showed her the ghost's last sketch—of the battle's conclusion, of the crowd gathered around Thorn and Beryl and Moon as they divined a word so that all the ghosts could finally die.

Her voice was still rough and whispery from the spelling, but Ticket managed a few words. "I wonder who will find the stories now," she said.

The courier gestured to where people were dancing between a dozen fires, while others leaned close to whisper or brought more wood to burn. "They'll find them," she said. "They've already started."


Most of the namers returned to the Number Twelve to sleep, and most of the players of the Black Square returned to their train, too. The courier slept on a blanket by the fire, with Seven and Beryl sleeping close by, and Oh curled up around them, providing more heat even as she sheltered them from the wind.

By morning, the waters had come far up the sand and taken what remained of Gray and his pyre. The courier delivered *tide,* and later that day she delivered *beach* and *dune.* Beryl divined that first two, and the courier divined the third herself. That was against committee rules, but there was no one to stop her, because officially—she reminded Beryl—the committee still had no chair.

The day was sunny and clear, though the wind coming off the sea kept those who remained by the shore bundled in jackets and blankets. Oh permitted the Gardener of Trees to look after her wounds. He cleaned them with seawater and patched a few of the worst gouges with bandages, held in place with long ropes. Most of the bandages fell off when the monster started playing in the waves.

In the midafternoon a small group of masked figures came walking along the beach. They kept their distance from the named, but the adults knelt beside the children and pointed as Oh leapt and dived, blasting steam into the air with her whistle.

The monster learned to hold still in the shallows, then snatch up fish with her claws. The courier was relieved to see her learning to eat something other than naphtha.

That night, the Black Square performed the story of Yarrow, the first dreams committee hunter, for the nameless in their city. Some preferred to avoid the noise and words of the show, but many gathered to watch. The courier declined a role and sat near the back with Beryl, Ticket, and Wolf. Oh was with them, a quietly rumbling presence, still crusted in salt from her day in the sea. The train stood on tracks close to the center of the city, and the lights were bright in this canyon among the tallest towers.

After, they gathered in the car of the Trees. The music was quieter tonight, the company more subdued. Some of the nameless came aboard, and after the players brought them food and drink, and the nameless took up instruments and treated them to songs without words.

While Shadow gave Beryl a tour of the train—she wanted to see the machinery that made the scenery move—Seven danced with the other players, and with figures in red masks trimmed with long purple feathers. Seven had been in the role of Yarrow that night, and she still wore the black-and-yellow quilted armor of a dreams committee hunter. The courier felt uneasy. She couldn't stay here, and she didn't belong on the Number Twelve, either. She left quietly and walked with Oh back through the city. She still had time to make another fire, she thought, and with the monster for company she'd be warm enough on the sand.

Along the way they passed several of those wild spaces between the towers. Out among the trees, the courier glimpsed nameless figures in blue masks with silver tears, still lighting candles for the ghosts, even though the ghosts were gone. Soon, she thought, they would need new masks to wear.

The next morning, the courier, Ticket, and Oh went to the switchyard to see the namers off. Scattered among the tracks were remnants of the army's presence: empty canisters and crates, lengths of chain, a few flatcars abandoned on the rails. Oh sniffed a pile of machine parts left beside the tracks, nosed bits aside until she found scraps of naphtha below.

The engineers had turned the train around on the wye at the switchyard's edge, and now the Number Twelve was aimed back at the nameless forest. How long would it be, the courier wondered, before her old committee returned to name these woods, these hills and scrublands?

Ticket, her voice almost fully restored now, told Beryl that the fifth committee would be looking after the namers. "Even with Frost gone," she said, "there will be questions about what happened here. We'll make sure the sayers can't make much trouble for you."

Beryl squeezed Ticket's hands and nodded. To the courier, she said, "You could still come with us. You could be a courier again, or a diviner, or something else entirely."

They both knew it wouldn't be so easy. The fifth committee could help the namers navigate inquiries into their actions. But as for the nameless courier who escaped deletion, then broke the army of the named from the back of a monster that breathed fire? The named had a word for her now, and it was one she'd delivered to herself.

The courier put her arms around Beryl. She felt something there that was almost like home. "Come visit me sometimes," she said.

"Visit you where?"

"I don't know yet, but I'll make sure you can find me."

The courier stood between Ticket and Oh, watching as the train pulled out of the switchyard. Only after it had vanished into the trees did she notice, abandoned on the wye, the last car of the Number Twelve. She had always known it would come loose someday, and now here it was. The dovecote was empty; someone had set the messenger birds free.

The courier said, "Oh, would you help me with something?"

Oh let them loop chains around her middle so she could drag the car down the tracks—and then clear of them. A few hours later, after the car had nearly tipped over and rolled down several slopes, they got it up into the dunes.

"Are you really sure about this?" Ticket asked.

From up here, they had a view of the sea, the city, and the beach of broken machines. "I'm sure," the courier said.

Oh sat on her haunches, more than twice the size of the car she'd dragged up here, taking in the view. Then she opened her mouth and spoke. "Oh," she said. The odd rasp of the monster's voice was oddly familiar.

"Two?" the courier said.

"I," the monster replied, her golden eyes bright. "I, Oh, I."

The courier pulled Oh's head down and put her arms around her neck. The monster rumbled with pleasure. When Oh had swallowed Two, the machine part of her must have absorbed the other monster's spirit, just as the war machines absorbed those of the monsters burned in their furnaces.

"Two," the courier said again. "Is that really you in there?"

"Oh," Oh said, and the courier knew that what she meant was, *It's both of us.*

Seven, Shadow, and Thorn joined Ticket and the courier by her car on the dunes. They ate food Shadow brought from the train and watched Oh splash in the waves below, her glass scales glistening.

The Black Square was preparing to go. Some of the soldiers who'd deserted the army had already drawn cards, so Juniper had more Shovels to fill the workshop car. No new Gardener of Stones, though, and no Rider.

"Will you be safe out there?" the courier asked Shadow. "After what the sayers have done?"

The monster's stars shimmered mischievously. "The sayers can say what they like," she said. "And we'll play the stories we want to play."

Ticket seemed unconvinced. "But the Black Square—"

"That was never really its name," Shadow said. "We were something else before, something bigger than those words. We're something different now."

"And maybe something bigger still," Thorn said. He winced and touched his wounded shoulder, but the courier knew the wound was only part of what hurt him. His eyes were on the blackened spot of sand where they had burned Gray's body.

The courier said, "I have something for you."

She'd been keeping it in the front of her boilersuit: the patchwork ghost's last sketchbook. Thorn took it gently in his hands and flipped through a few pages. "You're sure?" he said.

"It belongs with the others," the courier said.

He winced again as he tried to open his jacket. The courier took the book back and slipped it into his pocket, patted it against his chest.

Seven was quiet, her silver hair down over her shoulders and shining in the sun. She sat with the stowaway in her lap, and each time he tried to slip away, she pulled him back. The courier was surprised that he kept letting this happen.

Ticket said, "Shadow, there's something else we have to talk about."

The monster sighed a frigid sigh and said, "I know."

"You can't keep Frost in there forever."

"Can't I?"

"Shadow," Ticket said.

"Then I'll wait until the world moves on without him. When I eventually spit him back out, he'll spend every minute of every day feeling like someone who just missed his train."

Ticket seemed about to argue, but then she shook her head and smiled. "Fine," she said.

They lingered over dinner until the sun began setting. Shadow shook crumbs from the blanket on which they'd set their meal. She presented the courier with a basket of extra food and supplies, then she and the others started down the dune.

Only Seven hesitated. She stood before the courier, looking at the car she planned to live in, which rested a little crookedly on the sand.

"It's going to need a lot of work," Seven said.

"Yes," the courier said.

"I should probably stay and help."

"I'd like that," the courier said.

Shadow's stars blazed warmly, and she tipped her floppy hat. Thorn waved. They headed down the beach toward the city.

A loud horn sounded from the far side of the dunes.

"That'll be Wolf," Ticket said. "He doesn't really know how to drive."

The courier and Seven accompanied her through the tall grass, down to where Wolf stood outside the front passenger door, arms crossed over his chest. Oh came barreling along behind them, running one loop around the vehicle before coming to a halt in front of the dreams committee hunter. The two gave each other a long look. Then Wolf climbed into the vehicle, closing the door but keeping his window down. Moss was in the back seat, along with two other members of the fifth committee.

"A little crowded," the courier said to Ticket.

"Maybe we'll take a shortcut," Ticket said.

She didn't say where they were going, and the courier didn't ask. But the courier knew the borders had changed and were changing still, and the fifth committee would need new safe houses, new plans. It would also need a new committee chair.

Ticket embraced her and said, "They might still come for you, you know. Watchers, hunters, other agents of the sayers."

"They'll come for me," the courier said. "But I won't be alone."

Oh huffed smoke from her nostrils, and the courier sensed Two's devotion mixed up with the big monster's fiery defiance.

Ticket drove away, and the courier and Seven watched as the lights of the vehicle faded. Oh chased it as far as the road, then circled back to the dunes. The courier sensed the stowaway out there, inviting his friend to hunt with him. They would be out all night, she thought, and probably sleep through most of the day.

Seven took the courier's hand, and they walked back through the dunes together. When the little car came into sight, the moon big and bright behind it, they started to run, and they were laughing by the time they climbed up to the deck and fell through the door—where they found themselves, for the first time since they'd met, completely alone.

The courier and Seven spent their days improving the place together, leveling the car with bricks, patching holes in its floor and roof. They scavenged wood and furniture from the abandoned village. They used parts of broken machines to collect rainwater and funnel it into barrels. And with Oh's help, they dragged part of the beetle machine's cabin up the slope, then stocked it with wood for the winter. The courier divined and delivered *caboose,* something to call the place, though most of the time they just called it home.

They went into the woods and foraged for roots, berries, nuts, edible leaves. Oh hunted fish, and she learned to catch them without swallowing them whole. She began to deposit a few at the caboose door every day. The courier taught herself how to clean and gut the fish. She cooked their dinners in the little stove inside.

The courier and Seven found a deck of cards in one of the derelict war machines and played rounds of Hand and Moon in the evenings while Oh and the stowaway roamed the dunes. Other times they sat in the dovecote and watched boats coming and going from the city. There were many such boats, of different shapes and sizes: some went out to fish, they thought, while others bore passengers and goods.

"Where could they be going?" Seven asked.

The courier had no answer.

Seven often pretended to be different people. With Oh she was Cirrus, a dreams committee hunter, stalking and chasing the monster over the sand, then being chased by her in turn. "Back, foul beast! I'll reduce you to cinders even if I must burn with you!" With the courier she was a captured soldier of the named, forced to build an outpost by her cruel overseer. "Silent you may be, my nameless captor—and beautiful, I think, behind that mask of stone— yet I will speak my words to the sky while I toil under your brutish yet oddly entrancing gaze."

Sometimes the courier played along, sometimes she only laughed. Sometimes she grabbed Seven in her arms, and then she was usually Seven again, a runaway from a border town with a head full of story and a knack for trouble— attentive, kind, a little scared, and shy in ways that surprised the courier every time, a woman with more wants than she could find words for.

They went into the city sometimes, and the nameless welcomed them. Without the ghosts, the purpose of the place was changing. The courier understood it in pieces, when her mind brushed those of the people who lived here. Many who fled from Hollow had made their home in the city. Some went by boat to other nameless places, while many others arrived to help remake the city—not as it had been hundreds of years before, before it became a refuge for ghosts, but into something new.

She came to understand that this city was not truly the last city of the nameless. The nameless territories were vast and more various than any among the named had dared to imagine. The named world was very small, really. An island in a measureless sea.

The courier and Seven joined the nameless for celebratory feasts, understanding only a little of what they celebrated. They listened to their wordless songs played on horns and fiddles, and on instruments without names. They watched figures in dark gray masks fashion sculptures on street corners. Watched others hang lanterns from the brightly colored cords strung between the buildings. More of those cords appeared every week.

When winter came and the snows fell, the courier cooked and mended and brewed, tended to the fire, tried to keep sand from blowing in. She was worried that the sea would freeze, and that Oh wouldn't be able to catch fish anymore. But the sea didn't freeze.

When it got too cold, Oh dug herself a warren deep under the dunes. Her wounds had healed, and the scars looked nearly as tough as her scales. The stowaway stayed with the monster sometimes, though usually he remained in the caboose. Occasionally, the courier sensed him down in the city, where he hunted vermin and kept company with others of his kind. She could have stowed herself away among his senses, but she preferred not to pry too deeply.

The junk dealer came by every few weeks, to check up on them. He had relocated his operation to the city by the sea. Business was good. "Fewer nameless things all the time," he told them. "But those that remain are prized."

He brought them little gifts, and they gave him dried fish in return. On one visit he brought them an old typing machine, along with stacks and stacks of blank paper. Seven used the machine to write stories she thought the Black Square might like to perform someday. These were unlike anything the courier had seen before, pretend from start to finish, unconnected to any known stories of the named. The courier thought the stories were dangerous, like monsters made of words. She couldn't get enough of them.

Seven couldn't stop writing them, either, and some nights the courier would drift off to sleep with Seven's wild clacking following her into dreams. Their dreams mingled, sometimes. And even awake, the border between their minds grew thin.

In the spring, the courier and Seven prepared garden beds close to where the scrublands met the dunes. A group of nameless with masks like red leaves brought sacks of seeds and demonstrated how best to sow them. With Oh's help, they scavenged more parts from the machines to build fences and a shed, and spouts to distribute water over the field. Plants grew, budded, flowered.

Seven was struggling with her stories. She tore half-finished pages from the typing machine and burned them in the stove. The courier overheard her talking to herself in the voices of other people, people who didn't exist, who had never existed. She wasn't sure which of them was happier to discover, pinned under a rock outside the door one morning, a sheet of rough paper inked with a black square.

The show arrived the next afternoon, train whistling as it rolled out of the forest. Oh hooted as she bounded alongside the engine, escorting the Black Square Show into the city.


The courier and Seven waited until after the performance was over before they climbed aboard the train. Shadow found them first, and threatened to eat them both as she hugged them. They joined the others in the stage car, where the party was underway.

Thorn was the Six of Trees again, still dressed in his poorly cut suit. Seven showed him her stories. Flipping through the pages, he looked confused, then frightened, then excited.

Backstage, the courier walked with the Gardener of Trees as he oiled and made little adjustments to the machinery. She didn't have to ask him about Juniper.

"She was at her worktable," he said. "You know how she was, always staying up late to weld some new thing. We were confused at first, because she'd seemed fine all that day. And because there was no ghost in the car. But, of course . . ."

"Of course," the courier said.

The new Gardener of Shovels was nameless. The courier had noticed the child in a pale yellow mask, examining the lenses of the light machine.

"The kid's a natural," said the Gardener of Trees. "Already has that old furnace fired up. Soon we'll have more fruit for the something tree."

The courier and Seven stayed up late with Thorn and Shadow, drinking and trading stories. By the time they left, most of the other players had gone to bed.

They were quiet as they walked home through the city, the stowaway making wide loops through nearby streets. Once they were back on the beach, the courier took Seven's hand and said, "It's all right. I know you have to go with them."

At first Seven said nothing. The courier sensed that she didn't want to agree—but that she couldn't deny it, either. Finally she said, "I'll come back. And next time I'll stay."

They sat up in bed together, watching the waves crawl up the sand. The courier slept a little, and Seven rose before dawn to pack her things. The courier walked her as far as the edge of the dunes. After Seven was gone, she lingered on the beach until the sun rose over the sea. She didn't want to see the train returning west over the rails.

She harvested summer vegetables, learned to pickle and preserve them. Oh began to wander farther and farther from the caboose. Sometimes the monster was gone for a day or two at a time. When she came back, usually emerging from the nameless forest as the sun was going down, she always caught more fish than the courier could possibly eat, as though to apologize for her absence.

The days were long, the sea restless, the sun almost unbearable on cloudless days. Sometimes the courier missed her life aboard the Number Twelve. The velocity, the clack and rumble, the smell of fresh ink in the printing car, her own small part in the naming song.

Beryl visited sometimes. The old laws were changing, and the namers were permitted to come and go from the train with fewer restrictions. But the new chair of the names committee couldn't afford to stray from the Number Twelve for long.

One morning they were in the garden, and Beryl was helping her repair the water spouts, damaged in a recent storm. "The words are coming so quickly, it's hard to keep up," she said. "Diviners will find three or four in a day, and most of the couriers are as fast as you used to be."

The courier gave her a look.

"Well, almost as fast," Beryl said.

She inspected the rest of the system they had built for catching rainwater. She was impressed, though she suggested a few improvements. She told the courier she had watched the Black Square perform again, but she struggled to describe what she'd seen. The story was a new story, and it was also something that had never happened.

"That's one of Seven's," the courier said.

"The sayers are blaming her stories for the uptick in new monsters," Beryl said. "But what the sayers think matters less all the time."

"What do you think?"

"I think she's trouble," Beryl said. "And I wish I didn't like her as much as I do."

"Sometimes I wish I didn't, either," the courier said, though she was able to laugh as she said it.

She spent more time among the nameless, and their minds were often open to hers. She felt their sadness for the city they had lost, and the pride they took in the city they were making. They regarded the named with pity more than scorn, concern more than fear. Many of them, as the courier had guessed, were considered strange among the nameless for wanting to live so close to the noise of the named.

The ones with red leaf masks, who had brought seeds for her garden, introduced her to another, more secretive group. Five in number, they lived and worked together in a structure built beside one of the city's many wild spaces, mixing herbs, flowers, roots, and other matter into medicines. They wore the grinning brown masks with beards of twine which the courier knew from the Story of Hand and Moon. They were jubilant and unpredictable, and while they worked they performed little dances that made the courier laugh. They seemed to know who she was. They welcomed her into their workshop and urged her, each time she was about to leave, to stay a little longer.

So she stayed a little longer, and she returned often, and she learned from them. The named knew them as the people who made drugs to help blue-masked dreamers make monsters, but that was only a portion of their knowledge. They taught the courier mixtures to heal wounds, to rid the body of diseases, to aid sleep and produce good dreams. They showed her where to collect certain herbs, though some grew only in distant places, and would arrive in bundles on boats from other nameless lands. They gifted her with the tools she needed, and soon the inside of the caboose was cluttered with pots and jars and mortars, with herbs hung from strings to dry.

Ticket, the first time she visited, wrinkled her nose at the smell. "What are you *doing* in here?" she asked.

The courier presented her with little bottles of salves and liquids. *Potions,* she said, delivering the word for them, explaining how each should be used.

The sisters went for a long walk along the beach. Oh was with them. She pranced with delight at Ticket's presence. The monster had found a tree limb in the surf, and now she carried it in her jaws, dragging it over the sand. The stowaway walked with them too. The courier could feel his disdain for the monster's behavior.

"How goes the work of your committee?" the courier asked.

"So much is changing," Ticket said. "Most of it in ways we still don't understand."

The named were having to remake their world, almost from scratch. Factories stood silent, emptied of ghosts. The wranglers were disbanded, and the ghosts committee existed only in name. With so much changing, people dreamed up more monsters than ever before.

They were frightened, Ticket said, but the courier could tell that it was worse than what Ticket was saying. There would be violence, she thought.

Confusion and loss. All because she had delivered one word, the word for a border they'd overlooked for so long.

"There's trouble everywhere," Ticket said. "But there's hope, too. The deletion committees have been abolished, and no one wants war with the nameless anymore. The sayers are changing because they have to."

The two were quiet for a while. The courier saw Ticket lose herself to the sound of the waves, saw her body relax as she walked. Up ahead, Oh traded up for a larger tree branch. She laid down and started chewing.

The courier said, "I want you to teach me spelling."

Ticket looked suspicious. "Why?"

"I can already spell a little," she admitted. "I just want to make sure I'm doing it right."

The first time had been an accident. The courier had woken in the night because her stowaway had knocked something over, a glass of water by her bedside. The glass broke on the floor, and the fire in the stove was almost out. She couldn't see where to step. She was still only half awake when she said, *Light,* speaking the word as Hand must have spoken it, when Hand delivered *light.* For a moment, the entire caboose was flooded with light, as though the moon had descended from the sky and come in through the window.

Ticket listened to all this with wary interest. "Does this mean you want to join the fifth committee?"

"I'm a committee of one," the courier said.

"Oh?" Ticket said, smiling now. "And what is your committee called?"

"I haven't figured that out yet," the courier said.

She did figure it out, some weeks later, when people started coming out of the named territories, seeking the nameless woman who lived in a train car by the sea.

The first group followed the tracks on foot and approached no closer than the edge of the dunes. The sound of the waves frightened them, maybe. Or maybe they'd heard stories about the monster that could breathe fire and tear apart war machines with its claws. They camped down there, that first night, and the courier's stowaway kept an eye on them, making sure they didn't get too close to the garden.

Some time the next day they crossed the dunes to the beach, still giving her house a wide berth. They stood on the sand, a man, a woman, a little boy—farmers, the courier guessed, from their mud stained boots and good, wide hats—gazing up at the caboose as though it was the strangest thing they had ever seen. And maybe it was.

Finally the courier went down to them. "Well?" she said.

"It's the boy," the man said. "Bad dreams."

The boy gazed up at her with big brown eyes. He looked very tired.

"Monsters?" the courier asked.

The man looked at his feet, face reddening with shame. The woman said, "Almost every night."

The courier saw the soot on her hands. She had taken care of a monster last night, in their campfire. She had taken care of others before. Hard work, but it would be worse if the dreams committee came instead.

"Wait here," the courier said. She fetched a blue glass bottle from the caboose. She knelt by the boy and put the bottle in his hands. "Take a sip each night, just before you sleep," she said. "There's enough in there to last you a few weeks. After that, you'll make no new monsters. But if you do—and this is very important—just remember that you've done nothing wrong."

The man frowned.

"Absolutely nothing wrong," the courier said. "You can come back for more if you need it, but just keeping the empty bottle at your bedside should be enough." She wasn't sure if that last part was true, but she thought it might help for him to think it so.

The woman looked at the man, and he held out a basket. The courier took it and peered inside: three jars of jam and a whisk broom. The courier had not expected payment, but she nodded as though to say that this would do, and the three left the way they had come.

They were the first of many. Some came by foot as the farmers had, others by steam speeder or handcar. The courier gave them potions for cuts and burn wounds, for coughs that wouldn't go away, for bad dreams and bad breath, for helping a child happen, for preventing a child from happening, for finding lost memories, for forgetting. She wasn't sure how they'd found out about her, or why they'd known she could help. Maybe Ticket had given potions from her batch to people who needed them, and word had spread.

*Witch.* She divined and delivered the word to herself, saying to nobody, *I am* witch. *I am the chair of the witch committee and I am its only member.*

Though Seven was perhaps a kind of witch. And there were probably others among the nameless and the named. Someday all the witches might find one another—if any of them wished to be found.

In the meantime, she was not alone, because she had her stowaway. She could have found the word for the kind of animal he was, but she left that word unspoken. Instead, she delivered the word for what he was to her alone.

*Familiar,* she said without words, *the moon is new tonight, and I sense a strangeness on the breeze. I'll need you to keep watch.*

*Fine, fine,* the witch's familiar said, still wandering off, but not too far.

He did catch someone sneaking up the dune that night, hands in pockets, barely making a sound, though more than enough for his ears to detect. The courier considered calling for her monster, but instead she went out into the dark and waited until the intruder reached for the deck at the back of the caboose.

*Light,* the courier said, illuminating the air with a pale white haze.

Stunned by the glow, the woman blinked, her silver hair brilliant in the dark.

"Seven?"

Seven took the Black Square notice from her pocket. "I delivered all the others first," she said.

The courier kissed her and pulled her inside. The light, like a little moon, followed them through the door.

The courier saw how this would go, with Seven returning every fall to fill their caboose with the clacking of new stories, leaving every spring when the Black Square returned to the city by the sea. Staying as long as she could, leaving as soon as she had to.

And Seven did stay with her that winter, and other winters, too, though sometimes she stayed a whole year at a time, and sometimes she went away for just as long. The arrangement seemed to suit them both.

The courier continued to receive visitors. Among them were agents of the fifth committee, who taught her new spellings in exchange for salves and potions. Ticket started coming more regularly, sometimes in her vehicle with Shadow, but usually by herself. Sometimes she came to her sister for advice, or to recruit her for especially difficult assignments. Thorn would have loved to make stories from their adventures, so the courier made sure to never tell him about them.

She was often lonely, but she had always preferred the places between. And in her caboose at the edge of the world, she had found a place between everything: nameless and named, forest and city, earth and sky, land and sea. Alone, she knew someone would be coming soon. With someone else for company, she knew she would soon be alone.

Sometimes, when she was most alone, she caught a glimpse of the patchwork ghost reflected in a window or out of the corner of her eye. She felt his presence often. Sometimes he appeared for a minute at a time, seated on the dunes or standing with his feet in the waves. She delivered *haunt,* and after that he appeared more often still.

Sometimes she sat next to him, and his hands moved as though he were sketching, but the courier couldn't see the sketches.

Meanwhile Oh's wanderings took her farther and farther from their home by the shore. She left for weeks, then months at a time. When nearly a year passed, the courier was sure Oh was gone for good, probably to join the monsters that lurked in the borderlands. The named, she'd come to know, made many more monsters than the nameless. She only hoped Oh would remember to keep away from the dreams committee hunters.

But Oh did return, on a warm day in late spring, and she didn't come alone. She had three little monsters at her heels, and they all looked a lot like her.

"But how did you—"

"Oh!" said Oh.

"You're right," the courier said. "It's none of my business."

Her familiar hissed at the newcomers and hid under the caboose. The monsters were only a little larger than he was. In her brood, Oh's machine parts appeared diminished to spines along their backs, knobs on their arms. And they had wings—a gift from their other parent, the courier guessed.

She knelt to greet them, and they nipped at her hands with pointy little teeth. "They're beautiful," she told Oh.

The monsters stayed for a few weeks, and Oh taught them how to catch fish. She squawked at them, bewildered, when they began leaping from the tops of the dunes to glide on their wings to the sand.

The courier could have divined and delivered a name for the kind of monster they were, felt the word on the tip of her tongue. But she thought it better to leave them as they were for now.


She was alone with her familiar the day she saw a strange little steam speeder, black and sleek with silver trim, come rolling into the switchyard. A dozen people climbed down from the spacious cab and hiked up to the dunes, pausing only for a moment to inspect the garden. Among them were watchers, surveyors, and others in official uniforms.

Ticket had warned her that agents of the sayers would come one day. But what surprised the courier most were the two familiar faces among the delegation.

Smoke walked with his hands clasped behind his back, no longer dressed in the garb of a speaker. He was something different now, but the courier wasn't sure what.

Beside him stood Ivy. She was in uniform, but not that of a courier. Beryl, during one of her visits, had told the courier that Ivy had survived her fall into the tunnel and was still a member of the names committee. She no longer worked on the Number Twelve, but had joined other namers in Whisper, serving in a new role created to keep up with the ever-growing rush of new words. An archivist of some kind, Beryl said.

The courier stood outside the caboose, watching them climb the dune, calling to mind every spelling she knew.

Smoke raised both his hands. "The stories are true, then," he said. "The witch in her train car by the sea, overlooking the site of her great victory, gathering power from the nameless places of the world."

"More power than you know," the courier warned him. "And if you think you can challenge me with a force this small, you are mistaken."

"I wouldn't dare," Smoke said, though something in his voice told her that he would have liked to. "You see—"

But Ivy pushed past him, cutting him off. "Please," she said. "We didn't come here to challenge you. We came to ask"—she shook her head, clenched her jaw—"we came to *beg* for your help."

"My help?" the courier said, still wary. "What could you need my help with?"

Ivy looked to Smoke, and Smoke shrugged. "That's the trouble," he said. "There are no words for it."

They convinced her to come with them. They would have her back home, Smoke promised, before sundown. She sat alone on a bench in the steam speeder, watching out the window as they passed through the forest and into the nameless parts of Hollow. Workers were restoring the roundhouse, and in the distance she saw smoke rising from a few of the smaller factories.

They switched to another line that went north and east out of the city, down into a valley she had never seen before. A river flowed along the valley's bottom, swelling as it passed farms and villages. And then, up ahead, she saw the river join the sea again. A large boat was anchored in the mouth of the river. Strange flags flew from its mast.

On the beach was an encampment, and this was where Smoke and Ivy brought her. Here people cooked food over fires and washed clothes in pots. They wore peculiar hats, and stitched to their coats were brightly colored insignias of stars, bears, birds, boats, trees.

Smoke greeted them and introduced the courier. The travelers responded with sounds of their own—*words,* the courier could tell, but none that she recognized. The noise of them dizzied her.

"Recent deliveries?" she asked Ivy.

"None of those words were delivered by the names committee," Ivy said quietly. "We don't have any of them in the archives."

Still trying to hide her confusion, the courier said to the travelers, "I'm sorry, I don't understand."

They responded with more strange sounds, musical and fluid. They seemed as baffled as she was, but also amused.

The courier did not return home that day, or the next. Instead, she remained at the encampment. They gave her a tour of their boat and showed her the tools and foods they had brought with them from far away. The travelers had different words for everything the courier knew—for *boat, water,* and *sea,* for *fruit, knife, pit,* and *rind,* for *mouth, word, listen, speak.* Gradually, they began to understand one another.

So the nameless regions were greater than the courier had known. But there were other named territories as well, full of people who had broken the Silence with their own words, and who spoke their own words even now. They were delighted to teach and to learn, pairing words that seemed to match. She knew this was only a start.

The courier divined and delivered the words Ivy and Smoke needed—*language, translate, foreign, emissary*—and they accepted them somberly. They must have known, as the courier did, that with these new arrivals the power of the sayers would diminish further, because the new words would loosen their grip on the old.

When they left, she declined the offer of a ride. If she followed the coast south, she knew, she'd find her way home in time.

Later that summer, Beryl arrived one cool sunny morning with a bouquet of flowers. She was wearing her nicest suit, the blue one with no oil stains. The courier thanked her and put the flowers in a jar on her table.

"So, are you ready?" Beryl asked her.

"I don't think I want to do this," the courier said.

"Of course you don't," Beryl said. "You're the witch who lives in a train car by the sea."

"That's not why," the courier said.

"Your power is unrivaled, but you aren't used to receiving special invitations," Beryl suggested. "People should come to you, not the other way around."

"I just don't want them looking at me. They think they know the story, but they don't."

Beryl took her hands. "After tonight, they will."

"I've seen the Black Square perform," the courier said. "I've *performed* with the Black Square. After tonight, they'll know *a* story. But they still won't know *the* story."

"It's the old problem," Beryl agreed. She took a yellow flower from the jar, bit off the stem, and stuck the blossom in her own lapel. "But none of that matters. What matters is that you be there for Thorn. And for your Seven of Stones."

The courier knew she was right. She knelt in front of her familiar, who lay curled in a sunbeam, and patted his head in a way she knew would annoy him. For Beryl's benefit, she said out loud, "You'll have to watch the place while I'm gone."

The animal blinked his golden eyes and yawned.

They took the garden path down the slope. As the courier passed through the gate, she turned. Seated atop the caboose, a figure in a patchwork suit was watching her leave. Then a cloud passed over the sun, and the ghost was gone. The courier closed the gate behind her.

Beryl had borrowed a steam speeder from a friend on the maps committee, and one of the two mechanics who might have been Beryl's father had volunteered to pilot it. As he and Beryl chatted, the courier watched through the window. Trees rose up around them, sinking the cab in deep green shadow.

During a lull in the conversation, the courier said, "When we get there, I'm sitting in the back."

"Fine," Beryl said.

"And I'm not talking to anyone," she said.

"Not even to me?" Beryl asked.

"Only a little," the courier said. "But I'm not going backstage after."

Progress through the forest was slow. They weren't the only people traveling this route today. Masked figures from the city by the sea walked alongside the rails or rode handcars toward Hollow. The mechanic kept the steam car in its lower gears. When they reached the nameless districts of the city, the courier said, "Let's walk from here."

They left the steam speeder on a siding and walked with the nameless toward the theater. Beryl had more flowers in a sack slung over her shoulder. The mechanic went ahead to meet some others from the Number Twelve.

Many people had returned to these neighborhoods in recent years, and the streets were bright under lanterns hung from the cords overhead. The theater was outside, with tiered benches overlooking a wide grassy space. There were train cars down there, but they weren't part of the Black Square's train. Nameless and named alike were already gathering for the show. The courier and Beryl took seats in the back. As the sun went down, the courier's heart beat as though she were among those about to perform.

When the show began, the sides of the cars opened, revealing interiors of what looked like the Number Twelve. In Book's office, the chair of the names committee turned a bottle of nameless spirits in his hand and said, "A bribe, obviously. And I won't get caught drinking a bribe alone." He poured some for himself, some for the courier.

"I could deliver the word right here," the courier said.

Book spluttered as he sipped. "We can't let the sayers think this is easy."

"Let the sayers think what they want," the courier said.

The courier knew that Seven was playing the courier she had been. That the Gardener of Trees, in a rare turn onstage, was playing Book. But she was soon lost to the story, and it felt more familiar—and more like a dream—than she'd expected. The monster who would later be called Two, the burning of the seventh car, the courier's flight to Jawbone. When the Black Square played the story of the courier's time with the Black Square, all the courier knew for sure was that Shadow played herself. Thorn had left a lot out, but the glass-blowers were there, and so was their monster engine, and the battle at the edge of the world, and the delivery that sent the ghosts away.

After the show, Beryl asked her, "Are you sure you don't want to go back-stage?"

The courier felt different now that the story was over. It seemed that no one had noticed her after all. Or if they had, they'd been too polite to say any-thing As they left their seats, she said, "I'll go. And you'll give those flowers to Thorn and Seven?"

"Some to Shadow, too, if she wants them," Beryl said.

"She'll want them," the courier said.

"And I'm sure Seven will get you out of there before anyone pesters you with questions about what it was like to see your own story onstage."

"She will," the courier agreed.

They started making their way down the steps, but the courier put one hand on Beryl's shoulder and said, "Wait."

Beryl turned and waited. The courier took a deep breath. "I want you to have something to call me by, when you need to call me something."

The old trouble between them, or a grain of it. Beryl looked wary. Before she could say anything, the courier spoke her own name, delivering it to herself.

Beryl repeated the name aloud. "I don't know that word. What does it mean?"

The courier smiled to see her puzzled. "It means me," she said, "and it doesn't mean anything else."

# ACKNOWLEDGMENTS

This novel was written with invaluable support from Yaddo, the James Merrill House, and the Massachusetts Cultural Council.

I am grateful to the Amity Circle, the Amity House, the Jolly Millers, and the Montague Bookmill, and to those in whose homes parts of the novel were written: Katharine Houk and Seth Rockmuller, Ellen Rockmuller and Joel Minsky, Kelly Link and Gavin Grant, and Holly and Theo Black.

I wish to thank Pieter Lips for answering my many questions about steam locomotives and their operation; all errors and fantastications are my own.

I am grateful to my agent, Esmond Harmsworth, whose insight is matched only by his patience. My editor, Carl Engle-Laird, is a true magician; this book tumbled into his realm and was wondrously transmuted. Many thanks also to Matt Rusin and the rest of the team at Tor Books and Tordotcom Publishing.

Thank you to the Wolf Pack and the Jar Boys, and to Tristan Chambers and Libby Reinish, for keeping me on my feet, in this world and others. Thank you to Morwen for showing up at the end and making my world so much bigger.

Thank you, Emily Houk—there are no words.

# ABOUT THE AUTHOR

Tristan Morgan Chambers

**JEDEDIAH BERRY** is the author of a novel, *The Manual of Detection*, and a story in cards, *The Family Arcana*. He lives in Western Massachusetts. Together with his partner, writer Emily Houk, he runs Ninepin Press, an independent publisher of fiction, poetry, and games in unusual shapes.